Title: *Jax Freeman and the Phantom Shriek*
Author: Kwame Mbalia
Imprint: Freedom Fire / Disney • Hyperion
In-store date: 10/1/2024
ISBN: 978-1-368-06473-6
Price: US $17.99 / CAN $24.49
E-book ISBN: 978-1-368-6479-8
Trim size: 5 ½ x 8 ¼
Page count: 480
Ages: 8–12
Grades: 3–7

We are pleased to send this book for review.
Please send two copies of any review or mention to:

Disney Book Group
Attn: Children's Publicity Department
77 West 66th Street, 3rd Floor
New York, NY 10023
dpw.publicity@disney.com

JAX FREEMAN

AND THE

PHANTOM SHRIEK

BOOK 1

JAX FREEMAN AND THE PHANTOM SHRIEK

BOOK 1

by KWAME MBALIA

FREEDOM FIRE

DISNEY • HYPERION
Los Angeles   New York

First Edition, October 2024
1 3 5 7 9 10 8 6 4 2
FAC-004510-24235

Printed in the United States of America

This book is set in Minion Pro, Cheddar Gothic, Adlery Pro/Fontspring;
Helvetica Neue LT Pro, Futura, News Plantin MT Pro/Monotype
Designed by Tyler Nevins
Endpaper illustration © 2024 by [TK]

Library of Congress Cataloging-in-Publication Data
Names: Mbalia, Kwame, author.
Title: Jax Freeman and the phantom shriek / by Kwame Mbalia.
Description: First edition. | Los Angeles : Disney-Hyperion, 2024. | Series:
    Freedom fire ; book 1terr | Audience: Ages 8–12. | Audience: Grades 4–6. |
    Summary: When twelve-year-old African American Jackson Freeman is
    forced to move from Raleigh, North Carolina to Chicago he finds himself
    suddenly in a world of talking glasses and clocks, magical inheritance,
    and daredevil train porters in a fight against a terrifying evil.
Identifiers: LCCN 2023017699 | ISBN 9781368064736 (hardcover) | ISBN
    9781368065092 (trade paperback) | ISBN 9781368064798 (ebook)
Subjects: LCSH: African American boys—Juvenile fiction. | Magic—Juvenile fiction. |
    Good and evil—Juvenile fiction. | Monsters—Juvenile fiction. | Railroad trains—
    Juvenile fiction. | Chicago (Ill.)—Juvenile fiction. | CYAC: African Americans—
    Fiction. | Magic—Fiction. | Good and evil—Fiction. | Monsters—Fiction. | Railroad
    trains—Fiction. | Chicago (Ill.)—Fiction. | LCGFT: Fantasy fiction. | Monster fiction.
Classification: LCC PZ7.1.M395 Jax 2024 | DDC 813.6 [Fic]—dc23/eng/20231031
LC record available at https://lccn.loc.gov/2023017699

Reinforced binding

Visit www.DisneyBooks.com

To Esther and Beatrice:
you send me strength every day

PROLOGUE

MOSES WAS CRYING BEHIND HIS FAMILY'S GENERAL store when two things happened.

A door opened where no door had been before.

A boot stepped out into the night.

In between those actions, his world changed.

The wind picked up. Slowly at first, in gentle swirls that brushed the weed clumps peeking through the asphalt, and then faster and faster still. The trees surrounding the store leaned and the windows rattled. Some dented metal trash cans thumped against one another, and the lone streetlight protecting that stretch of road from the dark flickered once. Twice. The third time, it turned off completely for a few seconds.

When the light returned, the boy clamped his hands over his mouth and choked down a sob.

Bricks were marching along the sidewalk.

They began to stack themselves in piles, clinging to each other tighter than any mortar could cement them together. Wooden planks peeled off the sagging fence surrounding the garden where Moses's mother grew her cucumbers and melons. The boards inched along the pavement like worms after a storm, crawling toward the middle of the field behind the store, on the other side of the old railroad tracks. Once there, the planks straightened again, nails driving them together as the bricks formed columns and buttresses, arches and pillars. Glass shards from old Coca-Cola bottles assembled themselves into glittering rectangles and joined the magical maelstrom on the fringes of the neighborhood. Dust clouds leaped toward the sky, forming one brief, furious funnel cloud that momentarily blocked Moses's view of the activity. Then it spun away, and everything fell still.

A train station now loomed next to the tracks, complete with a new elevated platform and an overhang supported by pillars. Long and with thin towers at either end, the structure reminded Moses of a castle he'd seen in a book once. Stained-glass windows lined the front of the building—six on either side of a tall red door with a polished brass doorknob.

The red door opened, and out stepped the boot. The boot became a leg, the leg became a person, and a Black face peeked out. A giant young man limped onto the platform. He wore a long navy blue peacoat that he clutched shut with one hand while the other grasped a pillar for support. His charcoal-gray slacks and polished black leather boots made him almost indistinguishable from the night, and the flat navy cap with black brim pulled low on his head hid his face. He paused to lean against the pillar and reached into an inner coat pocket, rummaging around.

"All wrong," he muttered. "All wrong. Not enough time to reverse it—need to delay. Got to delay."

Moses slid quietly off the overturned barrel he'd been sitting on and began to inch his way to the back door of the general store. He'd seen enough to know that a strange man appearing out of nowhere in the middle of the night in Wilmington, North Carolina, wasn't something you wanted to stick around for. He was almost to the door when he heard something he hadn't heard in all his thirteen years.

A train whistle.

The man on the platform heard it, too, and he whirled around. "No!" he whispered loudly. "Not yet! Not yet! She'll be here."

The train whistled again. Moses stood still, forgetting for a moment that he was supposed to be minding his own beeswax. There hadn't been a train on the old tracks behind the store for years! His daddy always complained about it. Said when the railroad discontinued the line all his customers went away. If the trains were coming back, that was a good thing, right? His parents wouldn't have to sell the store, and Moses wouldn't have to leave to go to live in Chicago with an aunt and uncle he'd never met. Trains meant business, and business meant money.

He almost jumped for joy as the train's whistle sounded

again. . . . Except this time, it seemed a little different. Not like a whistle at all, but more like . . .

"Boy!"

Moses flinched. He'd been spotted! The man on the platform was glaring in his direction. The boy let out a whimper and recoiled, but the man didn't notice. He threw something, and Moses caught it out of reflex. It was a metal pin with a train car in the middle. BROTHERHOOD OF SLEEPING CAR PORTERS, it read, and it seemed to glow in his hand.

"Run!" the man said, just as the train whistled again, and it sounded like . . . screaming? Like a hundred voices tied together with wires and nails! Like something horrific! "Take this and tell them I'm sorry. I tried to stop her, tried to stop the spell, but . . . I'm sorry."

The horrible shrieking came closer, and the platform began to shake and rattle. And the man, instead of running away like Moses planned to do, he limped down onto the tracks, turning *toward* the thundercloud of horror that raced at him as it screeched and screeched and screeched. Shadows boiled, and the night splintered into a hundred different pieces.

The thing rumbling down the tracks wasn't a train at all. It was a kaleidoscope of terror, and Moses began to scream, too, his cries merging with the oncoming scourge. For a few seconds longer the man stood tall against its approach—thirty feet away, twenty feet, ten—and then he was gone.

They found Moses the next morning in a ditch beside the tracks, his eyes red and his voice raw, still screaming and clutching the metal pin.

CHICAGO DEFENDER, VOLUME XV, ISSUE 02, SEPTEMBER 1920

One Year Later: The Riots of 1919

The esteemed reporter Thomas Williamson spoke with severa
city officials as well as transplants from Southern states in an
attempt to garner more inf

FAMILIES WITH SOUTHERN CONNECTION AT CENTER OF THRIVING CHICAGO COMMUNITY

Hiram Davis was once a tobacco farmer, but now he and his
family, along with other transplants, find themselves serving
as community leaders in Tenement Building E on the South
Side of

JOY AND CELEBRATION AS FIRST AFRICAN AMERICAN UNION ESTABLISHED

Philip Randolph called the day a "historic and a crowning
achievement" as the Brotherhood of Sleeping Car Porters,
a union serving the porters employed by Pullman
Railroad, was born. A crowd of hundreds cheered

NEW DISPATCH RECEIVED . . . IF YOU ARE SEEING
THIS, A NEW DISPATCH FROM THE SPIRIT
REALM IS BEING HELD IN YOUR NAME AT YOUR
NEAREST ALTAR . . . PLEASE ACKNOWLEDGE
RECEIPT AT YOUR EARLIEST CONVENIENCE . . .
YOUR ANCESTORS THANK YOU. as history was made.

CHAPTER
ONE

IT'S BEEN SEVEN HOURS AND NINETEEN MINUTES since I, Jackson Freeman, turned twelve, moved across the country into a house of doom, and abandoned everything I ever knew and loved, only to be accused of tomfoolery. Me! Tomfoolery! I've never been more offended in my life. But I'll let you be the judge. While everyone is discussing my "actions," let me tell you what really went down.

And before I start, no, I'm not being dramatic. I'm a theater kid, feel me? Or I used to be. Tried it for two weeks right after everything happened. But still, it counts, and as such, we emphasize! There's a difference between emphasizing and being dramatic.

Oh, I know, I know. What, you may ask, is a nearly six-foot, two-hundred-pound Black kid from the South doing in the theater and not playing football? Well, Sergeant Stereotype, for one, I'm good at it. Turns out acting comes naturally to me. Suck it, broad generalizations.

And two . . . well, I got kicked off my football team after . . . everything went down. Injustice, right?

Anyway, all that pales in pasty comparison to what actually happened when I turned twelve. Now listen, I'm going to try and keep it tame, but it was pretty gruesome. I'm talking *gas station toilet after burrito-bowl Tuesday* gruesome. I'm talking *pimple-popping a tree zit* gruesome. (DO NOT GOOGLE *TREE ZITS* IF YOU EVER WANT TO EAT AGAIN.) Still interested? Cool. Allow me to get you caught up real quick.

January 2. Union Station. Downtown Chicago.

It was the day before my birthday. Minutes before my birthday, actually. I was at the front of the line to the passenger-assistance window. Everyone, including me, was tired and cranky after our forty-hour train ride had been even longer because of delays.

"Name?" asked the agent.

I leaned closer to the mic on the window. "Jackson."

"First name?"

"That *is* my first name."

The agent—an old lady with warm brown skin, a faint island accent, and two pairs of glasses on her head—sighed. I shrugged. If she didn't comment on me having two last names, I wouldn't say anything about her two pairs of glasses. Plus, it's rude to comment on another person's appearance, feel me?

"Last name, then."

"Freeman. Jax Freeman."

A bell chimed in the distance, and across the room, a man in a conductor's uniform glanced over. I couldn't tell exactly, but it looked like he was frowning.

Join the party, I thought. *This is the worst week of my life.*

"Okay, Mr. Jackson 'Jax' Freeman, what are you running from?"

"I'm ... sorry, what? I'm not running."

The agent didn't look up. "It's eleven p.m. Everybody here is running from something. What's your problem?"

I blew out a frustrated puff of air. Fine. Where to begin? With the fact that I'd been forced to uproot myself from my home in Raleigh, North Carolina, and move here? To live with a bunch of relatives I hadn't seen in years? All because of something that wasn't my fault?

Maybe it was because Mom and Dad hadn't known ahead of time that kids under thirteen couldn't travel on the train without an adult. When we found that out at the Amtrak station in Raleigh, the two of them exchanged a look—*the* Look that they always give each other when they're about to ask me to lie about my age. Most parents say their kids are younger to get discounts and stuff like that. Mine? They tell me to say I'm older, on account of my size.

There, I said it. I'm big. Nothing wrong with that; it is what it is. Sometimes people think I'm my dad (handy during parent/teacher conferences) or that I'm trying to scam Happy Meals (really?), but most times they leave me alone.

Until they find out I'm just a kid. Whatever. At least I'd made it to Chicago without getting in trouble.

Yet.

But you know what? Maybe my problem was the fact that I'd gone to passenger assistance to try to locate my two oversized, heavily taped-up camouflage-print duffels. Hand-me-down bags from Dad, who'd helped load them onto the train before he waved me off. I didn't know how I was supposed to lug both of them to meet my favorite uncle (technically my only uncle, but who's counting?), Uncle Moe. I hadn't seen him in a few years, not since the last family reunion, when he bought me a wizard's cape and a wand that shot out glitter. Mom had complained, but Uncle Moe had said *Black boys can be magical, too* with a weird look on his face. Anyway, he was supposed to pick me up here and drive me to my new house in Chicago. Or old house, depending on how you looked at it. Me? I tried not to look at all. Things were so bad I shouldn't have had to face them head-on. *Wriggle past your problems*, that's what I always say.

The point is, I figured I'd get a baggage cart when I got off the train. Except . . . my duffels didn't get off with me.

"Yeah, my bags went missing," I said to the agent. "Five feet long, camo print, really beat-up? Look like somebody packed their whole life in them?"

She stared at me. "Mm-kay, sweetie, just a sec." She perched one pair of glasses on the bridge of her nose while she consulted her computer.

I stood in front of the passenger-assistance window and tugged on my too-small shirt again, trying to loosen it a little.

Then I rubbed my arms. It was freezing here. Winter in Chicago was apparently in full force, and snow flurries drifted in from the train tunnels as I blew into my cupped hands. I'd packed my coat in one of the duffels, since it had been a balmy seventy-two degrees when I left Raleigh, and the wind now knifing through my chest was a cruel reminder of how silly an idea that had been.

Everything I needed was in my bags. The three brand-new school outfits I'd begged Mom to get me for my first week. My good phone charger (I have a backup coiled up in my pocket, but when I use it, I have to hold it at a certain angle and it smells like burned waffles). My lucky cleats, even though the new school didn't have a football team. Those cleats went with me everywhere. Well, except for today. The only things I had on me were a crumpled ten-dollar bill, a cheap cell phone with a nearly drained battery, a wonky old phone charger, and a handwritten note I double-checked every few minutes.

Oh, and a full bladder. Just an hour left in the eleventh chapter of my existence, and I couldn't wait to release the horrible vibes of the last year along with the Dr Pepper I had drunk two hours ago. New year, new me, and all that, right? Hopefully year number twelve would be better.

"Hmm." The passenger-assistance lady adjusted her glasses, then pulled them off and rubbed her temples. "Hmph."

Or maybe year number twelve would be more of the same.

She sighed. "Sweetie, it looks like there was a problem back in Carolina. Your bags didn't make the transfer."

"The transfer?"

"Mm-hmm. You needed to take them with you when you changed trains."

I groaned. All my stuff! I didn't want to mention that I'd thought train stations had baggage handlers, like at the airport. "Can someone send them here?"

"Wellll…let's see if I can track them down through Lost and Found.…I believe that train went to Atlanta.…Hmm. No, wait." She paused. "Let me see, that can't be right."

Pay attention now. This is when things got weird.

The clock in the corner hit midnight, a bell rang in the distance, and all of a sudden, I was twelve years old. Glorious. Cause for celebration, right? Wrong. WRONG. It was at this point that things really went south. I'm not talking Interstate 85 to Atlanta like my duffel bags—I'm saying things went downhill with no brakes. They took a turn for the worse without putting their blinkers on. I'm saying it was bad, feel me?

"You shouldn't have come."

I blinked. "Excuse me?"

The agent looked up. "Yes?"

"Did you…" I began, then cleared my throat. "Did you say I shouldn't—"

"Just give me one more second, young man," she said, putting her glasses back on and turning to her computer monitor. I stared at her, befuddled. I was going to chalk it up to being sleepy and nearly frozen when the voice came again. This time I saw the speaker, and I wish I hadn't.

The pair of glasses still on top of the lady's head—the bright blue ones on a silver chain, those glasses, a totally normal thing that exists—blinked. And *spoke*. I swear, even though I didn't know where their mouth was.

"You don't belong here," the glasses said. *"It's too soon. No training, no heirloom, no chance, no way."*

"Um…"

The agent looked up, which took the judgmental (unfairly, in my opinion) glasses out of my view. But before she could comment, another employee—an old man with graying hair and half of his uniform shirt untucked—limped over. It would've been reassuring to have someone else see what I was seeing, to confirm that my brain hadn't froze along with my fingers and toes, except…

"Everythang all right?" he asked.

"OOOHHH, THIS IS GONNA BE A BAD ONE, Y'ALL!" his belt buckle said. *"GRAB THE AIR FRESHENER AND PLUNGERS—WE MIGHT BE HERE A WHILE!"*

That's right. The man was wearing two belts, and on one of them, the silver buckle resembled the face of an old man. It was grimacing in pain, twisting into knots as if it weren't made of metal, and talking. Let me repeat that: HIS BELT WAS TALKING!

"What… is happening right now?" I mumbled.

The shimmering blue glasses twisted on top of the passenger-assistance agent's head. *"Wallace, don't nobody want to hear about your toilet troubles—you're dead! Save it for your spirit spades game later."*

"Wilma, I can't," the belt buckle said. *"I swear, this is gonna be the death of me and the generations that come after. It's*

genetic. A lavatory lineage. A bloodline of bowels. It's something I ate, and now my whole family's gonna pay. Oooh, call the fire department—it's getting smoky in here!"

"You haven't eaten in sixty years, you hunk of junk," said the glasses. *"You're dead!"*

"I am haunted by the toilet-clogging troubles of my past!" The scowling belt buckle twisted toward me. *"Young man, I'm gonna hire you. Find my next of kin. Warn them! Warn them of the colon crises they'll face if they don't change their diets. Please!"*

"Hush," the glasses—Wilma, I guess?—said. *"You can't hire him—he's not a summoner. Now go about your business before you attract too much attention. Gonna get this boy in trouble."*

I rubbed my eyes furiously, trying to scrub away the weirdness unfolding in front of me. Clearly, I was overtired. Imagining things. What I needed to do was to get my bags back, then go find a warm place with an outlet where I could charge my cell phone and call my mom to tell her I made it. Find my bags, then call Mom. Find my bags, then . . .

"Oh, my goodness!" The agent sat up straighter as she read something on her monitor.

Her coworker peered over her shoulder, then whistled. "Well, I'll be," he said.

"Is everything okay?" I asked, the talking accessories forgotten.

The woman jerked backward in her seat as if something had thumped her in her chest. She inhaled sharply, and her face twisted in horror as she reread whatever information had popped up on her computer. "Lord almighty, are you serious? That can't be. That...Oh my word."

"What?"

She didn't answer, just tapped on the keyboard and mumbled prayers as she squinted at the screen. Finally, after an anxious minute, she sighed again and shook her head. "I'm sorry, sweetie, but it looks like your bags ain't coming this way at all."

"Why not?"

She hesitated, glancing at her colleague as if deciding whether she should tell me, then sighed. "Because, apparently, they were pulled off at...Greensboro? Yep, Greensboro. Says here they were considered a...'possible threat.'"

The man turned toward me. "You, a threat? How old are you? Nineteen? Eighteen?"

"I...I'm—" I stammered out, backing away from the window before cutting myself off. If they found out I was twelve, I'd get in trouble. The other people in line stared at me suspiciously, and I swallowed my comment. "Okay, thank you! I'll be fine," I blurted out, then turned and walked away.

As I left, I heard Wilma—the pair of blue glasses still perched on the agent's head—call after me. *"Like I said, you shouldn't have come."*

I was losing it. Hallucinating. That was it. I had to be hallucinating. Was that a side effect of hypothermia? Of starvation? I hadn't eaten solid food since breakfast, when I'd snarfed all my snacks because I was nervous.

I needed to get out of there.

How old are you?

That question followed me wherever I went. I guess when you're bigger than people expect, they think you're grown, that you're out of place, or—even worse—threatening. It happens, feel me? You get used to it.

Sort of.

I went up to the street level. The digital clock in the middle of the waiting area ticked over to 12:10 a.m. I pulled the note out of my pocket and, for the hundredth time, read the instructions I had jotted down.

Great Hall, marble staircase to Canal St. city buses

Simple enough, right? No way I could miss that. I walked over to the stairs where Uncle Moe was supposed to meet me. Mom had insisted on having at least one person from the family be with me on my birthday. You know, since my parents couldn't. They were still back in North Carolina because Dad had injured his back planting begonias. (More like *back-gone-ias*, amirite? Right? It's fine; I'll wait here while you figure it out.) I could've been there, too, in the middle of the Carolina Panthers' winter football academy for top prospects. I'd saved up my allowance and birthday money and begged and borrowed to pay for my spot. I'd just finished my first semester at Ligon Middle School with a bunch of friends I'd grown up with, and in December I showed out at the offensive-lineman camp. It had been the best four months of my life.

Followed by the worst week of my life.

"Attention!" came an automated message over the station's

public address system. *"Union Station will be closing at one a.m. Please exit the building. Attention..."*

Closing? What?! What was I supposed to do now? Where was my uncle? Had he gone back home because my train was so late? I needed to call him before I got kicked to the cold, cruel curb.

I scanned the walls for an outlet where I could charge my phone for a few minutes. But the only thing I saw was a display on the other side of the floor. It was a replica of the inside of a train sleeping car, and two smiling Black people in uniform, a man and a woman, stood and waved in a digital projection in front of it. A glass case to the side held various memorabilia, including a hat, a folded coat, a metal pin, and even some old-fashioned train tickets. Two boys my age were checking it out. Thinking one of them might have a phone I could borrow, I drifted over.

"The Pullman sleeping car porter," a voice narrated from a speaker mounted on the train replica. *"The lifeblood of the rails. For decades, African Americans helped usher in the luxury and efficiency of train travel across America as porters, touching the lives of many. Also..."*

The narration continued, but the display flickered as a bright orange light flared nearby. For a second I thought I saw a large silhouette of a hand fall across the train replica before I had to squint and turn away from the strobing effect. When I turned back, both the light and the shadow were gone.

The two kids walked away with their hands in their pockets.

"Hey, wait," I called to them. "Did y'all see that?"

They turned, and the nearest to me frowned in confusion. "See what?" he asked.

"That weird shadow hand?"

"You saw the—?" the second kid started to say before the first one elbowed him.

"Nah, you're tripping," the first one said and pulled his friend away. They exited so fast I didn't have a chance to ask them about borrowing a phone.

I turned back to the display. It was no longer flickering, and the voice continued to narrate, but there was something different about the setup now. It took me a minute to realize that one of the items in the memorabilia case was missing—the pin. I looked at the empty space, then shrugged. Had one of the boys taken it?

If so, that wasn't right. But it also wasn't my problem. I had too many of my own already.

I made my way to the Canal Street door, hoping Uncle Moe was waiting outside. That was it—he was out there in his car, and because it was my birthday, we'd stop on the way home for midnight cocoa, just like my parents and I did on special occasions. Like when Mom became a principal. Or when Dad's begonias successfully bloomed before Mr. Barnes's did across the street. (Don't ask—it's like a whole grown-up competition with unwritten rules and lots of sulking.) I loved those outings because it was like we were between yesterday and tomorrow, and nothing existed except for us three. The Freemans. That's all I wanted for my birthday—for things to be like they used to be. All of us. Together. Home.

But if wishes were fishes, no one would go hungry, so instead, I was all alone.

Do you like that saying? I've got a million of them.

As I'm sure you've guessed, nobody was waiting on Canal Street. Apparently, Uncle Moe had given up on me. No bags, no family, no ride. The only car was a police cruiser parked at the curb.

I turned and stared around the Great Hall, consulted the note again, and checked the exit sign to make sure I was in the right place. But no one was there to greet me. No one to shower me with kisses, wrinkle their nose at my outfit, or even ruffle my hair, all of which I hated, but, you know, at least they proved I existed.

I sighed.

Maybe Uncle Moe would come first thing in the morning, after my mom called looking for me.

"You there. Hey! You know we're closing, right?"

I looked around, confused. All the passengers and employees had left the station, so where was . . .

"Up here!"

A face appeared on the digital clock, the colon between the hour and minutes wrinkling like a nose. *"We closed now, you hear? You one of those summoners, ain't you? Or close enough. Look here, I gotta job for you, and ain't no time like the present. Get it? Time? Present? Hoo-boy, Imma mess."*

"No thanks," I said, dazed and exhausted. "I'm . . . going to go now."

"But that's the wrong way!"

Since it was too cold to wait outside without a coat, and I didn't want to get snagged by a cop, I hightailed it up the stairs to find a place to hang out until Uncle Moe finally figured out I needed him. I'd thought I left all of my troubles back in North Carolina, but I was wrong.

New year. New me. New problems.

CHAPTER
TWO

"A STRING OF BURGLARIES ACROSS SOUTH CHICAGO *and into Naperville has left authorities puzzled. Victims report that the stolen items are worth very little money but have personal significance. Also, the search for a missing couple on Chicago's West Side has been called off, as it has been unsuccessful after several days. And now, the weather. Severe blizzards…"*

The news echoed from video monitors spaced across the mezzanine level of Union Station. I guessed they were always on, even when the place was closed. Maybe the custodians had to come and turn them off?

Maybe the weird inanimate talking objects needed something to watch, I thought. *Did the candelabra from* Beauty and the Beast *watch television?*

I passed a giant mural showing workers in overalls lifting hammers above a shiny set of railroad tracks. "'The Gandy

Dancers,'" I read aloud. The faces of men and women in all shades of color beamed with pride. "'The workers who connected America.'" At that moment my stomach grumbled, and I turned away from the image to deal with more pressing concerns.

I stared longingly at the sandwich stalls and snack shops—all now closed—lining the hallway on either side of me. There were spots selling pretzels, ready-made turkey subs, even a burrito joint. I was scanning the price lists—grimaced at one, made a strangled sound in my throat at another—and tightening my belt (Not literally, I wasn't wearing a belt. More like, pulled the drawstrings on my shorts even tighter, right? You get the point) when I remembered that it didn't matter anyway. Everything was closed.

I left and was just about to make do with my last stick of gum and some mint-scented pocket lint when I saw a tiny shop tucked between a utility room and an out-of-order restroom. (Seriously . . . the world needs to have a conversation about the lack of working bathrooms. If my mother were here, she'd have the whole administrative staff of Union Station sitting on the floor around her while she yelled at them about accessibility. My mother can be scary when someone isn't fairly treated.) I nearly walked past the shop, except I smelled something so familiar, so delicious, that it stopped me in my tracks. Why was someone still cooking when everything was closed? Then my feet decided to head toward it on their own.

"'Miss Ella's Pecans 'n Spreads,'" I read off the handmade sign. The shop was barely the size of a closet. A glass display with a heat lamp warmed caramelized pecans, cinnamon-dusted almonds, boiled peanuts, and—for some weird reason—empty glass bottles lined up in neat rows. Next to the case was a raggedy piece of cardboard with a crude picture of what I thought was a dusty ice cream cone at first, until I realized it was a mound of pecans rolled up in paper. "'Two dollars or best offer.' Best offer? What does that mean?"

I didn't realize I'd spoken out loud until a tiny old Black woman popped up from behind the display. "Simple," she said.

"AAAAAH!" I shouted, nearly jumping out of my shoes. Where had she come from?

"Quiet, boy, you gonna wake the neighborhood!" she snapped in a country drawl.

"aaaaaaaah!" I shouted in lowercase.

"Better." She nodded. "Now, the sign means that for two dollars you can get some of the best pecans on this side of the river, plus a one-card spread to reveal your fortune for today. Unless you got somethin' better to offer."

The woman had on her Sunday-best wig, tucked beneath a hairnet and pinned in place. She wore an apron that was nearly larger than her body and carried a wooden pole that towered over her head. The top of the pole was carved with faces wearing various expressions—scowling, smiling, crying, and shouting.

"Well?" the lady asked, her dozens of bracelets rattling as she folded her arms across her chest. "Get a good look?"

I flushed, because I'd definitely been staring. "Sorry."

"Don't be sorry, be better."

She sounded just like my grandmother. "Yes, ma'am," I said.

Miss Ella (I assumed) studied me for a few extra seconds, then tapped the counter with her pole. With a muttered grunt, she lifted it, and I realized it wasn't a pole—it was the largest wooden spoon I'd ever seen. It had to be almost as tall as me! The old woman began to stir a giant pot next to her. I inhaled another whiff of vanilla and cinnamon and clove and other spices, and I swear my stomach threatened me, that's how loud it grumbled.

"Sounds like you gotta belly full of thunder over there," Miss Ella said with a short laugh. "You gonna get you somethin'?"

"I guess so," I said reluctantly, gripping my ten dollars. It was supposed to be for emergencies. Did being hungry count as an emergency?

"You guess? You don't want my pecans?" She put both hands on her hips, and I swear the spoon kept stirring.

"Um…" I said, squinting at the spoon. "No. I mean, yes, I do."

"No, yes… Make up your mind, child, before you get dizzy. Is your money a little tight?"

I opened my mouth to protest, then closed it. She hadn't said it with any judgment or anything, like other people would. Like my friend Mikey back in Raleigh, who'd joke about how I should only look for WIC snacks when we hit up the stores on the weekend. Or the afterschool-care lady in fourth grade, who would always leave reminder-to-pay notes in my backpack even though Mama always paid on time.

"You ain't got a better offer?"

I looked up. Miss Ella was tapping the sign with the handle of her giant spoon. "Two dollars for the pecans, or a better offer. Now, I'm an old lady, and working this here spoon gets mighty tiring. So I'll cut you a deal. While I stir this next batch, you can tell me a story 'bout yourself, and we can have us an arrangement. How's that sound?"

"It sounds like charity," I said.

Miss Ella sucked her teeth. "Child, charity ain't nothing but another word for help. Look, closed mouths don't get fed, so if you wanna eat, I suggest you get to talking. Shop's closing soon."

I wanted to say no and walk away, because I wasn't gonna be a burden on nobody. In fact, I'd made up my mind to go drool next to a vending machine when Miss Ella flicked a pecan at me. I caught it out of reflex. It was still warm and smelled incredible. My hand popped it in my mouth before my brain could come up with an excuse to hand it back.

Oh.

My.

God.

The taste of sugar and spices exploded on my tongue like sweet fireworks. Crusty and chewy and with a hint of salt—these were better than the ones they sold back at the Carolina State Fair, and we used to stand in line for over an hour to get those.

"Now then," Miss Ella said, "we got ourselves a deal?"

Finally, after several seconds, I nodded.

She clapped once. "Well, don't just stand there like a frog on a log in a bog, gimme some tales, child! And none of them new-fangled whiz-pop adventures you kids like these days. I want a good story. Something about you. Gimme that Earl Grey."

I stared at her. "You mean . . . you want some tea?"

"Don't correct your elders, young man."

"But . . ." I said, "what if I don't really know any good stories? Not about me."

"Everybody has a story. A memory, a dream, a vision—"

I looked up. "Visions? Like, seeing stuff that isn't there?" Maybe she'd seen strange things, too, and heard them. Could it be something in Union Station making me see stuff? A gas leak? At this point I'd take reassurance from anyone, including a random tiny old woman.

"Ooh, child, dreams and visions are the best stories. They're the ones our subconscious is trying to tell us. A direct line to the spirits. You just gotta answer the collect call and open yourself up to what they're saying."

Hope flickered inside me. "And you can understand them?"

"Child, you're in luck, because deciphering visions is my specialty. Speak." She slid a paper cone of pecans across the counter and watched me closely as I took it.

I took a deep breath. Despite the strangeness of it all, I really *did* want to tell someone about what I'd seen, just to make sure I wasn't losing my mind. Okay, I could do this. "So . . . I've been seeing things here in the station ever since I arrived. I thought I was sleepy, but maybe . . . I don't know, they felt real."

The spoon stirred faster. "Hmm. Could be powerful

messages," said Miss Ella. "Or could be you need glasses. Hard to say. Keep going."

"Well, actually, earlier I thought I saw..." My voice trailed off because it seemed too silly to say out loud. "I thought a pair of glasses talked to me."

The spoon paused. "A pair of glasses?" Miss Ella frowned.

"And a belt. A gassy belt."

She raised one gray eyebrow. "A belt...with gas."

"Well, more the belt *buckle*, but still, that's wild, right?" I spoke in a hurry and through a mouthful of pecans. It was like the snack had removed the mental dam blocking my words. "Probably stress or something like that, right? That's what I figured. Moving cities, changing schools, no football, no friends—"

"These glasses," she interrupted, "and the belt buckle. You heard them talking?"

I nodded. "I know it sounds ridiculous. I thought so, too. But I was just, I don't know, stressing about my bags, and now no one's here to pick me up. This has been the worst birthday ever."

"A birthday!" Miss Ella scooped up another newspaper cone of nuts and handed it to me. "Then you *must* accept this on top of your other new gift. I insist."

I took it, juggling it with the first cone, a little dazed from the sudden change in conversation. What did she mean by my 'other new gift'? But I wasn't about to refuse free food. "These things are really delicious. Did you put something addictive in them?" I asked as a joke.

She sniffed. "Ain't nothing in my pecans except for brown sugar and a little luck powder."

"Luck powder?"

"Or maybe that was my laxative..." she said, pausing her stirring and examining the pot critically.

I stopped chewing. "Laxative?" I squeaked.

She shrugged. "We'll know sooner or later. Best not to stray too far from a toilet. Now then, these visions..."

"They're nothing, right?" I rubbed my stomach. I wasn't sure whether she was kidding about the powder or not. Was that an extra-tingly rumble I felt?

"Nonsense," Miss Ella said, resuming her stirring but now keeping one eye on me.

I breathed a sigh of relief. "Nonsense. Great. So I was just imagining things. I guess that makes me feel bet—"

"No, your vision is fine."

"It is?"

"Yep." She checked the consistency of the next batch, then turned her full gaze on me. "You can see spirits, including the ancestors of some folk, I reckon. A powerful gift, that is. This reading suddenly got a lot more interesting."

Words wouldn't form in my brain. Me, able to see spirits? That was the most ridiculous thing I'd ever heard!

She pulled an old deck of cards from her apron's front pocket. Not like the cards Dad used to play spades. These were larger and thicker. And... older. "Take one card but lay it flat on the case. Miss Ella will connect it to your story after you finish. Well, go on now, don't keep an old woman waiting."

She stirred the giant pot with increased energy while she peered at me expectantly. The wind howled outside as I hesitated. Then I reached over the case, plucked a card from the deck, and set it in front of me. Slowly, carefully, Miss Ella extended her right hand and placed a single wrinkled brown finger on the card. The wind quieted. Miss Ella set her spoon in the pot, then flipped over the card and held it up. It had a drawing of a man in a long coat striding out of a tomb in a graveyard. His face was blank, and yet it drew me in. But when I looked up to meet Miss Ella's eyes, she was wearing a horrified expression, as if she'd just realized something important.

"You have a mission," Miss Ella whispered. "You are on a path that forks. One direction will lead you to safety, alone, but others will suffer. The other path leads to others' safety, and the righting of a wrong, but *you* will suffer. Who do you want to suffer, boy?"

Her voice deepened.

The noise around us faded.

Her eyes bored into mine.

"You have a responsibility. A legacy to fulfill. Can you do this, child? Are your shoulders wide enough to carry generations of expectations? Of hopes? Of dreams? Souls of all ages fled here from deep in the swamps to the forests of steel and concrete, and they hide here still."

"Um..." I whispered, taking a step back. "Miss Ella?"

"This is your destiny!" she hissed. "Will you accept it? It comes soon. Sooner than you expect, sooner than you hope, sooner than you fear. A mission. A decision. Stay here when the call comes, and I can help you. Teach you, prepare you. You cannot go it alone, and I fear—"

"*JAX FREEMAN TO THE INFORMATION DESK,*" the public address system blared from the speakers in the ceiling. "*JAX FREEMAN TO THE INFORMATION DESK. YOUR PARTY IS WAITING.*"

The announcement jolted me out of a daze. A half-empty cone of pecans rested in my right hand as I stared at the speaker. I thought the station was closed. How did they know I was still here?

Then I put all that aside. My "party" had to be Uncle Moe. He'd finally arrived!

When I glanced back at Miss Ella, she shrank back. "Freeman?" she whispered. "You're a Freeman? Then it's time."

"Um, I have to go now—"

"I wouldn't."

"Okay . . . right." I started backing up. This was too much. It was definitely time to scoot. "Sooo . . . thank you for the pecans?"

Miss Ella scooped another cone of nuts and shuffled around the counter to get closer. Her eyes were wild, almost desperate, as she pulled a packet from her apron pocket and poured powder into the palm of her hand. Not a laxative, I hoped!

"Listen to me, child," she said. "Your ancestors have a job for you—today! You can see spirits, and your ancestors need your help! Even if you're not a summoner yet, you can do this."

Now I was all the way creeped out. This was the third time tonight someone—or something—had talked about hiring me or sending me on a mission. "No, thank you, I don't need any more lax—I mean, pecans. In fact, here's the rest of the other cone. I'm sorry I ate them—AAAH!"

I ducked as she hurled the dust in her palm at me. It missed and fell on the floor. That was it. I was gone. Skedaddling. Scramming. Outta there. For the second time that night, in what was quickly becoming the story of my life, I turned and ran.

CHAPTER
THREE

I TOOK THE STAIRS DOWN TWO AT A TIME, ALMOST at a dead sprint. Half the lights were still on, but the rest had been turned off as the employees began to leave. The station was practically empty, and I thought I was too late. I put on a burst of speed and was relieved when I rounded a corner and saw the information desk come into view. But I didn't see Uncle Moe. Instead, a tall, skinny man in a conductor's uniform and hat stood waiting for me. His face was pale, almost gray, and his mouth—when he smiled at me—was missing several teeth. A silver name tag was pinned to his breast pocket. BUCK was all it said.

"Ahh, young Freeman?"

"Yes," I said suspiciously.

"Perfect, perfect. They're ready for you."

"Who's *they*?"

JAX FREEMAN AND THE PHANTOM SHRIEK

"Your bags, of course! There was a mix-up. We found them. Got them at the platform downstairs if you can identify them."

A huge weight was being lifted off my shoulders. My bags! They hadn't been lost forever! I could get my good charger, plug in my phone, and call my parents. "Really? Thanks! Sure, I can identify them."

"This way, then."

I followed him to a service elevator, grateful that he was still working after hours, and we descended to the arrivals platform below. He pressed a button and beamed down at me, and I flinched. His eyes were red, and his fingernails were long and curled, ending in . . . well, in points. Plus, in the cramped space, he smelled like . . . I can't even describe it really. Something old. Not like old people, but like something that's been sitting in an attic too long. Mildewy. Rotten. And then, to make it worse, he'd tried to cover it up with body spray, but the smell still lingered. When the doors opened, I almost sprinted out, so happy to breathe fresh air again.

It took me several seconds to realize Conductor Buck had stopped walking.

"Where are the bags? I'm so glad you found them," I said, eager to get to them and grab a hoodie. Or two. It was bitterly cold down on the platforms. Chicago was not playing—any colder and someone was gonna have to warn Jack Frost that it was on sight.

I was breathing into my cupped palms, trying to get some warmth into them, when a chill colder than the night air ran down my spine.

"Hmm, yes, we're glad, too," the conductor said from behind me. "Glad to be living again."

I turned to see Conductor Buck pulling a piece of string out of his chest pocket. No. Out of his . . . *chest*? I must've been seeing things, because I could've sworn he was pulling out stitches. He sprinkled the string with a pinch of dust (Come on now, what was with all the dust around here? What if I had allergies?), and it began to glow.

Seriously.

It began to *glow*. And grow. It stretched, shining like a coil of LED lights, and curled up at his feet.

"Come here, little birdie," he sang, leering at me as he lifted the string with one hand and coiled it like a lasso. With the other hand, he pulled a needle out of his pocket. Long, pointed, wickedly sharp. "Come, I'm gonna stitch us back together. It won't hurt none at all. Well, not me, at least." He giggled.

As he stepped closer, the clothes on him began to fall apart, as if the string he'd pulled was the only thing keeping them intact. First went his hat, then his coat. Underneath he was practically skin and bones, thin and drawn and flapping, and very, very terrifying.

I backed up, searching for an exit but finding only train tracks on either side of me. The elevator closed, and Conductor Buck now stood in front of the stairs. He flung out the string and it raced toward me like a python, slithering on the floor and leaving a trail of silver dust in its wake.

"Hey!" I shouted, jumping aside. The sound of rattling

breath was the only warning I got before Conductor Buck shoulder-charged me, sending me reeling backward.

"Rotten child!" he snapped. I guess he didn't realize I was actually bigger than him. The impact had forced him back several paces as well. "Give me your skin!"

"What?! No! What sort of weirdo man are you?!"

"Weirdo? Man? None of the above, none of the above. Not yet. But this skin is fading. Been a wraith too long. Just you wait, though. My time is coming, right after I peel you like a nasty fruit." He giggled again and lunged at me, and only me tripping over my own feet saved me.

Wraith? This night was surreal. I was in a fever dream. That had to be it. At any second, I'd wake up and still be on the train, and my uncle would be waiting for me at the station. All I had to do was wake up. I had to wake up. I had to . . .

"Get over here!"

I blinked and ducked as the string whistled over my head, missing me by mere inches. The tail end of it stabbed my cheek, and I felt a sharp pain, like a hook had embedded itself in my face. I grabbed the string with both hands and yanked it out, yelping as the pain burst across my jaw. The same pain stung my palms as I tried to shake the string loose.

But I couldn't.

"Gotcha now, boy," Conductor Buck crowed in triumph. He stalked toward me, the skin around his mouth starting to fall away in flakes. Soon I could see bone, and even his eyes were gone. Only hollow sockets filled with unfathomable darkness remained. "Ooh, I can't wait till your skin is mine. You know how long it's been since I felt the wind? Touched grass?"

"Forever," I muttered. I couldn't help it.

"Close enough!" he snapped. "But that changes tonight. When I put on your skin and string your bones around my neck, I'll be back, and better than ever. The power of a summoner is a mighty thing, and I want it now, no matter what she says."

"She?" I said, scooting backward, trying to buy some time. "I don't know who you're talking about! You got the wrong guy, I swear. I don't even know what a summoner is."

Conductor Buck laughed even as more skin peeled away, revealing his few yellow teeth. "You can't hide it, boy. I saw you talking to the spirits earlier. The ancestors don't speak to just anyone. Gotta be powerful to hear, but to talk to them? Don't play sly with me, Freeman. Yesss, a Freeman summoner, too! Oooh, she's been looking for you. But if I get you first, we'll see who gives the orders. We'll see! I've been cooped up in this station for decades, but soon, ooh baby, soon! Now come HERE!"

The last word came out in a roar as he pulled himself forward on the string still stuck to my palms. Without thinking, I kicked out in a panic, trying to keep the wraith away from me. My right foot connected with his left shin. WHAM!

He shrieked in pain as some of his bones clattered to the train-platform floor. He hopped on one leg, trying to remain upright as he glared at me. "Repel powder!" he shouted. "That's a dirty trick. Dirty! You been talking to that witch!"

A rumble sounded, and my eyes flicked to the clock on the far wall. I knew, as sure as my name was Jax and water was wet, that a train was going to come through in one minute. Express. From Gary, Indiana. How I knew this I don't know, but now wasn't the time to question it, nor was it the first question I'd ask if given the opportunity. Plenty of weirder things to investigate. What I did know was I had to move.

"GIVE ME YOUR SKIN!" Conductor Buck shrieked, hopping toward me.

I took off my right shoe and flipped it over to see glittering black grains embedded in the sole—the same powder Miss Ella had thrown at me and I'd apparently stepped in. Whatever that powder was, laxative or not, it was protecting me.

As much as I hated to sacrifice a low-top Chuck Taylor special edition, I launched my shoe like a missile and watched it land square in the emaciated chest of the shrieking skeleton man.

WHAP!

Conductor Buck was blown backward off the platform in a tangle of bones and shredded uniform bits, clattering in a scattered heap on the tracks below. I ran, one foot bare, toward the elevator as he shouted threats.

"That's a dirty trick, Freeman! When I pull myself together, Imma find you and wear you like an evening coat. I been stuck here eighty-nine years, boy—you ain't getting away. I'm not foolin' with you! You are mine! Get back here! You hear me?"

The elevator dinged, and I leaped inside. I punched the

button for the ground floor over and over, willing it to close. *Eighty-nine years? This isn't happening! It can't be happening!* When I looked up, Conductor Buck had shoved his left arm into his right leg socket and was crawling along the tracks like a misshapen crab, or a twisted, nightmarish spider from a horror movie. He dragged himself closer, howling in rage.

"Gonna wear you like a dinner jacket, boy, you hear me?"

"Come on come on come on, close!" I shouted at the elevator doors. Why were they so slow? Was this it? The end? In a new city with no friends and one shoe?

"Don't you dare run, boy!" Conductor Buck shouted. "I'm gonna—"

Here it comes, I thought.

SPLAT!

A train rolled into the station, bashing the wraith to pieces. Trash, dust, and bits of an angry ghost rippled outward, and too late I realized it was all heading toward me. The shock wave slammed me against the back of the elevator, and as I slid down, my head hit the handrail. Stars exploded in my eyes, and then everything went dim. Faintly, I could hear one final howl being carried by the wind.

The elevator doors closed. My brain was spinning as my chest heaved from all the running. Wraith. Summoner. Spirits? Someone was playing a huge joke on me. *Welcome to Chicago, Jax. Here's your free hallucination with a concussion on top.* So far, being twelve sucked. At least things couldn't possibly get any worse.

The elevator doors slid open as I struggled to my feet, just in time to see a sour-faced Uncle Moe, an Amtrak security officer, and a tall, severe-looking Black woman marching toward me.

Gran.

"JACKSON JOSIAH FREEMAN, WHERE HAVE YOU BEEN?!"

CHAPTER
FOUR

YOU CAN SEE SPIRITS, AND YOUR ANCESTORS NEED your help.

The words of Miss Ella kept echoing in my ears on the ride home. I hadn't had time to process them, though, other than to note that it was more like *I* was the one who needed help. Gran kept lecturing me about representing our family in the right way and apparently being the poster child for Black children everywhere. I did my best to listen, but between the worn-out suspension on her old Ford pickup and the way Uncle Moe considered the speed limit only a suggestion, I was fighting for my life in the back seat.

"You're fortunate to even have this chance," she said as Uncle Moe grumbled and whipped a 270-degree turn to cut through an alley.

"Hurgggg," I agreed, the seat belt nearly decapitating me.

"I keep telling everyone. I say, I can't keep collecting all y'all's problems."

"Glarrrgh."

"And where is your shoe? This is our turn, Moe."

At Gran's instruction, and without even checking the mirrors, Uncle Moe slid the car across four lanes of traffic to speed through the parking lot of a department store.

Gran side-eyed him. "You sure you got your license reinstated?"

Uncle Moe grunted. "I know how to drive. Been doing it for years. No piece of paper can change that."

I gulped. It must've been one of those cartoonishly loud ones, because Gran tutted at me from the front seat. "Don't worry, honey. Your uncle didn't lose his license because he's a bad driver—just because of some paperwork."

Okay, I guessed that wasn't too bad.

"It's been what, fourteen years now, Moe?"

Never mind. It was *absolutely* bad.

Uncle Moe grumbled and wrenched the wheel left so hard that we skidded around a perfectly safe and law-abiding minivan filled with what I'm sure was a family with their seat belts on and long lives ahead of them.

Meanwhile, Gran continued her lecture as if this were a normal occurrence. "Been taking care of cousins and nieces and nephews at the Freeman House for years, because family need to look out for family. Freemans sure do attract trouble, Lord knows it. Look at Moe! I have a soft spot for the troubled, sure do, sure do. But you . . . You'd better be on the straight-and-narrow path to rehabilitation, young man, or I won't save you from the hole you dig yourself into next time, hear me?"

"Gznnnng."

We practically drifted fast and furious into a parking spot in front of the Freeman House, as Gran called it. I had finally arrived, and I was still in one piece, though she had made me regret both with her lecture. Uncle Moe put the car in park, then leaned back and pulled out his phone. "I'll text your mom to let her know you arrived safely. Since your phone is dead."

"Thanks. Could you also let her know my bags went missing and I'm gonna need new stuff?" Better him than me. I wasn't looking forward to *that* conversation.

"Welcome to your new home," Gran said. "What do you think of it?"

I took in the Freeman House for the first time. Located on the west side of Chicago, on top of a hill overlooking abandoned factories and empty train tracks, it was the only house on the block.

"What happened to the other houses?" I asked. In the glow of the streetlamps, I could see that the neighboring lots were overgrown, with weeds poking up through the cracked sidewalks in front.

"They were torn down for an urban-renewal project that never got final approval," Uncle Moe muttered while typing. "Typical around here."

Looming high above it all like a fortress, the Freeman House looked like it could use some renewal, too. It was five stories tall, with a redbrick exterior and a dingy gray roof.

There were more windows than I'd ever seen on a building that wasn't a skyscraper, and they came in all shapes and sizes. The one on the top floor was tiny, and on the second floor, huge bay windows looked out over what used to be a garden. The detached garage was so run-down you couldn't pay me to go inside, and the wraparound front porch sagged in the middle.

"See that turret?" asked Gran, pointing to the southeast corner. "That's where you'll be staying."

"Turret?" I perked up at the word, picturing part of a spaceship, but then I realized she meant the little tower attached to the home. *Womp, womp.* Still, it could be cool to live in a tower, I guessed. I hoped.

Then there was the painted wooden sign propped up next to the front door and illuminated by the porch light. You've seen them before. They usually say something like HOME SWEET HOME, right? Well, not this one. This one read YOUR ANCESTORS ARE WATCHING.

Talk about creepy.

"It's big," I said finally. "And old."

Gran snorted. "It *is* big, and it *is* old. Your great-great-grandfather, Portis Freeman, built this house one hundred years ago. Wanted a place he and his buddies who worked on railroad sleeping cars could rest their heads without being discriminated against. Traveled the country, saved up some coins, then showed up in Chicago running from a pile of trouble. Sounds familiar, huh? They used to say, 'You use a compass to find north, but you use Portis Freeman to find trouble.'"

That *did* sound familiar.

* * *

"Speaking of trouble, you should be thanking the Lord that Amtrak didn't want to press charges," Gran said.

It was a little after two in the morning, Uncle Moe had gone to bed, and she and I were sitting in the kitchen as I devoured a hastily made PB&J sandwich. I was exhausted but curious about my surroundings. The cupboards were painted this really ugly orange color, and dirty rainforest-themed plates were stacked in the sink. A piece of paper had been taped on the faucet: HOT WATER NOT WORKING. So that's why the dishes hadn't been washed and why I was eating off a paper towel. Apparently, this house was as big a mess as I was.

"But I didn't do anything!" I protested. "Some weird zombie guy attacked me!" How was this being blamed on me?

She sighed. "They saw on a video monitor that you were walking barefoot down by the trains."

"I still had one shoe on, and I never lost my socks. . . ."

"They let you go with a warning because of the luggage mishap, and they're waiving the usual fine."

"The conductor told me they found my bags, but—"

"When Uncle Moe talked to Amtrak before we left, they said there isn't a Conductor Buck or anyone with a similar name employed at Union Station. Maybe you saw someone, maybe Amtrak was covering their butts, I don't know. Either way, you have to watch yourself."

I slouched in my seat, freezing when it squeaked ominously. "He *was* real."

Wasn't he? Was that thing even a *he*?

"Just...go get some sleep." Gran got up to take something out of the fridge. "In the morning you'll meet a neighborhood kid who can walk with you to school and show you around. Be good to know somebody before you get up there."

Oh yeah. In all the excitement I nearly forgot I'd be starting a new school tomorrow. Today. When I woke up in a few hours. *Nearly* forgot, because I still carried this knot of fear and worry in the pit of my stomach. Starting a new school was terrifying! Doing it in the middle of the year, with friends already made and teachers already picking favorites, was downright miserable. Then add in the fact I didn't have my best clothes, didn't have a complete pair of shoes, and would be looking like something cats leave on carpets in the middle of the night, and we had a recipe for disaster. Two servings of disaster. With sprinkles of awkward on top.

Gran pulled a small plate from a cupboard and fussed with something, her back to me. "Your uncle has your schedule. Pre-registered you and everything. Thank the Lord Moe's here. I don't know what I would do with this house if he wasn't. Every day something else is falling apart! Just don't talk to him before he's had his third cup of coffee. And, Jax..."

She turned around and held out a plate with a homemade cupcake on it, her other hand shielding the flame of a single candle.

"Happy birthday!"

*   *   *

"Maybe things aren't that bad," I said aloud to myself, panting as I climbed the stairs that wound up the turret. "Lots of cool people live in towers. The Avengers. Eiffel. Rapunzel." I stopped to take a breath. "I could be Bruh-punzel."

When I reached the landing, I paused. Another sign had been mounted above the hallway entrance: YOUR ANCESTORS BELIEVE IN YOU. After the evening's events, I was starting to think the house was trying to encourage me. And, if I was being honest, a house comforting me would be the least strange thing to have happened since I arrived.

"I'm glad someone's on my side," I muttered. "Thanks, Freeman House." I opened the door at the end of the hallway, then sighed. "Or maybe not."

My room was at the tippy top of the turret. It had its own separate staircase and was actually on two levels, the fourth and fifth floors. In any other tale, a kid with a two-story bedroom would be excited. Privacy, my own bathroom, and even a special pipe system that let me call down to the kitchen. It should've been an awesome room, right?

Not this one.

First off, the top floor of the turret (on the fifth floor of the house) was fake. The staircase just came to an end at a blank wall covered with spiders that looked like they'd jump me if I stayed too long.

The bottom floor of the turret was covered in cobwebs. Thick, spooky cobwebs. There was a lamp in the corner, but the bulb had burned out, so all I could see were sharp shadows and whatever the thin light from the moon outside the window landed on, like:

1. A bed that creaked almost as much as the floorboards.
2. A wooden dresser with peeling stickers from generations of Happy Meals.
3. A tiny bathroom with a rusty sink and a stained toilet bowl.

The pipes in there randomly clanked and clanged, giving me a heart attack. Imagine someone holding a pair of cymbals right by your ear and waiting until you were sitting on the toilet before they crashed them together. Yeah. Marvelous. The sounds startled me so bad I ran out the bathroom with my shorts around my ankles, tripped over a warped floorboard, and fell face-first into the thickest bunch of cobwebs I'd ever seen.

4. Finally, there was another sign hanging next to the dresser: YESTERDAY'S PROBLEMS ARE TOMORROW'S FUEL.

"Thank you, Freeman House," I choked out as I lay on the ground, pants down, toilet paper in my hands, spitting out what tasted like depression-flavored cotton candy. Yeah, maybe the house was right.... It was time to call this day a wrap.

* * *

In the morning, after hours of the pipes fighting in the walls, I was lying in bed, debating whether to get up ever again, when a Black kid popped his head around the door. He had sandy-brown skin, a mop of curls with a fresh fade, and owl eyes that darted around the room.

"What's shakin', bacon?" he said after a second. "You Jax?"

I grunted.

"I'm s'posed to be your lee-ay-zone or something."

"Or something."

He looked at me.

I looked at him.

When he continued to blink, I sighed and sat up. "What's your name?"

"Toussaint." He pronounced it *Two-Sahnt*.

"Like the city in Arizona?"

"Like the general of the Haitian Revolution. *And* the city. But it doesn't matter—no one *ever* calls me that. Everybody calls me Two-Saint." He held up two fingers, then pressed both hands together and tried to look angelic. "Get it?"

Nope. "Sure."

"Two-Saint James. Metra-preneur. Need a Metra card?" He pulled a stack of small plastic cards from out of nowhere, like a magician. "All stops, all zones, hit your buddy on the phone, I got you." He posed, then shrugged sheepishly. "Sorry, I'm still working on the catchphrase."

"Right. Right. So... are you, like, a cousin of mine? You live here?"

"HA!" He slapped his leg, and I raised both eyebrows.

People still slap their leg when they're amused? "Nope, I'm just someone your uncle helped out once who never went away. Plus, your gran's food is the best, so whenever a new Freeman kid comes to town, I show 'em the ropes. I guess it's my way of repaying my debts."

That's right. Gran had mentioned that a kid would be here to help me out. I guess I was expecting someone more . . . normal. Then again, after what had happened to me at the train station, who was I to judge anybody else? I wouldn't trust another pair of glasses for the rest of my life.

Two-Saint tossed a bag into the room. "Here, I'm supposed to give you these. I'm also supposed to tell you your grandmother left some bacon and a phone charger for you down-stairs, and she's off to go play some video game with some other retired old people."

A charger? Sweet. But I blinked at the bag. "What's that?"

"Your uncle had some extra clothes that might fit, and a pair of shoes. What happened to yours?"

"Amtrak decided they were a terrorist threat," I said.

Two-Saint raised an eyebrow at that but wisely decided not to comment. He disappeared back into the hall to give me privacy, and I pulled out the clothes: a pair of old jeans and an oversized, faded black button-down shirt, plus a bright orange hoodie for warmth. Okay, not the best, but I'd worn worse. Like the time my practice jersey shrank in the wash and it looked like I was wearing a crop top. This was nothing I couldn't han-dle. I pulled on the jeans, which were only a little snug around the waist. Fortunately, the shirt was long enough to hide that fact, and though the hoodie didn't zip, it was comfortable. The shoes were a pair of wheat-colored boots, and surprisingly, they looked the best out of everything. Like they'd never been worn.

I was just about ready to go downstairs when I noticed that the sign next to the dresser seemed... off.

MAY YOUR ANCESTORS GUIDE YOU TODAY

I squinted. "Weren't you saying something different earlier?"

"You say something?" Two-Saint popped his head back in, then snickered. "You look like you're about to go pour concrete."

"I wish I could," I said. "Then at least I'd feel useful."

"Sure, sure. I'll be downstairs trying to smuggle out some bacon."

After he left, I glared at the sign near the dresser. It hadn't answered my question. Of course not. Signs can't talk. Then again, signs shouldn't be able to change their messages, either, but I was willing to cut the house some slack. Plus, I'd been really tired last night; I could've imagined it. Yeah, that was it. An overactive imagination. Best to put it out of my mind.

Except, when I left the room and started to head down the turret stairs, something told me to look back. I really wished I hadn't, because the sign over the hallway had changed, too.

IGNORE THE ANCESTORS AT YOUR OWN PERIL

CHAPTER
FIVE

Two-Saint was on the porch watching Bulls highlights and eating three pieces of bacon at once when I arrived down in the kitchen. I started charging my phone and made a mental note to find outlets at school when Uncle Moe walked in. He limped, favoring his left leg, as he carried a little brown boy who couldn't be older than two. The kid sucked his thumb and tugged his ear while he stared at me curiously. Uncle Moe waved at me without looking, then sat the kid in a chair on top of a stack of books and scooted him to the table. After that, Uncle Moe busied himself making pancakes.

The kid sucked his thumb and waggled his eyebrows.

I waggled mine back. Cute kid, though I wasn't aware of any cousins living here, too. I was about to ask his name when my uncle spoke up.

"His name is Booker," Uncle Moe said, "but we always call

him Boogs, both because of this little dancey-dance he does when he's eating, and because at any given moment you'll find his finger shoved so far up his nostril he could smell his fingerprints. He's gonna be staying here, too. Parents got in a bit of trouble."

That was a doozy of an opening. "How many other people are staying here?" I asked.

"Hm. Just us four. For now. Never know who might need a place to stay in our family. You sleep okay?"

"Well ... yes. Had to get used to the pipes, though."

He grunted. "After a couple of weeks, you won't be able to sleep without their noises. Ask Boogs. Them pipes are like a lullaby for him now. Cries if he can't hear them. I see the clothes fit. Boots, too. Good. Now, don't be late for school. Your friend is walking with you. I gotta stay here with Boogs."

Not once did he look at me. His eyes lingered on the pancakes, then on the plate in front of Boogs, where he cut the food into tiny triangles. He glanced at the dented and scratched coffeemaker, loaded it with a heaping spoonful of grounds, and shoved a chipped mug underneath.

I remembered what Gran said about Uncle Moe and coffee. "Is that your—"

"Fourth cup. Yep. Coffee is essential to my productivity. A necessity. If it ain't brewing, I ain't moving. Everything waits till the beans percolate." For the first time a smile cracked his face, and he even whistled a bit. Was coffee that powerful?

Uncle Moe was a mysterious dude. Like, I'd met him before at family reunions, but he kept to himself, always had his nose in a book or was scribbling something in a journal. Not so interesting when spades tournaments and rib cook-offs were unfolding around me. The only thing I really knew about him was that Mom said he got into some trouble up here a few years back and had to lay low. I wasn't supposed to bother him about it. But he seemed normal enough, like an old, retired nerd. Yet every now and again he had the habit of cocking his head, as if trying to listen for something, and . . .

Uncle Moe cleared his throat and glanced at me, almost as if he could hear my thoughts. "Jax, listen, I know this is difficult for you, being here away from your home and all. I get it, really I do. But we're gonna try and help, as best as we can. Just let us know what we need to do, or even if you want us to stay out of your way."

I nodded, not really sure how to answer.

"We all make mistakes," he said, turning back around to continue cleaning the counter. "I sure did. Bunch of them. But it's about how you try to fix them that matters. You get it?"

"Yes," I said. Then the rest came flooding out: "It feels like I made one mistake and that's it. No second chances, no 'Try and do better, Jax.' They sent me out of town so they can forget I exist." I folded my arms and tried not to whine, but it was hard. "I want to be at home. Get ready for spring football camp. See my friends!"

Uncle Moe opened his mouth to say something, then thought better of it and sighed. "We all wanted to go home when we first got here. But we couldn't. Besides, this school you going to is the best thing for you. Trust me."

Fat chance. But then Boogs sneezed, and a delightful spray of pancake snot went everywhere, and Uncle Moe groaned as he had to clean the counter again.

Bzzt

My phone vibrated, which scared me for a second. It's so old, I'm always worried it'll explode. Seriously, if it's off the charger for longer than thirty minutes, the screen turns a weird purple color. Also, I've never had the same ringtone twice. The last time someone called me, I spent ten seconds looking for the dying cat I was sure had crawled into my closet.

Was Mom texting me? I was just about to call her....

No, it was my old gang from back in Raleigh, in a group text we'd created while on the football team together. The three of them were my closest friends—family, really—and now they were hundreds of miles away. I dropped an emoji in the chat—the smiling cowboy, don't ask why.

Yooo, look who it is! Marcus typed. Could it be? Jax, you survived the move?

Funny, I replied.

Marcus was my best friend, and after everything that had gone down before I left NC, I'd thought that was in jeopardy. It was a big relief to hear from him. I needed to hang on to something familiar, despite what my parents thought.

Everything cool up there? BG asked. Quiet, short BG, who could leave defenders in his dust when he took off.

Cold, bruh. Like, angry cold. Type of weather where you walk outside and get mad.

A bunch of crying and laughing emojis flooded the chat,

and I felt something loosen in my chest. My friends were the only thing holding me together at this point. Giving me some normal at a time when everything else was spiraling out of control. New town, new school, new set of expectations that I had to juggle with the same old stress that never seemed to take a break. Grades, Mom's new job, Dad's back injury. It felt good to just be a kid.

But talking about the cold reminded me of something. "Uncle Moe!" I said. "Do you have a coat I can borrow?"

"Yeah, I should. Gimme a second."

While he cleaned up Boogs, I started to go back to my room for some privacy. I climbed the stairs, still texting away, laughing as everyone posted pics for our daily fit check. When it was my turn, I took a deep breath and posted a selfie, then rolled my eyes at the flood of mind-blown emojis, skull emojis, and uppercase comments I could hear.

NOOOOOO!

BRO YOU GOTTA GO TO SLEEP AND TRY AGAIN TOMORROW

MY MANS LOOK LIKE SOMEBODY ATE ORANGE KOOL-AID

LOOKING LIKE TIGGER AFTER A ROUGH NIGHT

LOLLLL, GOING TO TONY THE TIGER AT 2AM LIKE "I FREW UP"

NOT I FREW UP, BROOOOO, I'M WEEEAK!

Jax for real, you can't go to school on your first day like that. For real bro.

Oh shoot, Coach is here, we gotta go. We'll catch you later Jax.

Later, I typed, still chuckling at their comments. Nothing makes you feel better than getting dragged by people who care about you. They were right, though. I couldn't go to school like this. But what choice did I have? Maybe...

My phone vibrated again. Marcus, in a private message.

What's up? I typed.

Yo man, it was good to hear from you. We were starting to worry, u know?

I caught myself nodding. It's cool, I'll check in more often. Time zones won't let me be great.

Yeah that's the thing. Coach thinks it'd be better for the team if we sort of let you do your thing up there, to give you space.

My heart skipped a beat. What do you mean?

Well, after everything that went down, coach just wants us to focus on school and football.

You're kicking me out the text chat?

We're not kicking you out, bro, come on.

They *were* kicking me out. My friends. Marcus. I couldn't believe it. Marcus? We did everything together! I'd known him since second grade. When he wanted to try out for quarterback, I was the one who caught passes until the streetlights came on. When he actually made the team, I was the one who blocked for him. We had sleepovers!

Fine. You want to know what happened in Raleigh? Why I got sent hundreds of miles north—out of sight, out of mind— to do my time away from everything I knew and loved? Sure. Here goes...

Wait.

I'd gotten distracted and gone up too far. I was at the top

of the stairs of my turret, on the second floor, and a frown wrinkled my forehead.

There was a door where the wall had been solid before. I could've sworn it wasn't there last night. It was an old-fashioned wooden door, the kind with a skeleton-key lock, and its knob was in the shape of a balled fist. It looked . . . old. Really old.

"Uncle Moe!" I called into the speaking tube in the wall of the landing.

"I said gimme a minute. I'll find you a coat."

"No, there's a strange door up here."

"Your door?"

"No."

"The bathroom?"

"No," I said. "It looks like a whole new room."

"What is it, a closet? Is there a leak or something? Or asbestos in the ceiling? If it's asbestos, don't go near it—we'll have to get the contractor back out here to remove it. They swore they'd cleared the whole house. . . ."

"No, it's not asbestos or a leak," I shouted. "But—"

"Good! See if there's a plunger up there. I can't find the one we keep down here, and *someone* just threw a dish towel in the toilet. Boogs! Put down that oven mitt! And hurry up, Jax. Also, come straight home after school today, I need you to help me watch this terror. BOOGS, NO!"

The sound of Boogs's shrieking laughter mingled with Moe's shouts of frustration filled the house, but it washed right over me. I could've sworn there was just a blank wall up here the night before. . . .

You can see spirits, and your ancestors need your help.

IGNORE THE ANCESTORS AT YOUR OWN PERIL

I licked my lips nervously, then reached for the doorknob. When I tried to twist it, it didn't move, but...I felt a shock. I sprang back, shaking out my hand. Had that been static electricity? I stepped back and glared at the knob, then shook my head and went back down to my lower floor. I was about to skedaddle out of there when I saw something folded on top of my bed.

It was a navy wool coat with double-breasted black buttons and a flared collar. Next to it was a matching knit beanie.

"Okaaay," I said under my breath. "Maybe...maybe Uncle Moe forgot he left them for me? Or Two-Saint did it?"

I stared at the coat, debating whether to put it on. On the plus side, it looked expensive, and it would cover the hand-me-downs I was currently wearing. Also, it would keep me warm in the brutal cold outside.

But all free ain't free.

I'm not silly. I know all the rules. And last night at the train station had reinforced them. For example: Don't invite a mysterious stranger with a serious overbite into your house—that's how you get vampires. Don't follow the weird noise, like someone breathing heavily, into the basement—that's how you meet chainsaw-wielding weirdos. And, most important, don't accept gifts from unknown sources without checking to see if there are strings attached. These are Jax Freeman's Three Rules for Success and a Long Life. And I knew that wearing a coat that had conveniently appeared out of thin air, in a house that apparently loved to spawn rooms and signs, was definitely breaking the third rule.

I gave my room one more glance to make sure there wasn't something else I could wear instead. I was doomed to freeze if I went outside with just the hoodie on. Though, to be fair, if I froze to death, I wouldn't have to think about being kicked out of the group chat. You have to count the little things as wins.

"JAX!" Uncle Moe shouted. "You've got four seconds to get down here, and the first three seconds don't count! Let's go!"

Translation: *Move it.*

The only problem was, I still didn't have a coat. Unless Uncle Moe had found one downstairs.

Or...

I glanced at the navy coat on my bed.

You know what? Fine. Putting on the coat felt like an acknowledgment that all the weird things I'd been experiencing weren't just coincidences, but intentional. There *was* something happening to me and around me. But if I had to choose between weird stuff happening to Warm Jax or weird stuff happening to Frozen Jax, I'd choose Warm Jax.

Frozen Jax had been dumped by his friends. Warm Jax had a chance for a fresh new start with a fresh new coat at a fresh new school. If that start came with...oddities, so be it. Nothing could make me feel worse than being left behind by my *former* friends. Spirits, zombie conductors or whatever Conductor Buck was, laxative nuts. Bring it on. Jax would be ready to chuck the deuces and deal with the consequences.

Before I could talk myself out of it, I snagged the coat and shrugged it on. It ... fit perfectly. The sleeves stopped just short of my palms, the hem came to the middle of my thighs (hiding most of my outfit), and most important, I didn't feel like the seams would rip when I flexed my arms. Do you know how hard it is for a boy with big shoulders to find a coat that fits like that? I put my hands in my pockets, then paused, feeling around. There was something in the right pocket. Something cold and metallic. I pulled it out and examined it. A gold chain with a locket. I flipped it over and saw that it was inscribed.

"'PF' and 'ER,'" I read aloud. That was interesting. Maybe it was an antique. I put it back in my pocket and resolved to ask Gran about it later.

"Jax, let's go!" I heard Uncle Moe yell.

I jogged out to the stairs, pausing to check the hallway. Sure enough, the sign was still there, and it had changed again. I shook my head and continued down the stairs.

YOUR ANCESTORS WILL HELP PREPARE YOU, it had read.

It wouldn't be until much later, after everything weird, everything wild, everything ... well, magical, that I would ask myself about that message. *Prepare me for what?*

And by that point, it would be too late.

CHICAGO DEFENDER, VOLUME XXXV, ISSUE 04, MAY 1950

Missing Man Is a Witch, Claim Neighbors

The search for Portis Freeman, a local south-side Chicagoan, has
extended into its third week, and new details continue to emerge.
Mr. Freeman's neighbors claim that the man spent a lot of time wit.
port weird sounds coming from behind his house, including trains
where no tracks exist. Freeman is a migrant from North Carolina w.

HOUSING RESTRICTIONS EXPAND AS BANK LENDING SHRINKS

Mrs. Eleanor Rogers of West 132nd Street led a group of
protesters to the steps of the E&W Bank yesterday morning
demanding answers for the lack of loans granted to African
American

LOCAL FESTIVAL CELEBRATES UNITY

The organizers call it Glimmer Fest, what they hope will
become an annual tradition throughou

IF YOU ARE READING THIS, YOU ARE CORDIALLY INVITED TO ATTEND THE TENTH ANNUAL MEETING OF EXTRAORDINARY INDIVIDUALS KNOWN AS SUMMONERS. PASSAGE BY USUAL MEANS AT THE WILLOW TREE. SEE MRS. ROGERS FOR AGENDA ONCE YOU HAVE ARRIVED AT THE SILVER TENT.

Downtown Chicago.
Games, prizes, and food and drink will be provided at

CHAPTER
SIX

"'DuSABLE MIDDLE SCHOOL,'" I READ OFF THE school's website. My phone was having a terrible morning and I was using Two-Saint's, since his Internet actually worked. "'Home of the Panthers. Where future minds shine bright.'" A photo showed a single-story building with towering brick arches, high glass windows, and a bright blue sky overhead.

"Welcome to your new home away from home," Two-Saint said, beaming next to me.

I lowered the phone and sighed as I looked at the actual building. Whoever had taken the photo had done an incredible job of cropping out . . . everything. I saw the brick arches and high windows, but the photo conveniently left out the miles of rusty, unused train tracks stretching around the building and even leading to the school. Weeds and overgrown grass poked up everywhere, a perfect complement to the giant smokestacks in the distance that flooded the sky with gray clouds. Cracked cement stairs led up to the front door, which was currently being held open by a watery-eyed, middle-aged blond man who pursed his lips at everyone.

So, the school was a little run-down. Plenty of schools were. Normal in a big city, right? All I had to do was lie low, make friends, and fit in. *Lie low, make friends, fit in.* That mantra was going through my head on repeat when I noticed the . . . more unusual additions to DuSable's exterior.

Like the giant stone panther over the main entrance, whose eyes followed me as Two-Saint and I approached. Every so often its tail would lash, or it would bat a paw at a student, but no one seemed to notice . . . or care. I flinched when it yawned suddenly. "Did you see—" I started to ask, then cut myself off.

"Hmm?" Two-Saint was trying to get the attention of a girl who clearly was ignoring him, and I was glad he wasn't looking at me. The last thing I needed was for everyone at my new school to know I was seeing things. Instant counselor visit. No thanks.

"Nothing," I said, and continued to scan my new school.

There was a railroad crossing near the teachers' parking lot. The barrier pole would lift and lower at odd times, often when there wasn't a car anywhere close, and again, no one paid it any attention. Wasn't that a safety hazard? This place looked like it hadn't seen trains in a century, so why was the barrier still working?

And if that wasn't weird enough, one of the custodians—a gray-haired white man with a mustache like a push broom—was adding a fresh coat of paint to a mural of the school mascot, a panther with glasses and a mock turtleneck in school colors, on the front stairs. Well, that wasn't weird, but the lunch pail floating by his side and singing Premier League fight songs sure was.

You can see spirits... and maybe more?

"I think Miss Ella was putting more than laxative dust in her pecans," I grumbled.

"What?" Two-Saint asked.

"Nothing."

"Oh." He sounded disappointed, like he was waiting on me to do something cool. Joke was on him and the rest of the world—the best you could get from me were bad puns and awkward silences.

No, that was the old Jax. New Jax would try, at least.

"So," I said, "how did my uncle help you?"

Two-Saint hesitated, then shrugged. "He was at the school getting his paycheck and saw some boys bullying me. Older students. They thought because I couldn't... um, I mean, they were just being mean. Your uncle yelled at them and then gave me money for the L since they'd stolen it all. He's pretty cool."

I frowned. Uncle Moe hadn't told me he worked at DuSable. I wondered why.

Two-Saint didn't stay down for long. He clapped once as he walked backward in front of me. "All right. It's time for your favorite show and mine—"

"*Jax Gets to Go Home*?" I asked hopefully.

"*Two Cents with Two-Saint!*"

I pursed my lips. I wasn't going to admit it, but that was a pretty cool name for a show.

"Okay," he continued. "Welcome to the segment where I give you my two cents about everything and everyone you should steer clear of in sixth grade. Starting with the legend himself, Professor Benjamin, or as everyone calls him, Professor *Ban*-jamin. You know, because he tries to get everything he doesn't like banned. I don't even think he's a teacher—he's a parent volunteer who changed his first name to Professor so he could seem important."

"Okaaay," I said.

Two-Saint pointed to the blond man standing at the front door of DuSable, his head on a swivel as he tried to peek at the books students were bringing into the school.

"Hey!" the man shouted at a girl. "Is that book on this year's Books Under Revisionary Procedures list? Make sure you check the BURP list from now on."

"Ban-jamin for sure," I said.

"Or Banthony Davis," Two-Saint replied.

"Bantonio Brown."

"Banderson Cooper."

We laughed as we headed up the front stairs, both greeting Professor Benjamin at the same time. He glared at us suspiciously but didn't stop us, and we burst into fresh laughter once we entered the school. I was still chuckling as Two-Saint headed to class and I went to check in at the front office. It felt good to laugh with someone. So what if a few weird things were happening? New school, new me. That was the goal. I mean, it was middle school, not medical school. What was the worst that could happen?

*   *   *

DuSable was the worst thing that ever happened. It was like playing musical chairs, except you couldn't hear the music, people kept pushing you out of the way, and instead of chairs there were twenty classrooms in one hallway that everyone was trying to navigate at once.

Okay, so it was nothing like musical chairs, unless you count the fact that somehow, I always ended up in the wrong place.

"Ouch!" someone yelped.

"Sorry," I called back, trying to squeeze through the crowd to find my homeroom.

"Watch it!"

"Whoops, my bad," I said, tiptoeing around the girl whose foot I'd just stepped on.

"Come on, bro, you're too big!"

"I'm new," I said, as if that explained anything. I don't know, I blurt things out sometimes when I'm nervous. Not that I was nervous. Who said I was nervous? Mind your own business!

I'd made it through the first few classes all right, but I was Stressed with a capital S. Last semester, my grades had been fine. I wasn't the best student, but I also wasn't the worst. I was average, mediocre. (I even learned the word *mediocre*.) When it came to grades, I was right there in the middle of the pack, and

I was perfectly fine with that. Science was probably my hardest class, but only because the periodic table has way too many elements, and their names all sound like superhero rejects. Like clearly Argon and Helium didn't make the Avengers' tryouts.

But here? Bro. It was like the teachers were speaking a completely different language! Math? Linear equations that added letters together and pie graphs that had nothing to do with dessert. Language Arts? *Tell the class what this dead author was thinking when he wrote this.* Man, I don't know! I can barely tell you what *I* was thinking five seconds ago! And it was only day one!

Now I had to find the cafeteria, and this place was a zoo. I'd planned on meeting up with Two-Saint outside the boys' bathroom, but the pandemonium was too much. Eventually I put my head down and pushed through the crowd, like a lead blocker for a running back. Thankfully, I managed to reach a section of lockers against the wall, where I tried to catch my breath. This place was nothing like my last school. So many people, so many classes, so many people, so many floors with train symbols on the walls. Speed breaks, tracks switching, origin and commodity and destination. The names and meanings popped into my head as I glanced at them, which seemed to almost calm me down, even though I was pretty sure I'd never seen some of them before. But it was better than staring into the crowds. Did I mention all the people?

Last semester, we sixth-graders had a whole wing of the school to ourselves. I'd stayed in one classroom, no changes— Mr. Craft's corner room, with the big windows and floor chairs he'd let us hang out in while we worked. The only times we left were for lunch and recess, and an occasional trip to the library. I knew exactly where I was supposed to be and when I was supposed to be there. And Mr. Craft was really chill.

But there was nothing chill about DuSable, and I wasn't even going to think about how I didn't have recess. Different classes on different floors and in a completely new state.

Speaking of different floors, there was no way I would ever be able to find my way to lunch on my own. The school building itself was a labyrinth. A maze. A cornfield in one of those scary movies where the car breaks down and a wide-eyed kindergartner emerges from the grass and predicts your doom.

Calm down, Jax.

Okay, the point is, it was easy to get lost, and it wasn't just me. As I stood there, I saw kids go down the stairs on the west end of the hall and then reemerge from the east end with dazed looks in their eyes. One girl took a selfie in front of an old railroad poster on a classroom door, only to stop and stare at the same poster across the way, where it had reappeared above a water fountain. And these kids had already been here for a semester. Imagine *my* confusion! But hey, when I'd checked in at the front office, at least they'd given me a neat little button that said I'M NEW! HELP ME! Perfect.

And then there were the restrooms. They looked like maintenance rooms, with smoked-glass windows that opened to reveal closets, ladders that climbed to the ceiling and then stopped, and stall doors that slid open and had recessed door handles like latches. A tall Black girl stood in front of one such restroom a few feet away from me with a weird expression on her face as she held her phone to her ear.

"Hey, Mom, just letting you know I sent you another invitation for my birthday party in a few weeks. You know, in case you didn't get the others. Anyway, hope you can make it. Call me?" She hung up and stared at the phone as if waiting for an immediate response. When one didn't come, she sighed, then glared at the restroom door. "I hate these."

I opened my mouth to agree—I'm pretty sure that's what I meant to do—but instead, a flurry of words erupted. "It's a slam door. Used on trains before automatic doors were invented. Very common before, like, 1960."

I clapped one hand over my mouth as the girl stared at me in confusion. "Okaaay," she said. "Good to know, I guess."

"Not really used on sleeping cars, but passenger cars? Absolutely." Why was I still talking? "I'm sorry," I said, backing up. "I don't normally talk to people about how the area between the doors of connecting cars is called the gangway."

Stop it! You're embarrassing yourself, Jax!

I covered my mouth again. This was it. I'd finally lost all control over my brain. Intrusive thoughts 1, Jax 0. No, I wasn't even in the game. I was riding the bench. Cut from the squad.

"Nnngrrmskffddmmb!" I called out behind the hand still covering my mouth.

The girl wrinkled her brow, which sent the two-strand twists swept to the right side of her face cascading over her eyes. She brushed them away in irritation. "What?"

My hand fell away. "I said"—*No, please stop talking. Why*

am I still talking?—"that they're called slam doors because of the sound they'd make—"

No. Hand back over the mouth.

"—when passengers—"

Two hands over the mouth?

"—would slam them shut."

Enough already. No more mouth. I was taking it back to the store. Going to Geek Squad to get it fixed. It wasn't working right! Maybe I could glue my lips shut and just communicate via written notes for the rest of my life. *The Boy Who Scribbled* would be the name of the documentary they'd make about me, a giant sixth-grader living in the Arctic whose only friends were the polar bears he played *Madden* with. (They'd be Bears fans, of course.)

A buzzer sounded as I retreated from the girl, and everyone started rushing around even faster. It was almost the start of the next period. I had to get to lunch, but where was Two-Saint? The girl was still staring at me strangely, and I was still mortified, which is probably why I bumped into someone. I turned around to see a tall, gangly Black kid with a sling pack worn in front.

He whirled to face me fully, five other kids fanning out on either side of him. My heart sank. They'd been in the middle of hemming in a familiar scrawny kid, and I'd interrupted whatever teasing had been going on. So . . . yay?

"Two-Saint?" I asked. "You . . . all right?"

He managed a squeak, which I took to mean *Maybe*, and then I had other things to worry about. Apparently, the tall kid I'd jostled was the poster child for popularity and style. Polo shirt, sunglasses propped on his fade, and a Nike sling tucked over one shoulder. He looked like someone I'd actually like to be friends with. When I checked out his gleaming white-and-blue Jordans—which I didn't think were even carried in stores—my heart dropped even further. He was holding a Starbucks cup filled with some foamy drink, and half of it had spilled all over his shoes.

He glanced down.

His friends glanced down.

I looked up and prayed to the gods of awkwardness to ignore me for just one minute. Hadn't they already blessed me enough?

"Deviiiiin," one of the larger boys said, the one who was still holding on to Two-Saint's collar. "Look at your shoes!"

"Yeah, Jalen, I noticed," Devin said, rolling his eyes. "Thanks for letting me know."

"No problem," his crony said happily before returning to scowl at Two-Saint.

Meanwhile, I had no time to help Devin clean up, because his eyes lasered in on the I'M NEW! HELP ME! button I wore. The anger on his face smoothed out into a neutral expression, and he took a step forward. His friends took up nearly half the hallway, but no one challenged them, instead choosing to break around the confrontation like a stream flowing past boulders. That was never a good sign.

"You're new," he said, almost as an accusation.

I nodded.

Devin relaxed and smiled. He reached into his backpack, pulled out a napkin, and quickly cleaned off his shoe. "Chill, bro, don't even worry about it. Happens a lot if you're not careful. Took me weeks to get used to this dump. But watch out, aight?"

"Right," I said, just as the buzzer rang again. The boy named Jalen shoved Two-Saint, who scurried behind me. Jalen glared in our direction before heading off with the rest of the group.

Two-Saint sighed. "That could've gone worse. Normally I end up in a locker somewhere. You're a good-luck charm! And Devin doesn't hate you—that's a plus. Come on, let's go eat. I'm feeling extra fortunate, so maybe they'll have nuggets today."

*   *   *

Lunch was . . . interesting.

Now, don't get me wrong. I loved lunch period at my old school. It was when you could laugh and joke and cram fries into your mouth at the same time and no one would call you out. Me and my boys had the same table in the same corner, and everybody knew that's where we'd cut up, no ifs, ands, or buts about it.

But that was then. I swallowed, hating how a lump of sadness knotted my chest. Whatever. *Figure out your seat, Jax.*

The thing about transferring in the middle of the school year is that everybody already has their clique. Weird word, though, *clique*. Like *click*. Like everyone is supposed to fit together into a group, all nice and neat. Twelve-year-old jig-saw pieces. Yeah, right.

When I stepped into DuSable's cafeteria, I was stunned. Not because it was huge—the cafeteria at my old school was probably bigger. They both had the same weird combination smell of cleaning spray and meatballs, which was at once reassuring and slightly scary. Like, were the meatballs swimming in Lysol, or did the custodians clean up after us with spray bottles of marinara sauce? The world might never know.

But at least they both had meatball subs.

Where was I? Oh yeah.

No, what was stunning about this cafeteria were all the trains. The sides of boxcars and tankers and even a locomotive lined the cinder-block walls, their wheels shiny and the sides freshly painted, like they were seconds away from rumbling off down the hallways. Railroad signs—bright yellow-and-red warnings—were plastered on the room's columns. So weird. And yet…at least it was cool. I mean, I thought it was cool, but I'm not sure the average student admired them the way I did. In fact, a few kids chose to stand and eat rather than sit at a table pushed against a mural of a diesel locomotive. Who decorated like that? It was just one more entry on the long, long list I called Things of Deep Distress. *TODD* for short. Don't look at me like that—you don't wanna end up on the TODD list.

"Hey, move it! You're blocking the aisle!" someone shouted behind me.

I dragged my attention from the strange decorations and

mumbled an apology. *Real smooth, Jax. Definitely going to make friends gawking at the scenery.*

I looked for a place to sit with my food while Two-Saint made his way through the line (seriously, how long does it take to decide between meatball subs and tuna fish?), but the friend groups had already been established. The baseball team wore their jackets and took up two tables; the basketball team had their matching slides and warmups. The drum line from band had taken over a corner and were beating out competing patterns on the walls, tables, and even each other with their sticks. (Several teachers on lunch duty were already cutting through the crowd in that direction.) A bunch of girls from the volleyball team were laughing and holding up phones as someone's lunch box got bump-set across the table, while the girls' soccer team rooted them on.

I guess this happened all the time. But that left me to figure out where I would fit in.

I scanned the space, trying to see if there was a table 1) with room for me to squeeze in, and 2) with someone with their nose in a book. People who read at lunch don't care who sits by them as long as they aren't bothered.

There, on the other side of the room—one kid alone at a table, flipping through what looked like an old dictionary. I shrugged. Whatever kids needed to do to get through lunch was not my business. And I was absolutely starving. The bacon I'd grabbed this morning felt like a faint memory. So I was halfway into that awkward leg hurdle you do to get into picnic-style lunch tables when I realized that the kid wasn't nose-deep into their book—they were glaring at me. And I recognized them.

"Are you serious right now?" the girl asked with a glare, pulling out an earbud. It was the same person I'd spouted train facts to like an information geyser earlier. Fantastic. Nothing like confronting your awkwardness. Goes great with a serving of panic and tall glass of hallucinations.

Right on cue, a train whistle echoed in the distance. I frowned. I was fairly positive there were no train stations or Metra stops nearby. Then I frowned deeper. Why was I fairly positive about that? Since when did I become an expert on Chicago's train system? I'd just gotten here. I was starting to wonder if someone was whispering train logistics into my ear at night. Maybe it was those magical wooden signs back at the Freeman House. I knew I shouldn't trust them.

But I had more pressing concerns at the moment—there was nowhere else to sit, and I had a perfectly good meatball sub waiting to be devoured. I plunked myself down, and of course banged my knee on a support beam under the table, because the lunch tables weren't built for people taller than 5'10". I choked back a curse and started to eat as if I weren't in stomach-clenching pain.

"Are you okay?" the girl finally asked.

"Me? Fine!" I managed to squeak out.

"Are you crying?"

"No," I lied, tears streaming down my face. "Maybe. It's the meatballs. Delicious. You meatball? I mean, eat meatballs? Here often you? Do eat? Do you eat here often?"

"In the cafeteria? Yes."

"Amazing."

Dear god of awkward encounters and embarrassment, rescue me from myself.

The girl stared at me for a few seconds longer, and I thought about asking her name and introducing myself, but she shook her head and then put her earbud back in, so it was too late. Oh, well. Plenty of chances to stick my foot in my mouth in the future. Apparently that was my talent. My superpower. *Hey Jax, can you fly?* No, but I can ruin the rest of my social life with gusto!

I was halfway through my meatball sub (it was really the best thing about my day so far) and three-quarters of the way through reliving my blunder in excruciating detail when a kid went flying across my table.

You heard me right.

A blur of limbs and food skidded across the table in front of me, knocking the sub out of my hands before both it and the kid ended up on the floor.

When I looked down at the mop of curly hair decorated with bits of fruit and splotches of condiments, I recognized it.

"Hey, Nina," Two-Saint whispered to my tablemate.

"Toussaint," the girl—Nina—said, not looking up from her book.

"It's Two-Saint!" he hissed.

"You can't give yourself a nickname—your friends are supposed to do that." She continued reading, then sighed and brushed her twists out of her eyes. "Who is it this time?"

"Devin."

"Again?"

"Well, not him, but his goon squad. They don't like being told about the repressed trauma they convert into bullying." Two-Saint got up on his hands and knees and crawled behind me, peering out like he was in trouble. Then again, with two kinds of mustard—yellow and spicy brown—splattered on him, I guess he was.

"Sorry," he muttered to me.

I nodded, too confused to say anything.

Nina looked over her shoulder and sighed. "Looks like they found you. Better skedaddle."

"I can't! They stole my notes about the new Metra line. I need them for my newsletter!"

He ducked just as a group of kids sauntered up to our lunch table. The same group as earlier, except Devin was missing. Now it seemed that Jalen was the leader. He propped one foot on my bench and brushed imaginary dirt off his fresh white-and-green Jumpman high-tops.

"Daaaang, y'all, did you see that?" he asked. "Tootsie, you need to watch it. So clumsy. See how he fell? Shame about his lunch."

"You tripped him," I said. Without thinking, I might add.

Nina glanced at me in surprise, and I could see Two-Saint vigorously shaking his head from his hiding spot. After a second I realized my mistake.

"What'd you say?" Jalen asked.

My mouth, apparently still detached from my brain, continued. "You tripped him. I saw you."

Jalen scowled for a moment before he forced out a laugh. "You're the one tripping, big boy. Your belt must be cutting the blood off to your brain, because I would never. That would be bullying, right, y'all?"

His cronies nodded along, even as the three of them crowded around, shielding us from the view of the lunch monitors, who were still dealing with the band kids. Jalen had some bigger kids with him, seventh- and eighth-graders. They were taller than nearly everyone else around, and with their wide shoulders, they looked like they ate toddlers for breakfast. I'd seen their type before.

I'd *been* their type before. But that was then. Now I didn't know *what* I was. . . .

"Man, this is the saddest table I've ever seen," Jalen declared. He shook his head. "Except for you, Nina. How'd you end up in this club? Where's Devin? You know you always got a seat saved for you next to me, riiiiight?"

Nina didn't answer. Didn't even look at him. Just flicked the pages of her book and nodded to a beat. I couldn't be sure any music was actually playing, but she was definitely vibing. I snorted, and the smile on Jalen's face faded as he looked at me.

"You laughing? You? You're a joke. A big—"

He cut himself off as Nina lifted her eyes and raised an eyebrow. "A big what? Go ahead, say it."

Two-Saint popped up, a fistful of napkins in his hand as he scrubbed the ketchup, fruit bits, and the rest of my meatball sub out of his hair. "'Cause that would be fat-shaming. And that is bullying."

I swung my legs out and stood. The posse actually took a step back when they saw that I was taller than any of them. It felt good standing up for someone else for once.

Jalen glared at his gang. "Really?" he said.

"Is there a problem here?"

We all turned to see one of the lunch monitors marching over, her eyes sweeping across the group. They landed on me and lingered for a moment before switching to Jalen.

The boy straightened smoothly. "No problem," he said, glaring at me. "Right, y'all?" I shook my head as his cronies parroted his response.

"Nope."

"All good."

"We're good."

Nina didn't say anything, just turned back to her book. Two-Saint got up off the floor and sat down gingerly on the bench, but he kept quiet as well. Jalen smirked, and something flickered inside me.

"Yeah, we're good," I said, turning to the teacher. "Jalen here saw I was new and was trying to help. So thoughtful. Such a good boy. So I thought I'd help him back and tell him how he's gotta watch out for shoe resale scammers. We had them all the time back in North Carolina. My old friend Marcus got scammed by one."

"What are you talking about?" Jalen snapped.

I pointed at his shoes, a clean pair of Jumpmans I'd seen

on the shoe fan pages I used to look through. "They're fake, bro. Authentic Jumpmans have stitching on the tongue. Yours don't."

"Yoooo," one of Jalen's buddies said, while another started laughing.

Jalen flushed and I shrugged. "Like I said, it happens all the time. Gotta watch out for the scams."

He clenched his fists, but the teacher was right there, so all he could do was pivot without a word. Just then the bell rang to signal that lunch was over, and he stomped out the cafeteria, his goons in his wake.

I let out a deep breath. The lunch monitor gave me a stern look before she moved on, too, but her lips twitched as if she were fighting back a chuckle. I think.

"Wooow," Two-Saint said, jumping up and down and clapping me on the shoulder. "No one has ever talked to Jalen like that. Right, Nina? Did you see that?"

"I did," Nina said with begrudging admiration. She stood and tucked her big book into her backpack, facing me for the first time as she pulled out her earbuds. "His dad owns a bunch of clubs downtown, so Jalen thinks he's better than everybody else. Like what he says goes. Some people agree with him." She shrugged on her backpack and adjusted her twists again before looking back at us. "Some. Not me."

"Me neither," Two-Saint said, his face brightening as he spotted a crumpled ball of paper on the floor near the table. "My notes! Anyway, we should do this again. Sit together with Nina, I mean, and not get bullied. Maybe even defeat bullies? I don't know, could be fun. Same table at lunch tomorrow? Nina? Can we? Pretty please with desperation on top?"

I glanced at Nina, who rolled her eyes and put her earbuds back in. But she shrugged, the ghost of a smile on her lips.

Two-Saint whooped, punching my shoulder like he was training for a boxing match or something. "Yooo, this is going to be great. You allergic to nuts? I eat peanut butter every day, but sometimes I switch it up with peanut butter and jelly, just because I gotta keep my fans on their toes. You like the Bulls? Whatchu think about..."

I grinned as we walked out the cafeteria, Two-Saint on my left, Nina on my right, one earbud in as she shook her head at his antics. I guessed I'd found my clique. *Maybe this school won't be so bad*, I thought. *One semester. Keep my nose clean, keep on the straight and narrow.* Maybe life would be perfectly ordinary. Absolutely forgettable.

Ha.

You know that wasn't gonna happen, right?

Right.

CHAPTER
SEVEN

So now you're all caught up on Jax Freeman's TODD list. (Things of Deep Distress. Keep up, mm-kay?) Let's recap:

1. A ghostly train conductor tried to turn me into a turtleneck.
2. Everyday objects said things to me. (I wish I could say they were imaginary friends, but who am I kidding? That's how hard it is for me to make and keep friends.)
3. I lived in a haunted turret. Again, not that kind of turret.

And you know what? All that was fine. I could've handled it. If the universe had stopped there and decided I'd suffered enough, things would've been straight. But apparently the cosmos looked at my life and said, *You know what? Let's send Jax Freeman to the weirdest middle school ever.*

But, by far, the strangest class I had was sixth period, right after lunch.

It was held in a small classroom—more like a large coatroom than anything else. No windows, no decorations, just fluorescent lights in the ceiling, bench-style seats lining the walls, and a giant bucket in the middle of the floor filled with sidewalk chalk. And from what I could tell, no teacher.

When I walked in, everybody fell silent. A few familiar faces stared at me. I saw Nina and Two-Saint, and that was good. Then there was Jalen, which wasn't so good. The complete opposite, in fact. Devin was also there, which I thought could be good, but the angry expression on his face had me second-guessing myself.

"Jax!" Two-Saint called, patting a spot next to him. "You're in this class?"

"What're *you* doing here?" Jalen asked, sneering.

I ignored him and sat next to Two-Saint, who hadn't stopped talking since he'd called me over. "I *knew* it," he said. "I had a feeling when I walked up to your house this morning. I thought, 'This time it's different.' What was your OOS?"

"My what?" I asked, still looking around the room.

"Your Origin of Spirits? The reason you chose this class."

I shook my head. "I didn't choose it—the office just gave me my schedule."

Jalen snickered. "This is gonna be hilarious."

"Your OOS," Nina spoke up, looking at her phone, "is what made you realize you were different."

"I had a whole conversation with my grandmother in her

bedroom when I was ten," Two-Saint said, bouncing his feet as he drummed on his legs. "Even though she'd died the night before in her sleep."

"Oh." What do you say to that? "Sorry?"

"Don't be! That was my Origin of Spirits. I was talking to an ancestor."

You can see spirits, and your ancestors need your help.

"Nina fought off a zombie," Two-Saint continued, counting on his fingers. "Devin summoned a giant when a neighbor tried to cheat at cards—"

"Stop telling people it was a giant," Devin said, rolling his eyes.

"And Jalen got uglier," Two-Saint finished with a whisper. I suppressed a grin, which wasn't hard to do when he turned to me and asked, "So, anything strange ever happen to you? Weird stuff? Ghosts asking you the time, or maybe a witch tried to steal your lunch?"

"I . . ." I swallowed. There was so much. Talking eyeglasses for one, and a mysterious room appearing out of thin air for another. I still didn't know what was real and what was a hallucination. "I got attacked by this . . . creepy man at Union Station."

"A creepy man? That's a typical Thursday afternoon around here."

"No, it was more than that. He was an Amtrak worker. In a uniform."

"So, you fought a train attendant?" Two-Saint asked. "That's why you're in Summoning?"

A tingle ran down my spine. *Summoning.* Why did that sound familiar?

"They're called conductors," Nina corrected him absent-mindedly. She was aiming her phone at the back of the room.

"What's summoning?" I asked, looking over her shoulder as she recorded a pair of students holding an impromptu dance-off as everyone waited for class to start.

More familiar faces walked in—some I'd seen in my morning classes. A short, sandy-skinned Afro-Latina named Vanessa. Sam and Simon Long, two of three triplets (the third had apparently gone home sick after a dare involving pickle juice and croutons, according to his siblings) came in arguing over who was going to win something called the Glimmer Fest Games, whatever that was. A giant transfer kid from Ireland everyone called Bull lumbered in after them.

"I thought this was Enrichment Period," I said. "That's what it says on my schedule."

Two-Saint scanned the room as he answered. "Summoning. You know, heirlooms?"

"No, I don't know." I turned to Nina. "What is summoning?"

Nina frowned at me. "How can you be here and not know what summoning is? It's literally this class."

"No, this is Enrichment."

"Yeah, because they had to call the class something so the reggies wouldn't freak out."

I threw my hands up. "Who are the reggies?"

"Regs. That's what everyone calls non-summoners," Nina said. "Short for 'regular people.' But . . . you should know that,

Jax. You should know all this, because otherwise you wouldn't be here."

"Well, treat me like I'm new to it," I said. "School isn't exactly what I'm best at."

"You mean treat you like the loser you are," someone said behind me. "Already done."

I grimaced as Jalen high-fived another student. Great. I noticed I wasn't the only one glaring at him. Nina stared daggers his way like he'd stolen her puppy.

"Back to the train conductor," Two-Saint said, pulling out a half-eaten bag of Takis from his pocket. "How'd you fight him off?"

"I didn't fight. I just... threw a shoe at him," I said. "And then he exploded. Sort of. No, definitely exploded, but didn't die. It was weird. He kept yelling about wearing my skin."

Everyone stared at me like I'd grown an extra lip. Even the dancers paused mid-handstand.

"Ewwww," said Sam. "What did you do to make him come at you?"

"That's the thing—I don't know! I've never been to Chicago before. Never left North Carolina in my whole life."

"Ahwundahooeythotchuer?" Two-Saint asked with a mouth full of corn chips.

"I don't know," I said after translating that to *I wonder who he thought you were?* "But once he heard the counter lady say 'Jax Freeman,' it was on sight."

Nina froze beside me.

Across the room, Devin looked up and stared at us with a fierce expression.

"Your last name is Freeman?" Nina asked, chewing her lower lip nervously. She opened her mouth to say something else, but Devin stood and knifed his way through the crowd like a shark that smelled blood.

"Freeman," Devin said, his voice a harsh whisper. "Your last name is Freeman?"

I stood up, confused. I don't know why he was acting so aggressive, especially since he'd been so friendly earlier today. It got quiet in the room as people realized something was happening, something bigger than a dance-off. Jalen cocked his head. Vanessa frowned. Bull stood up as well, one hand rubbing his reddish hair as he looked between Devin and me.

"Yeah," I said. "It is."

Devin's fists bunched, then unclenched, then clenched again in that way that I just knew was going to make something pop off, when the door to the classroom slammed open and ricocheted off the wall.

WHACK!

In marched a brown-skinned Black woman straight out of an action cartoon. Or maybe a slice-of-life anime. Either way, she was the last person I'd expected to be our teacher. She was younger than any I'd had back in Raleigh. She wore coveralls stained with what I hoped was strawberry jelly and not blood, and her brown hair had been done up in two curly buns. She wore aviator sunglasses and had eye black smeared under each eye. She was simultaneously the coolest and the scariest teacher I'd ever seen.

"Okay, students! You all know the routine. Line up, single file."

Everyone stood, and after a moment's confusion I did the same, not wanting to be obvious about how out of the loop I was. The teacher hadn't noticed me yet, and I thought maybe I could blend into the crowd. Whatever Devin was about to say (or do) had been momentarily put on pause as he backed away and got in line, though he shot me a look every few seconds that I pretended to ignore. I followed Two-Saint as the teacher pulled a blue piece of chalk out of the bin and, to my surprise, closed the classroom door and began to draw on it. When she was finished, a blue symbol covered half the surface—a circle intersected by a cross, except there were two horizontal lines instead of one. She promptly yanked open the door, and I paused, causing the student behind me to bounce off my back.

"Where'd the hallway go?" I blurted out. So much for blending in.

Bull, now a few feet in front of me, stopped. "First time through a summoner link? Messed me up, too. Pretend you're stepping off a sidewalk curb. That way you won't fall when you get to the other side."

"I'm sorry," I said. "But what does that even mean?"

Bull patted me on the back and ignored my question. I stumbled forward through the doorway. There was a drop in the pit of my stomach...

...and then I was in a brightly lit abandoned factory.

Dust-covered skylights in the vaulted ceilings let in plenty of light, old assembly lines had been disassembled and shoved against the wall, and a circle of desks and chairs awaited us in the middle of a giant concrete floor. Columns and pillars stretched off into the distance, while chipped and broken statues were clustered in a corner, almost like they were waiting on us. Which was silly, of course, because they were statues. When I looked behind me at the door we'd just come through, I saw the closet-like classroom. But... but... I closed my eyes. Where exactly *were* we?

"Butts in seats, phones on silent, get out your heirlooms," said the teacher, shutting the door again. "Eyes up, mouths closed. Time to summon." As she swept to the center of the space following those cryptic instructions, a few things ran through my head.

1. Why had Nina and Devin freaked about my last name?
2. What was an heirloom?
3. Did I forget deodorant? (This one had been bugging me all day.)

"Um, excuse me?" I called to the teacher. Clearly, blending in wasn't going to work after all.

All the activity in the old factory paused around me. Well, the students' activity. The teacher continued to get ready...I think. She peeled off her stained coveralls to reveal a pristine cream pantsuit underneath, complete with a thin gray scarf she tied around her neck. She also pulled out a purse, a mirror, and several bottles of leave-in curl-enhancing conditioner. (Trust me, I've accidentally knocked over enough of my mother's hair products to recognize a leave-in conditioner when I see one.) How she managed to fit all that in the coveralls was beyond me, but within a few seconds her hair was done in elegant sweeping curls tied above her head in a crown with the scarf. The eye black stayed. Cool.

"Yes?" she finally answered.

"Miss—" I began.

"*Doctor*," she interrupted. "Dr. Clayton."

"Sorry, Dr. Clayton. I think I'm in the wrong class."

She swept her old clothes and supplies into a drawer in the bottom of a large desk and shook her head. "Impossible. This school has yet to place a student in a class they weren't intended to be enrolled in."

"But I don't even know what I'm supposed to do here!" I hated the fact that it sounded like I was whining, but my frustration had built to near-unmanageable levels. It was like everything confusing in my life had combined into a thug and decided to jump me in the parking lot: hallucinations, new school anxiety, and now a class that I was in no way prepared to take. My emotions were getting their butts whupped right now, and no one wanted to help. They'd probably end up on YouTube later.

Dr. Clayton didn't seem to notice my frustration, however. I don't mean she was ignoring it; I mean she acted like it was normal.

"Perfect," she said, flashing a frazzled smile at me as she

continued to prepare for . . . whatever she was preparing for. "The first step to becoming a student is acknowledging what you don't know. I'm proud of you. Your name?"

"Jax," I said. "Jax Freeman."

Was it me or did her smile dim juuuust a tad when she heard my last name? What was it about the name Freeman that made people act strange? I made a mental note to ask Gran about it when I got home.

"Well, Mr. Freeman, since you're new, and since I've been away for the past month handling a will-o'-the-wisp outbreak in Naperville, now is the perfect opportunity for a refresher."

As I processed *that* information, Bull raised his hand. "We're going to shower?"

"No," Nina whispered. "A recap. Going over what we've done before."

"Ah." The giant freckled kid nodded. "Sorry, still learning the correct words."

"No need to be sorry, Mr. O'Connor," Dr. Clayton called out cheerfully. "Learning is filled with mistakes, and making mistakes is learning. Now then: energies. Who can name them?"

I pulled out my phone to google the answer while a couple of hands shot up.

"Ah, Miss Velasquez, go ahead."

Vanessa ticked her answers off on her fingers as she recited them, and I followed along on the list on my phone. "The two main categories are potential and kinetic."

"Very good! Examples?"

Vanessa thought for a moment. "Thermal and electrical are kinetic, while chemical is potential."

"Nuclear," Two-Saint said. "That's potential, too."

"Mechanical," Nina added.

Dr. Clayton clapped. "Excellent! Great examples, everyone. Now, let's move on to the third type of energy. Can someone provide it for me?"

I frowned. Google didn't list a third type, just potential and kinetic. What other—?

"Spiritual," Devin said, sighing.

"Excellent! And its explanation?"

Devin brushed off his shoe and stared up at the ceiling. "Potential energy is stored energy, and kinetic energy is working energy. Spiritual energy is the ability to do both—access energy stored in the spiritual realm and channel it to do work."

"Brilliant, Devin. Wonderful job." Dr. Clayton pulled off her scarf and flapped it to unfurl it. "But we must also address the limitations, shouldn't we? The constraints. All systems have constraints."

Bull stood up in excitement, and in the process, knocked over several desks. He stacked them back neatly as his face reddened and the class snickered, and then he stepped into the middle of the factory floor. "I know this one! I think. It's from a lesson my nan taught us when we were little. She said power will be provided, not purchased."

Dr. Clayton lit up. She grabbed a blue dry-erase marker and moved to a whiteboard propped up on the teacher's desk, where she wrote that sentence and underlined it several times.

A couple other kids pulled out notebooks and jotted it down, so I snapped a picture with my phone, stifling a groan when the screen blanked and the phone shut down. I really needed a new battery.

"I like that," Dr. Clayton said. She then wrote a symbol on the board, the same circle bisected by a cross, and touched it with her fingers for several seconds, muttering under her breath. The symbol flashed . . . I think. Or maybe it was the sun glinting through the skylights? I couldn't trust anything anymore. "Power is provided, not purchased. Meaning what? Anyone?"

One of the kids I hadn't met yet raised a hand. "It means that spiritual energy isn't ours for the taking. We borrow it from the spirits willing to lend it, and no matter how badly we want more or think we should have more, we only get what we are given."

"Exactly!" Dr. Clayton wrote something on the board, and I squinted to read it. "The first rule of summoning: We *borrow* power from the spirits and ancestors—it is not ours." She pointed at her circle drawing. "Take this symbol—the one we use for our summoner links. It's a kosmogram, representing our realm adjacent to the spirit realm, and the lines symbolize the power we share. Now, who can tell me how we channel that power?"

"Heirlooms!" someone yelled from the back.

"Good," Dr. Clayton said.

She steepled her fingers, forming a triangle that she held in front of her chest. A glowing silver circle surrounded by smaller circles appeared in midair, and my jaw dropped open. What was that? A hologram?

"Is that the only way?" she asked us.

"Small acts of power can be performed without an heirloom," Two-Saint chimed in, "but we need heirlooms to perform stronger spells. And if we use up too much energy, we go *pfffttt*, like a lightbulb burning out."

"A wonderful analogy," Dr. Clayton said wryly.

Two-Saint wasn't done yet. "Our own ancestors are much more likely to lend us power than spirits we don't know are, and heirlooms strengthen our link to them. Like the super gaming Wi-Fi we have at my dad's house, instead of the janky hotspot my stepdad lets me use when I stay with him. Better connection. Same thing with heirlooms. The older the heirloom, the stronger the link, and the more powerful the summoner."

"Pretty smart for someone with *no* heirloom," Jalen muttered.

Two-Saint shrank down in his seat as things slid into place in my mind. I spoke up. "So I . . . uh, a summoner is someone who can channel spiritual energy through an heirloom, whatever that is, and . . . do what? Magic?"

Dr. Clayton laughed. "That's a simplified answer, since the power of each family's heirloom is unique, but yes."

I leaned back against the desk and stared around the classroom. The other students imitated Dr. Clayton's hand positions, concentrated, and in a bloom of light, their own symbols appeared in front of them. Devin's was a deck of playing cards, while Nina summoned a purple designer handbag. Vanessa had an unlit candle floating in a gentle spin. Bull unbuttoned his sleeve to reveal a bandage on the inside of his forearm, with a shining tattoo peeking out. Everyone had a glowing symbol—an heirloom, I guess?—obviously prepared for whatever we were about to do in class.

"Good, good," said Dr. Clayton, nodding at everyone in turn. "Focus, Priyanka, as if you are gathering energy from the spirits around you in front of your heart. Excellent!" She wandered around the room, correcting positions and whispering feedback, before returning to the front of the class. "Now, then, dispel them until I call on you."

"I'm dreaming," I muttered. "This is wild. Wild! You're telling me this sixth-period class is about doing magic?"

Dr. Clayton frowned. "Again, reductive and simplistic, but in a sense, yes."

"Okay, that's it," I said, throwing my hands up. "Ha-ha. Real funny. I'm definitely in the wrong class, but y'all could've said that instead of playing an elaborate practical joke on me. Hilarious! I'm not the best student, we get it. Scheduling mix-up! I'll let you AIG kids do your thing."

"Mr. Freeman..." Dr. Clayton began, but I'd reached my limit.

"Nope, we're good. No disrespect, ma'am. Obviously, I'm not supposed to be here, or y'all are pranking the new kid, or you don't like Freemans, so Imma just go."

I headed to the door, my hands shoved into my coat pockets and my cheeks burning as everyone watched and whispered about me behind my back. I'd tried. Honestly, I had. And that's what I'd tell Uncle Moe and Gran, since clearly they were in on it, too. But this place wasn't for me. I didn't belong, and I should've known.

Those were the thoughts circling in my brain when I felt a whisper of air on my face. Out of the corner of my eye, I saw Dr. Clayton's weird heirloom circles flare bright silver again, and then, in front of me, the scuffed tile floor bulged, as if something were digging up from the ground beneath it.

Which is exactly what was happening.

A thick green sprout poked out, snaking upward like a time-lapse video of some giant vine growing in a rainforest.... Except it wasn't in a rainforest—it was here, in an inner-city middle school. The vine twisted up to the ceiling and brushed the fluorescent lights before curling back down. A pod swelled at the end of it before bursting into the most spectacular blossom I'd ever seen. The petals were the size of my head, and they alternated cream and orange. Dewdrops glistened on them, and tiny insects bumbled their way along the stem, carrying pollen off to some unknown location. Others gathered in the disklike center, which was a gorgeous deep yellow and as unblemished as the morning sun.

At least it was unblemished until a slit appeared in it and the flower spoke, its words chilling my spine.

"*Tell me, Mr. Freeman,*" the flower said in Dr. Clayton's voice, "*have you seen anything strange lately?*"

CHAPTER
EIGHT

I STARED AT THE GIANT FLOWER.

The flower stared back at me.

Silence stretched between and around us. The other students held their breaths, and even Dr. Clayton seemed to wait on what happened next. I licked my lips, my mouth suddenly dry, and leaned in close.

"Petey Piranha?" I whispered.

Someone groaned in the background. It might've been Devin. But I ignored it and inched closer.

"Petey, is that you?" I looked at Dr. Clayton. "Did you trap him here, too?"

Dr. Clayton was stifling a sneeze or trying not to laugh—either way, it took her a few moments to regain her composure. "Did you just call my summon a Super Mario character?"

Nina put her head in her hands, and Two-Saint pulled

his shirt over his face in secondhand embarrassment. Devin looked bored, while Jalen was smirking and whispering in his ear, probably talking more trash.

I straightened and cleared my throat. "Of course not. I was surprised, that's all. So that's what you inherited? Growing stuff?"

"Oh, come on, be for real?" Devin blurted out. "Dr. Clayton—"

"Now, now, Devin, there's no such thing as a silly question."

Two-Saint opened his mouth like he was going to contradict her; then he changed his mind.

The teacher checked the symbol on the whiteboard, which was still pulsing between blue and silver, and then walked over to stand by the flower. "Extra credit to anyone who can answer Jax's question. You look ready to say something, Toussaint."

"An heirloom is the symbolic manifestation of power granted by the ancestors," he recited. "Its energy form. Like you said earlier, everyone's is different. An heirloom is not the only power a summoner can channel, but you can't do the really cool stuff without one!" He paused, took a breath, then, when he looked around and realized that everyone was staring at him and his excitement, he slouched in his seat. "Or so I've heard."

"Wonderful!" Dr. Clayton beamed. She wrote the words *SUMMONER* and *HEIRLOOM* on the board, all capitalized like they were important. "Anyone else?"

Bull stood up. "It's the way spiritual power is represented and given to a summoner."

"Correct! Keep it going!"

More students stood and shouted out answers.

"It's your family legacy."

"It represents generations of support and love and dreams."

Nina called out, "You use your family's heirloom as a link or a channel. Then a summoner accepts power from the ancestors along with all their guidance and invokes their power in a unique way."

Dr. Clayton clapped. "A perfect summary, class. I think that'll do for a pop quiz; everyone passes." A few kids cheered as she made notes. Then she walked back over to her giant flower. Her unique, magicky flower.

"Let's use this as an example," she said, patting the flower like it was a pet. "This is an *Echinacea pallida*, also known as a pale purple coneflower. Native to the Midwest, it has been used for centuries as a medicinal supplement. When my powers began to show, I was given my heirloom, and Petey, as you called it, Jax, appeared shortly thereafter. With it, I can communicate with any spirit who previously inhaled its pollen."

As if on cue, the flower's mouth (weird, weird, weird) opened and blew a puff of pollen into my face. I coughed as I raised my hand. "With your heirloom?"

Dr. Clayton pivoted and marched to the center of the classroom, but it was her flower that answered. If you ever want a sanity check, try listening to a lecture from a giant flower with a reedy voice. *Exactly! Now you're cooking with fire! Simply put, an heirloom is what summoners use to channel power from the ancestors and act with it. There are, of course, other ways to channel power: a community or group of family members could use a ring shout, for example. But for the individual, the heirloom is the only way. A symbol of your family and heritage, but also a powerful tool. Like a wand from those lovely wizard stories."*

"Or a flashlight," Two-Saint added. When the class turned to stare at him, he shrugged. "It's how I think of it. The batteries are the power from the spirits, and the heirloom is the flashlight that uses the power to create a beam of light."

Dr. Clayton tapped her chin. "An interesting analogy, Toussaint."

"It's Two-Saint."

"Let's ground our theory with practice, shall we?" She pointed at Nina and Jalen. "You two, come with me. I think this is the perfect time to simulate your EOG exam. Less lecture, more practice, as I always say."

"What's an ee-oh-gee?" I whispered to Bull.

"EOG. End of Grade." He gulped, and suddenly the gruff expression on his face was replaced by something more like fear. "Tests at the end of the year. There are two parts, I think. A group project, and a one-on-one demonstration of our abilities. Like a Glimmer Fest duel. If we don't pass . . . our heirlooms must go to someone else."

He turned away to focus on what was happening in the center of the classroom, and I frowned. A final exam that determined if you could keep doing magic? Talk about pressure!

Dr. Clayton stood between Nina and Jalen. The taller boy grinned smugly and folded his arms across his chest while Nina ignored him. Dr. Clayton clapped to get everyone's attention and then swiveled between both students.

"All right," she said. "Practice rules: Summon your heirloom, then gather power through its link to the spirits. Remember, the most important thing is maintaining control, now and during your EOGs. Jalen, you first."

Jalen flashed a nasty grin. He steepled his fingers and a large fang appeared in midair between them, pulsing with a sickly green light. "Ready, girl?" he sang at Nina, then closed his eyes. He hunched his back and curled his arms, as if trying to rip his shirt by flexing.

"What is he doing?" I whispered to Two-Saint, but he wasn't paying attention to me. The whole class was focused on Jalen. I looked around the factory. The lights flickered and dimmed, and I flinched. Someone laughed in a corner. I gritted my teeth and ignored it.

A deep, rumbling sound, like a growl from something bigger than I wanted to imagine, echoed around us. Then Jalen stood upright, and the lights went out completely. "Monday's walkin'," he said.

Except it wasn't his voice. It was . . . almost animal-like. Jalen looked . . . larger. Bulkier. His skin had gone from a medium brown to a mottled gray-green, and one of his eyes had turned a bright golden orange, like a burning coal. His grin was wider, sharper, and I swear I saw his fingernails grow another inch.

Fear gripped my chest. Thick, lung-stopping fear. What in the world was going on? I hadn't signed up for this! I thought I'd be doing worksheets, or taking notes, or watching a lecture and trying to stay awake. Not seeing kids morph into monsters!

Jalen—or whoever he was now—took a step toward Nina.

I'd just noticed that she hadn't moved. She stood with her arms crossed and yawned. Jalen noticed, too, and he growled and dashed forward.

I gasped. How could something so big move that fast? One minute he was on the other side of the room; the next he was a step away from Nina, one taloned hand raised, ready to slash her to pieces.

Casually, almost without a care, Nina steepled her fingers and out of nowhere summoned her purple purse. She dipped her hand inside and withdrew what looked like a handful of glitter. She scattered it in an arc around her, and almost as an afterthought, spoke a single word: "Repel."

Jalen put one foot on the glittering powder, and it was like a wrecking ball had slammed into his chest. He yelped in pain as he was launched across the room. The rest of us ducked when he hit the wall so hard the ceiling shook and dust rained down. I stared at the powder. It looked eerily similar to the stuff that old lady at the train station had thrown at me.

"And that, class," Dr. Clayton said, all amusement in her voice gone, "is why you have to maintain control. Try a stunt like what Jalen just did and you'll lose any chance at becoming a summoner. Is that understood?"

A chorus of *Yes, ma'am*s answered her, and she whirled on Jalen, who was staggering to his feet. He was shivering, and his skin had taken on a blue tint. "You, come with me to the nurse's office. Bringing Uncle Monday here was one of the more foolish things you could've done. We're practicing control and intention, not ridiculous shows of power! The rest of you, pair off and practice summoning with your heirlooms until I get back. Control! You must maintain control."

After she left with the whining and limping Jalen in tow, everyone immediately began to gossip about what had just happened. No one seemed very concerned about Jalen getting hurt, so I guessed this kind of thing happened regularly (hopefully only to Jalen... kidding, kidding... sort of), but my head was reeling as I tried to make sense of everything. Magic was real, spirits gave us power (who was Uncle Monday?), and, apparently, we could summon giant flowers or turn into were-gators. And this was an actual *class*!

In the meantime, the other students paired off. Bull seemed flustered as Vanessa dragged him off to practice, her friends giggling as they went. Devin looked annoyed when Two-Saint puffed out his chest and marched in front of him. I wasn't positive that was a good look, but I wished him the best. That left me and...

"Hey," someone said. It was a thin kid with glasses, the most forgettable member of Devin's group. Though the more I saw him, the more I thought he didn't fit in with them.

"What's up," I said. "Look, I have no idea what we're supposed to do, so..."

The boy shrugged. "I can't participate because I don't have my heirloom with me today, so I thought I'd introduce myself. Vernon. Everyone calls me V."

"Jax. New. I'm still taking it in."

"It's wild, right? The first day is always strange, and they just threw you into the mess."

I raised my hands in mock outrage. "Exactly! I'm struggling over here, bro. This is all wild."

Vernon nodded. "Let me know if you need some help. What's your heirloom?"

"I don't have one," I said. "At least I don't think so."

"That can't be right," Vernon said, frowning. "How'd you get into this class? They normally scan your heirloom to register you. And you can't be a reggie—the wards prevent them from seeing this class."

His words only made things even more confusing. It didn't help my confidence that not only was I behind in . . . whatever we were supposed to be learning in Magic 101, but also, I probably wasn't even meant to be here in the first place. Was I supposed to be in another class and got marked absent? If I got too many absences on my record, the school could kick me out. That couldn't happen—it would be the last strike! I had to stay in school; that's what the judge in North Carolina had said.

My stress level rose even higher when, at that moment, one of the broken stone statues in the corner of the room turned to look at me. *"You there,"* it said in a gravelly voice. *"Have you seen my nose?"*

"No," I muttered under my breath. "Now leave me alone."

Vernon was looking at me weirdly. I started sweating. Had he heard me talking? I panicked. "Actually, I think I *do* have an heirloom. It belonged . . . to my great-uncle." I hurried to add, "Here, let me try to channel my talent."

"I thought you said—"

"Nope, ha-ha, just joking!"

"That's not—"

"Oh, it totally is," I said, probably too loud, since a couple heads turned our way. "I can totally summon. Got my heirloom, gonna show you. Any second now."

Vernon stared at me. I smiled to reassure him, but maybe it looked like I was constipated, because his worried frown deepened. My hands were sweating as I dropped into an offensive-lineman stance (don't ask me why this was my magical stance—it was the first thing I could think of) and took a deep breath. Then, with a flourish, I wiggled my fingers. "Heirloom!" I shouted.

Nothing happened.

Well, that's not exactly correct. Everyone in the room started laughing, my ears burned, and a sudden desire to have the earth swallow me up in a Jax-sized sinkhole filled my chest. But aside from that, nothing happened at all.

"You did not just do jazz hands to summon," Devin called from the corner, where Two-Saint was currently doing his best to avoid a strange giant made of fog. Devin shook his head and turned away, dispelling the creature with a wave of his hand. He made everything he did look easy. I whirled back around to see Vernon tiptoeing off, as if he wanted nothing to do with me anymore. Fine. Perfect.

Suddenly it was all too much. I stuffed my hands into the coat I hadn't taken off all day and marched toward the exit. I didn't belong in this class. It was obvious. I knew it, and I was pretty sure everyone else knew it, too, and if they didn't, they'd soon find out. I could feel my face and neck flushing with the

JAX FREEMAN AND THE PHANTOM SHRIEK

heat of embarrassment the longer I stayed. My skin was prick-
ling, and the laughter was still echoing in my ears, and I didn't
know what I was supposed to do. So . . . I did what I always did
whenever things got to be too much. I ran. Well, not literally,
but I had to get away. The sooner I got out of this place, the
better. I shoved the door to open it.

"Wait!" Nina shouted.

But it was too late. I'd already smudged Dr. Clayton's circle-
and-cross symbol.

"That's a portal," Nina said, her face torn between anger
and fear. "Our way back! And now we can't get out!"

The mark shimmered, then disappeared. Immediately
afterward, the lights blinked once. Twice.

"Yeah, and now other things can get in," Devin whispered.

Something shuffled in the dark, and a cold draft raised the
hairs on the back of my neck.

The lights flickered back on.

Someone screamed. Was it me? Who knows? That's not
important right now. All I know is that it was justified.

In the middle of the room, floating two feet off the floor
and wearing a tattered suit, was a thin, gray-skinned man with
sunken eyes and no mouth. He wore a necktie made of bones
and carried a briefcase that bulged from time to time, as if
something inside were trying to escape. And if that weren't
freaky enough, I could see through him, straight to a grim-
faced Devin on the other side. The man didn't seem to notice
us . . . not at first. He just dangled there in midair, bobbing up
and down as if waiting. But I couldn't help it—I took a step

backward, and as soon as I moved, the thing's head whipped around to look at me...while the rest of his body remained facing forward.

"Now you've done it," said the broken statue in the corner.

"Is that—?" I started to ask.

"A spirit!" Two-Saint shouted.

"Look out!" Bull bellowed.

Too late, I realized the spirit was rushing straight at me.

CHAPTER
NINE

"MOVE!" SHOUTED NINA, SHOVING ME OUT OF THE way. "Don't let it touch you!"

I tumbled to the floor and a gust of cold air enveloped me as the spirit rushed over the spot where I'd just been standing. If it hadn't been for Nina, I would've been ... Well, I don't know what I would've been, because NONE OF THIS MADE ANY SENSE! Not that anyone wanted to take the time to explain it to me at that moment.

"Move, *Freak*-man!" one of Devin's buddies growled, leaping over me.

Devin himself didn't say anything, but his eyes flashed in annoyance as he sidestepped my crablike scramble and summoned his foggy-yet-fashionable giant ... creature again. Was brogre (*bro* + *ogre*) a term? I think brogre *should* be a term, and that's what appeared in front of him. It roared a silent challenge at the spirit, who hesitated, seeking a path around this new obstacle.

I bumped into someone else who was cowering—Two-Saint. "Why don't they just let this thing leave?" I shouted at him.

"We can't!" he answered, ducking behind a statue (which didn't seem to appreciate it) as a chair went flying across the room. "It's a sycophant!"

"A sick-of-what?"

"Sycophant," someone answered on the other side of me. Vanessa. She'd summoned her own heirloom, a translucent unlit candle, and her brown curls were floating behind her as she clasped her hands as if praying. "Mariana," she muttered.

I yelped as a pair of ghostly hands, each twice as large as an adult's hand, emerged from behind her. They joined Devin's brogre in attempting to corral the spirit—the sycophant—in the middle of the room.

"Sycophants are unbalanced spirits that attract other unbalanced spirits," Two-Saint said, popping up from behind another statue. "Too many and they'll drive themselves into a frenzy, and then a malevolent spirit might appear, and the whole city will be in trouble!"

"But they're just spirits," I protested, even as Nina dodged the sycophant's attempt to engulf her. "What can they do?"

"Unbalanced spirits? Drain your soul, shred your will, take over your body and turn you into a husk, steal your skin . . ."

Two-Saint kept rattling off nasty-sounding tortures as we hid, but something he'd said triggered a memory. *Steal your skin.* That's what the spirit at the train station had tried to do!

"... give you hives, steal your identity and buy a boat," Two-Saint was saying. "You don't want to mess with unbalanced spirits, especially malevolent ones!"

In the center of the room, the rest of the class had cornered the sycophant. It floated back and forth, agitated, as Vanessa, Bull, Devin, and Devin's brogre all inched closer to it.

"Now!" shouted Devin.

Nina slipped into the circle, spinning like an ice skater, both of her hands glittering, and hurled two waves of silver dust outward. A shimmering cloud began to form around the sycophant. The spirit struggled, flailing this way and that, but it couldn't move far as the cloud grew denser, until finally we couldn't see the sycophant at all. The cloud shrank to the size of a car, then a bike, then a toddler, then my fist, until, with a small *poof*, it fell to the floor as a small mound of dust. Nina pulled a small amber bottle from her purse, swept the dust into it, corked it, and tossed it to Devin.

"Is that it?" he asked her. "Did it call anything else?"

Nina shook her head. "No. We should be clear."

The two of them acted like they'd done this before. They made a good team, and I was going to say that out loud after Devin dispelled his brogre. But before I could, he stomped over to where Two-Saint and I were hiding and erupted. "Way to go! Way. To. Go. Now there are *two* useless people in this class. Him, and you!" He pointed at me. "What were you doing back here? It was your fault—you should've been out here helping!"

I looked around. Vanessa and a couple others were checking to make sure everyone was okay. Nina was taking pictures of the stain pattern her powder had left on the floor, like some-thing straight off *CSI*. The way she'd been so calm, even saving me from the sycophant, replayed in my mind. Maybe she could give me some tips. Tutor me?

Who was I kidding? I had a better chance of making friends with the spirit.

Bull was lifting chairs and desks with ease to put them back into their original spots. Everyone had contributed something, and they all knew what they were doing. Me? I'd been worse than useless.

Two-Saint puffed out his scrawny chest. "Leave him alone, Devin. He doesn't know anything."

I sighed as Devin scowled and walked away. "Thanks, man," I said to Two-Saint. "I think."

"Anytime," Two-Saint said. "Not everybody's first spirit encounter is with a sycophant. That's pretty rough."

"It is?"

"Oh yeah. Normally you'd be introduced to a minor spirit just to get used to being around them. Sycophants are for advanced students. Good thing Nina was here—she's prac-tically the heir of her tree. Or she would be, if it weren't for Devin."

I didn't know what that last part meant, but what he'd said about *a minor spirit* bugged me. "How many different types of spirits are there?"

Two-Saint paused and started counting on his fingers, which was never a good sign. "Well, there are all sorts of vari-ations, depending on which family trained you, but everyone mostly agrees on a few categories. First are the minor, which are like house spirits. Then there are the lesser—your river spirits, forest spirits, and stone spirits."

I could've sworn the statue in the corner winked at me when Two-Saint said that.

"Then there are the biggies—the named and the ancestral—"

"What are named spirits?" I interrupted, frowning.

"Oh, like spirits who are really important to a neighborhood—help out the local people. Like there's one named Tia Rosalina you can see wandering around Chicago sometimes. She protects children while they are walking home, just like she did when she was alive. Rumor is, if she grants your heirloom her power, you can always find a safe space if you're in trouble. It comes in handy when you're hiding from bullies."

It sounded like he was speaking from experience with bullies, so I left it alone. I thought he was done, but Two-Saint had paused to pull a small, crumpled notebook out of his pocket. He flipped through it like an old-school detective about to pull a gotcha moment. "And ancestral spirits are, obviously, your own ancestors. Like I said earlier, they're really powerful because they're connected to you, and you're their representative here on Earth."

"Minor, lesser, named, ancestral," I listed. "Is that it? Are they all dangerous like the sycophant?"

"They all have different levels of power, and we haven't gotten to the greater spirits yet. Again, there are different variations, like a sycophant is a kind of lesser spirit, while a malevolent spirit falls in the greater category. Malevolents are rare, though." He consulted his notebook. "Let me see . . . I thought I— Oh, there it is! Yep, the last malevolent recorded in this area was in 2008, after something happened with money and the stock market and blah, blah, blah, news stations went off the rails. And apparently, a greater malevolent spirit created a lair under the Dan Ryan Expressway. Since then, nothing."

"Wouldn't a sycophant who wants to take your skin be a malevolent?" I asked, thinking of Conductor Buck. I shuddered at the memory.

"Oooh, good question. Most skin-stealers are wraiths, another kind of greater spirit. They're super rare because the congregation and their stewards keep a close eye out for them. Wraiths are attracted to the power that summoners have. And word is if a wraith ever got control of a summoner's body, the wraith would be able to summon, too. Why do you ask?"

"I . . . think I saw one."

"Oh, that can't be true. I hope not, at least. Wraiths haven't been seen around here in almost a century. Maybe the spirit you saw was just really, *really* unbalanced. You probably stumbled into its path after something else riled it up."

"Probably," I said aloud. Inside, though, I wasn't so sure.

Suddenly, someone groaned. Devin. "I can't fix the summoner's link," he said, standing in front of the door, his arms folded in frustration. Priyanka rushed over and yanked open the door, and I cringed, but the only thing waiting was another long, dim hallway.

I stepped forward. "There's gotta be a way back, right? How far are we from the school?"

"Not far," Nina answered.

"As long as nothing else is out there..." Priyanka said. She and Vanessa peered through the cracked-open door.

"I told you," Nina said, annoyed. "The spirit didn't get a chance to lure anything else here. As long as no one does anything ridiculous, like try to summon before we're back inside the school's wards, we should be fine. But to be safe, we should probably go in small groups, in case our heirlooms still have a little power left in them."

As everyone gathered up their things, Two-Saint elbowed me, and together we inched closer to Devin and Nina. Vanessa and Priyanka headed out with Bull, which left the four of us last.

Devin rolled his eyes when he saw us but didn't protest. Nina just nodded when we were all together, and without a word, she led us through the door. I took one last hasty look over my shoulder at the factory and shivered. The stone statue lifted a hand, and I automatically waved back.

Life was getting weirder by the second.

CHAPTER
TEN

IT TAKES A LOT TO FRIGHTEN ME.

I'm not talking about being nervous. I was nervous that morning as I got ready for school. I was nervous the last time I went to the guidance counselor's office back in North Carolina, when Marcus was still my best friend for at least another ninety minutes, and my life was on the brink of being turned upside down and inside out.

I hadn't been frightened then.

Then there was that one time when I got lost at a car show at the state fairgrounds. I think I was seven or eight years old, and I got distracted by this truck with the engine on the outside and an ice cream dispenser on the inside. By the time I realized I'd lost Dad and Uncle Moe, almost five minutes had passed. But I didn't cry or freak out—I wandered around until I saw a car with the biggest subwoofers I'd ever seen, then climbed inside and cranked the volume up on the only radio station I could remember: 93.9 FM. When my dad and uncle found me, me and the entire Cadillac wing of the show were doing the electric slide.

So I'm not bragging when I say I don't get scared easily. But ever since last night at Union Station, it seemed like the world I knew was completely different. Changed. Or *I'd* changed. Everything I knew to be true was a lie, or at least not the complete truth. Either way, it was like I was learning how to exist all over again.

That was scary.

Then there was the journey Two-Saint, Devin, Nina, and I had to make to get back to school. They told me that the factory we'd traveled to through the summoner's link was only a few blocks away from DuSable, but the windowless corridor we were walking in seemed endless. And with every step I took, I felt that someone—or some*thing*—was watching me. Following me. Waiting for me. Did it help that Two-Saint trembled next to me while reciting all the gruesome ways a spirit could harm you?

"There's possession, yeah, but then there's leeching, spirit harvesting, ghost ear—which is like the wet willy of haunting—and that's just the lower tier of afflictions. On the higher tier . . ."

No. No, it did not help.

Devin stalked forward at the front of our group. Every now and then he'd shoot glares back at us. No, back at *me*. Normally I'd ignore it. I was used to people getting annoyed with me in public. But when he wasn't glaring at me, Devin would scowl at Nina. As if he was disappointed in her for some reason.

I dropped back to ask Nina what was wrong. "Nothing," she said, frantically scrolling through her phone. She attempted to make a call, but there wasn't any reception, and she shook her head at Devin, whose scowl deepened. It was like they had their own secret language. But who was I to care that they had such a close relationship? I'd only been here a day!

I fell back in line with Two-Saint.

"Has the summoner link ever been ruined before?" I asked him.

"We've done drills," Two-Saint said. "What to do if a reg catches you, who to call if you come into contact with a spirit at a higher level than you are, that sort of thing."

Something skittered behind us. "We shouldn't be here," I muttered.

Devin snorted. "Only two people don't belong here, and that's Two-Saint and you, Freeman."

"Bro, what is your problem?" I stepped in front of Nina to address him.

"You!" he said. "Your family is always messing something up, and now you go and follow in their footsteps. You're lucky we didn't leave you behind. So shut up and stay out of our way, or else."

Two-Saint was tugging my arm, but I was riled up now. "Or else what?" I asked, getting into Devin's face. He smirked, and then his fog giant suddenly appeared beside him. This close, I could see it stomping up to me in cloudy Timberland shoes, its wispy hand raised in the air. I didn't know if it was going to shove me or pull Devin away. I never got the chance to find out, because at that moment Two-Saint inserted himself between us.

"Be careful with the summoning!" he said. "Remember when Nina said . . ." He looked up and down the hallway. "Hey, where'd she go?"

That dragged my attention away from the dingleberry duo for a moment. "What?"

"Nina. She was with us, and now she's gone."

Sure enough, Nina was nowhere to be found. But there was a trail of footprints that stopped abruptly in the dust just ahead of us, near one of the few light fixtures mounted on the cement walls.

To my surprise, it was Devin who reacted first, though not how I expected. He muttered something under his breath and spun around, shoving the brogre away from him. "You were supposed to be watching her!" he snapped at it. Then he pulled a gray drawstring bag out of his pocket, reached inside, and took out a pinch of what looked like dirt. He scattered it on the floor, examined it for a few seconds, and then took off without a word into the gloom ahead. The brogre lumbered after him.

"Should we follow them?" Two-Saint asked, taking a few hesitant steps forward.

"Yeah," I said. I glanced behind me, hoping that this was just a trick and Nina would be there. "Yeah, let's—"

When I turned around, I was alone. Two-Saint was gone,

too. Just another set of footprints that disappeared after several feet.

"Hello!" I called out. "HELLO?"

I started walking forward, then stopped. I had no idea where I was going. *Maybe I should stay put*, I thought. *Let someone come and find me. Better than tearing off through an unfamiliar place and ending up who knows where.* I mean, it wasn't like I was afraid, I was only gravely concerned ... that I was heading to my grave.

Something scraped behind me.

My body froze as my eyes scanned the ceiling, studied the floor. Nothing but gray, damp cement under an occasionally flickering lightbulb. Then I started walking again, stopping every few steps to strain my ears for the sounds of my classmates. After ten minutes of this, I finally saw something different—an intersection of dark hallways a few feet ahead of me.

"Hello?" I called again. "Anybody?"

CREEEEAK

I whirled around, but there was nothing there but shadows and stone. I licked my lips, walking backward while still calling out for help.

"Can anyone hear me?"

Another scrape. This time a shadow rippled across the stone ceiling.

"Who's there?" I shouted.

"Freeman?"

Full disclosure ... I yelped and ran. Not far, but enough

for the echo of my startled shout to bounce back to me. High-pitched, like a cartoon character falling off a cliff. Not my proudest moment. But when I finally stopped and looked around, no one was there.

And yet...

I scanned the area again. Squinted into the dim light. Still nothing. Some dingy lockers the color of burned rice on one side of the corridor, stained brick on the other, but that was it. And it wasn't like there was any place for someone to hide here. The intersection I stood in was shaped like the letter T—the hallway behind me led back to the factory, I thought. The hallway in front of me stretched out into darkness, and the hallway to my left...

I stared.

About two-thirds of the way up the walls, the weird brick pattern stopped, replaced by smooth gray cement that continued to the high ceiling. And right before the wall ended, protruding every few feet, were these weird gargoyle-like sculptures. Some were shaped like animals. A lion, a horse, a dragon. Some had faces like people. I pivoted slowly in a circle and saw there were dozens. Maybe a hundred! But they were only in this one hallway, almost as if they'd been removed from the school and stored here. But that was silly. They were gargoyles, right? I mean, of course they were. They couldn't be moved.

My coat flapped, and I pulled it tighter without thinking. Then it flapped again, and I looked down. Where was the breeze coming from?

I heard someone snicker.

My heart leaped into my throat. "Okay!" I shouted. "Quit playing! I'm serious! Who's there?" Something shifted in the corner of my vision. A small movement. I walked deeper into the side hallway, angry now. "I know you're there! You think this is funny, huh? Playing jokes on the new kid. Well, you're too late! Join the club! Get in line! Jackson Freeman, the world's punching bag! Get your laughs in now! Get your—"

I stopped talking. Not because I was done complaining— oh no, there was plenty more where that came from. No, I stopped because when I'd said my name, it had started echoing down the hall, traveling through the darkness and bouncing back toward me, louder and louder and louder.

Freeman?

Freeman.

Freeman?

I pictured Devin's and Nina's startled faces when I'd told them my last name. Then I couldn't picture anything, because the echo built in volume, going from weird to spooky to downright terrifying.

Freeman.

Freeman?

Freeman!

I covered my ears as my own last name seemed to burrow into my skull. Stumbling, I started to run. I didn't care where I was headed, as long it was away from that accusing chorus. It felt like the choir from my church was chasing me, shouting my name over and over, and I fled.

Freeman.

Freeman?

FREEMAN.

I almost ran headlong into some old double doors that appeared out of nowhere. A rusty chain kept them shut, but there was enough slack in it to pull them open a bit. I squeezed myself through—first my shoulders, then my stomach, then my legs. As soon as I was inside, the chorus stopped. The only thing I could hear was my own breathing. I was panting, less from the exertion than from the sheer terror coursing through my veins.

I backed a few steps away from the doors. The light from the hallway didn't extend far into whatever room I'd entered, so I pulled out my phone, my breathing echoing in my ear. After three tries (Like, seriously, what if it was an emergency? OH, WAIT!) the raggedy thing finally turned on, and I used the feeble glow to examine my surroundings.

I was standing by a railing at the top of a small flight of stairs. Below was a giant room, from what I could see, and there was some huge shape in the distance. Water dripped somewhere in the dark, and my coat continued to flap, despite the lack of a breeze. I slowly raised the phone higher, trying to calm myself as I completed a circle. It was okay. I was okay.

I felt silly. This was ridiculous! I was way too old to be afraid of the dark. Didn't I just say I didn't get scared easily? Nina and Two-Saint were probably watching me from somewhere next to a light switch, holding in their laughter. And it was sort of funny. I'd run from my echo. Who does that? I snorted, then started to chuckle. I went back to squeeze through the double doors when something extending from the stonework above the doorframe grabbed my attention. Another gargoyle. This one was a snarling, sharp-tooth boy. I relaxed...

...until it turned in my direction, stone grinding on stone.

"Freeman," it hissed.

I shrieked and leaped backward, tumbling over the stair's handrail into the darkness below.

CHAPTER
ELEVEN

"Do you think it's dead?"

"Poke it and see."

"I don't have hands, boulder brain."

"Why'd you have to go and hiss in its face, Rufus? You know they're fragile creatures."

"Oh, lay off. Rufus only has one face, and he can't help that it's hideous. Besides, he got excited when he thought it was Pothole."

"Do you think it knows Pothole?"

"Only one way to find out. Hey, flesh creature! Are you dead? And, on the off chance that you aren't, do you know Pothole?"

"Keep it down, you-know-who is right over there."

"Oh yeah, sorry. HEY, FLESH CREATURE, ARE YOU DEAD?"

This conversation was the first thing I became aware of

when I blinked my eyes open, but it was quickly driven away by a painful throbbing on the side of my face. I felt like I'd just been blindsided by a bus. Once I was sure my jaw was still working and my teeth were all there, I noticed a second curious thing, which was the lights. I guess they were motion activated and my graceful tumble had switched them on, because several large, recessed bulbs in the ceiling were growing in intensity from a warm yellow to a bright white. But it was what they illuminated that drew my attention.

I'd fallen into the largest garage I'd ever seen. I knew it was a garage because of the tools scattered everywhere, the machine parts, and the smell of oil and metal. My friend BG's dad is an auto mechanic back in Raleigh, and sometimes he let us help out on the weekends during the offseason, when there wasn't anything for us to do but get in trouble.

Keep the hands busy and they won't do what they shouldn't, he'd always say, right before giving one of us a wrench. Marcus would watch and laugh—the pretty boy couldn't get *his* hands dirty—and afterward we'd have iced horchata, which is a cinnamon rice drink that tastes like joy.

But this garage was a little bit . . . different. While I climbed to my feet, I could finally see how huge it was. The ceiling stretched high overhead in a vaulted arch that had to be at least a jillion feet tall, maybe a jillion and five. And it wasn't just the space that felt huge, but everything in it as well. I walked over to a workbench and gawked at the tools. I'd never seen a wrench that big—when I picked it up and stood it upright on the floor, it was almost as tall as me. And there were parts that looked like they belonged to a supersized vehicle of some sort. Picture a tire rim the size of a kindergartner and you'll know what I'm talking about.

"Is it me?" I muttered. "Did I shrink? Oh Lord, I've shrunk. It finally happened. I knew *Gulliver's Travels* was a horror movie. I'm a Lily Pad."

"Actually," said a voice behind me, *"I believe they're called* Lilliputians, *not Lily Pads."*

I nearly jumped out of my socks. When I whirled around, however, there was no one in sight. Just the landing I'd fallen over, a cement square lined with rusted railings, and a few dusty stairs. Seeing how short the drop was, I felt kinda embarrassed for screaming like I had. But the gargoyle had frightened me, and . . .

Wait.

The gargoyle.

I slowly looked up.

I could see more gargoyles over the door now. A half dozen. The statues were clustered together like the sparrows trying to stay warm on the electric wires near my house. I recognized the one that had surprised me, and I flinched. It looked like a rottweiler head with ram horns. I took a step back, ready to find another exit, when the voice spoke again.

"See, Rufus? It's still scared of you."

And that's when my brain, probably knocked loose after the fall and still trying to get up to speed, finally returned from lunch break and clocked back in to work. The voices were coming from the gargoyles. They were like the statues back in the main room of the factory.

"*Poor thing*," the gargoyle on the far left said. It had the face (including the mustache) of an old-timey circus strongman and the voice (and hairstyle, amazingly enough) of someone's aunt who is concerned about your skinniness. You know the kind, the ones who stuff your pockets with two-year-old hard candies when you leave. "*I think it's dazed.*"

The one on the far right grinned, but not in a friendly way. More like an *I can't wait for you to blink so I can get closer* way. "*Let's put it out of its misery.*"

The aunt gargoyle clucked. "*Hush, Carver. You'll frighten it to death.*"

Carver's face, that of an older boy with a permanent gap-toothed smile of razor-sharp teeth, twisted. "*Excellent.*"

I made a noise in my throat. Something between a yelp and a sob.

Auntie frowned. (Have you ever seen a gargoyle frown? Terrifying.) "*What did it say?*"

"*I think it said 'Homigawd,'*" Carver said.

"*Of course! That must be its name. Hi, Homigawd!*"

I scrambled backward on my hands and knees, knocking over buckets filled with bolts the size of my shoe and jostling carts with tools scattered on top. I was being pranked. Had to be. No way was this happening. No way, no way, no way, no way.

"*It keeps muttering,*" said the gargoyle they (as in the other statues!) called Carver. It frowned. "*Is that normal?*"

Auntie nodded. *"Of course! Portis used to do the same thing."*

"Are you sure? It looks afraid."

"Excuse me, I am the expert here. Me. Portis left me in charge of watching over the Shriek until it finds a new summoner, and that's what I plan on doing." Auntie glared at Rufus and Carver before flipping her hair back (with no luck, of course, because it was made of stone) and turning to me. *"Now, Homigawd, before we get down to business, would you like to have lunch with us? Remind me—do you prefer gravel or concrete in your salad? I know you humans are particular about what you eat."*

This was... No, this was too much. Words failed me. My balance did, too, because I kept stumbling in my rush to escape whatever nightmare I'd fallen into this time. Maybe I'd hit my head too hard. Yes, that had to be why I was seeing and hearing things.

"Hey, be careful!"

When I looked up, the statues were grouped closer together and shaking their heads in warning. But whatever they were cautioning me about couldn't have been more upsetting than TALKING GARGOYLES! I spun around and crawled under a curtain, pressing my back against a rounded metal wall as I tried to catch my breath. This was a nightmare. A bad dream. I'd wake up at the bottom of a flight of stairs outside the cafeteria any moment now.

I squeezed my eyes shut. "Wake up," I whispered. "Wake up. Wake UP!"

I opened my eyes and moved the curtain aside, slowly. Peeked out.

Nothing.

The wall above the entry stairs was empty. No gargoyles.

I let out a deep sigh and leaned back. My head rested against the wall as I inhaled and exhaled for the next few seconds. It was over.

My coat fluttered.

"Freeman..."

The wall behind me began to rumble. The vibration hummed through my chest and made my teeth vibrate.

I turned around slowly, one hand still on the curtain.

It wasn't a wall. Not even close.

Towering above me, steam escaping from its triangular grille, wheels freshly oiled and wickedly sharp, smokestack billowing with gray clouds, was a black-and-gold train engine.

My mouth opened, but the scream never came.

The engine's door slammed open and I caught a glimpse of a shimmering cloud of silver blue before someone grabbed my coat collar and yanked me up.

CHAPTER
TWELVE

"YOU'RE LATE."

When I opened my eyes, I noticed three things. First, I wasn't in the old garage anymore. I don't think I was even in Chicago. I lay sprawled on a stone bench in the middle of a train platform. It rose out of a grassy field like ruins, and rusted train tracks zigzagged around it. An old doorframe with a sagging door leaned haphazardly on the far side of the platform. But that was it. No other buildings. No cars. No houses.

But I wasn't alone.

A man sat on the opposite side of the stone bench, facing away from me while peeling a potato with a knife. He looked young, maybe around college age, and he wore a uniform. Navy blue pants, polished black shoes, and ... I squinted. Yeah, he was wearing a coat just like mine.

He was also still talking.

"Now, I expected you to be late, because when have you ever been on time, so forgive me if I leave this figment instead of meeting you in person. I gots duties and all." The man held up the potato without lifting his head, chuckled, then resumed peeling it.

"Figment?" I breathed. "What's a figment? Who are you?"

He didn't answer.

"Hey, excuse me? Sir? Where are—?" I sat up and scooched over to tap him on the shoulder...but my hand went right through him.

"Oh, no. No thanks. That's it," I said slowly, sliding off the other end of the bench. "I hit my head. I'm tired. I'm stressed! I'm dreaming. I'm...I'm..." This was entirely too freaky. Talking gargoyles, a train hidden in an underground garage, and now teleportation? Mixed with hallucinations? Telehallucination? No. Maybe I was unconscious. My real body was sprawled out back in DuSable Middle, probably laid up in the nurse's office with a cold pack on my forehead. I was fine. Fine. Perfectly fine. That had to be it. But how could I wake myself up? Pinch myself?

"YOWCH!"

Okay, so no pinching.

"But it's also getting dangerous for us to meet," the strange not-man continued. I rubbed my arm and eyed him warily. He wasn't making any sense, and now he was moving his hands like he was chopping something invisible. "The families are starting to pull apart. Skulls and Wands, Knives and Baskets, all of them are squabbling, and the Coins...well, I don't have to tell you about them."

Skulls and Knives and Baskets? What was he talking about?

The man got up and began to walk toward the sagging door at the end of the platform, still talking to...me, I guess? Or whoever he thought I was. "All this is to say that now ain't the best time for some high-powered spell. I can't help you, Portis."

Portis?

"And then there's all these strange disappearances. I just don't think—"

He reached the door and went through before he could finish his sentence. I ran over and stumbled inside. But the man's voice had faded away, and even worse, so had the platform and the grassy field. At the same time, it felt like someone reached inside my stomach and pulled me forward...

*   *   *

...and I crashed to the floor of a moving train!

"Hey! You there! George!"

A middle-aged white man in a conductor's hat was shouting at the end of the car. I stood up and found myself in the middle of a passenger car. But it wasn't anything like the Amtrak I'd taken to Chicago. This train was older—much older. I could tell by the carpet on the floor—it reminded me of my great-aunt Jendayi's house. Felt like I should take my shoes off before somebody fussed at me. Also, the lights on the walls were brass and fancy, and the seats were polished wood with burgundy cushions. Like church pews. The cushions had this weird flower pattern on them, same as the carpet, and everything smelled like peppermints.

Like I said, really old.

"Not this again," a voice behind me said.

I turned around and froze. The same young man from the train platform was behind me. I guessed his name was George. This time he was pulling down the overhead berths, fluffing the pillows and turning down the sheets. There were a few other passengers in the sleeping car—men and women in fine hats and embroidered dresses. None of the passengers were Black, and none of them paid any attention to me. For that matter, they didn't look at George, either.

"Look, I gotta make this quick, Portis," he said.

I frowned. This was the second time he'd said *Portis*. That was my great-great-grandfather's name. And hadn't Gran told me he worked on the sleeping cars? I looked around hopefully but was quickly disappointed. Portis wasn't here. So why was George talking to him like he was?

"You gotta stop with that ritual! It ain't gonna work, man! I'm tellin' you, the..." George paused as a customer squeezed by, then continued in a whisper, "The spell you trying to make ain't nothing to be foolin' with. I talked to everybody. Talked to the congregation, to a couple conjurefolk I know, and even that new Coin boy—they all hunkering down. I hope this figment ain't too late and you ain't biting off more than you can chew. Leave it alone, you hear me?"

Figments again. Is that what this was? Some sort of magic

voicemail? This was too freaky, man. I needed to get it together or...

"George! No more dillydallying!"

"Oh man, not this guy," said George.

I looked up, automatically feeling defensive, but his last sentence had been about the burly, red-faced conductor stomping angrily toward us down the aisle. George plastered a smile on his face, but that did nothing to calm his supervisor. The conductor's eyes seemed to laser right into me, and I took a step back, then another.

"Don't. Complete. The ritual," George whispered to me. When I glanced at him, fear filled his eyes. Whatever Portis had been planning to do, it terrified his friend. I didn't know who this congregation was, or "the Coin boy," or what my great-great-grandfather had been a part of, but it seemed like no one wanted him to succeed. I thought about that for approximately three seconds, right up until someone barked an order into my ear.

"George, hurry up with those beds!"

I jumped in surprise and twisted at the same time. The conductor was inches away from my face, and I yelped and fell over my own feet trying to back away. I lost my balance, and I tried to put my hands out to soften my fall...

* * *

...but I slammed into wooden floorboards.

"Uuuugh," I groaned, my face smooshed against the hard

wood. "I hate this. If this is a dream, they aren't supposed to hurt. I'm never dreaming again. Martin Luther King can keep them." I sighed, then sat up. "I didn't mean that. Sorry, ancestors."

But if the ancestors responded, I didn't listen (They'd probably say I never do. Oh, well.), because I was taking in my surroundings. This time I'd teleported into a small, dark room with a lone window high up by the ceiling. I could just make out a desk in the corner, and that was it. No other furniture, only a few boxes stacked against the wall. The room felt tight, like I was struggling to breathe in there. The air was still, and the smell of mildew stung my nostrils.

I climbed to my feet and my head knocked against something. A dangling lightbulb. If there was a bulb, there had to be a switch, right? I felt the wall with my hands, grimacing at the dust I could feel gathering on them. When I found the switch, I flicked it on...

...and immediately wished I hadn't.

"Whaaaaaaat...?"

The room was actually much larger than I'd assumed. I could see at least ten feet of walls before they continued stretching up into darkness beyond the dim glow of the lone lightbulb. But it was what was *on* the walls that held my focus. Hundreds of old newspaper clippings. Some were a few inches wide; others were an entire front page. A few were crumbling, yellow fragments littering the floor beneath them. It looked like the set of every movie with a conspiracy in it. But I didn't want to solve a mystery right now. I wanted to get back to school before some teacher marked me tardy. Could you get marked tardy for hallucinating? I was never gonna eat a meatball sub again.

And then I made the mistake of reading the clippings. All of them had horrific headlines in bold letters.

GARY SCHOOL ROCKED BY EXPLOSIONS
Bus Overturned Near Racine, Children Missing
NEIGHBORHOOD SEEKING ANSWERS AFTER GRAVEYARD HORROR

Each article was dated from decades earlier, and they had to be from local newspapers, because I didn't recognize any of their names. "*Gary Crusader,*" I read off one. "*The Wisconsin Weekly Blade. The Chicago Defender.* Wait, I know that one."

The Defender. The Defender. Why did that name sound familiar?

Something fluttered in the corner of my eye, and I turned toward the desk. Above it, someone had mounted a giant map. Not of the city, or the USA, but of railroads. At the center was Chicago, and different Metra lines were highlighted, but there were also lines that went out to the surrounding area, as far as Indiana. Someone had circled the stops with a thick gray marker and crossed them out aggressively.

A tiny note was jotted next to one of them. "'Gray Line stop removed,'" I read aloud. I scrunched my face into a confused frown, then reached into my pocket and pulled out the transit map of Chicago I'd written my school-supply list on. I unfolded it and compared the two. There was no Gray Line on my map . . . and the stops the mysterious occupant of this room had circled weren't there, either.

I was racking my brain trying to figure out why the two maps differed when I heard voices approaching. *Crap*. Were they coming to this room? I needed to hide. I stuffed my map into my pocket, took out my phone, and called it all sorts of names as I tried to get the camera to work so I could take a picture of the wall map. Once technology graciously allowed me back into the twenty-first century, I scrambled behind the stack of boxes.

The voices stopped outside the door, and I held my breath. Maybe they wouldn't come in. Maybe they were doing security rounds. Maybe . . .

Wait.

Maybe I recognized those voices?

"Should we go in?"

That was Uncle Moe.

"I . . . Not yet." That was Gran. What were my relatives doing in my magic teleporting dream-hallucination?

"He hasn't done anything yet," she was saying. Were they talking about me? "And you heard his parents. Gotta trust the boy."

"I know," said Uncle Moe. "And I agree. I . . . I'm worried about what he did. You know I can't stand bullies. Only the weak hurt the weaker."

"Your sister said those boys down South messed up his head *so bad*. Turned him into something he's not."

Marcus. BG. Their faces cycled through my mind, and my fists clenched.

"He made his choices, too," Uncle Moe said.

Gran sighed. "But that's his room. We stay out unless it's an emergency."

Uncle Moe sighed. "And we trust him."

"We trust him," Gran agreed. "He has to accept his power on his own terms. Trust in the ancestors. They know what they're doing, even if they're a bit . . . fickle about it."

"Especially *our* ancestors," Uncle Moe grumbled.

I stood slowly. They *were* talking about me. About all the strange magic. And the brawl back in Raleigh.

They were outside my bedroom in the Freeman House. And also *this* room. Which meant . . .

I looked around and inhaled sharply. I was inside the locked room that had appeared out of the blue this morning. Maybe then . . . this wasn't a dream. But . . .

"Come on, let me make you some tea," Gran said.

I could picture them. Gran standing with her arms folded, gazing at the door to my bedroom. Uncle Moe bouncing and rocking a sleeping Boogs. The two of them turning and heading toward the stairs, concern on their faces.

Suddenly all I wanted was to go to them. Hug them, tell them that I *was* doing better, that I had stood up for someone in the cafeteria, that I was making good choices, and I'd be the best student they'd ever seen.

I burst out from my hiding spot and ran to the door. Somehow I knew it would open, even though it had been locked before. It would open because I wanted it to open. I *needed* it to open.

I turned the knob.

The door creaked open.

The world around me started to fade.

"NO!" I shouted when I realized what was happening. But it was too late.

CHAPTER
THIRTEEN

WIND HAMMERED MY FACE AND YANKED ME FOR-
ward, flinging me off-balance and nearly sending me flying
into the night. I scrabbled against what felt like cool metal and
yelped in pain as I crashed into a bar of some sort. I was outside, on top of something moving really, really fast. That much
I could tell, but I couldn't even open my eyes to take a peek,
that's how hard the wind was blowing.

Screams echoed in the distance.

I managed to roll over onto my stomach, still gripping the
bar for dear life. Now I could shield my eyes and open them,
just a bit.

"Oh crap. Crap, crap, crap!"

I was on top of a speeding train! It was night, the moon
hovered bright and silver overhead, and all around I could see
children running through tall grass.

Yes.

You heard me right.

We were speeding through a valley, heading toward a huge body of water. A sea, maybe, or a giant lake. The train tracks were slightly elevated, so I could see for miles to the left and right, and what I saw was straight out of a horror movie. Grasses parting as kids scrambled through them, racing toward the train. Hundreds of kids, maybe thousands. On both sides. Short, tall, wide, skinny. Some in wheelchairs or with other mobility aids. And it was obvious they were all running for their lives.

But from what?

"Not important, Jackson," I muttered. "Just find a way down!"

I was on a passenger car, and there weren't any handholds or anything along the roof. I peeked over the side, then wished I hadn't. Nothing down there but an instantaneous and painful demise. I'd turn into a Jax smoothie if I tried to jump off. And besides...

"Help! Help me!"

I looked over to see a kid burst out of the grass. She was in unicorn pajamas and a matching bonnet, and she had on cute bunny slippers. But something was chasing her. At first I thought it was a fire, because orange sparks leaped into the air and smoke billowed along the ground. But then I saw the eyes behind her. Bright, red-rimmed, and glinting through the smoke.

"MOMMY!"

That shout came from my left, where the train whizzed past a boy cornered by two of the . . . things. Creatures? Spirits? The malevolent kind Two-Saint had told me about? Unbalanced? Whatever kind they were, they were menacing. Gray, scaly skin. Claws like hooks at the ends of their four feet. Velociraptor-like heads that belched more noxious fumes. I couldn't make out their bodies because the smoke obscured them. And then the train zoomed onto a bridge over the water, leaving the children behind. More screams filled the night, and I wanted to plug my ears, because I couldn't do anything! I didn't know how to turn back.

Why was this happening to me? I needed to find another door, another escape into a different hallucination, because this one was a nightmare. I scrabbled toward the next car.

CLUNK!

Something landed behind me on the train.

I gulped. Turned.

One of the spirits/creatures hissed menacingly. Its claws gouged the roof, leaving smoking scars in the metal, and the smell of sulfur and ash stung my eyes. It hissed at me again, then slammed one front foot into the roof and moved closer.

"No," I said. "Nope, no, no, somebody help me! HELP ME, PLEASE. I NEED HELP!"

Nobody answered.

Another foot clawed closer. And another. It was figuring out how to move on top of the speeding train, and I needed to do the same thing. I pushed myself to my hands and knees, angling forward into the wind, and started to crawl away from the thing while still keeping an eye on it. I needed to climb down and find a door, fast. That's how this hallucination worked, right? Find a door, find a new reality to hop into?

I came upon a hatch in the roof and tugged on it, but it wouldn't budge. "COME ON!" I shouted. I banged on it, still keeping an eye on the burning lizard that was inching closer. "Can anyone hear me?"

Nothing but wind and screams.

I kept scrambling along. It wasn't until my left hand slipped that I realized I'd reached the end of this train car. There was one more in front of me, and someone was standing on its roof. A woman.

"HEY!" I shouted, waving. When I looked back, the smoking spirit was still coming toward me. It hissed and opened a mouth filled with teeth of all shapes and sizes. Pointy, yes, but also molars where they shouldn't be, sticking out at wild angles. It flicked its tongue like a snake, and I shuddered.

"EXCUSE ME, MA'AM? HELP!"

The woman never turned around. She was wearing a long white dress that flapped behind her like a flag in the wind. Amazingly, she also wore a hat. A big floppy one, the kind the ladies in my church wear on Sunday. How it stayed on in the wind I couldn't understand. But she wasn't struggling at all, I realized. She stood upright without so much as a waver. The skin on her arms was as smooth and dark as the night sky we traveled beneath.

I crawled closer to her. The lizard spirit was moving faster now, and it was only a dozen or so feet away! I remembered what Nina had said in class: *Don't let it touch you!* I had to do something. It was either jump to the next car or pray that the spirit just wanted to play tag, and it wasn't looking particularly playful. That meant...

"Okay, spirits, ancestors..." I said. "If you're there, if you exist and you're listening, I will light a hundred and eleven sticks of incense for you if I don't die." I thought about it, then added, "And I'll never make fun of plastic-covered couches again. They're clearly holy. Just...help!"

And I flung myself across the gap.

For two horrible seconds I hung in midair, thinking I'd misjudged the distance between the cars. The train was curving around a bend toward the smoky haze on the horizon, and I was sure I was going to fly off and fall thousands of feet to the lake below.

"Oof!" I grunted as I face-planted onto the roof of the next car. I skidded a few feet before I managed to anchor my toes and fingers on the roof. The lizard spirit hissed angrily behind me, but I didn't look back as I made my way toward the lady in the hat. Adults meant safety, right?

Oh, please let me be right, I prayed.

"Hey, lady, you gotta help me," I shouted into the wind as I crawled up to her, not trusting myself to stand. "There are these things chasing kids, and one of them—"

My voice broke off. Not because she'd said anything. She hadn't even acknowledged me. No, I stopped talking because the haze we were speeding toward started to shift. The clouds thinned into wisps of nothing, like ripples in water fading so you can see what lies beneath the surface.

A pair of doors.

Giant ones.

Hundreds of feet tall, silver, and glittering like stars. They rose out of the water as if they were part of the lake. I could see that they were secured with multiple black chains and padlocks, and across the top of the doors were words in a language I'd never seen before.

The lady in front of me finally moved. She raised both arms and spoke, yet I couldn't understand her, either. Her words were whipped away, and the doors shuddered. Peals of thunder shook the earth. Lightning lit up the sky. Amid this fury, the giant doors opened a crack and more wind came rushing toward us. The woman laughed, and then she turned.

"Oooh," I moaned softly in terror.

The top half of her face was covered by a thin white veil. But her mouth . . . It stretched, widened, growing from a smile to a grin to something otherworldly. Behind her, the winds increased. Behind me, a thousand hisses erupted at once, and I knew without looking that more of those lizard spirits were now standing all along the train, on the roof of every car, just waiting for me to run from whoever this woman was.

But I never got the chance.

Three things happened all at the same time:

1. The giant doors in the lake burst their bonds and crashed open.

2. The woman spoke two words: "Not. Yet."

3. And she pushed me off the train.

I fell, screaming, into the night.

*   *   *

"AAAAHHH!" I continued screaming as I fell out of my desk chair.

Wait.

Desk chair?

I stared up in confusion at the familiar tiled ceiling of my Social Studies classroom. I'd recognize that gray-and-white pattern anywhere. Every school has it. Why? Who knows? The more important question was, how was I back? What had happened? Where were the talking gargoyles, the vengeful spirits, the secret room in the Freeman House, the woman on the train, the giant doors in the lake...? None of that had been real? I *had* been dreaming after all?

"I was dreaming," I said, sighing in relief.

"Mr. Freeman," a dry adult voice said. "While I'm just as horrified as you at the idea of having to pay a tax to vote, perhaps we can save the dramatics for what I'm sure will be a stellar essay you turn in."

Several kids snickered as I scrambled back into my seat. The teacher, Mr. Brown, a young Black man with locs and glasses, had one eyebrow raised in the universal expression of *This boy is tripping*, but he didn't say anything else as I fumbled with my notebook and pencil. He tucked a loc behind his ear and continued. "Now, similar to what Mr. Freeman so wonderfully demonstrated, there were immediate reactions to the poll taxes enacted around the country. In fact, a few miles south of us…"

I waited to make sure Mr. Brown was well into his lecture before I snuck a glance around the classroom. He was so engrossed in his lesson that I saw kids passing notes without getting caught. But I wasn't interested in writing. Nina was sitting one row back and to the left of me. Devin was all the way at the front, in the right corner. The last time I'd seen them, they'd been in the passageway between the warehouse and the school, and then they'd disappeared before my eyes. *Was* I tripping?

"Nina," I whispered. When she didn't answer, I grabbed a tiny piece of scrap paper off the floor and crumpled it into a ball. I tossed it at her, and it bounced off her arm. I know she felt it because she flinched. But what did she do next? Nothing! Just hunkered down lower and started scribbling in her notebook. Seriously? Now wasn't the time to be a good student!

Devin wasn't any better. It was almost as if neither of them wanted to make eye contact with me. But why? No way we could all go through something like disappearing in a tunnel and pretend it didn't happen, right?

Had they had weird visions of their own? Why did mine always seem to revolve around my great-great-grandfather Portis? He must have been a summoner. But what spell had he been trying to cast? It must have been important, since he'd continued to try it despite everyone telling him to stop. I wanted to learn more about it. I could ask Gran, or search that…

Just then, out the corner of my eye, I saw Devin glance back at me.

No. Not just me. Me *and* Nina.

Where is he? he mouthed.

At first I was confused. What was he talking about? But as Nina passed me a note, I remembered that we three hadn't been the only ones in that hallway. I unfolded the paper and read what I already had come to realize.

Two-Saint is missing.

CHAPTER
FOURTEEN

WHEN THE BELL RINGS TO END THE SCHOOL DAY, it's like the running of the bulls. Have you ever seen those video clips? In Spain and a few other countries, there's this annual event where they let bulls loose in streets that have been blocked off, and people choose to run in front of them. They *choose* to do this! Can you imagine? I was once trapped in an apartment hallway with an excited Chihuahua and had to run for my life. I still have nightmares about my ankles getting nibbled on.

Anyway, that's what it was like at DuSable Middle when school let out. A bunch of kids with backpacks the size of other kids wobbled toward the exits while teachers stalked after them, probably just as ready to get home and do whatever it is that teachers do when they're not shoveling fractions down the throats of terrified children.

(Imagine this: A boy trembling before a whiteboard with improper fractions written on it, while a teacher cackles wildly in the background like a Disney villain. I call it *Snow White and the Seven Fourths*.)

All this is to say that I wasn't surprised I couldn't catch up to Nina when we left Social Studies. Hordes of sixth-graders were trying to leave at the same time. But I was surprised (and a little hurt) at what happened when I finally spotted her hurrying to the exit.

"Nina!" I called out. If Two-Saint was missing, we needed to tell someone, like a teacher, or Batman, or the principal. Yes, one of those is fictional, but when the principal gets a cape, she'll move up in the rankings.

Nina heard me. I know she heard me because she started to turn around. We made eye contact, and I began to wave, but she immediately turned away and walked toward the door even faster. I stopped in my tracks. Weird. Maybe she hadn't seen me. I cupped my hands around my mouth, ready to shout to her, when, for a brief fraction of a second, the sea of students between me and the exit parted. Just a tad. And you know what I saw? Yes, there was Nina, marching steadfast and determined out the door. But there was someone beside her.

Devin.

And almost like he could feel me looking at him, he turned his head for a moment, and we made eye contact too. He scowled, then continued walking.

I was moving before my brain could catch up with my feet. Students squawked as I shoved my way forward, but for once

I didn't mumble any apologies. Then the double doors were in front of me, and I pushed through them into the sharp glare of the January sun. *There.* At the bottom of the snow-covered stairs, Devin and Nina were arguing—I could hear their voices from up here, but not the words. A few kids around them were watching curiously, though most were fleeing to their carpool or bus stop or starting the trek to the L-train stop a few blocks away.

But not me. I stomped over to the duo.

"Bro, what do you *want*?" Devin asked. "You stalking us now?"

I didn't answer him. "Are you okay?" I asked Nina.

She didn't look at me. "Fine."

"Is he bothering you? Because I can—"

"You can what?" Devin interrupted. "Finish that sentence. Please."

"You two are being clowns," Nina hissed. "Everyone's looking. You going to argue right here? Jax, leave it alone; this isn't about you."

"Oh, it's about him, all right," Devin replied. "He made it about him. Right?"

The two of us were inches apart now, and everything else was about to fade away. The other students, the school, the cars inching along the street—none of that mattered. Just me putting this boy on his back, and hard.

Then Nina inserted herself between us, shoving Devin and then rounding on me. "You. I don't need you 'defending' me. I can take care of myself. Understand?"

I blinked. "Oh . . . I didn't mean—"

"No, of course you didn't. And you," she said, spinning to confront Devin. "Just because you're related to Granddad doesn't mean you can be a jerk, because I *will* tell Grandma."

Granddad? Grandma?

To my surprise, Devin actually flinched. He scowled at me, then shrugged and turned his back on Nina and me. "Whatever. Do what you want; I don't care."

I looked back and forth between him and Nina. This felt like a conversation they'd had before. "Y'all are related?"

"We're cousins," Nina said.

Cousins. Cousins? "So you're not . . . He's not, like, your boyfriend? Ex-boyfriend?"

"Ew!" Devin said, shaking his head in disgust. "Bro, I'm done here. Is this really who you want to hang out with?" he asked Nina.

I felt my neck grow hot with embarrassment. All thoughts of asking about Two-Saint evaporated from my brain, and instead it immediately kicked into flight-or-flight mode. Yes, you read that right. I'd thought . . . well, I didn't know what I'd really thought. I'd overreacted. Again. And in front of half the school! There was a crowd around us now, watching and recording on their phones. It was time for me to leave. This day was eating at my sanity, and I just needed to get home and flop facedown on my bed for about three centuries.

I was about to make a beeline for the L when an all-black luxury SUV pulled up to the curb and stopped in front of us. Nina stiffened beside me, and Devin inhaled. The rear passenger-side window rolled down partway. It was dark inside. Really dark.

"Get in," came a voice.

Nina quickly moved to the other side of the car and pulled the door open. I hoped she knew who was driving this thing. Devin started to follow her, but the voice spoke again, stopping him in his tracks.

"Were you fighting again?"

Devin hesitated. "Dre..."

"Were. You. Fighting?"

I watched, fascinated, as Devin seemed to deflate. Whoever was in the SUV had him shook, and I both wanted and didn't want to know who could do that to him. Morbid curiosity. As if he could sense me watching, Devin glanced at me, furious, before shaking his head.

There was silence from Dre. Then: "Better not be lying. Pops will be disappointed."

Devin flinched again. "It's not my fault—it's his! Ask Nina!" He pointed at me, and I felt, rather than saw, the mysterious passenger shift toward me in their seat. Whoever it was didn't like what they were hearing. I didn't, either. I was just angling myself to leave when the voice in the car sighed.

"This ain't the time to be losing control, Brother. Heirlooms being stolen. That mess with the spirit at the train station. Gotta be careful. Pops already thinks you're not ready. Get in. I want you to tell me everything that happened."

"Dre..." Devin started to protest.

"Get. In."

Devin walked around to the other side of the vehicle, following Nina, but I was still hung up on something Dre had said. *The spirit at the train station* . . . "Conductor Buck?" I wondered aloud.

Nina and Devin stared at me. My face flushed again. I shouldn't have spoken. Once again, that heavy pressure of attention from the passenger seat turned on me.

"Sorry," I said. "Didn't . . . mean to say that out loud. Don't know what came over me. In fact, forget I said anything. Train station? I don't even know . . . what that is. Like, I take buses. Silly, right? Wild. Anyway, y'all have a lovely day. I'm just going to . . ."

The rear passenger-side door opened, and if I'd ever had any doubt of magic, of summoners, of spirits, of anything outside of the ordinary existing, the person who emerged put it all to bed. No question. Dre was a tall young man who looked to be in his twenties, with the same dark brown complexion as Devin, the faint hint of a beard, and waves that would make movie stars jealous. I mean, I got seasick when I looked at his hair. He wore gray slacks, a white polo, and polished black loafers with a sprig of some plant tucked in the penny slots.

But it wasn't his looks that overwhelmed me—it was his presence. It felt like he moved the wind as he stepped forward, and a melody played as he looked around—something catchy with a bass line and hook. Finally, a chain untucked itself from beneath his collar as he shut the door and approached me.

You heard that right. He didn't untuck a chain—the chain untucked *itself.*

"You were there," Dre said. Not a question. I nodded anyway. He pulled a worn purple-and-gold card out of his pocket and began flipping it between his fingers. It was larger than Devin's, though similar in color and design, and I wondered if that was because they were brothers. "Tell me about it."

It didn't sound like a request but a demand. I cleared my throat. "Um ... you know ..."

"I don't."

I looked around. There were still a few students lingering, and Dre waved at them dismissively. The card flicked in his hand, from knuckle to knuckle, and out of the ground rose a crowd of spirits. Dozens of them. They were people, wearing everything from overalls to pantsuits, and I could see right through their bodies. At a gesture from Dre, they flitted around us, each one taking a different student. My jaw dropped as the spirits cupped their transparent hands over the kids' ears.

"Now they won't be able to hear us," he said. "And they won't understand why."

"Whoa" is all I managed. Dre let a flicker of amusement cross his face, then became serious again.

"Andre Bell," he said. "But you can call me Dre. Now ... talk to me."

"Right," I said, and cleared my throat. "Well, it was, like ... midnight, and I couldn't find my bags. Well, it's not that I couldn't find them—they weren't there, feel me? And then—"

Dre was rapidly losing interest, studying the crowd and tapping his card on his thigh, so I sped it up.

"This ... *thing* in a train conductor uniform pretended to

have my bags, when it really wanted my skin! Like 'I'm gonna wear you like pajamas, Freeman!' or something like that. Weirdo."

Dre whipped his head up and his eyes narrowed. "Freeman?"

I didn't stop, because I was just gathering steam. "And I didn't mention the old lady who glitter-bombed me, but I guess I should be thankful, because it wasn't glitter. I think it was the same stuff Nina uses, because the skin thief whined about repel powder and—"

I stopped at the intense look on Dre's face. Devin was scowling, as usual, and Nina was considering me curiously, the way you look at someone who's about to get into trouble but you don't know how much. I really needed to work on keeping my mouth shut.

Dre took a step forward until we were almost face-to-face. His eyes roamed over me and took in the coat. Then he whistled silently. "Freeman?"

I nodded again.

"What else did this skin thief say? Who sent it?"

"I don't..."

"Anything else happen to you, and only you, in the last couple days?"

I shrugged, then hurried to add, "Some, yes, but I can't really explain it."

His eyes burned into mine. "Try."

I took a couple of deep breaths, closed my eyes, and tried to bring up memories of the weird dreams. "This afternoon, when we were coming back from summoning class, we got separated and I saw these...visions, of people talking, and a train, and these giant doors in the middle of a lake or ocean. And also my friend Two-Saint is—"

"Who?"

"Toussaint, but he calls himself Two-Saint. He was with us, and then he wasn't, but he should've been. When I woke up in class, everyone was there except him. He's missing, and I don't know what to do or...I just don't know."

I paused and took in a deep breath before I did something I'd really regret, like start crying. My hands were shaking. I clenched and unclenched them, closed my eyes, and exhaled. So much had happened in less than two days, and talking about it had made me relive it all. Made me remember that I was...a summoner. Whether I wanted to be or not.

Was puberty like this for everyone?

Meanwhile, Dre remained silent. His gaze swept over the crowd, then he pivoted suddenly and walked to the SUV. He opened the rear door. Inside, Nina and Devin were already scooting over to make room, but I didn't understand what was happening until Dre nodded at the back seat.

"Get in," he said. "Let's take a ride."

CHAPTER
FIFTEEN

I HAD A FEW CONCERNS.

Hidden speakers pumped the catchy rhythm of some rap artist whose name I couldn't think of because, well, I had more pressing things on my mind. Like why was I in this SUV, would I ever see home again, where was Two-Saint, and why do chip companies fill their bags with so much air? Such a rip-off.

Also, because of all those concerns, I was sweating. Like, a lot. My pits felt like I was in one of those infomercials for industrial-strength deodorant hosted by a guy who never stopped smiling.

My biological waterworks aside, there was also Dre to make me nervous. If Devin thought he dressed tough, his brother actually pulled it off. Andre Bell—Dre to everyone who knew him—was effortless with his style. His watch matched his belt, which matched his shoes, and the sunglasses he pulled out of a hidden storage compartment in the middle row of seats were the coolest ones I'd ever seen.

That same style apparently applied to the cars he rode in, too. The inside of the SUV was much larger than it appeared on the outside. Cream leather seats with red trim had me sitting perfectly still, because I was scared of getting them dirty. It also had couch seating, meaning that the second and third rows were facing each other. Nina, Devin, and I sat on one side and Dre sat on the other.

Which brings me to my final concern. You might wonder who was driving the car. I'm so glad you asked. NO ONE! WE HAD NO DRIVER! Not a living being, anyway.

Dre straightened the rolled-up cuffs of his sleeves around his forearms. "You probably got some questions, huh, big man?"

I jumped in my seat. My attention had been glued to the steering wheel and the lack of a butt sitting behind it. But yes, I had tons of questions. Like, was this a self-driving SUV? Why did I have to come along? AND WHO WAS DRIVING THIS SUV?

"Nope," I said. "No questions, not at all."

"Oh, come on. You've got to be curious. You ain't a little curious?"

"How come y'all don't get pulled over?" I finally asked, pointing at the driver's seat. "Isn't that a little suspicious?"

Dre laughed, then took off his shades and tossed them to me. "It's a glimmer, big man."

"Glimmer?"

"A constructed hallucination. A disguise. Check it out.

These glasses are under an inverse reveal spell I developed. Helps show me what the reggies see. Really helpful when I'm designing glimmer spells. Go ahead, put them on."

I slid on the shades and almost had a heart attack. I lifted them up to my forehead, then put them back down again. "This is amazing," I said. When I looked through the glasses, there were two people sitting in the front seats—a man driving, and a woman next to him. Their appearances changed every time I put on the glasses, but you know what stayed the same? They always had on expensive clothes and jewelry, and they smiled and waved at onlookers as we drove by.

I shook my head in wonder and started to pass the glasses back to Dre, but he flapped a hand at them. "Hold on to them for me. We can consider it a down payment for your cooperation. I answered one of your questions—now it's my turn. See, I'm a little curious, too. Let's start with this: Who are your people?"

"My people?"

Dre leaned forward so his forearms rested on his knees. "You ain't Coins. I would know. Are you Skulls? Wands? Baskets wouldn't dare be this bold, and Knives were wiped out in the last feud."

My mouth opened, then closed. The man in the vision had mentioned those names before, but I still had no idea what he was talking about. "I . . . have baskets. Laundry baskets? Two, actually. One for dirty and one for clean clothes, but I mostly use the one for clean clothes because every time I try and fold my stuff, it ends up wrinkled. Plus, the dresser in my room smells like hair grease. I found thirty combs in the top drawer when I moved in, and I think they're my grandfather's." I stopped because everyone was staring at me like my armpits were angrily sweating. I clenched my arms tight to my sides just in case. "Sorry. I talk a lot when I get nervous."

"Really?" Nina said sarcastically.

"My dad has a perm," I blurted out.

Dre stared at me. "You think this is a game?"

"No, sir. I don't think. At all."

"And now you're cracking jokes."

I threw my hands up, then quickly dropped them in case my pits were really leaky faucets. "I'm not joking! I don't know what's going on! I only learned about...magic...yesterday. Now, today, you made me get in the car, which I'm pretty sure is kidnapping, and you started talking about Skulls and Baskets and Knives, and I'm not allowed to use a knife unless I'm buttering a roll or something! What do you want me to say?"

Devin looked at his brother like *See what I'm saying?* Dre leaned back in his seat and tapped one finger on his knee. He had a shrewd expression on his face, and after a few tense moments of silence, he started chuckling. It wasn't a reassuring sound.

"You really don't have a clue, do you? Just wrong place, wrong time."

I nodded as quickly as possible. "No clue. I followed Nina to ask her what happened after the class where the spirit broke in. She and Devin and Two-Saint disappeared, and—"

"It didn't break in," Devin said. "You *let* it in."

"Not on purpose! You think I want these things near me? It's bad enough I keep having these freaky visions...."

Dre raised an eyebrow. "Freaky visions?"

"I don't know how to describe them. Some parts were like dreams, and others were like memories, but not any of mine, because everything seemed so...old. Like, this guy named George talked to me like I was someone he knew or was expecting. Like a dream-voicemail."

"A figment," Dre said, his gaze sharpening.

"That's what he called it!" I said. "The man in the first vision. He said...um, something like he would've been there in person, wherever *there* was, but he couldn't get away, so he left a figment."

Dre nodded, then glanced at Nina and Devin. "You two know what figments are?"

"The spiritual essence a summoner leaves behind to accomplish a specific task," Devin recited. "Usually something about communication."

"Everyone uses figments," Nina added. "They're like DMs between summoners. Reggies can't even see them. Before today, our teacher in Intro to Summoning was a figment Dr. Clayton left behind as a substitute." She glanced at me. "Today was her first day back after a month."

"Not everyone uses them," Dre corrected. "It takes a high-class summoner to carve off a bit of their essence and give it a task. Really skilled stuff. Your teachers can do it because only the best summoners prepare the next generation. The congregation uses them, too. So do the heads of the four summoning families. Are you going to the Glimmer Fest Games at the end of the week? You'll see some top summoners show off their figment control there."

I was hopelessly confused, but he didn't stop to explain. Instead, he added, "And you'll see more figments during your end-of-grade placement exams. Again, it takes great skill to create them, and the summoner on the receiving end triggers them with their presence. Which makes me wonder how you, Jax, triggered a figment that—according to you—seemed really old. Older than you are, if my guess is correct."

Dre studied my face, and I tried to look as innocent as possible. I wasn't ready to tell him that I, apparently, was receiving messages from long-dead people. He frowned, then leaned forward and held the purple-and-gold card out to me. "Tell me what you see."

I took it and flipped it over, but both sides were blank. It was larger than a playing card, too, now that I looked at it up close. Almost twice as big, and the paper felt rougher. "What is this?" I asked, looking up in time for Dre to blow a cloud of dust into my eyes. "Hey!" I shook my head and wiped my eyes with the back of my wrist. "What'd you do that for?"

"Now look at the card," Dre said, then muttered something under his breath.

"How? You threw dirt in my eye!" I blinked tears away. Great. Now they were going to think I was crying.

"Not dirt," Nina said. "It's part of a spell."

"I know, but it's easier to call it dirt." I looked at the card. "It's blank...."

I paused, because as I studied the card, something gradually appeared on it. A symbol—one I'd seen before. The circle with the cross in the middle that Dr. Clayton had called a kosmogram.

Dre stared at me as if he was puzzled. He sat back and pursed his lips as he dusted off his hands into a pouch hanging from a cord around his neck. He tucked the pouch back beneath his polo, all while never taking his eyes off me.

"You're telling the truth...and yet you're not," he said. "There's something...messing with the card."

My eyes went wide. "Is it my phone? I once saw a YouTube video that said phones are a tool Bigfoot uses to control us."

The car went silent. Nina, Devin, and Dre stared at me, and I squeezed my hands together again. "That's what the video said, not me," I mumbled. "Can you just drop me off at the nearest Metra stop? I've gotta get home—my gran and uncle are gonna be worried. And I have to find Two-Saint. Unless he's already there..."

Dre let a half smile cross his lips. I shivered. For some reason, I preferred his soulless stare to that smile. He checked his watch. "Chill, big man. First, I know somebody who will want to hear about your 'freaky visions.' And we'll keep an eye out for your friend. We have people for that. You help me out, we'll help you. I'll even throw in these." He held up his right hand, which I swear was empty, and then, with a flourish, he produced a bunch of Nike gift cards. "Five one-hundred-dollar gift cards to the Nike store on Michigan Ave. Deal?"

Nina's inhale and Devin's involuntary gasp told me they were thinking the same thing I was: That was a *lot* of money.

I licked my lips. "Five hundred dollars?" I could completely change up my wardrobe. Be the coolest kid in class for once. My hands rubbed the knees of Uncle Moe's hand-me-down pants on their own, as if they couldn't wait to get into a fresh pair of joggers with a matching hoodie. And the shoes—I could get the new Jumpmans I'd been eyeing. Real ones, not the counterfeits like Jalen. Five hundred dollars...

"Five hundred dollars," Dre said, as if repeating my thoughts.

I reached for them, but his hands flicked again and then they were gone. He leaned back and closed his eyes. "First, you gotta talk to someone."

"Who?"

His eyes became slits, all traces of amusement gone. "My grandfather."

CHAPTER
SIXTEEN

THEY CALLED HIM PAPA COIN.

Deep in the heart of Chicago, just south of Calumet Heights and a hair north of Trumbull Park, he ruled a three-block area with an iron fist and had done so for three generations. At least that's what Devin told me as we drove on. Dre was talking in hushed tones with someone on his phone, and Nina tapped nervously on her knees.

"He owns like five restaurants, three barbershops, and a limo service," Devin whispered. He'd put his headphones down when we apparently got close to our destination, and if I didn't know better (which I didn't), I'd say he was almost as nervous as I was. "We're riding in one of his now. Specially crafted for the summoner on the go, but reggies use them, too. Everybody wants to be seen in one. Rappers, basketball players, politicians..."

I frowned as we crossed a set of railroad tracks, and a faint tingle went up my spine. Must've been the bumps. "I've never heard of him."

Nina leaned in. "Well, of course not. It's one of those *if you know, you know* things. Like parties for rich people and shopping without looking at the price tag. But he's the head of the Coins, and we—*they* are pretty much the biggest tree in the Midwest."

"Tree?"

"Family, house, whatever you want to call it. Organization. A community of . . . well, you know."

"Summoners?" I guessed.

"Exactly."

"I'm not built for this," I muttered.

Devin nodded. "I agree."

"Shut up, Devin," Nina and I both said at the same time. She showed me her phone and swiped through her photo gallery until she found the picture she wanted. "Look. You were there, Jax. You saw them."

It was a picture of two of the gargoyles—Carver and Rufus. I recognized Carver's leer and Rufus's butt-ugly face, and I recalled their voices.

"Yeah, I saw them," I admitted. "But why are some stone gargoyles important?"

"That's what we need to figure out. Those aren't just gargoyles—they're spirits that protect the school and the summoners who attend. You triggered them. You're involved in some strange summoner activity, and Papa Coin is going to want to know why. We *all* need to find out why."

I shrugged. I didn't get why everyone cared so much, but at least Nina was talking to me again. That had to count as some positive news, right?

The SUV pulled to a stop in front of a barbershop flanked by old brick homes. It was a lively neighborhood, with squeals of laughter coming from a daycare across the street, cars driving by blasting jazz or rap or blues, and pedestrians chattering as they strolled down the sidewalk.

"Let's go," Dre said, sliding his phone into his pocket and straightening his shirt cuffs before getting out. Devin quickly followed, but Nina hesitated. She glanced back at me, and I could read the worry in her eyes.

"Remember," she warned. "Forget what you think you know."

She slid out the door, and I followed. What had I gotten myself into now?

*   *   *

The barbershop was packed, every seat taken. Customers were getting fades, or lined up, or their locs re-twisted while barbers cracked jokes, and the people waiting their turn held their sides and laughed and laughed. Music played from a speaker near the front, and a couple of kids with fresh cuts shared a box of fries in a window seat piled high with magazines. The walls were completely covered with posters of singers and rappers, photos of different hairstyles, or giant mirrors that seemed to magnify the energy inside the shop to infinity.

Just for fun, I slid on the reveal sunglasses Dre had given me to see how many of the people inside were a part of a glimmer. Nothing changed. I leaned over to Nina and asked if any of the customer were summoners.

She shook her head. "No. Not that I know of."

"I think a few clippers are enchanted to never get dull, though," Devin said. "Saves time."

Dre led us to the rear of the shop. Conversations trailed off as we walked past, and nearly everyone nodded or murmured greetings to Dre and Devin. A few people smiled at Nina, while everyone eyed me curiously. A boy in a hairstyle photo taped to the wall nodded at me as if to say What's up before turning back to his three-quarter pose. I nodded back, slightly bewildered. Then we were through a storeroom and Dre pushed aside a curtain of vines.

"Whoa," I whispered. It didn't feel right speaking at a normal volume here. Like . . . something would be disturbed.

Nina stepped up beside me. "Yeah. That feeling never goes away."

We'd entered an alley of some sort that had been converted into a garden. Planters decorated the high brick walls on either side, the pots and boxes brimming with herbs and flowers. The scents of earth and plants filled the air, like a forest fresh after a storm. I closed my eyes and inhaled. It reminded me of our garden back in North Carolina, where the soil was black as twilight and everything we grew tasted twice as good as what you'd get from a store. When I opened my eyes, I could almost see my mother weeding.

At the far end, in front of an old repair shop, there was a huge chair with carvings of animals, plants, and even faces in the polished wood. Strange symbols decorated the walls overlooking us, and they pulsed, growing dimmer and then brighter every few seconds.

I shivered. It was warm in the alley—warmer than made sense, considering the time of year—but seeing that chair and those symbols gave me a chill for some reason.

Next to the chair was a rickety workbench where an old man was grinding something with a mortar and pestle. He wasn't dressed for repair work. He wore gray dress pants, gold suspenders over a navy button-down shirt, gold loafers, and gold-rimmed sunglasses. He must've really had a thing for gold, because even his walking cane—hanging on the table next to him—was that color.

The air around him seemed to twinkle as sprinklers misted water down on a cluster of potted plants on the floor beside him. Every so often he'd stop grinding, add a pinch of something he pulled from a jar on the workbench, and then start up again. He reached into a different jar each time—the bench was covered with them. Dusty jars. Tiny jars. Broken jars and topless jars. Jars full of liquid and jars full of gnarled, twisted things that I couldn't identify. Blue jars. Green jars. Jars on top of jars and inside other jars. I felt like I was losing myself in a jar that was big enough to swallow me whole, and that if I blinked, I'd open my eyes and...

"Pops," Dre said softly.

A chuckle rasped out of the old man's chest, and suddenly I was blinking and shaking my head. *What had just happened?* For a second there, a wave of dizziness had swept over me. When I looked up, the old man was still working at the bench, but now there was only one jar. A small blue one filled with chunks of what looked like a root of some kind. The container shimmered as I looked at it, and I quickly turned my head away. This garden was more than it seemed... like Papa Coin himself.

"Andre tells me you were fixin' to fight, boy." It wasn't a question. Papa Coin addressed Devin in a low, grating voice. Hoarse, like he'd been shouting all day. Yet I heard every word.

Devin shuffled in place. "Yes, but—"

"What is your responsibility?"

"But Pops, he—"

"*What* is your responsibility?"

Devin sighed. "To secure the future."

Papa Coin's hand dipped into the mortar, brought out a pinch of fine grayish powder, and sprinkled it into a small pouch. "Whose future?"

"The family's. But, Pops, I tried!"

"Mmm. Our tree depends on dreams, and you've put everything at risk." He worked silently for a few seconds. "Go help Mrs. Córdova prepare tonight's deliveries. Then sweep the shop and close up after everyone's gone."

Devin tried one more time. "But..." His voice trailed off, however, when Papa Coin's head moved ever so slightly, just enough to reveal a glint in his right eye. Devin shot a furious glance at me and then turned and stalked back the way we'd come.

Silence filled the alley garden. Then Papa Coin carefully dusted off his hands, making sure to not waste any of the powder, and cinched the pouch closed with a leather cord. He wrapped it in a cloth and placed it gently on the edge of the bench.

"Andre," he said, "have your cousin run this to Mr. Albert across the street. Tell him it's been recharged."

Dre nodded. Then he patted Nina on the back, and she stepped forward. She took the pouch and glanced up at Papa Coin as if she wanted to say something, but he never met her eyes. Instead, the old man began cleaning the workbench.

When Papa Coin had said *your cousin*, had he meant Nina? If so, why hadn't he just asked her directly?

Nina waited another second, then turned and followed Devin out of the alley. She didn't look at me as she brushed past. To my surprise, Dre followed her. He *did* meet my eyes, and there was a hint of sympathy in his expression as he left me alone with Papa Coin.

"Do you know what this is?" the old man asked.

I was in the middle of inching my way back to the vine curtain we'd entered through, and I jumped when I heard the question. He had his hand on the lone jar on the workbench, the one with the gnarly roots inside.

"No, sir," I said. Didn't hurt to be respectful. Not when dealing with wizard gardeners. Trust.

Papa Coin lifted the jar and turned to face me. I gasped,

then clapped my hands over my mouth. His sunglasses had slipped down the bridge of his nose, and his eyes—they were glowing! A bright silver, like a full moon at midnight. He chuckled again as he pushed up his frames. He shuffled to the side, and I saw one of those magnifying lamps on the table next to him. I let out a shaky breath. That must've been a reflection I'd seen. Right?

"Stop with the dramatics, boy. It's just a charm to help old eyes see the energy of the world. Now this here... this is John de Conquer root. Powerful indeed it is. Can boil it, grind it, even just hold it whole. In the right hands, it can bring wealth and health. Money and survival, boy—two thangs our people been chasing after since we were stolen. You think?"

I struggled to keep up. "I do think. I think, I think."

"Do you agree?"

"Oh, yes. I mean, I guess so?"

"He guesses so." Papa Coin snorted. "Just as I thought. No training. Talent and ignorance—a recipe for disaster."

Coming here had been a mistake. This old man wasn't going to do anything but insult me, and I could get that anywhere. "Okay," I said, still inching back to the vines. "I'm gonna let you get back to... glowing. Sorry to interrupt. No, don't worry, I'll catch the Metra back; no need for the InvisiDriver to give me a ride."

I was almost to the vine curtain when Papa Coin spoke again, freezing me in place.

"Jackson Freeman," he said. "Great-great-grandson of Portis Freeman." When I turned around, a pouch dangled from his hands. "Made a bunch of mistakes. Dealing with the consequences. That about right?"

"How do you know that?" I whispered.

Papa Coin laughed. A harsh cawing sound, like a crow. He gestured to the alley walls. "Because I been dealing with your family's foul-ups for decades, boy. Decades. Anytime I think I've got a handle on things, a Freeman shows up. A firecracker in the stew. Well, this time I was prepared."

"I don't . . ." I said. "I don't mess with firecrackers. Too dangerous and unpredictable. Bottle rockets? Horrible."

"Dangerous is right," Papa Coin snapped. "The people outside them walls depend on me knowing how to keep them safe. Things that summoners know."

I hesitated. I could leave right now. Get on the Metra and head back to the Freeman House. Put all this behind me and get on the straight-and-narrow path to success like I was supposed to. But even though my brain said that would be the smart thing to do, I didn't move. "What . . . exactly are summoners?" I asked.

"Us," Papa Coin said with a sharp smile. "You and me. Summoning is in our blood. The belief in the natural and the spiritual and the power they give. Like this root. We can use it to do powerful things, but it ain't the only tool we use. We got many ways to help our survival. Other spells, other remedies . . . other charm bags, like the one I just finished. We got spells and rituals and bargains. And we got the people who came before."

"The ancestors," I said, and he harrumphed. I got the

feeling he wanted to tell the story his way, without interruptions. Whatever beef he had with my family, it must've been serious.

"That's right," Papa Coin was saying. "The ancestors. Though Portis Freeman nearly ruined that for us, too."

I stepped back into the space, my curiosity overruling the internal alarm bell telling me it was time to go. "You knew him?" How was that possible? It would mean he was, like, a hundred years old!

"I did." Papa Coin stared at me for several seconds, one clawed finger raised to point at my chest. "Your great-great-grandfather nearly killed us all."

CHAPTER
SEVENTEEN

PAPA COIN'S WORDS ECHOED IN THE ALLEY. MY great-great-grandfather had nearly killed all the summoners? Why? How? Questions bubbled up inside me, fast and furious. I may have had my own issues with being a Freeman, but that didn't mean I would let anyone just talk trash about my family, ancestor or living. That's not how we play.

"What do you mean?" I finally asked. "How could he nearly kill a whole group of y'all?"

The old man turned back to his workbench. "Tell me what you know about spirits."

"Before yesterday? Not much. Didn't think spirits were real."

"Not real?" He slammed his cane into the ground. A crack of thunder echoed in the sky, and I glanced up. It had been clear moments before, but now storm clouds were bunching on the horizon. The temperature was dropping, too, and I shivered as a gust of wind knifed through the alley garden.

"Not real?" Papa Coin repeated. *Slam* went the cane, and car alarms went off up and down the block.

"Not real?"

SLAM!

He pulled his shades down, and though his eyes looked normal now, they were hooded and full of anger. "Reality is what we make it, Jackson Freeman. Not how someone else defines it."

I shook my head. "Yeah, but spirits and charms and stuff? That's something from a movie or video game. At least, that's what I used to think. I'm still trying to figure this out."

Papa Coin pointed at me with his cane. "You want to figure something out? You want real? Let me tell you something real. About a hundred and fifty years ago, five families worked together on a farm. Planted rice all day. Picked rice all night. Down in the low country they worked, in clouds of skeeters as big as hawks. They split the work, they did, 'cause it made it easier. They were sharecroppers, see, working someone else's land for a small share of the profits, if there were any. The man who owned the farm, a white man, died after a while, but the five families kept on working. Nowhere else to go, see?"

Thunder rattled the bricks beneath my feet, and I jumped. Was it just me or was the day turning to night faster than usual?

"Now, stories say these five families knew some of the conjure. Spirits had hitched a ride with them from the Old Lands, made their homes in the water and the stones, in the forests and the trees, and also in the graveyards. The families took care of them, and the spirits lent them their power. Power to weave spells and charms. Make tisanes and potions. Cure illness and bring fortune. The families passed that knowledge down through generations."

Papa Coin turned and began disassembling and cleaning another charm bag, still talking as he worked. "When word got 'round that the farm owner had died, people didn't like the idea of five Black families working for themselves. Rumors spread. Nasty rumors. Saying awful things about how the farm owner died. Well, as the saying goes, rumors and fires spread faster than they can be put out. A bunch of townspeople got it in their minds that those five families had to go—one way or another."

I gulped. That didn't sound good at all. "Were they—?"

I couldn't finish the sentence, but Papa Coin understood. "They ran, them conjurefolk. They ran out of town in the middle of the night, carrying nothing but their children and their hopes. For three days they ran. Only stopped to bandage their feet. But the townspeople followed. Chased them on horseback and in wagons, with dogs and rifles. Cornered them in the marshes by the ocean, with nothing but water on one side and a rusty set of train tracks cutting through high grass on the other."

Train tracks through high grass? Like the visions I'd had earlier! Had I seen the past?

"Yessss." Papa Coin nodded, watching me. "You're hearing me. That was it. The conjurefolk had nowhere else to go.

Any second and them townspeople would have them dead to rights."

Lightning flickered in the sky at the word *dead*. I shivered. Everything in me was telling me to get out of there, but I had to hear the end of the story. "And then what?" I whispered.

Papa Coin finished cleaning the charm bag and removed the frayed cord. He threaded a new one through the loops of cloth, then held it in both hands. "And then the spirits answered," he said.

I waited for more, but the old man fell silent. "That's it?" I asked. "What does that have to do with my great-great-grandfather?"

The storm was nearly overhead. Wind was howling through the streets, and the clouds blocked out the sky like gray mountains. I heard shouting in the distance, but I couldn't make out any words. Lightning flashed again, and thunder boomed. My heart pounded along with it.

Papa Coin picked up the charm bag and grabbed his cane with his other hand. He walked toward me slowly, and I realized just how frail he was. Every movement seemed to send out waves of pain that twisted his face and left him short of breath.

"No, that's not it," the old man said, limping now. I stepped forward to help, but he waved me off. Instead, he clutched the pouch and inhaled deeply. "Stories say there was a train."

I froze. "A train."

"Covered in silver and sunrise. An engine and two cars. That's it. Came rumbling out of nowhere along them tracks just as the posse of townspeople arrived. Picked up them conjure-folk and carried them out of harm's way."

I instantly thought of the dream I'd had of the silver train with the veiled lady on top. That had to have been a coincidence, right? Right?

"Portis Freeman was a talented man, Jackson. When he was born at the turn of the century, some say he had the sight. The power. Well, nearly two decades later, a lot of folks say it was him who called that train, who rescued them conjurefolk. Yes, he was talented . . . but also greedy. He was always looking for new spells to create, or new ways to communicate with the ancestors. But he went too far, and he put us right back into harm's way. Took too much power for some secret he never saw fit to share, and he—and all us summoners—paid the price. We could have cemented our legacy for generations to come, but instead I'm hacking and scraping in this garden all day, struggling to charge these simple trinkets!"

WHACK!

His palm slammed down on the workbench, and I jumped. Two-Saint had said heirlooms are like a flashlight, *and the batteries are the power from the spirits.* What happened when the batteries were all used up and you had no way to recharge them?

The dark creeps in, I thought.

"That's why I had you brought here," Papa Coin said.

"To the workbench?" I asked, eager. "You need my help?"

Whatever hope bubbled up in my chest was popped by his harsh, cawing laughter. "No, boy. I'll be a cold body in the ground before I take help from a Freeman again. No, it's why I had you brought to Chicago."

The storm thundered... or maybe it was my heart pounding in my ears. "You... what?" I asked.

Papa Coin gripped his cane with one hand and tapped his chest with the other. "You're a Freeman, boy. Know what that means? There is a chance, the smallest chance, of you inheriting Portis Freeman's power, so I had you brought here, where I can watch you. Decades ago, I could've kept tabs on you no matter where you were in the world, but these days I gotta conserve my power. So you came here like all the Freemans do."

"But... but..."

"It's not like y'all are difficult to find. You can always count on a Freeman to foul things up. Either their life, like your uncle, or someone else's, like your grandmother." He leaned in close. "Like you."

"But my parents... They sent me here because the judge—"

Papa Coin waved a hand. "Nothing a call to some folks who owe me favors couldn't arrange. Could've left you down South, out of sight, out of mind, but a sore on the behind will eventually become a pain in the rear, you understand me? You're a headache, Jackson, wherever you go. And what do people want headaches to do?"

"Go away," I whispered.

He nodded. "Go away. So, here's the deal—the same deal every Freeman gets when they show up in my city. You stay low. Real low. Crawl along the ground if you gotta. No heirlooms, but minor summoning is allowed. You go to class, stay out of trouble, stay *away* from my grandchildren, and keep your nose clean. In return, I'll keep the congregation from stripping you of your magic and banishing you to the farthest corner of the earth."

No heirlooms... Minor summoning... Congregation stripping me of my magic... My head was spinning.

"But if you attempt to leave the Freeman House for good, I'll find you. You try to run, I'll find you. You do something I don't like, even if it's rolling out of bed the wrong way on a Sunday morning and disturbing the neighborhood, so help me, boy, I. Will. Come. After. You. And you don't want to find out what a summoner's life turns into when he's cut off from the spirits and his ancestors. Just ask your uncle."

Uncle Moe, listening to something only he could hear, appeared in my mind.

Was he trying to hear spirits talk to him again?

Papa Coin had done that to him? Why? How? I didn't want that happening to me. All I had to do was lie low and follow the rules, right? That's what my parents had sent me to Chicago for, anyway.

Except they *hadn't* sent me, apparently. Papa Coin had set the whole thing up to keep an eye on me because I was a Freeman. But Freemans foul everything up—that's the family curse—so it made sense, right?

Then why was everything inside me screaming that this was wrong?

Papa Coin's fingers squeezed the handle of his cane. "Do we have a deal?"

I had to do this, right?

Just as I extended my hand to shake his, thunder rattled the garden workbench again. My eyes were drawn to the table over Papa Coin's shoulder, and I gawked as the symbols drawn on the wall above the giant chair and the workbench began to fade.

More shouts echoed now, and they were growing louder. I could hear them over the storm. Papa Coin looked around, frowning. "What in all—"

BOOM! BOOM!

Pounding interrupted whatever he'd been about to say. A few seconds later, Dre ripped through the curtain of vines and grabbed Papa Coin by the arm. "We gotta go, Pops. Something isn't right." He turned to me. "You can come with us until the storm is over."

I never got a chance to respond.

In a brilliant flash, lightning streaked across the sky. A bolt struck the alley in a burst of flame and booming thunder. The ground beneath my feet slid sideways, and I fell to my knees. The world went white. I couldn't see or hear anything! My ears were ringing as I blinked furiously. Slowly, my vision returned, and the ringing began to fade.

"Jackson!"

"Jax!"

It took me a few moments to realize that people were calling my name. There were other shouts and screams, too. The alley was bathed in smoke. Had something caught fire? I turned around, slowly, still dazed, and saw Devin and Nina helping Papa Coin into the storeroom. The vine curtains had been destroyed, and several hanging planters had crashed to the bricks below. I could hear people in the barbershop and the surrounding neighborhood shouting in the chaos. Whatever was going on, summoners and regular folks alike were in trouble.

I staggered slightly, and a hand reached out to steady me. I turned to see Dre looking over my shoulder with a grim expression. He had two of his cards in hand, and he flicked them to the ground, one after the other. The images on them—a man with a scythe and a skeleton dressed in a suit—disappeared.

Spirits matching the images materialized in the air above the cards.

"Wha—" I began to say.

Dre gripped my arm tight. "Don't speak, listen. We're being attacked by avarice spirits.... You can't fight them. Not right now. You take Nina and Devin and run, and don't look back. Nina knows where to go."

He pushed me toward the barbershop, just as . . . well, something skittered over the alley wall behind us and dove into the smoke billowing along the ground. I couldn't make out what it was—a cat? It had to be a cat, right?

Too many legs for a cat.

My eyes widened as Dre reached into his pouch, pulled out some glittering black dust, and sprinkled it on the end of a broom next to Papa Coin's workbench. Before my eyes the broom seemed to catch fire from the inside, bristles glowing red hot at the tips.

Something hissed and charged forward out of the smoke.

NOT A CAT!

"Jax!" Dre shouted, just as a snarling, twisted face filled with knifelike teeth exploded from behind the vines. I knew that face. I'd *seen* that face. It was from the visions I'd had—the burning spirits chasing the children, the ones that had cornered me on the train. They were real?

"JAX!" Dre screamed. "RUN!"

CHAPTER
EIGHTEEN

CHAOS.

The evening sky was smudged with purple smoke clouds as more and more avarice spirits appeared. They swarmed like sharks that smelled blood. Out on the street, screams filled the night air as people were attacked. Two spirits scaled the alley wall right in front of me, cutting us off, dropping down to join the one currently battling Dre.

Devin's older brother was poetry in motion. Violent poetry. Combat haiku? You get the point. He was smooth and efficient. The broom twirled in his hands like a staff, the glowing bristles slicing through the spirits like . . . well, like they weren't even there. One spirit swirled around him, snarling and swiping with its smoking claws. I held my breath as they whistled within millimeters of Dre's neck, but the Coin heir twisted away at the last second. Dre's summons, the scythe-man and the skeleton, surged forward, battling the avarice spirits and keeping them occupied while Dre planned his next attack.

I could've watched him fight for a while, except, you know, I was supposed to be running. At that exact second, one of the spirits broke off to hurtle toward me, and I took that as a sign to skedaddle. Get on the good foot. Dip out.

I raced into the storeroom of the barbershop and nearly collided with Devin. "Where's my brother?" he demanded. "Where's Dre?"

"Back there," I said, chest heaving as I tried to catch my breath.

"We have to help him!"

I shook my head. "He's trying to give us a chance to—"

"Watch out!" cried Devin.

I looked behind me to see that the same burning avarice spirit had materialized in the doorway. I spun around to head toward the front room of the barbershop, but another floated into view, trapping us in the small space.

"Now what?" I groaned.

Devin didn't answer. He'd summoned his card deck—his heirloom—and two cards appeared in his right hand as he muttered, "Reunion."

Not just one but two brogres manifested—the Timberland-wearing mist giant and another wearing a Cubs cap and holding what looked like a Louisville Slugger . . . which must have been made out of all the trees in Louisville. That club was monstrous!

I shuddered as the brogres leaped into action. The misty

bat met smoky claws, and semi-transparent boots smashed into snarling fangs.

As the brogres went to work, I pulled at Devin's sleeve. "Come on," I said. "We need to get out of here."

But he shook me off. "No! I'm going to help Dre. You run. You Freemans always run."

He dashed to the alley, slipping around the melee as I stared after him. Whatever. He had a way to defend himself—I didn't. I ran the opposite way, heading into the main room of the barbershop. The employees and customers had obviously fled in a panic. Chairs were overturned, and clippers and other equipment lay scattered on the floor. The lights had gone out, and one of the mirrors had been smashed, a spiderweb of cracks radiating from a corner. Screams continued to echo from outside, and I kept my head on a swivel. Every nerve in my body screamed at me to run, run far away and never come back. Run all the way to Raleigh, North Carolina, and into my old bedroom, dive under the covers, and stay there forever.

Something flickered outside the window, and I heard glass shattering. Darkness descended.

I immediately ducked behind a toppled barber's chair. There was another broom on the floor next to me, and I grabbed it. Who knew where Dre had pulled that superpowered powder for his broom, but maybe all the brooms in the shop were already enchanted. I was grasping at straws—broom straws, even—but at this point I'd take any encouragement I could get.

A shadowy figure stepped in front of the window. The glass shattering I'd heard must've been a streetlight outside.

Whoever it was didn't want to be seen. Another avarice spirit? No, they hadn't cared about being seen before. Why start now?

The shadow raised a hand. It was holding a burning torch—an honest-to-goodness torch. What was next, pitchforks? But all trace of ridicule left my brain when smoke began to boil out of the flame, twisting and writhing...until an avarice spirit floated in midair. It hovered for a second, then dropped to the ground and dashed off, snarling.

My blood turned as cold as ice. "They aren't just appearing..." I whispered to myself. "They're being summoned!"

A hand landed on my shoulder.

I jumped and opened my mouth to scream, but a hand clamped over that as well, muffling it to a whimper, and I dropped my broom in terror.

"Shush, boy!" a familiar voice whispered, tickling my ear. I peeked back to see Nina. She was stifling a smile. "You real scary, huh?"

"I thought you were the evil summoner," I snapped.

"Evil what?"

I pointed out the window, where the shadow summoner could still be seen, torch in hand, face still hooded, bringing forth another avarice spirit.

Nina's hand tightened on my shoulder. "Oh, this is bad," she said. "This is really bad."

"Well, yeah." I peeled off her fingers and rubbed my shoulder, scowling at her.

"No, you don't understand," she said. "Random spirits showing up could be a mistake. But if they're being sent...if we're being *attacked*, that means the truce has been broken. The feud is starting up again."

The storeroom door behind us exploded into shards of wood. Devin came tumbling out, followed closely by his two brogres and Dre, who was still twirling the broom, keeping four snarling spirits at bay. His scythe-man and skeleton followed shortly after, swiping at the avarice spirits and forcing them back. When Dre noticed Nina and me crouching on the other side of the room, he was livid.

"What are you still doing here?" he spat. "I told you to run!"

"But—" I started.

"Get them out of here, Freeman," Dre said, cutting me off.

"Freeman?! You're putting him in charge?" Devin asked in disbelief.

"We can help here!" Nina said at the same time.

A grunt of frustration escaped Dre's lips as he swiped through two of the avarice spirits, scattering their forms to the ceiling, where they disappeared into the vents. "I know you want to," he said, "but you can't. Not this time. You're capable, but I need you to get out of here. There's something—"

"They're being summoned!" I blurted out. "We saw one. A summoner! Using a torch to— See?"

The shadow summoner was looking straight through the window, right at Nina and me, just as more of the avarice-spirit attackers began to manifest in the doorway behind us.

Dre's face paled, and he shouted, "Quick! Out the back!" Shoving Devin at me, he brought the broom whistling in front of him, shielding us as the bristles began to glow again. He was spinning it so fast a circle of purple sparks appeared, but even I could tell that there were too many spirits for him to hold off as we retreated through the storeroom and into the alley.

Two jars landed on the ground next to us—small, dusty jars the size of coffee mugs—just as swirls of mist rolled over the alley walls.

Behind us, the avarice spirits materialized fully and snarled.

Footsteps and the click of a cane echoed out of the mist, and Papa Coin emerged, limping, but his eyes were narrowed, and his voice was strong. Had he thrown the jars?

"Bones to soil," he called out. "In the end, that's where we all go. Bones to soil."

The jars that had fallen on the ground cracked, and dirt fell out, more dirt than I expected either container to hold. Thick black soil seemed to boil out of them, and it grew into many little hills, until I couldn't see the concrete floor of the alley at all. It was mesmerizing, and if that were all that had happened, I still would've been impressed. But it wasn't all.

The pile nearest me trembled, and a bony finger poked through the dirt.

"Bones," Papa Coin whispered. "To soil."

Every mound in the alley began to tremble.

Someone gripped my shoulder and spun me around. It was Dre, and he seemed panicked. "You have to go," he said, eyes wide. "Don't stop or come back for anything. For *anything*! Understand, Jax? Get them out of here!"

I shook my head. "But why me? I can't do twirly tricks with cleaning tools! I can't even summon! I'm just Jax!"

Dre brought the broom behind his head like a samurai preparing for one final strike. Outside, the shadow summoner raised their torch. Dre looked at his brother, then at me. "Because you're a Freeman. Freemans run. They run. Now go!"

Soil erupted in showers as skeletons crawled up into the alley. Papa Coin began to laugh—harsh cackles that grew in volume as the bony reinforcements leaped at the avarice spirits, grappling and clawing and biting. I dodged one battling pair, backing up to the doorway, speechless at what I was seeing. This was one high-level summoner fight!

Glass shattered. I turned and peeked into the barbershop, then yelped and fled back into the alley as the shadow summoner broke through the window and hopped inside.

Dre rushed by me to attack, sweeping the broom in a massive arc. The bristles glowed white-hot as they sliced through the air and shredded avarice spirits into puffs of gray smoke. His efforts forced the summoner back, but not for long, so Dre followed the momentum of the broom into a spin while taking one hand off the handle to reach into his pocket for more repel powder. In one smooth motion he blew it onto the bristles and swung the broom in yet another wide arc. This time the concussive blast exploded outward, sending the shadow summoner tumbling head over heels into the alley wall.

"GO!" Dre shouted, and his voice was so powerful I was on my feet and moving before I realized it. I grabbed Devin's arm with one hand and Nina's with the other, and I pulled them into the night.

We raced past the fallen shadow summoner, their face still hooded.

We slipped between still more avarice spirits emerging from the dropped torch.

We sprinted past onlookers, past buildings and cars and houses.

We ran.

CHICAGO DEFENDER, VOLUME LXXII, ISSUE 11, MAY 1977

Hundreds Attend Sit-ins for Disability Rights

Local community leaders celebrate Saturday's sit-in, calling it "movement forward for equality."

in
the
s a
ion
was

t to
and

uld
ne

MINI-SERIES HIT SUCCESS INSPIRES LOCAL FILMMAKERS TO TRACE THEIR OWN ROOTS

The success of *Roots*, released this past January, has inspired many local artists to trace their own lineage, and many are learning more about their personal histories. Wilhelmina Freeman, a high school student and aspiring artist, explained how tracing her own family tree brought her and her mother together.

LOCAL RESTAURANT SERVES FREE MEALS AND THE COMMUNITY

Southern Fried Love, newly arrived on the South Side food scene, is rapidly becoming a local favorite as they serve hearty meals in addition to managing a free community garden. The owners IF YOU ARE READING THIS, SUMMONERS WITH HEALING TALENTS ARE NEEDED AT ALL CROSSROADS. AGAIN, SUMMONERS WITH HEALING TALENTS ARE NEEDED AT ALL CROSSROADS AS SOON AS POSSIBLE. YOUR ANCESTORS THANK YOU. hail from Wilmington, North Carolina, and bring with them

PART
THREE

CHAPTER
NINETEEN

"We need to go back," Devin said dully for the fourth time.

"We can't," Nina answered yet again.

I didn't say anything. They both trudged behind me as we crossed a dark residential street. A gas station sign flickered down the block, advertising diesel prices and two-for-one Lay's chips. My stomach grumbled at the thought of snacking, but I shoved the hunger down with the other things I didn't have time to think about, like where was Two-Saint? Or what were summoners doing with the lizard—avarice?—spirits I'd seen in my visions? Or...

"Why was the broom glowing?" I muttered to myself for the thirtieth time.

The other two didn't hear me. They were still arguing, even as we cut across the gas station's parking lot and headed toward what sounded like a major intersection. Out of habit I checked my phone again, but the battery had long ago given up its shaky hold on life. The dark screen stared back at me as I tried to figure out where we were. Something told me to keep going in the direction we were headed, but I still wanted the assurance of knowing exactly what was ahead of us.

"They need our help," Devin argued.

"Your brother told us to go," Nina said. "And he's the strongest one in the family—they'll be okay. Plus, our granddad—"

"I don't care!"

When I turned around, the two of them were face-to-face. Devin looked furious, and Nina was angry, too, her arms folded across her chest. I sighed. We had to keep moving, but the way these two were shouting, someone was gonna call the cops on us.

"Y'all—" I started to say, but Devin talked over me.

"I should be back there helping," he said, pounding a fist into his other hand. His shirt was stained with dirt, and his shoes were scuffed. Gone was the pretty boy from school, though none of us had escaped unscathed. Nina's locs were streaked with dust, and her arms were scraped up. I felt like I'd swallowed an entire cloud of smoke, and the urge to cough tickled my throat. There was also this weird tingling in my chest, as if instead of a heart I had a glowing coal that would start a fire inside me if I breathed wrong.

Devin was still shouting. "That was an attack! An *attack*, Nina. Do you realize what that means? The truce is over. Over!

Who knows when another attack will happen? I need to be there to help with a counterattack, or—"

"Or how 'bout help the injured? Rebuild?" Nina's eyes blazed as she glared at her cousin. "You think I don't want to strike back, too? Of course I do! But if the truce is over and the feud is starting up again, an actual war between summoners, we need to regroup and make a *plan*. Not rush in blindly. We don't even know who attacked, or if it was even one of the families."

Devin scoffed, but before he could continue the argument, I stepped in. "What is the truce? Y'all mentioned it before but never explained."

"Because we were *attacked*," Devin said with a snarl.

Nina ignored him. When I turned to keep walking, she moved up next to me. After a second or two, I heard Devin following us and I breathed a sigh of relief.

"So, there were five summoning families that came to Chicago," she said.

I nodded. Papa Coin had mentioned them. "On a train, right?"

"Right. When they first arrived, they stuck together, but then something happened. Some kind of argument turned them against each other. No one really knows what it was about... or at least they don't talk about it. The families split up and established their own territories around the city. Coins, Baskets, Skulls, Knives, and Wands. Wealth, harvest, memory, power, and wisdom. The Baskets and Coins live near each other, which brings its own tension, but usually they leave each other alone. Mostly. Wands are north, almost in Wisconsin, while Skulls are in the Loop."

This was all so much to take in. Territories? Conjure gangs? I felt like I was in a movie. "And...the Knives? They're gone, right?"

Nina shrugged. "Right. They sort of faded away. Their last head, Eleanor Rogers, stepped down from the congregation almost two decades ago, according to Granddad. No one's heard from her in years."

"Maybe until now," Devin grumbled. "Who knows, they could've planned this."

We reached the intersection: 95th Street, just beneath the Chicago Skyway. Cars and semis rumbled overhead as we entered the shadows. Water dripped into sewer grates as we walked past graffiti tags and concert posters plastered on the walls. The storm clouds had drifted off and the sun had disappeared beneath the horizon, but even with the streetlights turned on, pockets of darkness lingered. The hairs on the back of my neck prickled, like someone was watching us, and I picked up the pace.

"This is ridiculous," Devin said, though some of the malice was gone from his tone. He stepped up so he was on the opposite side of Nina, and he glared at me. "And why are you in charge? Do you even know where you're going?"

I shrugged. "Actually, your brother said Nina would know where to go."

"Dre means my house," Nina said. "Dad should be able to

come get us. But let's find a place to hide while we wait. I don't think we should be out in the open."

Devin groaned. "Your house? You've got to be kidding me!" When I looked at him confused, he rolled his eyes. "Dre wants us to go to Basket territory. I don't believe it. And after the truce was broken! We might as well advertise ourselves as hostages. *Here, come take us!*"

"My mother's a Coin," Nina explained to me. "But Dad was a Basket."

"Like oil and water," Devin added.

Nina shrugged. "Granddad didn't approve of the marriage, but they didn't care. When Granddad found out Mom was pregnant with me, he was so angry. *Everybody* was angry—well, except for Andre—so much so that Mom . . . well, she left a year or so ago. It's been just me and my dad ever since."

That seemed ridiculous to me, and really sad, but I guess it explained why Papa Coin wouldn't talk to Nina directly.

"But we're not going to be hostages," Nina went on. "Dad mostly keeps to himself these days because his family didn't like him marrying a Coin, either. He runs a little flower-and-herb shop."

Devin muttered something under his breath, but we both ignored it.

"So, we go to your house and try to figure out what exactly is going on," I said. "Like what are avarice spirits, and why even summon them? Those things are vicious! And why is all this happening to me?" I knew I was complaining, but I felt I'd earned a pity party. Just a small one. A pity get-together.

"Oh, stop whining," Nina said, pulling up our location on her phone. "If you have the ability to summon, it was bound to happen. Regular people don't see spirits. There's no way you could've seen any of what's unfolded if you didn't have the power."

"Unless he's a spy," Devin said.

I ignored him. "Even if there *is* something like that in me, why's it coming out now?"

"Power meets power," Devin answered, and Nina nodded.

"What does that mean?" I asked.

"The ability to summon comes when you need it most."

That reminded me of Papa Coin's story. "Your grandfather said that a train rescued the summoning families," I said slowly. "It came when they needed to escape a posse that was chasing them. . . ." And when I needed a warning in a train station?

"Exactly!" Nina flashed a grin.

But I still wasn't sure why I was part of all this.

She put her phone to her ear. "Let me call my dad. He's not a part of the congregation anymore, but he'll still know what to do. Hopefully he can get someone else to babysit the plants for a few . . ."

I didn't hear the rest of the sentence because my heart leaped into my ears and started thumping like crazy. *Babysit.* I was supposed to help Uncle Moe watch Boogs tonight! Oooh, he was going to kill me! And on my first full day here, too. Or, even worse, he'd tell Gran, and she would yell at me, and *then* Uncle Moe would kill me.

"Y'all, I have to go," I said, interrupting Nina's call.

"Go?" Nina frowned. "Jax, you can't. Are you serious? We need to figure out what just happened!"

I was already backing up, desperately wishing my phone hadn't died so I could call the Freeman House and tell somebody I was on my way. "Sorry, y'all. I'll Google it."

Devin threw his hands up. "Are you for real? You can't Google how to summon, bro! There's no YouTube channel for working power."

But I shook my head. I was already going to be in so much trouble. "No, I'm done. I'm going home. Underground wars and broken truces are too much for me, plus I promised your grandfather I'd lie low. He already thinks I'm bad news because of today. And, oh yeah, my uncle is going to ground me for a year."

Nina stared in disbelief. "How are you going to get home?"

"Oh, that's easy. Metra Electric to Van Buren, walk ten minutes, then catch the Green Line to Conservatory-Central Park Drive. If I catch the next train leaving in eight minutes, I can be home by seven. Maybe I'll live to eat dinner. If I don't, delete my phone's browser history at my funeral, okay?"

The two of them stood there speechless. I looked between them. "What?"

"You've been in Chicago how long, and you have both the Metra and L schedules memorized?" Nina asked.

I opened my mouth to explain, then paused. "No, I don't. I just know. Don't ask me how." I started walking again, shoving my hands in the pockets of my coat.

"You just know?" Devin asked, his voice dripping with skepticism. "You don't know how to summon, but you—"

"Yeah. I feel like there's a Metra station on the other side of the highway. If we hurry, you can call your dad to come get you there and I can catch the next train."

"You *feel*?" Nina echoed.

"I don't know how to explain it! Now you're making me sound weird."

"Because you are," Devin muttered. "I've never heard of a summoner who can sense public transportation. Does it work with buses, too?"

"Remember the girl in Dre's class whose ancestor was a taxi driver?" Nina asked him. "The girl's heirloom was a badge, and she never got lost. Now she helps find missing persons. Maybe Jax has a power like that."

The two of them stared at the underpass wall I'd pointed at. It *did* feel like there should be a train platform right on the other side, as if I'd been here before and was remembering my way around. Just like I was positive a train was coming in eight minutes. Seven, now. It was the same feeling I'd gotten at Union Station, when I absolutely knew the train that smashed Conductor Buck into smithereens would be rolling in. So I kept walking, and the other two fell in behind me again, holding a whispered conversation. And when we emerged from the cement to see the bright M sign shining a half block away, even Devin looked impressed.

Nina made me promise to call her once I'd gotten home and charged my phone. Six minutes later, a train came rumbling along. I clutched the day pass Devin lent me, found a seat in the middle of the car, and waved good-bye. Devin sorta raised a hand, which was cool, and Nina waggled hers furiously, which was even better.

But I couldn't shake the little voice that whispered *You should've stayed with them.*

CHAPTER
TWENTY

I SPENT THE ENTIRE TRAIN RIDE COMING UP WITH excuses—every excuse I could think of, and the more dramatic the better. Anything to keep Uncle Moe from grounding me.

I took the wrong train, I thought as I got off at Van Buren street and walked to the Green Line.

No, he'll ask why it took so long to realize my mistake.

Maybe I was tutoring someone in math!

I immediately discarded that idea. The day I tutor someone in math is the day a pig will teach someone how to fry up bacon.

Got it! I'll say I was working on a group project at school and lost track of time! Devin and Nina will back me up.

My walk from the Green Line elevated train (*The L, Jax. No one calls it the elevated train.*) to the Freeman House took about ten minutes. I went over my story again, then a third time, just to make sure it all added up. Adults can sniff out a lie like they've trained their whole lives for it. It's wild.

I was so focused on making my excuse perfect as I crossed the street to my block that I almost didn't realize that the air had become incredibly still. I mean, for a place nicknamed the Windy City, it felt like nothing was stirring in my neighborhood.

The bodega on the corner behind me was closed, and all its lights were off. That was strange. It wasn't even seven in the evening yet. And with no other houses on my block, only weeds, trees, and bad intentions, it was darker than I expected. Really dark. In fact, the only light I could see came from the end of the block, where the light on the front porch of the Freeman House beckoned like a signal.

Or a warning.

After the day I'd had, I was a little skittish. I turned and looked back the way I'd come. Down the street, cars drove past the intersection and leaves skittered across the pavement. I stepped up on the curb behind me and felt a breeze whip past. Then I put one foot on the street again and the breeze disappeared, like someone had hit an off switch.

"Huh," I said. "That's . . . abnormal."

Maybe I was just weirded out. Between almost getting into fights with both humans and spirits, falling asleep in class, learning about weird turf wars, and seeing creepy brooms, I was about at my limit, feel me? I could honestly say that I was glad when the Freeman House came fully into view. It still leaned a bit to the left, and the front stairs were warped and creaky, but there was something about the pots of herbs on the porch that brushed the worries off my shoulders. Even the sign mounted next to the door didn't scare me anymore. If anything, it actually made me feel a little . . . I don't know, safer?

CHANGES AWAIT, it read.

Well, maybe not too much safer.

"Jax? Is that you?" I heard when I went inside.

Gran. At least *someone* was babysitting Boogs! But she had trouble with the stairs, so maybe that's why Uncle Moe had wanted me to help. I hoped she wouldn't be mad that I was late.

I took a deep breath, then exhaled slowly. I could do this. Tell her like I practiced, then go watch Boogs until Uncle Moe came home. Easy. I hoped.

"Yeah," I said. I straightened my shoulders and put an apologetic smile on my face, then headed through the front sitting room and into the kitchen. Gran was working at the kitchen table while Boogs, in his high chair, scribbled on a slate with some chalk.

"Sorry I'm late," I blurted out. "We were working on a project for school and— What's wrong?"

Tears were running down Gran's face.

Oh no. "I didn't mean to worry you. . . . I—"

Then I saw that she was chopping onions. She looked up at me and smiled. "Welcome home."

"Oh, never mind. I thought you were upset."

"Maybe I am," she said with a little huff. "But it has nothing to do with you. It's your uncle."

I thought back to the things Papa Coin had said. *You can*

always count on a Freeman to foul things up. Either their life, like your uncle, or someone else's, like your grandmother.

What exactly had they done?

"Thinks he's twenty again," she said. "He's been messing around with... Well, never mind. I'm just mothering, I guess. He's been different ever since..."

Her voice trailed off. *You don't want to find out what a summoner's life turns into when he's cut off from the spirits and his ancestors,* Papa Coin had said. Is that what she was talking about?

Gran cleared her throat. "Anyway, you make sure you take care of business in school." She glanced at me and hesitated, as if weighing whether to say what she was thinking, before continuing. "This family needs a summoner; upon my soul it does."

I met her eyes as my own widened. "You know? You know that I'm... a summoner?"

She nodded. "I don't think you'd be here if that weren't the case. I told you Portis Freeman built this house for his railroad buddies, but he also built it for the summoners in his family, because he was one, too. Just like you. You would've liked him, and y'all would've been troublemakers together, I know it."

That fed my soul with something I felt like I'd been craving. Validation. Acknowledgment. Belonging. But as soon as that feeling arrived, it was followed by a thought that put a damper on everything. "I met Papa Coin today. He... told me about what happened to Uncle Moe."

Gran harrumphed. "Don't get me started on *Dennis*. He's the reason Moe is acting up now, trying to do too much. That man has had it in for our family as long as I can remember, and he and Moe especially butted heads. Papa Coin. Hmph. Can't give yourself a nickname."

"Oh," I said, "that reminds me—have you seen Two-Saint? He went...I haven't seen him since school earlier."

For a second I hoped that Gran had news, but she shook her head. "That boy ain't been here, and I'm making all this food, so he better stop by. Speaking of which, I need to keep making dinner if we're ever gonna eat. Looks like it's just you and me and the tornado toddler. Take Boogs upstairs while I finish up this spaghetti and garlic bread."

"Umm..." I hesitated, thinking of all the mysterious goings-on up there. I didn't want the spirits messing with him or vice versa. "Can't we watch TV down here?"

Gran shook her head. "No, I don't want him watching a bunch of TV yet. And I need to focus."

"But, Gran—"

She shot me a look. "By the way, where were you this after—?"

I snatched Boogs and was halfway up the stairs before she finished asking the question. "Sorry, Boogs wants to go play!" I said. "What's that, Boogs? You wanna play the scream game? AHHHHHH! TOO BAD I CAN'T HEAR ANYTHING, OH NOOOOOOO!"

Gran snorted as we scampered up the stairs, Boogs cackling as he bounced on my shoulders, and I breathed a sigh of relief when we got to my floor. My bed remained in the same state I'd left it in that morning—like a tornado had slept in it instead of a kid. I blew out a puff of frustrated air as Boogs immediately headed for a pile of laundry (clean...I think) in a basket on the floor. Uncle Moe must've left it for me to sort through until someone could take me to buy new clothes. With a pang of guilt, I remembered all the gift cards Dre had promised me. What had happened to him?

The little dude dove into the laundry basket like he was on the Olympic swim team, splashing clothes all over the place.

"Might as well pick up," I grumbled. "Are you gonna help?"

"Dabba dugga no," came the toddler's reply from deep within the shirts, and I rolled my eyes.

"Traitor."

"Bulablah two!"

"You better watch your mouth." Once I was sure he was good and distracted by something nonhazardous (my two-day-old socks do not count as hazardous material, thank you very much), I began to make my bed and organize the day's schoolwork. As I tidied up, my mind wandered. The events of the day had been overwhelming, but it was hard to believe they had even happened now that I was back with family and in the Freeman House. Summoning...magic...figments...Papa Coin...avarice spirits...And Devin and Nina...had they gotten home safe? And Two-Saint...maybe he'd gone home, too? Yeah, that had to be it.

We don't even know who attacked!

I shook my head. This was ridiculous...wasn't it? A whole underground magical community about to go to war using powerful spirits as weapons? That was straight out of a comic book, or a movie. Stuff like that didn't happen in real life. No, real life was medical emergencies and getting in trouble at school. The only way a kid like me could become a wizard was if he was drafted into the NBA.

Power meets power, Devin had said.

I sat down in the rickety desk chair and leaned back so I could let my thoughts drift in the silence.

Wait...silence?

I sat up with a jolt and spun around. Toddlers aren't silent! That's an undisputed fact. Like gravity. Or the two-flush rule in public bathrooms. The only time toddlers are quiet is when they're doing something they're not supposed to.

"Boogs!" I whisper-shouted. I didn't want to be too loud, just in case Gran heard me. Like I needed to give her more ammunition in the *Jax isn't responsible* case file she was probably building. "Boogs!"

The laundry basket was now empty. A trail of socks and tighty-whities led to the door, where they were replaced by...

"Chalk," I groaned.

Two lines of chalk, one blue and one red, swirled along the wall and floor and led toward the hallway. I followed them quickly, suddenly horrified that a little boy, who couldn't walk five steps without tripping over something, was headed for the steep and twisty stairs that led downstairs.

"Boogs! Where are—"

I stopped. The chalk lines didn't lead to those stairs. That should've made me feel a hundred times better...but it didn't.

That would've been predictable. They would've made sense. Back to Gran, back to food—I could totally get that.

I felt a cold shiver run through my whole body. Because instead, the chalk lines led upstairs. When I followed them up, they ended next to the weird room from this morning. The mysterious locked room. The room I'd visited in what we all agreed was a daydream that I didn't have to be concerned about.

Except the door wasn't locked anymore. It was cracked open.

And Boogs had gone inside.

*   *   *

I guess the good news is that I found Boogs right inside the doorway. He didn't even complain when I picked him up, just started sucking his thumb and gazing around wide-eyed. Meanwhile, I was repeating the same thing over and over like I was stuck in a loop.

"It was a dream," I whispered. "It was a dream. It...was a dream, wasn't it?"

I flicked on the light switch. The room looked exactly as it had when I'd visited it in my vision. Well, almost. I don't know what bothered me, but something was off. What was it? The newspaper clippings still covered the walls, and the giant map of the Chicago area's Metra and L lines still stretched from one side of the room to the other. A mortar and pestle rested on a door-turned-desk, and there were some glass jars, but everything seemed to be the same . . . so why did it feel like everything was different?

Freemans run.

Boogs lifted his head and removed his thumb. "Ja book?"

"We'll go draw in just a second," I said. Boogs wriggled in my arms, and I put him down so I could pull out my phone. "I promise." I pulled up my photos and found the one I had taken of the wall in my vision. (So it *had* been real. . . . How was any of this possible?)

"Ja? Ja, ja, ja?"

"Yes, fine, we can draw." I squinted into the room one more time. It was like one of those visual puzzles where you had to spot the differences between two pictures. I hated those because I always ran out of patience before I found all the things. Or Where's Waldo? I don't know! If Waldo wanted to be found, he'd let us know!

"Ja?" Boogs asked.

I sighed. "Okay, let's go draw."

"Ja!" He held something up in a chubby fist and grinned. "Jax ja?"

My heart stopped. It was a newspaper clipping—he must've grabbed one of the loose ones on the floor and thought it was scrap paper he could draw on. Chalk swirls decorated the yellowed edges, and I was pretty sure that was a *B* he'd drawn in the middle (at least I hoped it was a *B*—otherwise we'd need to have a serious talk about why drawing butts was inappropriate, no matter how funny it was). But what caught my eye were the silver letters glimmering at random throughout the article.

The more I stared at them, the brighter they got.

"'G,'" I read aloud, "'A-R-Y.' Gary?"

I tugged the clipping out of Boogs's hand and replaced it with my phone before he could get upset. As he immediately began to swipe left and right with no regard for whatever app he opened, I smoothed out the piece of newspaper and read the handwritten scrawls that appeared beneath the headlines. Then I looked at the other clippings on the walls and saw more notes.

GARY SCHOOL ROCKED BY EXPLOSIONS
GARY ATTACKED NEXT?

Bus Overturned Near Racine, Children Missing
CHILDREN OF CONJURE?

NEIGHBORHOOD SEEKING ANSWERS AFTER GRAVEYARD HORROR
GROUND DOGS?

There were messages hidden in the clippings . . . with magic! And again, these were from newspapers I'd never heard of. I stared at their names, committing them to memory, making a note to ask someone about them. Maybe Mr. Brown at school would know.

And then there was the map on the wall. The Gray Line shimmered just like the magical letters in the clippings. Maybe being here in person, and not in a vision, made a difference. Also, the rail line was really long! It included not only all the L stops and the Metra as well, but also a few stops that didn't seem to belong to either one. These glowed a faint silver like someone had traced them with a magical highlighter—before slashing a giant X across them. And now, unlike the first time I'd been in this room, I could see that someone had written additional messages next to the crossed-out stops.

GULLAH JACK STATION INFESTED WITH INVASIVE HOOP
SNAKES, TEMPORARILY CUT OFF FROM GRAY LINE.

IF SEPARATED FROM OTHERS, USE TRACKER SPELL TO FIND THEM.

TRICK LAID AT VESEY STATION. SEVERAL MINOR SPIRITS
DISCOVERED UNBALANCED. STATION MANAGER UNABLE TO
FIX IN TIME. TEMPORARILY CUT OFF FROM GRAY LINE.

RUMORS OF MULTIPLE CURSES AFFLICTING MULTIPLE STATIONS.
IS IT THE FEUD, OR SOMETHING ELSE? GRAY LINE TEMPORARILY
SHUT DOWN AND GREATER SPIRITS RELOCATED UNTIL PRAISE HOUSE
RITUAL IS COMPLETED. THE RING NEEDS MORE SHOUTING, THE
WORDS DON'T MATTER. FIX THE RITUAL, END THE FEUD. PF.

I reread the last note. There were what looked like a few verses of a poem or song below it, but the words had been scratched out. They'd been written next to a park that was circled in red.

I backed up, my brain racing. *Gray Line shut down.* My great-great-grandfather had disappeared a century ago.

PF.

Portis Freeman.

Freemans run.

Papa Coin had said my great-great-grandfather had nearly killed all the summoners.

The newspaper crumpled in my hand as I made a fist. Whatever mystery Portis Freeman had been trying to solve, it affected the whole community. He was attempting to fix a problem, even in the middle of a feud. But...what had happened? My eyes landed on the last message.

Until Praise House ritual is completed...Fix the ritual, end the feud.

Maybe that was it. That was the key. I would follow Portis's clues. Figure out the ritual and complete it. Maybe, just maybe, if I could fix whatever it was that my great-great-grandfather broke, this newest feud would end as well.

Tomorrow, I had to find this Praise House.

CHAPTER
TWENTY-ONE

"Wait, wait, wait, slow down," Nina said. "Your great-great-grandfather did what?"

It was the next day at school, and she and I were sitting in the gym bleachers, waiting for our turn to launch missiles of doom at a helpless student. Okay, that wasn't really the objective, but it might as well have been! Coach Breland, our PE teacher, said we were practicing penalty kicks, since there was a big soccer tournament happening in the spring, but I knew the truth. Missiles. Of. Doom.

Bull was up now, and both Nina and I winced as the poor kid in the net tried his best to survive. Maybe in Art we could design *Get well soon* cards for him. And also for Jalen, who hadn't been seen since he got decked in yesterday's Summoning class. Maybe a *Get well at some point, no rush, take your time and heal* card.

On a more positive note, Devin had confirmed that Papa Coin and Dre had fared better against the avarice spirits, even though there was a lot of mess for them to clean up. He and I seemed to be vibing today, which was fun. I think.

On a less positive note, Two-Saint was still missing. But! Thanks to Portis's messages, I now had a plan for that.

I waited for a burst of noise to cover what I was about to say, tugged on the charcoal-gray sweat suit I'd borrowed from the laundry pile, which was mysteriously increasing in size in the basket on my bedroom floor, then leaned in and showed Nina the photo on my phone. "See?" I zoomed in on the image of the wall map. "All those crossed-out stops on this mysterious Gray Line?"

"Vesey Station . . . Gullah Jack Station . . ." she read off. "Wait, I know them. Those are"—she looked around and lowered her voice—"summoner communities. Or they were. Granddad said the people moved away years ago to get closer to places of power."

"Or maybe," I whispered, "that's what they said to cover it up."

"Cover what up?" Devin asked, reclining on the bleachers behind us.

"The attacks! Isn't that what Portis meant by 'trick laid' and 'multiple curses'?"

Nina bit her lip. "The feud. But what's the Gray Line?"

"I don't know," I admitted. "That's what I'm trying to figure out. Maybe some secret railroad? After I do this ritual at the

Praise House, whatever that is, maybe we can find the answer and—"

Devin interrupted. "What about Two-Saint? He's still missing, remember?"

I nodded. "Portis Freeman's notes say there's a tracker spell that can be used if someone gets separated. Maybe the instructions for that's at the Praise House, too. Learn it, use it, find Two-Saint."

"Just like that?" he asked. "That's convenient."

I glared at him. Why did he have to be right? I knew it was just a hunch, but even still, let me dream, you know?

"Anywaaaaay," I said, turning back to Nina, "do you know who the Praises are? I figured you would, since you pretty much know everyone in the community. If you can introduce me, I can try to figure out my great-great-granddad's ritual and finish it. Do you think they'll let me do it in their living room?"

Devin burst into laughter. It was so loud that Bull, who was on penalty kick number five, missed the goal and sent the soccer ball whistling toward Coach Breland. She ducked and the ball slammed off the wall, bonked a girl named Siobhan on the head, bounced up into the air, and swished through a basketball hoop.

"Meant to do that!" Bull shouted. Meanwhile, Siobhan growled and picked up a dodgeball from a storage crate. She took a huge windup and flung it at him, thumping him square in the back and sending him tumbling forward with a shout. "I've been hit!" he cried out.

"BALL FIGHT!" someone yelled, and suddenly the air was

filled with dodgeballs, soccer balls, and even soggy spitballs whizzing around everywhere.

Devin was still chuckling as I tried to keep one eye out for stray missiles while also frowning at him. "What's so funny?" I asked.

But he just shook his head and tried to catch his breath. It was Nina—who was also smiling, by the way—who ended up explaining. "Jax, there's no Mr. or Mrs. Praise. A praise house is like a tiny church. Granddad said they were built long ago as safe places for Blacks to commune and worship. They're powerful spots—if you can find one. According to everybody, the last praise house in this area was demolished when some luxury townhomes went up."

"Does this place still exist?" I asked. I held up my phone, pointing to the area circled in red on the map.

Devin peered at it. "Yeah, I think so. . . ."

"My guess is that I'll find something there," I said.

"*We'll* find something," Nina said.

I paused. "What?"

"We. I'm coming with you." She shook her head before I could protest. "Have you ever performed a ritual before? I didn't think so. Do you even know what steps you need to finish this one? Double I didn't think so. Besides, if I can help you with this, maybe certain people will finally take me seriously."

"You've gotta be joking," Devin said. He sounded annoyed. "You don't have to prove—"

"Don't I?" she interrupted. "He doesn't even look at me.

Doesn't talk to me, won't acknowledge me—he thinks I'm a joke!"

Devin's face softened. "Nina..."

"I don't think you're a joke," I said. Now what in the world made me speak up at that moment? Jeez, Jax. "I also probably shouldn't've butted in, so I'm going to ramble on for a bit and then just stop talking all of a sudden."

Both of them stared at me, and I twiddled my thumbs. I'm a good thumb-twiddler. The best.

"See?" Devin said. "This is why I can't take you seriously, Jax. Also, this whole thing is ridiculous!"

"Which is why you're coming, too," Nina replied.

"I am?" Devin asked.

"He is?" I asked.

She nodded. "If the prodigy of the family witnesses us completing a ritual, people will *have* to believe us. Granddad will finally come around."

I got why this was so important to Nina, I really did. When I talked to my mom and dad after the brawl back in Raleigh, I'd tried to convince them that the property damage at the mall wasn't my fault, even though Marcus had let everyone think it was. But my parents didn't listen. Even in our text chats and phone calls since I'd arrived in Chicago, the conversation always tended to end up with another lecture about control and setting an example and other adult-isms. I hadn't even had a chance to ask them if they sent me here because they knew I was a summoner, and that was always the plan, or if they even knew anything about summoning, or if they just wanted to get me out of town and out of more trouble. If they didn't know anything, would they even believe me if I told them? I mean, let's be honest, so far I wasn't proving to be a very good summoner. Maybe if I could show them, they'd *actually* listen to me about the other things. That was it. I had to prove to them who I was.

If only I could figure it out.

"And three is a powerful number, remember?" Nina went on. "We're going to need it."

I frowned. "Why?"

She looked at me in surprise. "Because of where the Praise House is."

"The park?"

Nina shook her head slowly. "That's not a park, Jax. It's an old, abandoned cemetery. And spirits love cemeteries."

* * *

When the bell rang to end seventh period, Nina and I hurried after Devin, who was stomping his way to our final class of the day, Study Hall, complaining the whole time.

"Nope," he said. "Forget about it. Are you even listening to what you're saying? Papa Coin would kill me. And then Dre would summon my ghost back from the afterlife and kill me again. A cycle of violence. One order of intergenerational trauma, supersized just for me. No thanks. I choose peace."

We entered the classroom and sidestepped a three-on-one arm-wrestling contest between Bull and the Long triplets.

Somehow Sam, Simon, and their brother Steven had rigged up a pulley system using hair bands, and Bull was panicking, as he was on the verge of losing. On the other side of the room, a bunch of kids were working on posters for this evening's basketball game, the first of the season. Between the constant bickering about how many puns they could fit ("An annoyed lobster is called a frustracean!") and the desks scraping as Bull struggled against his inevitable doom, no one was paying attention to us as we schemed. Or as Nina and I schemed and Devin complained.

"And besides," he continued, slumping into a seat and immediately tilting it back on two legs so he could balance and rock, "that cemetery is on the other side of the city. How are you going to get there from here?"

"*We*," I emphasized, "aren't going to leave from here. Not exactly. I have it all planned out."

Both of them looked at me. "You do?" Nina asked skeptically.

"I'm offended that you seem so surprised."

"It's just that seconds ago you thought a praise house was a neighbor to the Proud family, and you got mad at Devin for laughing. Now you have a master plan?"

"I'm not coming," Devin said.

I ignored him. "I personally think Devin can go gargle a bag of marbles..."

"Hey!"

"...but he might actually help out. And it's not a plan—it's a scheme. And, if I do say so myself, which I am doing, it's brilliant."

"I'm not coming with y'all," Devin said.

"A scheme?" Nina asked.

I grinned and rubbed my hands together before spreading them wide, like a magician calling for the audience to pay attention to his next trick. On the gym floor, Bull howled in frustration as the Longs celebrated their win, and I used the opportunity to lean in close and make sure only Devin and Nina could hear my plan.

"Picture this. The first basketball game of the season is tonight, right? Everybody's excited about it. I even heard Mr. Alston talking about it in art class. Apparently, some people from the school board might be there, and every teacher and staff member is freaking out. So it's the perfect cover! We duck out the back door while everyone else is shouting and jumping and all that stuff during the pep rally. Now, normally it would take two buses and a long walk to get to the nearest L train, but not with our favorite prodigy here."

"Please don't touch me."

"Instead of the bus, we're gonna catch a ride with, dun, dun, duunnnnnn, Coin limo service! We take it to the five-fifteen Red Line L and ride that crosstown. Easy-peasy."

"Why not take it all the way to the cemetery?" Nina asked.

"I'm not going," Devin said.

"If we take the limo all the way, Papa Coin will figure out where we've gone. But if we go to the L stop right next to Target, we can say we needed to get more markers and posterboard for the pep rally. Always have an alibi, in case anyone asks. It will take us approximately seven minutes on the L to get to the

119th Street Metra Station, and we can catch the Rock Island southbound train at five twenty-five p.m."

"No, not 119th Street," Nina said. "We're not allowed over there, not since a couple summoners went missing."

"Okaaay, 111th Street, then. We'll get off near Thornton, and boom, we're there. Almost. A twenty minute walk to the cemetery. Perform the ritual and find out how to fix the Gray Line. We'll be back at the basketball game before halftime."

"And again, just letting both of you know: I'm. Not. Going."

"And then we're done. Feud over, all thanks to us!"

"I hate you . . . so much," said Devin.

"You can't hate me," said Nina, "or I'll tell Grandma."

"And you can't hate me, either," I said. "We're best friends now!"

CHAPTER
TWENTY-TWO

"I CAN'T BELIEVE YOUR PLAN ACTUALLY WORKED," Nina said.

"I can't believe you conned me into joining you," Devin said with a groan.

I was going to cheer him up with another pun, but something made me pause, and it wasn't the exasperated look he was shooting at me. No, it was more like... the feeling of being watched. Again. I looked over my shoulder, but only curtained windows and an empty intersection stared back.

The three of us stood on a cracked sidewalk in a quiet neighborhood. We weren't in Chicago anymore, but Thornton, Illinois, a suburb to the south. A row of ranch houses squatted behind us, their yards hidden behind grayish-brown fences and thick, gnarled trees with branches that twisted like claws. Every so often the wind would gust through the branches and send them knocking against each other, making a sound eerily like chattering teeth. I shivered. The sun had set, and the shadows had shifted from cute and hilarious to creepy and scary.

And I still couldn't shake the feeling that someone was staring at us. I shoved my hands into my coat pockets and started across the street. "Come on," I whispered.

"I think it's closed," Devin muttered.

"Of course it isn't," I said, not even looking back as I reached the opposite curb. "You're just scared."

"What about the fence?" Nina asked.

Okay, so Mount Forest Cemetery *was* closed, technically. I say technically because, yes, it did have a high, rusted chainlink fence topped with barbed wire that sectioned it off from the rest of the community. I could see a few grave markers scattered inside, and they looked really old. But this had to be the right place. And I wasn't turning back, not after we'd come all this way. The gate sagged so far off its hinges I was sure I'd be able to squeeze through, so why not take a peek to be sure?

"That's just to keep the animals out," I said, trying to put some reassurance in my voice.

They both looked at the thick stands of trees on both sides of the fence, practically hiding the cemetery from view. Some of the trees were growing through the pickets, making gaps so big that anything from a bored squirrel to a blindfolded elephant could get inside.

"And the sign?" Devin said.

He pointed at the rectangular piece of metal lying facedown on the gravel driveway a couple feet away from the fence.

When I examined the gate, sure enough, there was an empty spot and rusted mounting brackets where a sign had probably once hung.

I shrugged. "That sign could say anything."

"Like 'Keep Out'?"

"Or 'Beware of Blindfolded Elephants!' Or 'Welcome!' You ever think about that, Devin? It could say 'Welcome.'"

Nina flapped her hand and crouched down. "Hey..."

Devin and I were face-to-face now as he held up his phone. "If you want to get yourself arrested, go for it. But I'm calling for a ride and getting out of here."

"Hey!" Nina said.

"Go ahead and call your car service," I snapped back. "Who cares, bro? Just admit you're scared! It's fine!"

"I'm not scared," he said through gritted teeth. "And if you call me scared one more time, I'm going to—"

At that moment, Nina stepped between the two of us. Her purse heirloom glowed in front of her as she reached inside and pulled out a handful of something. She raised it to her mouth and blew a cloud of glittering dust at the fence. Devin and I coughed and wiped our eyes as we stumbled back. It felt like I'd swallowed a spoonful of cayenne pepper mixed with cinnamon. Tears streamed down my face as I frantically wiped my sleeve across it.

"Nina!" I said, coughing. "Why..."

My voice trailed off as my vision cleared. It was like the world had exploded in color. The weeds glimmered and the concrete shone. Purple moths fluttered to miniature golden suns that used to be streetlights. And the cemetery! The gate was still there—but it wasn't alone. Another gate, a larger one, now joined it, arching high overhead, silver in color and shimmering like stars in the sky. It must've been as tall as a house! Thick walls replaced the old chain-link fence, and yet they were transparent. I could see through them to the graves beyond . . . and there were so many! Emerald tombs and ruby pedestals, giant sapphire headstones with gargoyles poised on top, but unlike the school's dusty gray stone versions, these statues were made of polished marble. There was even a fountain with a statue of a lady in a dress and church hat standing in the middle. Her dress was amber and her hat rose quartz.

"What did you do?" I whispered. Whispering felt like the right choice.

Nina brushed the remaining powder on her hand back into her pouch, then dispelled the heirloom before pointing at me and Devin in turn. "You were so busy arguing, and he was so busy whining, neither of you saw the spell."

"Spell?" Devin continued to wipe his eyes as he squatted and examined the gravel driveway. "Like, to conceal?"

"Exactly."

I scratched my head. "I'd want to hide the place, too. What if some Indiana Jones dude came around and started stealing statues or digging up graves? It'd be the Egyptian pharaohs or the Benin bronzes all over again."

Devin raised an eyebrow. "How do you know about the Benin bronzes?"

"My dad."

"Respect," he said grudgingly.

Nina had crouched down and was rubbing soil between her fingers. "The problem is, none of this should be here. This is fresh graveyard dirt—I don't think this is an old spell. Somebody cast it recently. Maybe even right before we got here."

"You can tell that by pinching dirt?" I asked.

Devin snorted. "They may be backstabbers, but no one knows more about rootwork than a Basket."

"Remember that when you come begging for another love charm for your crush," Nina said, but she was distracted, so there wasn't much heat in her reply.

"Well," I said, dusting off my hands and walking up to the double gates, one real, one spiritual, "we'll have to keep an eye out for more spells. Come on, let's find that Praise House."

"The spells aren't what worry me," Nina said. She moved next to me on my right and Devin joined me on the left, and together we entered the cemetery. "I hope whoever cast them isn't still here."

* * *

The journey through the cemetery made me feel as clumsy and clueless as a toddler.

"Watch out for that trick!" Nina hissed, scattering more reveal powder across what I thought was a harmless bit of graffiti.

"Trick?" I asked.

"A magical trap set by a summoner. This one is like a tracker, and it's incredibly difficult to remove."

When her dust bounced on the spray-painted magical trap, the yellow paint bubbled and boiled like a pot on the stove before fading away as if some giant invisible hand had erased it.

Another time I got yanked into the air by a different trick. I cut through a stand of trees because a log had fallen across the cemetery's main path, but I missed the work doll pinned to a branch above. Suddenly hands erupted out of the night— wooden hands with knotted fingers and thorny fingernails— and they gripped me around the upper arm and hauled me up into the air. It all happened so fast I didn't even have time to scream for help. If it hadn't been for Devin, I would've ended up somewhere in the trees, being squeezed like an orange on a Sunday morning. But he'd been right behind me, and he slapped one of the summoning cards from his heirloom onto the ground like a winning hand of spades. One of his brogres erupted out of the earth, wrapped me in a giant, foggy bear hug, and dragged me back to the ground. It was touching, even if Devin waited a little too long to release me. Truly, I was ever so grateful.

Anyway, I could see things, but I couldn't tell the difference between what was safe and what was dangerous. Like Papa Coin had said, I knew enough to get myself in trouble, but not enough to help us navigate the cemetery.

"Whoever set these traps really doesn't want anyone visiting," Nina grumbled. She pulled cobwebs out of her twists as Devin and I stumbled back toward her on the path. Spiders had burst out of a rotten tree when we walked by, and the furious blast of repel powder she'd unleashed had knocked everything ten yards back, including us. She scowled at the cloudless night sky. "Now I *do* wish that the spellcaster was still here. Mist spiders? That's low." Then, "Watch out, Jax, don't move."

She tossed a pouch (a no-look pass, by the way) to Devin, whose brogre spiked it against a thorny vine that had started to wrap around my ankles. I yelped and fell backward onto the seat of my pants as the vine zipped back into the trees and something skittered away into the underbrush.

"That's ten," Devin commented.

"Ten what?" I asked, still squinting into the shadows for any more ninja vines.

"Ten times we've saved your butt. I'm gonna start charging you."

I stood up and brushed off my pants, my ears burning. "Yeah, well, joke's on you—I'm broke. You charge an arm and a leg, and I might have to give you a literal arm and a leg."

Nina shuddered. "Don't even play," she said as she stooped to examine a piece of vine that had gotten caught under a stone. Her heirloom still hovered in front of her, and Nina plucked the plant from the ground and dropped it, still wriggling, into one of her purse's many pouches. "Some spells might actually take you up on that."

Before I could process *that* little nugget of info, Devin— who'd walked ahead of us up the hill—raised a hand as if in warning. "Hold on," he said. "Do you feel that?"

Nina and I paused. "Feel what?" she asked.

"I don't know.... Something seems...different."

But when I climbed past him to where the path crested the top of the hill, I didn't see anything dangerous. Just a small clearing with a tiny shack that had peeling white paint. I checked to make sure the path didn't take a turn to lead to someplace more exciting, but nope. It went straight to the shack. What a dump.

"Are you for real?" I muttered.

Meanwhile, Nina and Devin reached the top of the hill. Nina let out a sigh of relief when she saw the shack. "Good, you found it."

"*That's* the Praise House?" I asked, full of disbelief. It looked like a shed that old lawn mowers would be stored in. This was the place where we were supposed to perform a powerful ritual?

Devin looked as surprised as I was, but Nina nodded. "Praise houses weren't these giant megachurches, you know. Papa Coin said they were supposed to be hardly noticeable because they used to be secret."

"When did he say that?" Devin asked.

"During a lecture he gave you a couple years ago, when you two were going over magic history. I eavesdropped with a whisperjar spell." Nina saw my frown and explained: "If you put a whisperjar in a room with the lid unscrewed, it'll collect conversations. Later you can open it, and voilà—a whole conversation will replay, same voices and all. Cool, huh?"

Devin snapped his fingers. "That's right! He said Black folk used them to worship in secret back during slavery. Something about too many of us gathering in one place would make slaveowners..."

"Losers," Nina said with a cough.

"Klancestors," I sneezed out.

"...suspicious."

I started walking to the Praise House, curious now. "So, basically, it was like any Black picnic."

"Or cookout."

"Or party."

The Praise House door looked like it was barely clinging to its hinges. A soft breeze would knock the whole thing over like a house of cards. If there was any wind at all. Come to think of it... I was a foot away from the door when I paused.

"What's wrong?" Nina whispered.

Devin smirked. "Not getting scared now, are you? Let's go in!" He couldn't maintain the cool image anymore—he was as excited as we were. Even his brogre was antsy, bouncing from foot to mossy foot.

Still... something was raising the hairs on the back of my arm. Is this what Devin had felt earlier? Try as I might, I couldn't see anyone around. Was it another spell, or was I just nervous? Whatever it was, I knew one thing—I wasn't going to let Devin steal the glory. So I pushed aside the little voice warning me to take it slow and shoved open the Praise House door.

A blast of wind, stale and full of dust, rushed out, swirled around my legs, then flew into the night.

"Did y'all feel that?" I asked, whipping around. "And can you hear that?"

Nina looked at me strangely. "Hear what?"

"That...sound. Like people chanting. A choir, maybe?"

She glanced at Devin, who shrugged. Then Nina reached into a pouch and cast a pinch of its contents in a wide circle around us. When she blew on her fingertips, I heard a buzzing near my ears, like a hundred mosquitoes had gathered there, and then the sound faded away. "There," she said. "That'll let us know if anyone other than the three of us speaks a spell. But right now, there's no one else here."

I nodded, ignoring the questioning look she exchanged with Devin again, and took a deep breath. Gingerly, I put one foot in front of the other and climbed the two tiny sagging wooden stairs to the doorway. Words had been carved on the wooden doorframe, and I read them aloud.

"'Though we may have forgotten the power of the ancestors, the ancestors haven't forgotten us.'"

"Deep," Devin said, and Nina and I snickered as we stepped into the Praise House, ready for whatever.

It was dark, darker than the cloudy night sky outside, and yet I could still make out a few details. Several warped pews lined the tiny space, and rickety-looking wooden chairs ringed the interior along the walls. Bits of yellowed paper lay scattered across the floor. Old hymns or something? There were no windows and no other doors. A metal bucket, dented and rusted, was overturned in one corner. And on the floor planks there was a faded pattern—nothing complicated, just a circle that traced its way around the pews. Almost like a path...

Something grabbed my wrist, and I screamed. "AAAAAH!"

"Relax, you baby," Devin said. He handed me something. "Tuck this into your pocket, and then I'll go get you a pacifier."

It was one of his summoning cards. The edges had a faint glow, and I noticed Nina was now holding one as well. The area around us *did* get a bit brighter, and I could make out a few more details. *Useful.* I stuck mine into the breast pocket on my shirt and cleared my throat, ignoring the others' muffled snickers. "Right. Anyway, how do we begin?"

"Don't ask *us*, Freeman—this was your idea," said Devin.

"What did your great-great-grandfather say about it?" Nina prompted.

I shrugged, then realized they probably couldn't see the gesture. "I don't know—it was really vague. Something about making sure to shout when walking the ring. Wait, I took a picture of it. Look." I pulled out my phone, and—after waiting for it to unfreeze after I put in my passcode—pulled up the last photo I took. "See?"

THE RING NEEDS MORE SHOUTING, THE WORDS DON'T MATTER.

The scribbles on the walls of Portis Freeman's hidden room seemed grainy in the photo, but Nina and Devin both nodded. "'The words don't matter...'" Devin said thoughtfully. "It's like Papa Coin's growth song."

He didn't explain, and Nina looked troubled, so I cleared my throat and asked, "His growth song?"

"Yeah, he hums it when he's working in the garden."

"He says the words don't matter, just the act of putting

power in the music," Nina added. "My dad does the same thing when he's preparing different pouches for his customers. Speaking or singing helps the spirits inject power into your actions."

I stared at the faded path on the floor. So, I wasn't supposed to shout, but sing? I gulped. Talk about being put on the spot. And what was I supposed to sing? But right then, my phone flickered and died. I groaned. So much for having the picture as a reference. Now what? I squeezed my hands into fists. I'd brought us all the way out here, and this is where it ended?

"Come on, Freeman, what're you waiting for?" Devin asked.

Nina moved next to me. "You okay?"

I exhaled in frustration. How was I going to tell them I had no idea what to do? *Spit it out, Jax—get it over with. They might get upset, but it's not like you've never had that happen before.*

I took a deep breath, ready to admit this whole trip was a failure, when something rattled in the corner. A slim stick. It reminded me of a drumstick. Maybe at one point there'd been instruments in here. I thought of the band at DuSable. The drumline wouldn't even fit inside this Praise House, much less the whole band.

The image of them gathered around the lunch table, drumming and singing when the lunch monitors weren't there, popped into my mind. I cocked my head. No way...

"'The ring needs more shouting,'" I murmured.

"Jax?" Nina asked, but I ignored her.

"Freeman has truly lost it," Devin groaned.

Now, what were the words? I thought for a second, then licked my lips. Just because I had a plan didn't make this any easier. I picked up the stick and handed it to Devin. "All right, this is going to sound weird, but I need a beat."

"A beat?"

"A beat! Like this." And I took the stick and started tapping. *Tap-a-tap-a Tap-a-tap-a Tap-a-tap TAP TAP TAP.* "And then repeat it. Got it? Go."

Despite looking at me like I was a couple pebbles short of an avalanche, he took the stick and kept the rhythm going. Nodding in time, I turned to Nina. "You. Clap along."

"Why does this sound familiar?" she muttered.

"The band was practicing it," I said. "For the basketball halftime show."

Devin choked and nearly missed a beat. "'Master Blaster'? You're using Stevie Wonder to cast a spell?"

"Stevie Wonder is a wizard on the keyboard, so yes!" I shouted. I took a deep breath, then started clapping. "Here we go. See, the spell—it's a ring shout."

Nina and Devin both looked at me like I was speaking Klingon. "Uhhh," Devin said, but I kept going. "A ring shout! Remember Dr. Clayton mentioned it? As a way to build higher-order spells?"

"Ohhhh," they both said at the same time. "But..."

"No butts! Not unless you're throwing it back to the beat."

Devin looked up. "Really?"

"Play!" I shouted. I started walking, dipping to the beat, trying to catch the rhythm.

"'*We're in the middle of the makings of the master blaster jammin'!*

"*'We're in the middle of the makings of the master blaster jammin'!'*"

"He's...actually pretty good," Devin said begrudgingly. Nina said something back, but I couldn't hear because I'd started over. I didn't know all the words, just that part, and only because "Master Blaster" was a song Dad would sing while cooking in the kitchen. If you wanted a snack before dinner, you had to recite the bridge perfectly, and there'd been many a day when I went back to my room empty-handed. He'd be proud of me for remembering it now.

Except...something wasn't right. Why wasn't it working? I tried to clap louder, or sing louder, but it wasn't quite gelling. Maybe if I stepped into the...

My foot touched the worn circle, and a flare of light rippled along the walls of the Praise House before fading away. "Did you see that?" I shouted, right as Nina whooped.

"Do it again!" she called out, while still keeping the beat.

Clap, CLAP, clap, clap.

Nothing.

What had I done? I'd stepped on the circle. On a hunch, I took a step forward and clapped.

"There!" Devin pointed, as a faint glow pulsed from under a pew. "I saw it!"

Realization dawned. "You have to walk the circle," I said. "Keep the rhythm and sing while you walk. I think. Watch."

Clap, CLAP, clap, clap. "*'We're in the middle of the makings of the master blaster jammin'!'*"

Sure enough, the floor beneath the pews inside the circle began to glow.

Clap, CLAP, clap, clap. "*'We're in the middle of the makings of the master blaster jammin'!'*"

But it wasn't enough. The floor would glow, and the papers would rustle a bit, but then the light would disappear. Like a flashlight with dying batteries. Maybe I didn't have enough power?

Nina stepped up. She watched me for a second, clapping and bopping her head to the rhythm, then joined in. She repeated the lyrics while walking a few paces behind me.

Clap, CLAP, clap, clap. "*'We're in the middle of the makings of the master blaster jammin'!'*" we sang.

Devin didn't join us as we walked the circle. Instead, he dropped the stick and then slapped down two cards and summoned his brogres. *They* walked the circle, their huge footsteps eating up ground as they silently stomped to the rhythm. Meanwhile, Devin pulled out a couple of pencils and grabbed the metal bucket. He sat in one of the chairs and started really going in on the beat. It was like a lunch-table session, except instead of rapping the lyrics to our favorite song, we were performing magic!

"*'We're in the middle of the makings of the master blaster jammin'!'*"

The rhythm built.

The floor began to glow. First amber, then gold, filling the space with brilliant light. Wind rushed in and swirled up and around, lifting the dust and dirt and leaving a gleaming bronze floor behind. The papers rustled, then flapped, then tore loose from the floor and gathered in a great cloud between us. The bits and pieces fit together like puzzle pieces, until whole booklets floated around us. They bobbed in time to the music, and if I didn't look too carefully, I could see the outline of hands holding them, as bodies swayed and feet stomped. It felt like there were more than the three of us and Devin's summons in the tiny shack. A dozen voices sang with us, and two dozen hands clapped.

And still the rhythm built.

Sparkling rays of light stabbed up through the circle on the floor, creating a ring that illuminated us like we were on a stage in concert. The chairs straightened, and the pews shook off their warping. The door rattled, and the wind howled.

And still the rhythm built.

"Look!" Nina shouted.

I opened my eyes (when had I closed them?) to see the ring shoot up through the roof of the Praise House. We ran out the door into the cemetery just in time to watch a bright pillar pierce the clouds, only for a second, before dropping to the ground, landing on the far side of the cemetery in a two-story arch, where it pulsed through the trees. Sparks continued to arc from it like falling stars, landing on the ground, and fizzling out of existence after a second. Inside the Praise House, the song continued. The spell would apparently keep going until someone turned it off, I guess, like an engine. We'd just had to get it started. But why? How would this end the feud?

"Do you think we did it?" Nina asked.

"That has to be it," I said, pointing at the glowing arch. "Whatever *it* is."

Devin dispelled his brogres and returned his cards to his sling pack, including the ones he'd given us to light our way. "I hope so. If I have to hear Freeman sing again, I'm swearing off magic forever."

I snorted, which turned into a chuckle. To my surprise, Devin laughed, too, and then we were all bent over double, gasping for air. We'd done it! With the Praise House active, we were one step closer to the Gray Line and also the tracker spell to find Two-Saint. All we had to do now was reach the arch and—

Run.

The single word cut through my thoughts, just as Devin straightened and pointed to the cemetery path. "What's that?"

Smoke billowed out of the ground where one of the sparks of light had landed. The dirt on either side of the path began to rumble, slowly at first, before shaking faster and faster like an avalanche building up speed. A small mound bulged out of the earth. It grew larger as the sound of hissing filled the air, until, with an eruption of soil and sod, a scaled lizard creature the size of a wolf, with gray-green skin and glowing eyes, crawled out of the ground.

"RUN!" I shouted.

CHAPTER
TWENTY-THREE

"WAIT!" SHOUTED DEVIN. "DON'T. DO. ANYTHING."

I was in mid-getupouttathere, just about to put my Crocs in sports mode (even though I was wearing boots), ready to abandon any and all forms of bravery and run like the coward everyone assumed I was, when he called out, and I glared at him like he'd lost his mind.

"Have you lost your mind?" Nina hissed.

"He must've," I said. "Someone doesn't watch horror movies. You don't freeze—that's how you get ate. You wanna get ate?"

"It's *eaten*," Devin muttered. "Now be quiet and *look*."

Moonlight fell on the clearing around the Praise House. What time was it? It felt like we'd been in the Praise House for hours, but my phone was dead, and even if it wasn't, I wouldn't dare reach into my pocket to check, because more of the lizard-like creatures were emerging from the ground, like zombies in a movie, or evil oversized earthworms. With legs. So maybe nothing like an earthworm, but you get the picture. At first I thought they were avarice spirits, but they weren't burning, weren't wreathed in smoke, and they were also sort of cute. Sort of. So. More importantly, there were dozens of them, tongues flicking and eyes glowing as they stood still around the cemetery.

But none of them were looking at us.

"Why aren't they attacking?" Nina whispered.

I licked my lips nervously. "Maybe they have bad eyesight. If we hold really still, we'll be invisible. I've heard that works."

"Really?" Devin said. "Every time I forget, you remind us."

"Of what?"

"Of the fact that you don't know anything. This isn't Jurassic Park."

"First of all, I know that movie is clearly fake. I'm not that naïve, okay? I was referring to the classic cinematic documentary *The VelociPastor.*"

"Jax..."

"Or was it *T. rex and Effects?*"

"The rapping dinosaurs?" Nina asked.

"Enough!" Devin shouted. "They're not attacking because they're waiting for someone else."

Nina said, "So we aren't the targets—"

"But we sprang the trap," Devin finished. He thumbed his cards, which I now realized was a sign that he was worried. "Maybe by doing that ring shout."

As he and Nina went all family huddle, once again leaving out yours truly, I inched closer to one of the weird lizard creatures. I was nervous, yet also curious.

But none of them moved a muscle. And hear me out, from a certain angle—and I mean only that one particular angle—they were kinda cute. So what if they were each the size of a rottweiler, and their wrinkly skin was gray and hairless? So what if their teeth looked like shards of glass and their tails looked like weighted clubs? They were like friendly Komodo dragons. Maybe I could teach one to sit or stay. Ooh, what if it followed me home and I snuck it into the Freeman House? It could live in the map room, and I would feed it leftover casserole. In the afternoons, when everyone took their dogs out walking, me and—hmm, it would need a name...maybe Chuck? Yeah. Chuck and I could...

"Jax. Jax!"

Nina and Devin were waving frantically. "Get back!" Devin warned.

"Why are you—" I started to say, then stopped as I heard leaves crunching underfoot and turned around. One by one, each of the creatures' tails began to whip furiously on the ground and their glowing eyes, every single one of them, all stared at me.

No, not at me.

At my *coat*.

"Duck!" Nina shouted.

I threw myself backward as one of Devin's brogres erupted from the earth, just in time to take the impact of a creature that had hurled itself forward. My heart was racing. If I'd been any slower, that would've been me getting shredded.

"Move it!" Devin shouted as he slammed a second summoning card down. This time the slugger brogre emerged, covering me as I ran down to the path where Nina stood. She was throwing powder that burst into puffs of grayish flames before fizzling out. When I reached her, she pulled me into a run, her face twisted in confusion. Devin followed close behind.

"It doesn't make sense," Nina mumbled. I had to return the favor and yank her out of the way of a tree branch because she was so focused on the patterns of the flames as she threw more powder. "Daddy's identi-fire says those things are ground dogs, but they can't be."

"Because"—I gasped, a stitch in my side reminding me that I even if I put my Crocs in sports mode, I wasn't a sprinter—"they're not dogs?"

"No, *ground dogs* is another term for *salamanders*." Nina slid down the side of a ditch, rolled over a log, and kept moving. Meanwhile, I tripped over a leaf. "Another type of trick. They were buried and left for a target to walk over. Then they were supposed to emerge and go after the person. But ground dogs can fit in a jar. These are huge!"

Devin sprinted by. "Less dissertation, more escaping!"

Together we raced down the path, the scrape of claws and the smell of burning leaves following us. I chanced a look back and wished I hadn't. A mass of lizards boiled over the hill after us. I put the cramp in my side out of my head and found an extra gear. No bloated magic salamanders were gonna eat Jax Freeman tonight!

We'd left the dazzling cemetery behind—only overgrown graves and worn stone markers remained. We cut through a stand of trees, then burst into the clearing by the rusted gate to the street. "Do you think . . . they'll stay in . . . the cemetery?" I gasped out, stumbling next to Devin.

A *twang* of metal sounded in front of us. A section of fence posts compressed like a spring recoiling, and a mass of ground dogs leaped through the opening like a tidal wave of terror.

"That answer your question?" Devin asked grimly, before turning around and sprinting along the fence line. "Come on!"

We abandoned the front gate and raced along the inside of the fence, the ground dogs keeping pace with us through the canopy, along both sides of the fence, and behind us. They were trying to surround us! Nina must've realized the same thing because she muttered under her breath and steepled her hands. When her heirloom appeared, she started digging fistfuls of powder out of the bag with both hands. She hurled them left and right, still muttering, and the powder began to glitter like diamonds as it made contact with the creatures. At first, nothing happened, but then . . .

CRACK!

A parking meter on the outside of the fence exploded, and a storm of coins slammed into the closest ground dog. It hissed in pain and tumbled into the feet of another. More meters exploded and launched their contents at the nearest creatures, and Nina nodded grimly as she continued to run. "Who said attract-wealth spells couldn't be dangerous?" she remarked as she passed me.

Devin snorted as his two brogres leaped into the trees and pummeled other giant magical salamanders. But even with his summons and Nina's rootwork, more and more of the creatures continued to gather behind us. There were too many to fight!

"Oh no," I said, skidding to a halt as we crested a hill.

"Keep going! Why are you stopping?" Devin snapped.

Nina slowed next to us. "What are y'all doing? Oh..."

We'd reached the arch. We were still inside the cemetery, hemmed in by the fence on one side and the ground dogs on the other. The arch rose in front of us, a glimmering portal to who-knows-where. On any other day, Jax's Three Rules would've kept me from going inside it, and I did hesitate, but... we were running out of options.

More ground dogs came hissing up the street on the other side of the fence, preventing us from escaping to the Metra. They crawled on houses and swarmed over parked cars. Good thing the streets were empty—otherwise people would've been freaking out. But that also meant there was no one around to help us as the ground dogs crawled closer and closer. Hisses came from the left and the right. They had us trapped.

But then...

"They stopped," Nina whispered.

Devin shook his head. "I don't get what's happening."

The ground dogs stood in place, tails lashing, eyes burning into us, but they didn't come any closer. Not the ones on the roofs of cars, up on lampposts, or even the cluster of them hissing right in front of us. It was like they were ... waiting.

Something caught my eye. A flash of white in the trees.

A woman walked out of the cemetery. I'm not sure how I could tell from such a long distance, but I knew without a doubt that it was a woman in white wearing a veiled hat.

"No," I whispered.

"Jax?" Nina asked. "What's wrong?"

I pointed, and Devin and Nina squinted. "Who is that?" Devin asked. "Do you know her?"

I was backing up. "It's her. The woman from my vision. She must be the one controlling the lizards—I mean, the ground dogs. Plus, those monsters in the vision obeyed her, too. This is all her doing."

In a blink, she was twenty yards closer to us.

"Did she just flicker?" Nina said with a gasp.

"Did she what?" I asked.

"Whoever she is," Devin interrupted, "she's powerful. Where are you going?"

I couldn't answer him. My whole body was trembling, and I wasn't in control of it. I was backing up, leaving Nina and Devin standing back-to-back as the ground dogs parted for the veiled woman. In another blink she was only fifty yards away. My teeth were chattering.

Nina was talking, trying to keep one eye on me and one eye on the woman. "Jax, stay close—you can't protect yourself."

I wanted to run. Whoever this lady was, she had something to do with my great-great-grandfather's tragedy, I just knew it.

I could literally feel fear grip my muscles and squeeze. I had to run. Run far away. Turn around and run. RUN!

The woman in white moved (flickered?) forward again, and now the ground dogs parted like troops for a general as she glided through. I could see the black lipstick, the glistening white dress and hat, and the veil that remained unnaturally still.

The pull of the arch beckoned to me, like I was supposed to enter it. It didn't feel dangerous, but isn't that when you're supposed to be the most careful? It felt like...like...

The force of a magnet pulling something into existence.

Pressure in your ears right before they pop.

A rip current trying to drag you into the ocean.

I ran forward and grabbed Nina and Devin by the shoulders again as the Veiled Woman reached out to us...to me. I pulled the other two with me and we plunged into the golden glow of the arch. A jolt of electricity went through me—a shock of energy that rattled my bones and teeth. I thought I would pass out because every single one of my nerves was on fire, and I couldn't take it much longer....

The world went white.

CHAPTER
TWENTY-FOUR

WHEN I OPENED MY EYES, I WAS SPRAWLED ON A weird bench and Devin and Nina were hovering above me. Nina held a paper cup in each hand, and Devin had an old metal bucket. Both looked ready to pour their contents on me.

"I'm up," I said groggily. "I'm up. Don't—"

Devin dumped his bucket on my head. Ice-cold water splashed onto my face and chest, and I howled as I shot upright and banged my head on the sloped ceiling. We were in some kind of outdated sitting room, and that head knock must've been serious, because it felt like the floor was moving beneath my feet.

"I said I was up, you goon!" I shouted at him, rubbing my head.

He shrugged. "My bad. I thought you were still talking in your sleep."

"I don't talk in my sleep!"

Nina set her cups down on a polished end table. "Actually," she said, "you do. It's pretty bad."

I paused. "What did I say?"

"Well, let's just say I'm not leaving you alone with Nina anytime soon," Devin said, flicking water off his hands.

My expression had to be one of total mortification, I mean absolute *Hurl me off a cliff immediately*, because the two of them looked at me and burst out laughing. Devin went so far as to fall to the ground. Was it really that funny?

"You... should see your face," he said, gasping.

"Relax, Cupid," Nina said, wiping tears from her eyes. "You just complained about someone eating your meatball sub."

"I would argue that's even worse."

"Shut up, Devin," Nina and I said at the same time. I cleared my throat, took the napkins she offered me, and rapidly changed the subject. "So where are we? And who designed this place? It's, like, straight out of an antique store."

"We were hoping you could tell us," Devin said. "You know, since you brought us here, then had the nerve to pass out. You sleep like our great-aunt Martha, by the way."

"Neat," I said, stretching my neck. "Is she a summoner?"

"She's dead, but yes. Snored, too."

Nina elbowed him. "We're on a train... but that's all we've been able to find out. The door to this car is locked, so we couldn't go far. Not that we were gonna leave you."

Devin looked like he was about to disagree, but he kept his mouth shut when Nina threatened him with an elbow.

A train.

Memories of the ground dogs chasing us around the cemetery came flooding back, along with the Veiled Woman. We were almost goners before that glowing arch sucked us inside. Had that been a train? Maybe it absorbed us. Were we in the train's stomach?

I took a look around. While I didn't see anything that resembled stomach lining, the walls were stained cherry red to match the cushions of the chairs. The train car reminded me of the one in my vision of George. Brownish-red plush carpets covered the floor, and brass fixtures gleamed above windows with the drawn shades. I walked over to one—a couple steps, really, because the space was *really* small—and reached for the window shade's drawstring.

"Don't open—" Nina shouted.

Too late. The shade zipped up, and a gray monster with razor-sharp teeth peered back at me. I shrieked and almost backflipped away. Instead, I fell onto my butt and scrambled backward, like those awkward crab shuttles gym teachers love to make you do. Devin lunged forward and yanked on the drawstring, dropping the shade back over the window.

"Was . . . Was that a shark?" I asked.

Nina nodded.

"We're . . . underwater?"

She nodded again.

"Now you see why I'm a little stressed," Devin said. He was standing over a small sink, refilling his bucket. "Because we've also traveled through rainforests and deserts while on board this nightmare train. Guess what? Chicago doesn't have rain-forests! Or deserts! That's a super-fun fact for you. So, if you don't mind, I'm going to need you to tell me what that arch did and what you did and then FIX IT, or you're getting another cold shower."

He brandished the water bucket, but I ignored it. Rain-forests? Underwater? This train was magical, no doubt about it. I shook my head. "What *did* I do?"

"Yes, what did you do?"

"I don't know!" I rubbed my head, still staring at the window. "I got us away from those freaky lizards and bridezilla. *I* did that! How? I don't know. I just don't! Why don't *you* tell me what I did, Mr. Expert-at-Everything?"

"I didn't bring us here," Devin said.

"No, because you're Prime Minister Perfect. Captain Correct. Señor Stellar. You never make a mistake. Well, I'm sorry, other people do, so deal with it."

Devin dropped the bucket, splashing water everywhere. "Don't tell me to deal with it. This was your idea, so it's your problem. You fix it, or else—"

"Or else what?" I said, turning to him. "Or what?"

Nina was standing to the side next to an oversized plush chair, tapping her chin thoughtfully as she held up her phone like she was looking for reception.

"Aren't you going to tell us to stop arguing?" I asked her.

"Me?" she asked, not even looking up. "Boy, please. I'm not your mother or your babysitter. You two want to fight, go ahead and fight. I don't have the energy to waste protecting fools from being foolish."

"Now that," said a voice from over by the door, "is the smartest thing anyone has uttered so far."

We all froze for a second, then whipped around to see a Black woman in an elegant floor-length ball gown and a silk shawl. She was lazily redoing her matching headwrap.

"But if you want to know what you have done, young Jackson," she continued, "it is what your arrière-arrière-grand-père could do. He was a porter, a transporter, an escort in dangerous times, and you are, too. You are a porter, and you help spirits make their way home. We are riding the Gray Line, and"—she paused, and it was at that moment I realized I could see right through her—"you never should have come."

The three of us looked at each other, then back at her, and screamed.

* * *

We all leaped into action at the same time.

Too bad everything we did was wrong.

Nina grabbed a fistful of repel powder and hurled it at the woman. Devin tried to summon a brogre . . . but he had run out of summoning power, so he kicked a couple of chairs toward the lady instead. I was just about to try to suplex her (a *booplex*, thank you very much) when she clapped sharply, like a kindergarten teacher trying to get her class's attention.

"If you're quite done?" she asked in a tone that meant any

answer except a *Yes, ma'am* would mean severe punishment. "Excellent. You, sir, kindly rearrange what you have knocked askew. And you other two children? Take a seat. We have lots to review, and time is fleeting."

We all stopped in mid-action. (Have you ever stopped in mid-booplex? It's tough!) After we exchanged glances, Devin quietly picked up the chairs he had knocked over, and Nina and I sat down on a pair of cushions on the floor.

"You're a spirit?" Nina asked.

"No, she's not," I said, having realized the truth only after all our efforts to subdue her had failed.

The woman pulled an enormous easel, a chalkboard, and several pieces of chalk out of a tiny purse. It was less distressing to see how much her little clutch could hold than it was to see the chalk float over and begin to make notes on the chalkboard in a neat script.

One, I didn't sign up for school outside of school.

Two, and maybe more important—we still had to learn cursive?

"No?" Nina asked.

"Well," I said, "sort of . . . She's a figment. Right, ma'am?"

"Ten out of ten, young Jackson." The woman performed a tiny curtsy. "My name is Madame Helene De La Croix, and I am indeed a figment. A spirit in the same way a half-dollar is a coin. Highly specialized to perform a singular job, as instructed by the leaders of Conjure Station."

"Conjure Station?" Devin asked.

"Do we still use half-dollars?" I whispered to Nina.

"*Shhh*, you two!" Nina said.

Devin joined us on the floor cushions, and Madame Helene nodded. "Conjure Station. The belle of this side of the spirit world; the junction where spirits and summoners together created a space safe from those who would harm them both. A place where spirits are escorted and ancestors deposit power for safekeeping until their descendants can channel it safely. A place of gathering. A place for journeys. A place that, unless I can do my job, you will never reach, and yet a place you *must* reach, young Jackson."

We were hanging on her every word, but her last sentence jarred me. Never reach? And why me?

"Now," the figment continued, "my role is to quickly educate you in disembarking from the Shriek before it's too late."

I raised my hand. "The Shriek?" That's what those creepy gargoyles had mentioned.

"The train you are currently aboard, Jackson."

Devin spoke up. "But we can't even leave this car.... How are we supposed to exit the train? Is there a key hidden somewhere?"

Madame Helene scowled at him, and he fell quiet. I started to smirk, but then she turned her gaze on me and I gulped. "And you call yourselves summoners. Really. I'm surprised you were not able to work it out. The *key*, Devin, is inside Jackson."

"My heart," I said, nodding.

"No, Jackson."

"My gall bladder?"

"It is the spiritual energy you possess! You are a porter, Jackson, and you have to remember that before it's too late."

Devin glanced at me. "You *were* the only one who didn't try to open the door. . . . You know, because you fainted?"

I rolled my eyes, but Nina spoke up before I could retort. "You keep saying that," she said, staring at the figment intently. "'Before it's too late.' Why?"

Madame Helene pursed her lips, then turned and walked toward the door at the end of the train car. She passed right through it before reappearing and beckoning. "Come. I'll show you."

We stood, and Nina and Devin looked at me. I realized they were waiting on me. *Great. More pressure. Totally fine! I'm a rock in a pond. A cave in a storm. A stick in the mud.*

"What are you talking about?" Devin asked.

Oh crap, had I been speaking out loud?

"Yes," Nina said. "And you still are. Now stop stalling and go open the door."

I swallowed and took a step forward. I was a porter. What did that even mean? I guess I'd find out if I could open that door. Portis Freeman had been a porter. Did my great-great-grandfather ever ride the Shriek? Could I be following in his footsteps? I wondered if he'd ever had moments of doubt. Was he the first Freeman foul-up?

I was at the door now. The doorknob was a dull brass latch, and I reached out. . . .

Maybe he *was* a foul-up. Maybe he'd made mistakes. But I'd seen his notes. He'd been trying to fix things. To correct a problem that the whole community of summoners suffered from. Even after they'd gotten upset with him, he'd still tried! Didn't that count for something? It had to!

Help me out, Great-Great-Granddad....

My coat rustled, almost like he was answering.

A roar like summer thunder echoed in the distance.

"I'm going into the next car," I said firmly. My hand grabbed the latch...and it moved! The door clicked. "HA!" I shouted, turning to gloat at Devin. "I got it! Take that, you—"

I paused.

"What's wrong?" Nina asked.

"My hand," I said, yanking at it. "It's stuck! I can't let go!"

It felt like my hand was glued to the latch, but that was ridiculous! I tugged and tugged again, but nothing happened. Devin and Nina grabbed my shoulders, trying to wrench me free, but that turned out to be the exact wrong thing to do. Because, at that moment, the hinges on the door disappeared, and I felt a force gather on the opposite side. Like the pull of a magnet, or a giant hand on the other side getting ready to...

"Hold on!" I shouted, just as the door was yanked open, and I—with Devin and Nina hanging off my shoulders like angry parrots—hurtled forward into the next car.

This car was more of the same—outdated seats, dim lighting, and cherry-stained trim. But as we flew through it—and I literally mean *flew*—something amazing happened.

"Look!" Nina shouted in my ear.

"It's changing!" Devin shouted back.

"AAAAAHHHH!" I screamed. Seriously, this was terrifying!

But it was also amazing, almost like we were leaving magic in our wake. Everything we passed began to blur, shimmer, and ripple, like water in a pond after a stone is tossed in. The chairs became leather recliners, and the lights morphed into recessed RGB strips that slowly changed color every few seconds. The old plush carpets dissolved, and modern ones grew up like grass on a lawn.

"How—" I started to ask, and then we were crashing into the next car. This one was like a mobile garden. Benches appeared out of the walls with terrariums on top. Mist floated from spouts in the ceiling, watering herbs and vivid flowers, while hanging plants dropped forest-green vines down on either side of the aisle. Near the back of the car were dozens and dozens of pots full of rich black soil waiting to be seeded and tilled. Glass jars and bottles, leather pouches, and flasks lined the shelves above them. It reminded me of Papa Coin's alley.

"It's a rootwork garden!" Nina said as we zipped by. "On a train!"

And then we were crashing through the next doorway. And the next. Again and again. We flew through car after car, marvel after marvel. One car had multiple altars to the ancestors, complete with offerings and incense. Another was a classroom with sleek desks and a projector. The Shriek was amazing, absolutely amazing.

We slammed to a stop against a wall and fell to the floor with a chorus of groans. We'd reached the last car before the engine of the Shriek. It was a double-decker, with windows that stretched two floors up on either side, casting the car in bright light and allowing passengers to enjoy the scenery.

"End of the line," a voice said, and we looked up to see Madame Helene floating above us, her face stern but with the trace of a smile. "For all of us, if you don't disembark. First lesson, and perhaps the most important, children. You wanted to know why we must rush, young Nina? Behold. *That* is the rush."

She floated up to one of the windows. I climbed to my feet, as did Nina and Devin, and together we took the car's spiral staircases to the top section and peered out. At first, I couldn't see anything, just a mass of gray fog that looked like rain clouds. Was this why it was called the Gray Line?

Then, for a brief second, we exited the formless gray and entered a valley of sunshine. I gasped. We were high up in the air! A city stretched out beneath us, and an automated voice said something, but it was lost as I looked back to where the silver train tracks curved behind us.

"Why are the clouds moving?" Devin muttered.

Nina squinted. "There's something coming. Is it another train?"

Chills raced down my spine, and my mouth went dry. Even without being able to see it, I was positive it wasn't a cloud or a train. I also knew, as surely as I knew my own name, that it was what had killed Portis Freeman.

"Do you hear that? Is that thunder?" Devin asked.

"No, child," answered Madame Helene. "It is the Gringemaw."

The clouds boiled apart behind us, and a *thing* emerged.

Nina covered her mouth and reeled away, like she was about to throw up. Devin actually gripped my wrist, squeezing it as if his life depended on it. (Maybe it did...) I swallowed, my heart pounding and my mouth dry.

The Gringemaw was ginormous. As big as a building! Its body was shaped like a distorted brain, huge and bulbous at the front, while dozens and dozens of arms, all different shapes and sizes and colors, protruded from the back. It pushed and it pulled itself along the tracks, howling into the sky with its many mouths as its hundreds of eyes followed the train.

No, not the train.

I don't know how I knew, but I did.

This was what had killed my great-great-grandfather, and now it was coming for me.

CHAPTER
TWENTY-FIVE

"No, no, no, child! It is a spin with a flourish—a *flourish*! And intent. Always INTENT! That is how I learned, and so shall you. Next!"

While the Gringemaw scrambled behind us, Madame Helene was trying to teach us how to disembark, which was a fancy word meaning *get off the train*. No one was getting it right. Even Wonder Boy was having trouble. And though the Shriek kept speeding forward, too fast for the monster to catch us, who knew how long that would be the case.

Devin collapsed next to me on the floor, where I lay trying to recover. Nina joined Madame Helene in the middle of the observatory car and began to turn in circles.

"No, NO! That isn't a spin—it's a twirl!" Madame Helene said. "AGAIN!"

"Intent is very loud," Devin grumbled.

As much as I wanted to disagree with him, I couldn't.

"I don't get it," Nina complained. She stooped, hands on her knees, to catch her breath. Her twists were tied up in a short ponytail behind her head to keep her neck cool. My—Portis Freeman's—coat was laying on the stairs to the upper section, and even Devin seemed slightly sweaty. Slightly.

Madame Helene floated to the window and glanced outside, and the Gringemaw must've spotted her, because a thunderous roar again shook the floor of the Shriek. I felt a stab of fear, followed quickly by a surge of anger. That thing was a killer! But I'd figure out a way to take it down. If I could ever get off this train, that is.

"You don't open a door a sliver and hope someone inside pulls you out of the train," Madame Helene said after a moment. "You don't stand on a sidewalk and wait for it to carry you to your destination. No elevator is going to come for you; no windows will automatically open. Summoners don't wait. The spirits do not wait. You move, you act, you use your power with intent!"

"Sounds like someone has accessibility issues," Nina grumbled.

I heaved myself up onto my elbows. "Is there some sort of magic word we should be saying? An incantation? *Abracadabra*, or *hocus pocus*? *Bubble gum, bubble gum in a dish*?"

"Words are irrelevant," Madame Helene replied with a sniff. She adjusted her headwrap and re-draped her shawl around her shoulders. "Speaking is antiquated."

"But Papa Coin—" Devin started to say.

"Aht-aht! You have a choice, young man. Listen to what I'm saying now or listen to me say *I told you so* for the rest of your life, because if you can't figure this out, we will be spending a lot of time together. I cannot leave until you do."

"Wait, you're stuck here until one of us learns?" I asked. "That doesn't seem fair."

"That is the job of a figment," Madame Helene said sadly.

I thought about the man who had waited forever to pass a message to my great-great-grandfather. Was he still there? I'd gotten the message, but I wasn't Portis Freeman. How many other figments were out there waiting to complete their missions?

Madame Helene was now marching back and forth down the aisle of the car—if floating spirits can march. Bobbing up and down determinedly? "Do you know what the Gringemaw is?" she asked.

"Ugly," I muttered.

"A spirit," Nina said with a sigh.

I looked at her in surprise. "Wait, really? That thing?"

"Yes," Madame Helene answered. "And no. It is an *amalgam*— many spirits combined. An exchange of power gone wrong. When we summon, we borrow power from the spirits and ancestors to complete a ritual."

"Right." I nodded. "It's the first rule of summoning. I remember that."

"The Gringemaw is what happens when that power is never returned. You are *borrowing*, not keeping. The energy, the power, is meant to be given back." Madame Helene's eyes latched on to mine. "Portis Freeman, your great-great-grandfather, attempted something that was beyond his skill, and he failed. The Gringemaw appeared as a direct result, and it feeds on the energy we channel from the spirits. It fed on many summoners before your ancestor's spell lured it onto the Gray Line, where it got stuck."

And killed him, I thought. Then something occurred to me.

"I know what Portis was trying to do!" I said, and everyone turned to look at me. "He was attempting to stop the feud by connecting the summoner communities. He tried to create the Gray Line so they could all be united, but he couldn't get it right. Issues kept popping up with each stop, like someone was messing with him. In his notes, he said he would try one more thing. That must be when he—" My voice broke off, and I swallowed a sudden lump.

Nina nodded. "He casts this big spell to do it all at once, but it doesn't work, and he is . . . gone, and the Gray Line shuts down."

"He was trying to help," I said softly.

Devin shuffled his feet awkwardly. "And we started it back up. Can we shut it down again?"

Madame Helene shook her head. "You would need to borrow a lot of power to do so, and you see what happened the last time somebody tried."

"So we just ride this thing forever until we figure out how to leave?"

"Exactly! Now, let me see if you've learned anything! Up, up!"

Devin and Nina groaned at the same time, even as they climbed to their feet to follow Madame Helene to the center of the train car. I stood, too, but instead of joining them, I walked over to one of the huge windows and peered behind us. The Gringemaw still followed, hauling itself after us, its many arms scrabbling for purchase and its many faces making a million different expressions. A tiny wisp of pity for it curled in my chest, but I stomped it down mercilessly. *No pity for murderers.* I wanted more than anything to scream in its face, to tell it exactly what it had done to generations of Freemans. Creating this thing was the first Freeman foul-up. The Gringemaw was the beginning of the family curse, and I wanted to make it know that. I could see myself yanking open the door and shouting into the gray fog. . . .

Wait a minute.

Yank open the door.

Open the door.

I could clearly see myself opening the door and stepping out.

With intention.

"INTENT!" I shouted. "I figured out intent!"

The others turned in surprise as I sprinted past them, heading for the slam door at the front of the car—the one that opened to the engine.

"Jax!" Devin warned.

"Jaaax?" Nina called.

Madame Helene said nothing...but was that a smile on her face?

I barreled straight for the door and grabbed the handle. I hesitated, thinking of exactly where I wanted to go. The kitchen? Not yet. Food later, magic first. The roof of the train, then. Let the Gringemaw see what was coming for it. I thought about me standing up there, triumphant, not worried about fitting in or being good at school...and I opened the door and stepped through, holding on to the doorknob just in case.

A man with a super fuzzy mustache screamed at the top of his lungs, then fainted. It was Mr. Jameson, a custodian at our school. I was back at DuSable! Somehow, I'd walked into the custodian's closet as he was wrapping up after the evening's basketball game. My right foot was stuck in a bucket and a mop had fallen on my head—I must've looked terrifying!

"Sorry!" I called. I retreated through the doorway into the observation car.

"Jax!" Nina shouted. "I thought you were—"

Devin punched me in the arm. "Don't ever do that again."

"—dead or injured, and—"

"Without you around, who would I have to hate?"

Madame Helene floated between us, cutting them off and saving me from any more punches. Once it was quiet, she tilted her head toward me. "Do you know what you did wrong?"

I nodded. "I got too distracted. At the last second, I thought about school, and that's where I ended up going."

Nina gawked. "You went all the way to the school?"

"And you actually came back here?" Devin asked incredulously.

"Yep. Might need to send an apology Edible Arrangement to Mr. Jameson. Think he likes pineapples?"

"Wait, the custodian? What did you do?"

"Pretty sure I scared him half to death." I hoped it was only halfway. "Anyway, I think I know what to do now."

Madame Helene stared at me, and then nodded. "I believe you do. But remember Jackson, you are a porter. But more than that, you are a Freeman. Your ancestors will help you if you ask. Just be sure you ask for what you need, not what you want."

"What is she talking about?" Devin asked, looking between the two of us.

"I understand," I said, waving at her. "Bye, Madame Helene!"

"Bye?" Devin said. "What do you mean, bye? What does he mean, bye?"

Nina studied my face. "Jax, what are you doing?"

"Like the teacher said, it's all about intent," I said. Then I linked arms with my friends' at the elbows. They were too flabbergasted to try and pull away, which was really good, considering that I didn't know what would happen if they did. I reached for the door, the words *Conjure Station* repeating in my mind over and over. That was my destination. That was my intent. *Conjure Station.*

"Jax..." Devin warned.

"Jax . . ." Nina said, gripping my arm with her free hand.

Oh, in case you hadn't caught up by now, I had figured out how to disembark.

"JAAAAAAX!" they both shouted as we plunged outside.

CHAPTER
TWENTY-SIX

I'VE NEVER BEEN TO DISNEY WORLD, AND I'VE never been to outer space. Conjure Station was like going to both at the same time.

"This is . . ." Nina said, her voice trailing off.

"Everything is floating," Devin said in disbelief.

I didn't speak. I couldn't. I'd forgotten how to do anything except at gawk at our surroundings.

Conjure Station was like a solar system of train platforms! We floated in a cloudlike nebula the same colors as a sunset. Rectangular train platforms made of frosted glass orbited around a giant crystal split-flap display with frozen arrival and departure times and destinations. Some I recognized; others were unfamiliar.

We stood on one of the platforms as the rest of the train station orbited around us. Another platform floated a dozen feet below, while a third drifted by overhead. Marble pillars grew up and out of the platforms, twisting and splitting before disappearing into the nebula. Ruby fountains with water frozen in mid-spray sparkled like stars. Rows of jade benches passed by like rockets. Statues of what I assumed were famous summoners trailed past like comets, briefly attaching to this platform or that before drifting off again into orbit.

And then there was the food.

Kiosks and food stalls painted in every color imaginable swirled around the platforms like moons, their pans frying and grills sizzling. Delicious aromas of every street food you could think of wafted down, switching from tacos to chicken wings to Korean barbecue, from po'boys to dumplings to donuts. It was breathtaking. And mind-blowing.

"There's no one else here," I whispered.

A chime echoed at the other end of the platform we were on, and I froze.

"*Welcome to Conjure Station!*" a warm voice spoke. It echoed around us, but I couldn't find a speaker no matter how hard I looked. "*Please watch your step. Platform one-nine-six— Oscarville Station—now arriving in orbit.*"

A platform spiraled into existence like a galaxy being born. Spinning up out of the purplish nebula, it appeared brick by silver brick, unfolding out of nothing. First came the floor, then the pillars, then the benches and arches. It glittered bright and sharp like the sun before slowly dulling to a soft glow. Train tracks appeared alongside it, running all the way to the platform's end before diving down like a roller coaster to disappear into the nebula below.

"*As a reminder,*" the voice continued, "*platforms two through two hundred are closed to arriving trains. Next departure: platform one, the Chicago express, in thirty minutes.*"

We all looked up at the signpost on the platform we stood on.

"This is platform one," I read. There were two hundred platforms here? But if each station was a community of summoners, then that meant the summoning world was huge! So many people like me, out there, waiting to connect to a community they might not even know existed!

"*Repeat, next departure is platform one, the Chicago express.*"

"That's our train," Nina said. "The Shriek."

Devin inched closer to the edge to peer down, then shuddered. "That gives us thirty minutes to ... do whatever we need to do, and then we can get out of here. I'm starting to get weirded out."

"We'll have to come back," I said. "Somehow."

Everyone nodded, though I was slightly disappointed. Thirty minutes wasn't enough! A half hour? That's all the time we had to explore Conjure Station, find my great-great-grandfather's tracker spell to help Two-Saint, and maybe figure out a way to get the Gray Line working again. If we could connect the communities like Portis had been trying to do, they'd stop fighting ... right? Then I had to get us back aboard the Shriek and take us home without getting caught by the

Gringemaw. And in the meantime, I thought as my stomach growled, I could grab a snack. Or two.

Nina looked around with a wide-eyed expression. "Two hundred platforms," she said. "Where do you think they all go?"

"Places like Vesey Station and Gullah Jack Station," I said after a second. "Remember? Those were two stops on the map in my great-great-grandfather's room. You said they were summoner communities before they were shut down."

"Two hundred communities?" Devin asked skeptically. "That's a lot. There has to be more at work here."

"Like what?"

"I don't know." He hesitated, scanning the other platforms drifting past. "But...I think we need to leave. There's something...creepy about this place."

I held my hands out wide and walked to the edge of the platform we stood on. "Leave? We just got here! We need to explore! Investigate!"

Nina was staring at her conjure-powder handbag with a strange expression on her face. I was going to ask her what was wrong when Devin walked over, his face twisted in annoyance.

"You want to investigate? Fine. Investigate this: Where is everyone? Why would any summoner leave this place?"

I flapped a hand at him, my attention distracted by a kiosk that had entered our platform's orbit. It was another unmanned food stall. Pans sizzled on a gas range, cooking something savory that beckoned me over. "You worry too much," I said as my stomach grumbled.

"And you don't worry enough!" he exploded.

"Jax, hold on a second," Nina called.

But I wasn't listening. The smell of whatever was cooking had consumed me. My stomach twisted in on itself again, and my mouth watered. I hadn't eaten since...lunch at DuSable. How long ago was that? Years? I wanted nothing more at that moment than to pile a plate high with the contents of those pans. It smelled so familiar, so achingly delicious, I...I had to have some.

I took a step forward, then another.

I reached out a hand.

"Jax!"

I looked back...

...and saw that the platform I'd been standing on before was now floating over a dozen feet away. Nina and Devin were still on it, staring at me in disbelief.

I was standing by the cooktop. "Uuuhhh, what just happened?" I shouted.

"You flickered!" Devin answered. His expression alternated between awe and envy.

"I what?"

"Flickered!" Nina said.

Then I remembered that Nina had used the word before. "You mean like the lady with the veiled hat?"

Nina nodded and shook her hands in excitement. "We're not supposed to learn about it until next year, in seventh grade, but it's an advanced summoner technique. Like teleporting, but you can only travel to what you can see. Watch!"

She seemed to twist in place, and then...she vanished!

Seconds later she appeared at the other end of the next platform over, which wasn't platform two as one might expect, but platform fifty-two. "See? Papa Coin taught us. Well...he taught Dre and Devin, and Dre taught me."

I glanced at Devin, who shrugged. "After a protest march turned violent, Papa Coin said we might need to learn how to get out of a place fast."

"So you can do it, too?"

Devin didn't answer. Instead, he folded his arms and glared at me.

Nina laughed. "Apparently not as far as you. We're not supposed to let anyone know we can do it because we could get in trouble with the congregation."

"They spoil all the fun," grumbled Devin.

"While you're over there, Jax," asked Nina, "anything good to eat?"

My eyes dropped to the cooktop in front of me. "Meatballs," I answered, drooling. Savory, dripping in sauce, ready and waiting to be heaped high on a sandwich roll and smothered in mozzarella cheese...which was all right there. I could make a meatball sub! I reached out and grabbed a plate, but as soon as I touched it, the food started to move on its own! A ladle dipped into the meatballs and stirred them as the roll trundled its way to a toaster. Seconds later, six savory meatballs were being scooped onto the roll as shredded mozzarella drifted down on top like an early winter snow. My jaw was on the floor. Flickering was cool and all, don't get me wrong. Like, moving instantly from one place to another? Amazing! But the perfect meatball sub? Mannnn...

"Do it again!" Devin shouted.

"Scrmff?" I said, not paying attention. I had just taken a monstrous bite out of my sandwich.

"Do it again. Try to flicker somewhere else."

"Uh, okay," I said. I reluctantly put the sub down. After checking the area, I noticed there was an information kiosk twenty feet above me, orbiting an empty platform fifty-six. I frowned. Something nagged the back of my mind. *Information kiosk.*

Lost and Found.

The tracker spell!

I reached out and spun around, my destination firmly in my mind....

One second, I was at the meatball-sub stall, and then, with a whirl of air and fog-like mist, I appeared in front of the information kiosk. Like magic! Well, it *was* magic. Summoning magic.

"Welcome!" a voice said from behind the desk, though no one was there. It was the same voice as the PA announcer. *"Please state your request."*

"Um," I said, not sure where to look, but settling on the empty chair behind the desk. "I need to find a friend?"

"Name?"

"Two-Saint, I mean, Toussaint James."

After a brief pause, the voice said, *"No registered summoner appears to be in the station."* My heart sank, but before I could flicker away, it continued. *"Please provide item of missing person to register summoner, and a locator will be provided."*

"Oh," I said. "Oh! I have one, not here, but at home. A Metra card."

A ticket with a kosmogram illustrated on it printed out of a dispenser on the counter. *"Please take ticket and place on missing person's item and a locator will be provided. Thank you, and please visit Conjure Station again."*

I backed up, a grin splitting my face from ear to ear. Finally, we were getting somewhere! I didn't know where Two-Saint was, but I could only imagine the loneliness and the fear he must have been feeling. Not for much longer, though. I was one step away from finding him, and I'd bet he would love Conjure Station, the Shriek, and everything else we'd found.

"Hey," I said, flickering back down to platform fifty-two. Devin jumped in surprise, which made me feel even better. I could do something Wonder Boy couldn't. "Guess what? I found the tracker spell...sort of. I need to get something of Two-Saint's from my house, but then we should be able to find him."

Devin whistled and Nina beamed, punching me in the shoulder. "Look at you!"

"I know, right? Impressed?"

"I actually am," Devin said. "You didn't screw up this time. I'm proud of yo— Hey!" He jumped and wiggled around after I'd flickered to a lemonade stand, grabbed ice cubes, and stuffed them down his shirt.

I grinned, then wiped my hands on my pants. "By the way, how does this work? Flickering, I mean."

"You mean you don't know how you're doing it?" Devin asked in disbelief. "What do you think about before you flicker?"

"I was hungry," I said, shrugging. "There was this delicious smell—oh, dang, I left my meatball sub up there. Anyway, next I thought about ice cream, and kinda twisted, and there I was."

"Unbelievable," Devin said. "Your stomach taught you! Of course it did."

"Magic man's gotta eat."

Nina, meanwhile, was looking confused. She was staring at her conjure purse again.

I raised an eyebrow. "What's wrong?"

"I don't know...." She hesitated. "But I think my purse is refilling. Slowly, but it's definitely refilling."

Devin peered over, suspicious. "Wait, what do you mean?"

"So, every Basket's conjure storage pouch, satchel, or purse, in my case, is linked to a home garden, where they plant and harvest their herbs, grind their powders, and make the rest of their preparations," Nina explained to me. "Mine is ... Mine is linked to the garden Dad planted for Mom before she left. He wanted someone to be able to use it. My purse is an heirloom from my great-grandmother on Dad's side. As long as we have the ingredients in the linked garden, the purse will restock itself when it gets low."

I whistled. "That's pretty cool."

"Yeah, except..." Nina looked in her purse again, and

her eyes widened. "I don't have ghoulweed in my garden. Or Carver's vine."

Now Devin was definitely on high alert. "Carver's vine? You have Carver's vine? Isn't that, like, worth a fortune?"

"Yes.... We could never afford to grow our own. But I'm positive that's what this is. And if it's not coming from our garden...where *is* it coming from?" Nina seemed shaken, and I didn't know if it was in a good way or a bad way.

"What's Carver's vine?" I asked.

"A rare plant discovered by George Washington Carver," Devin said, and the fact he answered without any snark or annoyance let me know how serious this was.

"The peanut guy?" I asked.

"The same," said Devin. "Rumor has it that he found a plant with two properties that are essential to summoners. For one, when Carver's vine is fertilized with spiritual energy and brewed in a tea, it can cure summoner's chills."

"That's what Jalen got after facing Nina in class yesterday, right?" I asked, remembering his shivering and bluish tint.

"I'm sure the nurse gave him diluted Carver's vine to get him back to normal," Nina said.

"Some people chew it like gum for a boost of summoning power," Devin added.

"But it's rare, really rare," said Nina, "and now—I mean, look!" She opened her purse to show us a twirling clump of string-like vine that was speckled orange and green.

Devin whistled. "That'll pay for your whole house," he said.

His cards were in his hand again, and he shuffled them back and forth, flicking one from knuckle to knuckle.

Suddenly Nina lashed out and snatched his wrist.

"Hey!" he shouted.

She ignored him. Her face had gone pale, and she gulped several times. "Look," she finally said. "Try to summon them."

"But I don't have—"

"Just do it!" she snapped.

We watched as Devin shrugged, then flicked out one card. Almost instantaneously, a brogre appeared, the one with the Timbs.

"Dispel him," Nina commanded, and Devin did. "Now summon him over there, on that platform. Platform twenty-two."

Devin stared at her, then looked at the platform she was pointing at. It was on the opposite side of Conjure Station, drifting downward behind a giant cube display. "Nina, come on. That's too far! It'll drain the deck, and you know how Papa Coin gets when he has to recharge one of our heirlooms prematurely."

"No," Nina said icily, "I don't know, because he doesn't recharge my conjure purse. I had to learn how to do it on my own. But let's skip past that. Pretend that I know what I'm talking about for two seconds and do it! Summon him on platform twenty-two!"

I don't think Devin had ever heard Nina talk to him like that before, which was probably why he did what she asked. He shrugged, muttering about how it wasn't going to work because it was too far, and then summoned a card and flicked it.

The brogre reappeared just as platform twenty-two dropped out of view. We heard the creature's roar echo across the station, and Devin's jaw dropped. "But...how? I didn't have enough charge to summon when we got on the Shriek, and now I can summon from a longer distance than ever before?"

But Nina wasn't listening. She had turned to stare at me, and the excitement in her eyes bordered on mania. "Don't you see?" she whispered.

"No," I said. "No, and I don't think I want to."

"Yesss," she hissed. Suddenly she reached into her conjure purse and began flinging handful after handful of different powders along the platform floor, muttering their names in rapid succession. "Repel powder, reveal powder, identi-fire, goofer dust..." She hurled them all. Then she flipped her purse, dumped its entire contents on the floor, and let out a piercing laugh.

"I...am so scared," I said.

Devin nodded, speechless.

"You guys," she shouted, "it's the station! It's charging our heirlooms. Don't you get it? It's like Madame Helene said—this is a place where the ancestors could store power for when it was needed." She turned over her purse and showed us the inside. It was once again full of powders and Carver's vine.

Devin's face blanched, and he stared at his deck of cards like he'd never seen them before. "No way," he said, his voice barely above a whisper. Then he yelled, "No way!" The two of them started jumping around, hand in hand. Nina actually shoved Devin so hard he fell backward onto the seat of his pants, and instead of getting angry, he laughed even harder.

"HELLO?" I finally interrupted. "I get why that's cool and all, but you guys are acting like you won the lottery. . . ."

"Jax," Nina said, grabbing me by the shoulders, "why did the feud between the summoner families happen?"

I thought about it. "Because there weren't enough heirlooms?"

Devin snorted from his seat on the floor, but for once it didn't feel like he was being mean. "There are tons of heirlooms, bro—they're just out of power. Remember Papa Coin's workbench?"

I wrinkled my brow. Papa Coin's table . . . piled high with glass jars, mortars and pestles, and . . . "The pile of junk wasn't junk," I said slowly. "Those were heirlooms. Heirlooms without spirit power."

Devin nodded. "And because Papa Coin has the most heirlooms left that can still channel power, he's the only one who can recharge them. Other families are jealous because theirs are running out."

"But even his are starting to fade now," Nina broke in. "And he can't recharge all the Coin heirlooms like he used to. He's getting older."

That was an understatement. He knew my great-great-grandfather! How long could summoners live, anyway?

I looked at the contents of Nina's conjure purse scattered across the platform—the powders, the glowing Carver's vine—and then watched as Devin's brogre came back into view, stomping up and down platform twenty-two and trying to punch the water in one of the fountains. I swear that thing was like a puppy barking at leaves. But if showing up at Conjure Station and hanging out could recharge heirlooms' spiritual power, that was huge! The attack on Papa Coin, the thefts Devin had mentioned . . . all that could stop. Once we told everybody about this place, we could end the feud, just like Portis had wanted!

"Attention!" the station PA system said. *"Chicago Express departing in five minutes."*

"That's us," Nina said.

"We need to get back to your grandfather and let him know," I said.

They both nodded. "Time for a piggyback ride," Devin said. He brushed off his pants and held out his hand. I stared at him for a second, then extended my own and helped him up. He shrugged when Nina stared at him. "What? That's basically what it is, isn't it? Jax is carrying us onto the Shriek."

"Please don't call it piggybacking," I grumbled. "Makes me feel like I'm babysitting."

"Aww," Nina said, laughing. "Poor Jax. He has to be responsible."

"Keep laughing," I said, "and I'm gonna tell Madame Helene y'all don't wanna *flourish*."

"Nooo!"

"Ay, bro, that's going too far."

"Yeah, well—"

A chime sounded on the platform. Another announcement?

I waited for it to pass before I continued to mock-threaten the two of them....But it kept going, getting louder and louder, until the station's automated voice returned. I grew still.

"Attention in the terminal: a hostile presence has been spotted on approach. Attention in the terminal: a hostile presence has been spotted on approach. Conjure Station will now go into shutdown until the presence has departed."

The three of us looked at each other. "Hostile presence?" Devin echoed with a confused expression.

Realization hit Nina and me at the same time. "The Gringemaw!"

"It's following the Shriek!" I said, smacking myself in the forehead.

"So what do we do now?" Devin shouted.

"Whatever we're going to do, we need to do it fast," Nina warned. She pointed off into the distance. "Look!"

My heart plummeted.

Conjure Station was winking out of existence. The platforms were folding in on themselves, as if the nebula were a black hole. Tracks, statues, and arches shivered, then twisted together before popping out of view. Platforms disappeared above and below us, and panic started to grip my chest. Then the floor began to shake beneath our feet.

"Oh no," I whispered. "We have to get back to platform one before the Shriek arrives."

"RUN!" Nina shouted.

We sprinted toward the far end of the platform as it shifted beneath us. Bricks shuddered, then compressed and shrank.

Water reversed into fountains, and lights dimmed. Food kiosks shriveled like balloons letting out air.

"Come on!" Devin shouted, pointing toward our right. A platform drifted beneath us. "Flicker!"

Without a second thought I slipped into the spirit realm and reappeared in a puff of mist a second later. Nina and Devin followed shortly after, and together we ran, even as this platform began to shake beneath our feet as well. A large fountain appeared overhead, and we flickered up to it one after the other, pausing there for a second to regain our bearings. Then we pushed off it to flicker onto another platform. But time was running out, and with each flicker Devin fell farther and farther behind, only catching up if we paused.

"Watch it!" Devin shouted. He yanked me back, and I tumbled away just as the floor began to disappear from beneath me. Nina yelped and flickered away. I was about to follow when I noticed Devin on the ground, panting from exhaustion.

"Come on, bro, sleep later!"

But he only shook his head. "I can't do it."

"Yes, you can—just flicker! We're almost there!" Platform 171 was literally drifting right next to us.

"It's too far," he said, closing his eyes in frustration.

I turned to look at the gap to the next platform, and a sinking feeling entered the pit of my stomach, because the distance between this platform and platform one was nearly thirty feet. We were almost there, but Devin looked like he didn't have another ounce of energy to use. I balled my hands into fists. We had to go, but we couldn't leave him here. I growled something totally inappropriate under my breath and ran back to him.

"You better never say a bad thing about meatballs again," I said, reaching down to pull him to his feet.

"What? Leave me, Freeman, I'll wait—"

"Cool story, bro," I said. "Wait over there."

And I shoved him off the platform.

"JAX!" Devin screamed.

"NO!" Nina screamed from platform 171.

Me? I took a deep breath, then ran and flickered. The platform shuddered and disappeared just as I left. I reappeared, not on platform one, but on top of a food stall that had been drifting midway between the two and slightly below. Devin fell, screaming, and I shoved off the stall, my hand reaching for him even as I began to flicker.

One moment I was reaching for his arm in the middle of a nebula. The next, I was on platform one, and Devin was screaming his head off beside me. "ARE YOU OUT OF YOUR MIND?!" he shouted. "YOU COULD HAVE KILLED ME! I'M TRAUMATIZED NOW. TRAUMATIZED!" He started punching my shoulder with both fists, before leaning against me and collapsing into hysterical laughter. "THAT WAS THE COOLEST THING I'VE EVER SEEN!"

Nina blinked into existence next to us, and her jaw dropped as I bit back a grin. A train horn blasted in the distance, reminding me of my responsibility as a porter, and I shook myself and focused on thinking about the Shriek.

"...*two*..."

Oh, right! The countdown! I whirled and reached out, grabbing Nina and Devin's hands as I thought about the rootwork car and the classroom.

"...one..."

Platform one trembled beneath our feet as I thought and visualized and imagined and dreamed about the train we'd arrived on, down to the updated carpet in the observation car. *Intent. Intent.*

"...and thank you for visiting Conjure Station. Good-bye..."

Everything went still.

And then I leaped into the air with my friends—a literal leap of faith. A slam door materialized in front of us and slid open. I pulled my friends through it as the Shriek tore past Conjure Station, mere moments before platform one disappeared.

CHAPTER
TWENTY-SEVEN

IF ANYONE HAD BEEN WALKING NEAR THE FREEMAN House around eight in the evening, they would've witnessed something incredible: three Black kids in near hysterics, laughing and sobbing, leaning on each other, appearing out of thin air like fireworks in the night. A sparkle, an explosion of mist, and there they were. But no one saw except the wind, and everyone knows the wind has been keeping secrets for centuries.

I took in a lungful of freezing-cold air and breathed out slowly as Devin sighed and put away his cell phone. Nina was frowning at hers, and mine—well, it turned on. That was the good news. The bad news is that somehow the language had switched to Wookiee text-to-voice, which meant if I got a text, everyone within a fifty-foot radius would be treated to Chewbacca trying to decipher the poop emoji.

I kinda hoped someone would text me. Because, you know

what? Even after everything that had happened, from the Veiled Lady and the ground dogs to the Shriek and the Gringemaw, I sorta didn't want the night to end. It was the first time since I'd left North Carolina and all that mess that I felt... I don't know, like I was a part of something bigger.

"What'd they say?" I asked Devin.

The first thing Devin had done when he caught his breath was call his brother. No, make that the second thing. First he had tried to call Papa Coin, but no one answered.

Devin shook his head. "Dre said... Well, he said a lot of things, but he wants me—us—to wait it out. Things are... well, they're still wild."

"That bad?" Nina asked.

"Granddad is... stable. That's what Dre said, whatever that means. Stable. Also, no one knows who the shadow summoners are. Apparently, someone let loose a hoop snake near the daycare. Mr. Reynolds, the guy who manages it, is blaming anybody and everybody, but low-key? I think he did it. You know he's always talking about his summoning skills."

Nina groaned. "Oh my god. A hoop snake?"

"What's a hoop snake?" I asked. Something about snakes tugged at my memory, but my mind was too fried to retrieve the info.

"A cryptid," she said.

"Isn't that Snoop's dance?"

"That's... No, Jax. A cryptid is basically a mythical animal whose existence has never been proven but we know it's real. Like the Loch Ness Monster, or chupacabras."

"Chupacabras are real?"

Devin nodded. "Ask Vanessa about them. She claims she rescued one last summer."

I whistled, which was more like me blowing an enthusiastic raspberry, but give me a break—it had been a long evening. Speaking of which, I needed to go inside.

"So where are y'all gonna go? Back to Nina's house?" I asked.

Devin glanced at Nina, who tapped something on her phone, got a reply in what seemed like only seconds, and then they both looked at me. "Dad texted me to say he went to go help Papa Coin," Nina said. "They may have issues, but this... Papa Coin isn't getting better."

"And the Coin car service is down," Devin said, balling his hands into fists. "I don't think we realized how much we all rely on Granddad. He likes to control everything, which was fine before, but now I wonder..."

Nina touched my arm. "Do you think your parents will care if we spend the night?"

I stared at her. Then Devin. Then back at her. "Seriously?" I asked.

No one had ever asked to sleep over at my house. Back in Raleigh, everybody always crashed at Marcus's house after a game or team activity. The one time I suggested people spend the night at my house, Marcus got angry. He said there wouldn't be enough food to go around because my mom and dad were too broke to feed everybody, and a bunch of other things. At the time I shrugged it off, even though it hurt, and said he was probably right. But he wasn't right. About a lotta stuff.

"It's all right," Nina said, her shoulders slumping. "I'll text Dad again—maybe he can get someone to cover—"

"NO!" I shouted. "I mean, no, it's cool. Really. I just... I mean, come on, let's go ask. Not my parents—I live with my uncle and Gran—but they'll probably want to call your parents."

"Good luck with that," Nina muttered.

There was pain under her words, but Devin cleared his throat before I could ask about it. "Dre can talk to them if he needs to," he said, and I nodded. I pivoted and headed up the stairs to the house. I couldn't help but grin with a little pride when Nina and Devin both gawked at the castle-like exterior. "This is where you live?" Nina said. "It's like some Gothic fortress."

"I don't know what Batman has to do with this—"

"That's Goth*am*," Devin said.

"—but yes. My room's in the turret right there. Not that kind of turret—it's only a tower. Not as cool, I know, but it's all right."

"Are you kidding?" Nina asked, climbing the million stairs up to the porch. "You're a wizard in a tower, boy. You gonna get us out the hood. Imma start calling you Randalf the Gray."

"Lamaruman the Wise."

"Larry Potter."

"*Brr*lin."

Everyone cracked up. It felt good to—for once—laugh

with friends and not be the joke. The only person missing was Two-Saint, and he'd be back soon enough.

*   *   *

I was already coming up with second and third arguments to use if Gran and Uncle Moe said no to Devin and Nina staying the night, but it turned out I didn't need them. Gran was in the kitchen, a gaming headset off one ear as she chopped bacon for a BLT sandwich and shouted at someone through the mic.

"Well, you tell Rosa Lee to put her glasses on and play for real! If we lose one more time because she's off looting an ammo depot, I'm gonna wrap this here cane around her good knee. Hold on, my grandbaby's here. What you need, sugar? How was the game?"

"Hey, Gran," I said, then gestured at Nina and Devin, who waved sheepishly. "It was ... fun. Lots of goals. Anyway, there was a problem at my friends' granddad's place, and now they need somewhere to crash while everything gets sorted out. Can they stay here?" It wasn't technically a lie, and I only felt a little bit guilty.

"Of course!" Gran exclaimed. "Poor things. Y'all hungry?"

"No, ma'am," Nina said.

"Okay, well, if you need a bite, we got lasagna and garlic bread in the fridge. Jax, make sure to keep the bedroom door open, and don't y'all be up to one in the morning. I wasn't born yesterday."

Devin opened his mouth to—I'm sure—say something slick.

Gran turned her gaze on him, leaning back against the counter and lifting her cane to point at him. "Try me, chile. Try me."

Devin's mouth shut with a *click*.

"That's better. Now go ahead, 'fore I change my mind." She watched as Devin and Nina took the stairs to the turret two at a time, hollering after them, "And there's some extra bedding in the second-floor closet, and toothbrushes in the third-floor bathroom! Don't want no funky-mouthed kids in this house!"

I lingered behind to ask, "Where's Uncle Moe?" I snagged a piece of bacon and dodged Gran's swat.

The smile faded from her face, and she didn't answer for a few seconds. Instead, she put her mic on mute and rested her hands on the counter, her gaze on the bacon. Then she sighed and shook her head. "Still out. Called to say he'd be late, that he ran into some problems. Another night of missing Boogs's bedtime..."

She shook her head and then cleared her throat. "Anyway, you go ahead and be with your friends—ain't nothing you need to be worrying about right now. Go on now, and I mean it, keep that door open."

Up in my room, Devin was shaking his head as Nina passed him pillows and comforters. "Grandmothers are scary."

"And cool," Nina said. "I like her."

"Cool, sure, but definitely scary," said Devin. "And was she playing *War Haven Legends*?"

I nodded. "Yep."

"Iconic."

He and Nina poked around my room curiously as I did my best to smush dirty clothes from the last couple days into a pile. I'd promised myself to do a better job of keeping things tidy, especially in a someone else's house, but so far that wasn't the reality. Once the floor was relatively clear, I draped a blanket over the mound of laundry. Voilà! Instant beanbag chair. I should become an interior decorator.

I wasn't sure what to do next as a host, so I started digging around the room to find Two-Saint's Metra card. Devin had summoned one of his brogres to help arrange his blankets and pillow, which seemed like overkill, but who was I to judge? I wasn't exactly an expert at summoner sleepovers. Back in Raleigh we would play video games or tell ghost stories or talk about who we liked at school. Well, here I didn't have any video games, our whole lives were a ghost story, and there was no way, I repeat, NO WAY, anyone was going to get me to tell Nina who my crush was.

Actually, you know what? Forget I had that thought. Let's pretend I didn't even have a crush.

"So..." Nina asked casually, flipping through the science worksheet packet I'd brought home yesterday. She was lying on her stomach on a blanket next to the door, her head propped on one hand. I'd offered her the bed, but apparently the sheets smelled like cheese. "Anyone at school you like, Jax?"

I was peeling back blankets on my bed, sure the Metra card was around here somewhere, when she spoke. I started choking on air. "What?" I said after a coughing fit. "Who, me? Like? I don't like things. At all. Hate everything. Why don't you ask Devin?"

"Oh, please. The only things that boy likes are sneakers and summoning."

Devin threw a pillow at her. "You don't know anything."

Nina caught it and used the pillow to prop up her head. "Do too. I know everything—we Baskets are observant. You have to be when working with powder spells. We're not as sneaky as the Tree of Knives, but close. Like, did you know Vanessa and Bull have crushes on each other? But neither one knows how the other one feels, so, like, you'll see them sitting next to each other and sneaking glances and then looking away. It's the cutest thing."

I pictured the giant Bull and tiny Vanessa holding hands and laughed. Who would've guessed?

"Yeah, well," Devin said, shrugging down into his blanket. He was propped up against the closet, his summoning cards shuffling rapidly in his hands. "No crushes here. People are a distraction."

"You can focus on being a super summoner and still like other people," Nina said. "It's not that big a deal."

"Maybe it isn't to you, but it is to me. And after everything that happened today, I can't afford to be distracted. Not for a second. Papa Coin may not trust—"

He cut himself off. Nina didn't look up from the science packet, but she grew really still.

"Sorry," Devin mumbled.

"No, say it," Nina said. Now she did look up. "Go ahead. You were going to say Papa Coin may not trust me, but you still have a chance to keep his love and affection, right?"

"That's not what I was gonna say."

"Well, it's how he's thinking!"

Silence fell again, and I looked back and forth between the two of them. Finally, I couldn't stand it anymore, and I sat up straight on my bed and stuffed the pillow between my back and the wall. "Why do you let Papa Coin treat you like that?" I asked. Even though the question was for Nina, I made sure to glance at Devin, too.

"Believe me, if I could change his mind, I would," Nina said angrily. "But he hates me."

"He does not," Devin snapped back. "So don't say that."

"You don't know!"

"I do, actually." He paused as if unsure if he should say anything else, then pressed on, apparently deciding that fixing this was more important than any secret he was about to spill. "I do know. Dre told me once, when I asked him about it."

Nina looked up at this. "You did? When?"

"A year or so ago. After . . . When it was just you and your dad. We were at that family reunion at that park, the one with the mural on the basketball court. Everybody was relay-racing, and I think you won four in a row."

"Five," Nina murmured, and a small grin slipped across her face. She dodged another pillow throw.

"Everybody was cheering for you during the last race," Devin went on, "and you beat me, remember? I came in third or fourth, and you were first and...so happy. We went to tell Papa Coin, and at first he'd thought I won. He started boasting that I was the best, that no one could beat me. But when we corrected him...when *you* corrected him, he shut down. Got angry and told us to stop messing around and go help get the picnic ready. You were so upset, but you know what? You didn't cry. You didn't shout or say anything—you just went and helped set up. After that I asked Dre why Granddad hated you. You know what he said?"

"No..." Nina whispered.

"Dre said it wasn't you. It was never about you. He said it was the fact that you look exactly like your mother and you're just as talented, if not more talented, than she was at your age."

Nina looked shocked. Crushed. I didn't know what had happened between her mother and her grandfather, and even though I wanted to ask, I could see that this wasn't the time. Instead, I slid off the bed and scooted next to her, propping myself up against the wall. I nudged her with my shoulder.

"Hey," I said, "it's fine. Once we tell everybody about Conjure Station, you'll be a hero. I mean, we all will, but he has to recognize you after this. He'll have no choice!"

Devin nodded and joined us, sitting on Nina's other side. "Jax is right. For once. Probably won't ever happen again, so cherish it, but yes, when we tell Papa Coin what Conjure Station can do, you'll be the only thing he talks about from now until Juneteenth." This time it was his turn to nudge her with his shoulder. "I'll make sure of it."

I rolled my eyes but didn't say anything. High road and all.

Then a glint of white caught my eye. It came from under the bed, and I shouted and dove for it. Devin and Nina looked at me like I'd sprouted horns and started neighing, but I just cackled and held up the Metra card. "I found it! This is Two-Saint's. We can use it to find him."

They both crowded around as I pulled out the printed kosmogram ticket from Conjure Station and pressed it to the Metra card. I was unsure if that's what I was supposed to do, and when a few seconds passed and nothing happened, I began to wonder if it was even going to work. But immediately after that thought, gold sparks sputtered from the kosmogram, and the paper disintegrated until only the symbol remained. The Metra card began to glow as the sparks etched the circle and cross onto it.

"*Tracker spell activated,*" came a tiny voice from the air above the card. It was the same voice as the PA announcer in Conjure Station. "*Now searching for subject.*"

We looked at each other, then leaned in over the Metra card as the sparks traced the kosmogram. A summoning loading screen. Who would've thunk it? We were all nervous. I could feel my heartbeat pounding through my chest, and Nina squeezed my arm as the seconds passed. Even Devin chewed his fingernails.

Ping!

The sparks erupted in a tiny shower of light, and then the voice came back. "*Subject cannot be found. Tracker spell has been blocked. Thank you for using Conjure Station's Location service. Good-bye.*"

I stared at the card as the kosmogram faded away. "Can't be found? Does that mean he's—"

Nina shook her head. "No."

"But it said—"

Devin leaned over and grabbed the card, twirling it in his fingers as he examined it. "It said 'Tracker spell has been blocked.'"

"What's the difference?" I asked.

Nina bit her lips, and Devin frowned. Finally, Nina sighed. "It means he's probably wearing a counterspell. Wherever he is, he doesn't want to be found."

We were right back at square one. No Two-Saint. No idea what he was doing or where he had gone. There was nothing left for us to do but tell Papa Coin everything, from Conjure Station to Two-Saint's mysterious absence. I should've felt excited about that conversation, but instead, the tracker-spell failure had soured our joy.

But you know what made everything seem alright? When Nina's hand found mine and squeezed. Even though, yes, she squeezed Devin's, too. So what? I pretended he wasn't there for a second. The point was, the three of had one another's backs, and after tomorrow, we could stand up to anything.

Looking back at that evening, I wish I had been right.

CHAPTER
TWENTY-EIGHT

CLASSES PASSED BY IN A BLUR THE NEXT DAY.

I spent more time thinking about how Papa Coin would thank us after school for discovering Conjure Station than I did about my lessons. Math was about multiplying fractions, but I thought about making the summoner community whole again. Social Studies had us talking about early Chicago history, but I spent the hour looking up stops on the Gray Line and wondering what the summoners who lived there did when they were cut off from Conjure Station. Fun fact: The Oscarville stop? It's buried under a lake now in Georgia—someplace called Lake Lanier.

Even Intro to Summoning came and went. Jalen was back, and though he shot scowls at us during class, he kept to himself. Two-Saint's chair was empty, and I must've been staring at it for several minutes, because Nina nudged me. "We'll find him," she said. I nodded, but inside I didn't feel so sure.

Dr. Clayton wasn't there today—instead, a tall Korean man from the Tree of Wands was our substitute instructor, and we spent the class period talking about how our Origin of Spirits, that moment when we were first introduced to the spirit world, was in part influenced by our ancestors.

"You must understand where your powers come from," Professor Jeon said. "Your ancestors appear at your OOS, and by tracing that moment backward through the summoners in your lineage, you can discover connections and communities where you thought none existed."

After school let out, a few of us gathered beneath the giant panther gargoyle (which was pretending to be asleep to lure some sparrows closer) as we waited for our rides. A group of seventh-graders jogged by, music blasting from a speaker tucked into one of their backpacks, and Devin sighed.

"I wish we could be like them sometimes," he said.

"Ignorant?" I asked.

"Innocent," he said, kicking at me as I skipped away. "Summoning is stressful."

"Just wait until we graduate," Bull said, stomping over with Vanessa's backpack slung over one arm. "When we'll get our own missions." He clapped once, and across the street some kids ducked as if a firecracker had gone off. "So, Jax, what's your ability?" He winked and I rolled my eyes.

"Ability?" I was still thinking about his missions comment. It felt like Nina, Devin, and I were so close to completing our own mission: reuniting the summoning community. Maybe they'd throw a party for us. With finger food. Like meatballs on toothpicks.

"Yeah! You know ours, right? Nina's, Devin's, even Vanessa's helping hands."

Vanessa threw a pebble at his chest. "Don't say it like that. You make it sound like I don't do anything by myself."

Bull lifted her backpack. "Well . . . Ouch!"

"You offered and I accepted," she said with a sniff, tossing another pebble in the air.

"Helping hands?" I asked in a low voice. Didn't want reggies overhearing.

Vanessa waved the pebble beneath Bull's nose just to let him know what was waiting for him, and then shrugged. "Sometimes, when I'm struggling with something, it's like one of my aunts is behind me, helping lift whatever I'm carrying, or keeping me steady when I might fall. It's like I have all the sisters of my grandmother and great-grandmother standing with me."

"That's . . . actually really cool," Nina said.

"So, Jax?" Bull asked. "What about you?"

"He can open doors on trains," Devin broke in.

"Whoa! Wait, what?"

I glared at Devin before answering. "First of all, it was *a* train. Singular. One. And there was a giant spirit-energy-eating monster chasing it."

Bull whistled. "That's pretty cool. The monster, not the train doors. Although I'm happy if you're happy."

"What about yours?" I asked, trying to get the focus off me.

Bull looked around to make sure no one was listening, then shuffled closer. "I also have . . . a door."

"A door?"

"Yep. Since I was little. One day I was playing in the field behind my granny's house. It started to rain and I began to run, but I got lost. I was so scared, right? But . . . then this door appeared. Huge and glowing around the edges, just standing in the middle of the field. It opened a crack, and the warmest air rushed out like a summer breeze. It smelled like baking bread and soup, so I went inside."

A teacher walked by, and Bull cut himself off. Once the coast was clear, I nudged him. "And?"

"And two hours later, my parents found me on my granny's doorstep sleeping with what they thought was an old blanket covering me."

I frowned. "They *thought* it was a blanket?"

Bull nodded. "But it wasn't. It was a cloak—a patchwork cloak with four symbols on it. A sword, a spear, a stone, and a cauldron. Granny says it was the Tuatha Dé Danann that saved me."

"Who are they?" I whispered.

"Gods of the old country," he said proudly. "Apparently they've been keeping an eye on our family for centuries."

At that moment Bull's host family drove up, and he waved to us before climbing inside. Soon after that, Vanessa's mom came, and then it was just me and Devin and Nina. Devin raised an eyebrow at Nina, and she flushed. "Dad will be here," she muttered.

Just as she said that, a minivan whipped a U-turn in the street and screeched to a halt beside us, spraying everyone with slush and ice. I gawked. Powder blue with orange flowers painted on the side, purple hubcaps, and a custom license plate that read RooT, it wasn't at all what I was expecting. The passenger-side window rolled down and a deep voice called out cheerfully. "Sorry 'bout that. Didn't winterize the tires. Get in!"

I tried the door, but it was stuck, and a grunt of realization came from the driver's seat. "Gotta pull like you mean it, son. Let Petal do it."

I was about to ask who Petal was when Nina stomped past me, grumbling. "Dang door has been stuck since before I was born." She pried it open and slid it back, then climbed inside. Devin followed, then I went last. It's a good thing I did, because I stopped in my tracks in absolute shock.

"Is that … a garden?" I asked.

"Sure is," came the driver's voice. I couldn't actually see him, because there was a small bush growing out of the back of the driver's seat. "Find a seat anywhere. Just don't sit on the stinging nettle back—"

"OWWW!"

"Never mind."

As I rubbed my thigh, I stared at the actual jungle growing inside the van. No, I'm not joking. I'm not talking about pots and planters—I'm talking actual plants growing out of the seats, out of the floor, and even out of the seatbelts!

The inside of the minivan was also larger than it appeared on the outside. When I asked, Nina seemed a little embarrassed.

"Yeah, we had to expand our garden, and the neighbors were already complaining about the smell of the medicinal garlic, so Dad got some summoners to charm the inside of the van."

"Spirit realm interior design," Mr. Green said cheerfully. "Talented folks. And in return, I send them some incense for their altars every month. Who needs money when you can barter?"

"Dad..." Nina groaned.

"I'm just saying, Petal, capitalism killed the bartering star."

"Sorry," I said. "Um... who's Petal?"

Devin snickered as Nina sank into her seat, but Mr. Green jabbed a thumb back in her direction. "You're sitting next to her! I've called her that since she was little. Found her in the garden when she was one or two with a rabbit in a headlock as she tried to put calendula petals on its paw. Apparently, the critter had stepped on some broken glass somewhere. But that's not the best part of the story."

"Daaaaad!"

Mr. Green ignored her and turned around, pushing aside the bush so I could get a look at his face for the first time: a huge beard, thick glasses, and a smile so wide I was actually concerned. He cheerfully ignored oncoming traffic and gestured wildly as he spoke. "The best part is that she said her grandmother told her it would help. But her grandmother had passed away a decade earlier!"

"Dad! Car!"

The minivan jerked back and forth as we avoided certain death, and when my heart rate had returned to normal,

I glanced at Nina. "That was yours, wasn't it? Your Origin of Spirits?"

She grimaced but nodded. "Yes, though if you call me Petal, I will bury you in this van and use you for fertilizer."

I grinned and sat back, careful to avoid the nettles this time. They were all lucky—Nina, Bull, and Devin—to have relatives who'd gone through the Origin of Spirits, too, and knew what summoning was. My smile faded. Devin had his brother, Nina had her father, and Bull had his grandmother. Who did I have? I wasn't sure Uncle Moe and Gran counted, since they couldn't summon anymore. Could it be Portis Freeman? When all the chaos was over, maybe I could ask Papa Coin to help me talk to my great-great-grandfather. The two of them had known each other once; surely there was a way to connect us.

I nodded to myself. Once we stopped the feud, I'd talk to him and try to speak with my ancestors. Maybe they could help me be a better summoner. There was nowhere to go but up.

* * *

Mr. Green dropped us off down the block from the Coin barbershop and daycare. The street was still closed off due to the damage done by the shadow summoners, and even though it had snowed overnight, you could still see the evidence of the attack. Houses had scorch marks on their porches, cars were dented and scraped, and more than a few lampposts had wicked gashes in the metal.

"Be careful, Petal," Mr. Green warned. "Go straight to your

grandfather and text me when you get there. I gotta drop this stomach tea over at Mrs. Allen's house before she comes looking for me. Last time I was five minutes late, I found her in the grocery store in her nightgown, confused and alone. Sure you don't wanna do this a little later so I can come with you?"

Nina was out of the car before he could even finish the question. "It's cool, Dad, I'll see you at home."

He chuckled as Devin scooted out, careful to avoid smearing dirt on his pants. I didn't mind the dirt so much. The minivan smelled like the farmer's market back in Raleigh, the one Dad and Mom and I used to go to every Sunday to get greens and fruit. It smelled like comfort, like home.

"Thanks for the ride, Mr. Green," I called as he waved and drove off. Then I smiled at Nina. "I like him."

She rolled her eyes at me. "He tells that bunny story to whoever will listen."

"It's a good story, Pet— Oof!"

Devin turned around and shushed both of us. He'd been standing still, head cocked, examining the neighborhood for the last minute or so. Now he motioned for us to be quiet. "*Shh!* Something's wrong."

Instantly Nina and I were at his side. "Shadow summoners?" I whispered.

"Avarice spirits? The Veiled Lady?" Nina asked.

Devin shook his head. "No...it's...I can't explain it. Come on."

As we walked down the block toward Papa Coin's alley garden, I started to get the same feeling as Devin. But it wasn't until I'd accidentally kicked a fire extinguisher left on the curb that I realized what was wrong.

"It's too quiet," I said, watching the red canister roll to a stop near a car's snow-crusted tire. "Where are all the birds, the traffic, the people yelling and laughing at each other? It's like everyone's gone."

"Maybe Papa Coin put a curfew in place," Nina said. "I heard they had to do that the last time a feud broke out."

"Maybe..." Devin said, but he didn't sound convinced.

We kept our eyes peeled for anything strange, but by the time we reached the barbershop we still hadn't seen anybody else on the streets. Just to be sure, I peeked into the daycare next door, but still nothing. No kids, no stressed-out teachers chasing them; only dark, empty rooms with toys still scattered on the floor.

"I don't like this," Devin said. He had his cards out, probably seconds away from summoning a brogre.

"Maybe they went on a field trip," I suggested, still staring back at the daycare.

"Someone's always here," he muttered. "Always. Let's go."

He led us into the barbershop—and instead of heading to the rear entrance, he took us to the wall opposite the barber chairs and stopped in front of a large shelf lined with shampoos, oils, and conditioners. He took five cards from his deck, muttered under his breath, then spread them in a fan cluster and pressed them against the side of the middle shelf. He stood back as several bottles of conditioner began to glow with purplish light in rapid succession, as if someone had traced a pattern on them.

"Follow me," Devin said. He pushed on the glowing bottles, and they fell away like curtains.

"Where does this go?" Nina asked.

"Papa Coin's office."

Nina made a face but didn't say anything, and I was pretty sure she was thinking the same thing I was: another family secret Devin knew and Nina didn't.

I pushed through the shelf (weird, weird, weird) and found myself standing in a small, dusty room. There was another workbench in here, and at one point it must have held supplies: tools, journals, and pens. I say *at one point* because it didn't have them now—not intact, at least. The place had been searched and turned inside out.

"Devin, I don't like this," Nina said.

"Me neither," he agreed. "I'm calling Dre." He pulled out his phone and punched a number.

A phone chimed nearby.

Devin looked at Nina, then at me. Almost simultaneously, the three of us sprinted to the far side of the little room. Devin did his five-card spread, and another door appeared in the wall. We shoved through together . . . and skidded to a stop.

We were back in Papa Coin's alley. The hanging vines lay in shreds on the ground. Glass from shattered jars crunched underfoot. The workbench had been smashed to pieces and now fed a small fire burning in the corner. The pots and planters were overturned, dirt spilling out and plants destroyed, the smell of herbs and flowers replaced by smoke and the coppery metallic aroma of blood.

And in the center of it all was the giant wooden chair, polished and gleaming in the firelight. A Black woman in gold heels and a patterned gray pantsuit with gold trim sat sprawled across it like a panther lounging on the branch of a tree. Her hair was done up in twists, just starting to turn silver, the tips capped with gold leaf. Green eyeliner arched out like wings from the corner of her eyes, giving her the appearance of a jeweled bird of prey.

From the way she stared at us, we were about to become her next meal.

Until her eyes landed on Nina, and her gaze softened. And when I glanced at Nina, shock had twisted her face. Devin's, too. They knew her. It wasn't until Nina took a shaky step forward, then a second, that I made the connection.

"Mama," she whispered.

"Hey, baby," the woman said, a small smile creasing her face. "I'm back." Then she lifted Dre's phone from her lap, followed by Papa Coin's walking stick, and tossed them to the floor. She stood, her movements smooth and graceful, and stepped down into the firelight. Though she spoke to Nina, her eyes met mine as she continued. "We need to talk."

CHAPTER
TWENTY-NINE

THE BURNING WORKBENCH CRACKLED, SPITTING bright orange sparks into the air. The afternoon sky was fading from blue to purplish orange as evening approached. The air chilled my breath, but it wasn't the temperature that kept me frozen where I stood.

The woman in gray and gold studied each of us in turn. As she did, I observed as much as I could. In the shadows I could now make out four other figures standing in pairs on either side of the wooden chair: a hulking bald man, an older woman with a cane, a teen boy in an oversized hoodie, and a stocky girl with pigtail braids that went down to her waist.

No, there were five. A tall man stood in the background. The figures were all dressed in some variation of gray and gold and seemed like they were ready for action—like, one wrong move and they'd jump me—so I watched them all as closely as possible.

"Mama?" Nina whispered again. "What are you doing here?"

"Auntie Naomi? What happened?" Devin asked at the same time.

The leader's smile, so warm and welcoming when she looked at Nina, faded as she turned toward Devin. She appraised him, judged him, and dismissed him with a single sweep of her eyes. She considered me next, and while her expression wasn't what I'd call welcoming, it wasn't hostile, at least. But she didn't speak to me, either. I could practically feel the tension and anger knotting in Devin's frame. I eased closer to him, in case . . . well, I didn't know. Just in case.

Naomi (I should probably call her Miss Naomi, or the ancestors would haunt me forever) only talked to Nina. "Nina Bean." Her voice was low and soothing, and I could see Nina's eyes glistening. This was really her mother? The person she'd been trying to reach for all this time? "I've missed you so, so much, baby."

"Why are you here?" Nina asked again, taking another step forward. Cautiously. Like this was a dream that could, at any moment, burst like the flimsiest bubble.

"Oh, baby, I had to come back. Things are happening, and I need to be here. With family."

"With me?"

"Yes, baby, with you."

The two of them were right in front of each other. Nina slowly reached out, and her mother dropped to her knees and swept her daughter into a giant hug. Nina's shoulders were shaking, maybe from laughing or crying or both, and Naomi squeezed her tight.

"Oh my god," said Nina. "I . . . I called you. So many times. And left messages. And mailed you notes and report cards . . . Was it the right address? Did you move? Did you ever get the Mother's Day card I sent you?" She was babbling, and Miss Naomi laughed and just hugged her tight.

"I'm here now," I heard her whisper. "And I'm never leaving again."

Devin stirred next to me at that comment. "Where's Granddad?" he asked. He moved forward, too, but a low grumble made him pause, and I realized it had come from one of Miss Naomi's companions (bodyguards?)—the giant bald man in a cut-off muscle shirt and jogging pants.

Muscle Man shifted his weight and folded his arms across his massive chest, and Miss Naomi shot him a look. Then she glanced back at Devin. "Nephew," she said, her voice cool.

"And where's Dre?" Devin continued. "Where's my brother?"

Miss Naomi stood but kept her arms around Nina, who was looking back and forth between her cousin and her mother. "Your brother's around somewhere," she said vaguely. "Your grandfather"—not *Dad* or *Daddy* or even *Papa Coin*, I noticed—"is getting treatment right now. He's not well. Hasn't been for a long time."

Devin balled his hands into fists. "You hurt him?"

"Of course not," Miss Naomi scoffed. "He's still my father.

Respect your elders and all that nonsense. No, he overextended himself. He thinks he's younger than he is, and after fighting off all those avarice spirits . . . Well, let's just say he wasn't himself by the time we arrived. And now I've decided that he's going to take the time he needs to get better. As long as it takes."

"*You* decided?" I asked, speaking for the first time.

Everyone's eyes turned toward me, and I flinched. Miss Naomi peered at me thoughtfully. "Yes, Jackson Freeman, *I* decided."

"You know who I am?"

"Of course I do. As the temporary head of the Tree of Coins, it is my responsibility to know all the new summoners in our territory." She narrowed her eyes, and once again I could feel her examining me closely. "Especially one hanging around my daughter."

"Wait," Devin interrupted. "Head of the tree? That's Granddad's job!"

"And, as I said, he is taking a temporary leave of absence," Miss Naomi snapped.

"But Dre is the heir, so—"

"Your brother left," she said, her tone harsh and angry now. "Ran away. Fled like a coward."

"You're lying," Devin whispered.

"Some heir. Not fit to rule, put into the position because your grandfather wanted a man to be head of the tree. Not the most talented. Not the most qualified. Not me, his oldest child, not even after your father died. No, never Naomi. Just like he brushed my Nina aside for you, a lesser summoner."

"Shut up," Devin said, his voice quiet.

Nina stirred by her mother's side. "Mom—" she began, but Miss Naomi stepped in front of her, cutting her off.

"Nina could be great—greater than me. But did your grandfather give her the time of day? Did he help her like he helped you, coached you? No. And look at the state of the tree now." Miss Naomi snorted. "A shadow of its former glory. Harassed by outsiders, losing heirlooms to thieves. Everyone's laughing at us."

"Us?" Devin snarled. "Where were you? You ran away and left your own daught—"

It happened in an instant. Miss Naomi's fingers barely moved, and the giant bald man lunged forward. There was a flash of light, like a mini explosion went off between his hands, and Devin reeled backward, stunned. The man reached for him . . .

But I caught Devin first, dragging him back to prop him against a wall.

"You . . . will . . . WATCH YOUR MOUTH!" Miss Naomi shouted. She stalked closer, snatching something off the ground as she approached us. It took me a couple of seconds to recognize that the object was a broom—the same one I'd seen Dre use when he was battling the shadow summoners. I was glad Devin was still too groggy to make that connection.

What had happened to Andre? I hoped he was okay.

The bald giant, who had moved like a panther moments ago, lumbered back to his position by the chair like a bear, silent and looming. The other four figures hadn't even moved, and my mind raced through worst-case scenarios about what they were capable of. Were they Naomi's super soldiers? Super summoners?

"I left," Miss Naomi continued, squeezing her words through gritted teeth, "because your grandfather did to me what he's been doing to Nina. He ignored me, so I taught myself. Hustled power. Conned spirits. Learned. Stole. Ran. I ran and ran. Not away, though. *Toward* power. I wanted it, needed it, but was denied it. I deserved it, just like Nina does, and anyone else who has been denied an heirloom because they aren't the 'right type' of summoner. We deserve it!"

Devin stirred, his glazed expression sharpening into something dangerous. Something foolish. I was gonna try to calm him down, maybe figure out a way for us to get out of there, when Big Baldy folded his arms again. He'd surprised me the last time he attacked, so I was keeping a close eye on him. Which was how I noticed the necklace tucked beneath his shirt.

Small white sparks fizzled around it.

I jerked my eyes away. Miss Naomi was still snapping at Devin, and I pretended to watch her for a moment. When I risked another glance over at the chair, Big Baldy was staring directly at me.

I waved weakly, then turned to one of the other underlings, the older woman with short white hair and a cane. She reminded me of an owl studying a mouse as she watched me, but I was focused on what was in her hands. When she shifted her grip on the walking stick, I saw a carving underneath. Sparks drifted up from it before she quickly replaced her hand.

My breath caught in my throat. Now I knew I wasn't imagining things. The cane, the necklace, and I bet . . . yep. There, on the hoodie of the third goon, was a large ornamental pin in the shape of a skull.

Realization clicked, and my mouth went dry. Miss Naomi and her gang hadn't come to deal with the shadow summoners and rescue her father. . . .

"You were stealing heirlooms!" I blurted out. "Are *you* the shadow summoners?"

Miss Naomi glared at me, but if I was right, we were in more danger than ever before. I couldn't tell them about Conjure Station—I wanted to stop a war, not give one side a weapon to make it even worse.

"What?!" Nina and Devin asked at the same time. Nina looked annoyed, but Devin seemed unsure.

"Think about it," I said. "The Coins are attacked, and the person with the biggest grudge against your grandfather suddenly appears to 'help out'? I don't buy it."

"You have no idea what you're talking about, child," Miss Naomi snapped.

But it made sense, didn't it? Who else would try to attack Papa Coin, a powerful summoner? Who knew his weaknesses and defenses as well as his own daughter? Who—

"The shadow summoners got past the wards . . ." Devin broke in.

Everyone paused. "Devin?" Nina finally said.

"The family wards. No one outside of us should know how to get past them. And yet someone did."

"And you think *I* did it," Miss Naomi said, her tone indicating it wasn't a question but quite possibly the most ridiculous thing she'd ever heard.

"I think you know how to disable the wards."

"Why would your grandfather teach me that and nothing else?" Miss Naomi's tone was light, but her eyes watched Devin like a hawk did a mouse, waiting for the right opportunity.

To his credit, Devin was equally focused. His hands were at his sides, and his fingers twitched as if eager to produce his brogres. "You just said you taught yourself everything," he pressed. "And conned and stole."

Miss Naomi took a step toward us. "I'm through being interrogated by a child."

"Child?"

"Devin," Nina said, inserting herself between us and Miss Naomi. "My mother wouldn't attack her own father."

"How do you know?" Devin said, his eyes blazing. "She just said she hated how he treated her."

"Because *I* wouldn't attack him, and I hate how he treats me!" Nina shouted.

Devin snapped his mouth shut. Nina took a second to inhale and exhale, then stepped toward her cousin and placed a hand on his shoulder. She whispered something, and though his face was still tight with anger, Devin nodded.

The tension in the alley seemed to lessen. Big Baldy unfolded his arms. Pigtails chewed her gum and blew a bubble. Beak Nose and the old woman were muttering to each other. I kept a close eye on them and those heirlooms.

"Wait," I said loudly. "Where's the other guy?"

Everyone turned to me as I peered around frantically.

"What are you doing?" Nina asked.

I continued to scan the area as I talked. "There was a fifth person here when we came. Didn't you see them? I couldn't get a good look in the dark, but they were here. A tall guy?"

Miss Naomi laughed. "And now what? You're going to accuse me of abduction? Clearly, you've stayed up past your bedtimes, and I've spent too much time humoring you. You three go home and do your homework. I have actual, serious matters to deal with."

"You saw him, right?" I asked Nina.

"Jax...I didn't see anyone else," she answered.

"Devin?" I said, whipping around to look at him.

But he shook his head.

This was ridiculous! I'd seen a man, I was positive. Well, maybe not *seen*, because he was in the shadows, but I'd noticed someone. My eyes weren't playing tricks on me...were they? Hadn't he been standing right behind...the old woman?

I turned to look at the woman with the cane and found her staring right back at me. Her eyes narrowed into a shrewd expression that I couldn't read but that didn't reassure me, and now every nerve in my body was tingling. Something was off. Either I was starting to lose my mind or...

Or Miss Naomi was lying.

Suddenly I wanted to get back to the Freeman House. There were way too many things in this world I couldn't control, and being surrounded by unfriendly-at-best summoners wasn't helping.

"Okay, you know what?" I said. "Maybe I'm just tired and seeing things. It's been a long day, I haven't eaten in hours, and I'm cold. I'm going to head on home. Nice to meet everyone. I hope I never see you all again."

Miss Naomi's eyes narrowed, the same way Nina's did whenever I said something suspicious, as I turned and—shoving my hands into my coat pockets—began walking to the alley entrance. I was almost at the back door of the barbershop, which was sagging off its hinges and covered in scorch marks, when Beak Nose slid in front of me.

"Not so fast, Jackson," Miss Naomi said behind me.

I turned to find her sauntering up while the rest of her squad spread out on either side so that I was surrounded. One of her hands gripped Nina's wrist.

"You know," she said, studying the fingernails on her free hand, "I will give you this: you are *interesting*. When you are forced to learn how to summon on your own, you have to figure out pretty quickly who has power and who doesn't. Who will give you what you want, and who you have to take it from. Who is *interesting*"—she raised her eyes to meet mine—"and who is hiding something."

"Mom," Nina said, "let him go. He's useless."

I didn't know whether to be grateful or insulted.

"Oh, honey, I'm disappointed in you," Miss Naomi said. "Of course he's useless. But even trash can be recycled, so better to be safe than sorry."

Trash?

"It's just—"

"Enough!" Her tone was sharp, and Nina fell silent. Miss Naomi cupped her daughter's cheek, but she was looking at me. "It occurs to me that one stranger has been conveniently around every time something important has happened. Attacks on my family? Spirits where they shouldn't be? A surge of power in the suburbs of Chicago? Nooo, there's more to the story here. And since coincidences are just plots we haven't discovered yet, I think he should stick around until I'm certain he isn't a threat. What do you say, Jackson?"

"I wish, but I really should be going," I said. "I have a curfew."

A smile slid across Miss Naomi's face. "Oh, Jackson," she said, stepping back as her goon squad moved closer. "I knew you'd make this fun."

She nodded at Big Baldy, and he stepped in front of her, blocking her from my view. As she continued like a sports announcer doing color commentary, his fingernails started to smolder. "You've already seen Cinder in action. When he's around, who needs a heater?"

Sure enough, the snow under Cinder's feet was already melting into slush. He lunged forward, and I had no room to run. As Cinder's fingers swiped at my chest, I flickered to the opposite wall, putting a pile of overturned planters between me and the brute. My lungs were on fire, and when I breathed it felt like someone was dragging coals across my skin.

Miss Naomi laughed in delight. "Brilliant! Oh, I knew you

were special. My daughter wouldn't choose just any old boy to hang out with. She must like you!"

Like. *Like?* Before that little nugget could sink in, something wound around my ankles and yanked, and suddenly I was hanging upside down in the air, my fingertips grazing the ground. I spun slowly to end up looking at the girl with the pigtails, and she winked at me.

"Oooh, but it looks like Mona might have snared her man first!" Miss Naomi said.

One of Mona's pigtail braids had come undone and was now wrapped around my legs like a snake. A copper heirloom shaped like a hairpin blazed in front of her, sparks sputtering into the evening. I struggled to kick free, but I was tied up tight.

When my fingers grazed the snow-covered ground again, I got an idea. I scooped up a pebble-filled slushball and hurled it at Mona's face. She shrieked and pawed at her eyes, dropping and freeing me in the process. I tried to flicker to the wall but ended up crashing into a charred plank behind the burning workbench. I dragged myself farther back, wheezing from the pain and effort.

On the other side of the alley, Devin had summoned his brogres and was attacking Cinder, but they couldn't get around the bald man's lightning-fast counters. As Mona recovered, the older woman with the cane stomped her foot, darkness spreading from her like ink in water as a purple-and-black heirloom bloomed in front of her. The beak-nosed boy in the hoodie summoned a silver skull as his heirloom, which elongated and twisted until it was a sword with a skull on the cross guard.

He slashed the air, and I retreated as he walked forward. The flames on the workbench flickered, then began to shrink with each step he took, leaping to the tip of his sword and wrapping around the blade.

"But you can't leave yet, Jackson," said Miss Naomi. "You haven't met my newest apprentice, Ty, a champion sword fighter, nationally ranked. Nor have you seen my mentor in action. Old Marie taught me everything she knew, passed the torch to me. The two of them have given me so much...."

Old Marie lifted her cane and slammed it into the ground. Once. Twice. Three times... And the flames disappeared, casting the alley into shadow, though I could still make out a few details.

When Miss Naomi spoke again, she sounded...different. Harsher. More menacing.

"...including their obedience. Hopefully my Nina will still like you when this is done, Jackson."

Ty lifted his sword, and despair curled tight around my chest as flames whirled down the blade. Then I heard a thud and Devin grunting in pain. I looked up just in time to see Cinder batting aside the brogres—*Three? Why were there three brogres?*—and flinging the boy in Miss Naomi's direction. Devin skidded to a stop in front of her as his summoned muscle disappeared. I swallowed a lump of fear and tried not to panic. We were surrounded. I could try to flicker over the alley wall, but even if I could make it (and from Mona's stare and the lashing copper coils in her hair, I seriously doubted it), that would mean leaving Devin behind. Nina would *probably* be okay, but Devin? Was Miss Naomi this determined to squash any threat to her power that she would hurt her own nephew? He was family!

I hesitated. Should I try? Go get some help? I could flicker to the tracks a few blocks away and...

"ENOUGH!" Nina shouted.

Everyone turned toward her in surprise. "Nina Bean," Miss Naomi warned, but Nina shook her head.

"This is ridiculous," she said. "I do NOT like Jax. Why would you say that I do? Ew!"

Nobody spoke. I think we were all stunned. Which was fair.

"Now," I said, the words wheezing out of my throat, "you don't have to—"

"His clothes don't match," she continued, marching over to me.

"I lost my duffels..." I tried to explain.

"He smells like meatballs."

"I mean, they're really good, and I had half a sandwich in my coat...."

"And he isn't even that cute!"

"Now, that's... kinda mean, don't you think?"

By this time Nina had stomped all the way over to me, eyes blazing, hands on her hips, shouting for everyone in the world to hear what she thought of Jax Freeman. I mean, even Miss Naomi's gang were wincing like they didn't want to be me.

Miss Naomi sighed. "Nina Bean, now isn't the—"

"I'm sorry, Mom, but I'm tired of this. Like, the only reason I'm here is because I like a boy. *This* boy. Not because I might want to develop my own power. It's not like I wanted to get stronger so I could find out where my mom, the person I cared about most in the world, had disappeared to. No. It's about how to impress a *boy*. Because that's all a girl with magic should want to do. Well, I'm SICK OF IT!"

Nina was shouting now, and everyone was riveted by her words.

So riveted, in fact, that they didn't see that when she stopped right in front of me, she'd summoned her heirloom. Or that she winked.

"I'll take care of him *myself*," she said, shoving me aside.

"Hey!" I looked over to see her pull out glittering black repel powder and hurl it . . .

. . . straight at Ty, who was nearly in range with his sword.

Oh.

I finally got it.

I ducked out of the way as the powder hit the boy like a linebacker, sending him squawking and tumbling to the alley floor. I sprinted away, and Nina chased me, yelling insults all the way. Did I conveniently run straight toward Miss Naomi's squad? Maybe. Did repel powder send them all tumbling backward? Perhaps. Was Nina doing it on purpose? Go ask somebody else, because I'm not telling.

"Get back here!" Nina ordered me.

Cinder grunted and staggered into a pile of debris.

"Stop running!"

"Watch it!" Mona shouted as she was blasted back into Old Marie.

I pivoted, swerved, and dashed all around the alley, until I finally made a beeline for Devin. He'd staggered to his feet, only to grunt in surprise when I shoulder-charged him, picked him up like he was a sack of potatoes, and flickered up to the top of a wall.

A train horn sounded in the distance. When I glanced down, the scene below was mayhem. Miss Naomi was marching toward Nina, who was stomping her feet and trying to hurl repel powder up at me, but somehow, conveniently, it only blasted the others who were chasing me.

"You'd better not let me catch you, Jax Freeman!" Nina shouted. "If you *ever* come back around here again, you'll be sorry. Do you understand? Leave me alone!"

I swallowed a reply and just nodded. Then, before Miss Naomi could gather her troops again, I summoned my last bit of energy and flickered off the alley wall and down to the street below, Devin still over my shoulder.

Leave me alone!

I understood all right. Nina was telling me not to come back for her. And I understood why. She'd finally been reunited with her mom. But that didn't mean I didn't feel guilty about leaving her behind.

I could hear Miss Naomi rallying everyone and coming after us. We needed to put some distance between us and them, but I was tired. So, so tired. My feet felt like cement blocks, my lungs were burning, and Devin was starting to weigh a ton. I'd only stumbled maybe half a block before I had to put him down. "Almost there," I said with a grunt. Where, I didn't know, but maybe I could speak it into existence. "Almost there."

It was only then that I realized Devin had passed out on my shoulder from the injuries he had suffered at Cinder's hands.

"There they are!" Mona shouted from behind us.

Pain and fatigue took turns swamping me in waves. The burning feeling had spread from my chest up to my throat and down to my stomach, like I was wearing a turtleneck of fire. It was hard to speak. Harder to move, but I had to... I had to...

A train horn sounded again. It was closer this time. Like down-the-street closer, which was weird, because as far as I knew—and I *did* know, somehow—no train was scheduled to arrive at the nearest Metra station right now. And yet, I believed the sound was real, and... for me. Sure enough, a set of railroad tracks appeared a few yards away.

Stories say there was a train, Papa Coin had said.

I picked up Devin again, groaning, and put one foot in front of the other.

He was a porter, a transporter, an escort in dangerous times, Madame Helene had said.

Just one more step. Then another step. Then another. Until the tracks were under my feet and I could feel them rumbling, even though I could see for a mile in either direction and no trains were in sight. I was in the right place. It was the right time. I just had to do the right thing.

Portis left me in charge of watching over the Shriek until it finds a new summoner, Auntie Statue had said.

Finds a new summoner.

I lifted my tired hands and imitated what I'd seen Nina and Devin and the other summoners do, steepling my fingers in front of my chest, like I was focusing energy in front of my heart. It hurt, and I was tired, but it was the only thing I could do. I gritted my teeth. My fingers were trembling. Even though I'd never done it before, urgency and need gave me the confidence to try. Slowly—*too slowly!*—a neon-blue glow appeared in front of me. And within it, a rectangular shape. A piece of paper...no, an old-fashioned train ticket. It grew and grew, and I could *feel* power radiating from it.

"Come on," I said, pleading. "Shriek. SHRIEK!"

Blue sparks erupted from the glowing ticket, just as my vision started to go dark, like curtains closing over my eyes. I stepped forward, Devin on my back, right into the path of a roaring locomotive, the sound of a train's whistle echoing in the night, and I passed out.

CHICAGO DEFENDER, VOLUME C, ISSUE 01, FEBRUARY 2005

The Centennial Celebration

All year, we at the Chicago Defender will be celebrating one hundred years of carrying all the news impacting Black Chicagoans. With historic articles, interviews with people behind the scenes

VIDEOS ON THE INTERNET?

Rumors swirl about a new video-sharing platform soon to launch over the World Wide Web. YouTube, as it's called, is set

10 RESOLUTIONS TO KEEP DURING THE NEW YEAR

With January firmly underway, the editors at ATTENTION, SUMMONERS: IF YOU ARE READING THIS, ALL CLEROMANCERS ARE NEEDED AT ONCE AT THEIR FAMILY ALTARS. AGAIN, ALL CLEROMANCERS ARE NEEDED AT ONCE AT THEIR FAMILY ALTARS. DIVINATION OF STORM FORECASTS FOR THE YEAR HAVE TO BE CONFIRMED AS SOON AS POSSIBLE. YOUR ANCESTORS THANK YOU. he Defender compiled their top resolutions for the new year and present

PART
FOUR

CHAPTER
THIRTY

WE WERE RACING THROUGH THE NIGHT. SICK BABIES.
Tired kids. Scared adults. All of us, in the middle of the night, run-
ning from the flames. Running from the past, what lay behind
us, what we'd had to do. I was tired. So tired. Hurting. Crying.
Collapsed on the ground as the others ran on. I wanted to sleep.
Wanted to rest. Wanted to stop... running...

"Get UP, Freeman. The spirits aren't done with you yet!"

* * *

I jerked upright with a gasp. I was on the floor of a train car,
covered in sweat and feeling like the engine had run over me,
backed up, and run over me again before I'd climbed aboard.
But I *had* made it aboard. I'd summoned the Shriek. The Shriek!
A train! I collapsed back to the floor and started laughing.

Nobody was going to be able to tell me anything from now on. *Oh, you summoned claws, Jalen? Let me back up so I can summon a TRAIN! Just wait until Nina and Devin . . .*

Nina.

Devin.

I lurched up and looked around. We were in the rootwork garden aboard the Shriek. I recognized the inside of the train car, and the planters and pots taking the place of benches and seats. The smells of drying herbs and fresh flowers should've brought me the same comfort they had the last time I was here. But all I could see was a body lying on a workbench.

"Devin!" I cried, stumbling to my feet as the train swayed beneath me. The car was brightly lit by the grow lamps mounted on the ceiling, and I could see how gray and still the boy was. I grimaced as I limped over to him, then grabbed his wrist and tried to see if there was a pulse, the way I'd seen in the movies. Nothing. I was on the verge of full-blown tears when I felt, more than saw, his chest rise and fall.

"Oh man," I said, cuffing the tears out of my eyes. "You absolute loser. Don't scare me like that!" He was still unconscious, but he was alive. We were alive.

A bone-rattling roar stabbed my ears. I winced and covered them until it was over. Then I peeked out of a window, my breath echoing in my ears and my chest pounding. The Gringemaw was still behind the train. The behemoth was even closer than before, and, like it could sense me (could it?), its many faces turned toward me and screeched again. I had to figure out where we were and get us someplace safe, and fast.

"Stay here," I said to Devin, as if he would get up and walk away. "I'll be back."

I limped forward through the train, slam door after slam door, until I entered the observation car. I stopped, confused. The gray clouds still raced by the window, but every so often something would pop through, like a skyscraper. Except they weren't all skyscrapers. They were various recognizable landmarks from different cities.... They'd appear suddenly and then disappear, like someone was changing the channel on the largest TV in the universe.

Bzzt. There was the Willis Tower.

Bzzt. There was the St. Louis Gateway Arch.

Bzzt. There was the Golden Gate Bridge.

What was going on?

The PA system crackled to life. *"Next stop: South Loop. Calumet. Naperville."*

I looked around, trying to find a map. There was a digital one on the wall, but it was glitching along with the view and the PA system. The little red sticker dude wearing a shirt that said YOU ARE HERE shrugged like it wasn't his problem.

"Next stop: Gary. Detroit. Flint."

"Wait a minute," I said as the map flickered and changed. "That's not in Chicago anymore. That's not even Illinois! I wasn't *that* bad in geography class."

The PA crackled as if to spite me. *"Next stop: Freetown. Durham. Saint Helena Island."*

I threw my hands up as the map changed yet again. "Oh, come on!"

The little sticker dude threw his hands up, too, and stomped away. I wanted to do the same thing, but I could barely walk, let alone stomp. It felt like my ribs shifted with every step. Devin needed help, and I wasn't too stubborn to realize that I also could use a doctor, and quick.

The lights dimmed.

A chill passed through me.

A breeze brushed my face.

Someone was here. No. More than one person was here. In the observation car with me. I scooted back against the far wall and hid behind the spiral staircase leading to the second floor, waiting and watching. Who was it? Madame Helene? Or Miss Naomi and her team? Had they followed us?

The lights flickered again. Then once more I heard... Were those footsteps?

"Boy, if you don't get your big head out my way..."

I jumped, ready to apologize, ready to beg for forgiveness and my life if necessary... only to stop and stare as the lights came back on.

A group of people stood in the middle of the train car. Men and women wearing overalls, coveralls, and steel-toed boots. They carried sledgehammers over their shoulders and had wrenches tucked in tool belts around their waists. Grease stained their clothes, their hands, and their faces. Faces that were dark, faces that were pale, and faces that were every shade in between.

Two of them, a man and a woman, jostled each other as

they moved through the crowd. The man pretended to shrink away in fear.

"Girl, I know you ain't talking about *my* head." The man elbowed a few others. "Ay, ay, y'all, listen, listen up. They said Turtle here has a head so big, if you put coal under her pillow at night, in the morning you get a diamond. Ol' heavy-headed-looking face."

The others laughed and fell out while the woman, Turtle, chuckled and shook her head in disappointment. "Now, Jock, come on now. Y'all hear what they say about Jock?"

"What'd they say?" the crowd yelled back.

"They say Jock's forehead's so big, you can surprise him in the morning and his eyebrows will still be traveling up his face in the afternoon! Ol' boiled-bean-looking face."

"Ol' wide-head-looking face."

"Ol' sprouted-potato-looking face."

"Face-built-for-radio-looking face."

I couldn't help it—I laughed at the last comment.

All at once, the conversation stopped, and everyone turned to look at me. The man called Jock, a skinny, dark-skinned man a few years younger than Uncle Moe, put one hand on his hip and strolled closer.

"Now I know you ain't laughing," he said. He put one foot on the stairs and rested his elbow on his knee as he peered at me. "You laughing? You?"

I flinched and waited for it. I'd already heard plenty of jokes about me. The big jokes. The fat jokes. The two-seat jokes, the eating-for-two-people jokes. Marcus used to rag on me like that. It got old, but after a while I realized he was just look-ing for me to react. If I got mad, he'd say he was joking and to lighten up, so I didn't get mad. If I didn't do anything, he just got bored. So I did the same thing here.

"Sorry," I said.

Jock snorted. "Don't be sorry, be better."

I frowned. Where had I heard that phrase before? But I didn't get a lot of time to think about it because Jock was ges-turing at me to join the crowd in the middle of the observa-tion car.

"It's your fault we're out here," he said. "You called us."

"I did?" I looked around, then my eyes went wide. I reached out slowly...and slapped Jock's shoulder.

He whipped around. "Now what'd you do that for?"

"Sorry!" I said. "I thought you were figments, or spirits, or ancestors, and that you weren't real."

"You go around slapping figments?"

"No! I thought my hand would go through you!"

"That don't make it right!"

Turtle, trying to hold back her laughter, interrupted. "Jock, I think the boy has been through some drama. Look at him! I don't know how he got aboard with them injuries."

Jock's frown disappeared, and he stepped back to get a good look at me. A low whistle emerged as he shook his head. "Turtle, I think you're right. Say, what's your name?"

"Jax," I said. "Jax Freeman."

"Well, Jax, you're a right mess, and you stepped into some-thing worse, by the looks of it. Here, take a swig of this." He handed me a dusty jug of something. "It'll put you right as rain on a Sunday evening."

"What is it?" I asked, lifting the bottle to peer inside, before taking a swig.

"Onion juice."

I coughed so hard I was sure I turned inside out. Everyone around me burst into laughter as I spluttered. "Onion juice? That is the nastiest thing I've ever tasted!"

"But I betchya feel a little better, don't you?"

I raised my hand to complain, then paused. My aches and pains weren't completely gone, but they weren't as sharp, either. But why did that stuff have to taste so foul? Like I'd licked the underside of a bus seat.

Jock took my silence as proof and nodded smugly. "Onion juice is onion-defeated. Get it? Onion-defeated . . . *un*defeated . . . Ahh, you'll get it in a little while. In the meantime, we'd better get on the job, 'cause we wouldn't have been called here if there wasn't something that needed fixing."

I shook my head. "But I didn't call you."

Turtle threw an arm around Jock, and when he leaned in for the side hug he thought was coming, she put him in a head-lock and squeezed. "You don't have to—the Gray Line calls us when a train goes wonky. Never thought it'd be the Shriek. Then again"—Turtle eyed me up and down—"I seem to remember Portis nearly running over a herd of cattle one of the first times he summoned it."

"I need a vacation," I said, rubbing my forehead in confusion.

"You and me both," Jock said, finally pulling himself out of the headlock. "But first we got business to take care of. Boy don't even know what he's doing. It's a wonder we're not in space right now. Lucky we just off the track."

"I summoned the Shriek off the tracks? How?" I asked.

"More like hopping tracks," Jock said. "Skipping around."

"Flapped up the rails," Turtle said.

"Out of alignment."

"Wiggling loose."

"Skedaddle rattlin'."

I stared at the two of them. "That last one isn't a thing, is it?"

Jock winked at me. "Nope. But it's still relevant. The point is, the Shriek is off the Gray Line, and we're going to get her back on."

"We are?"

"Yep! Well, not you. You and your friend back there need some doctorin' help, but fortunately for y'all, we know just where to take you, don't we?"

"Fortunately?" someone shouted. "More like *un*fortunately."

"Hope you can pay," said someone else.

"If not, you gonna work, work, work, work, work, work so much Rihanna gonna owe you royalties."

I looked out the window. "Are you going to be safe out there on the Shriek with the Gringemaw following us?"

Everyone grew still, as if I'd said the worst thing ever. "Can't let fear stop us from doing what needs to be done, now can we?" said Jock. "Otherwise, the world would stop."

"Can you at least get the monster off the tracks?" I asked.

But Turtle shook her head. "Don't you think we tried?"

"Lost a few good ones the last time," Jock added. "Can't risk it again. But that don't mean we can't make sure this train outruns it. You summon; we fix trains, big guy. That's what we were born to do. Y'all follow the tracks; the tracks follow us. Nobody hits harder or shouts louder, you hear me? We don't have veins; we got steel for bones and grease for blood, you feel me?" Jock whooped, swinging his hammer in the air, and the others joined in until the train car was filled with noise and energy.

When Turtle and Jock lifted their hammer and wrench high and the others followed suit, I had the weirdest sense of déjà vu. Like I'd seen this exact image before.

And that's when it hit me—I had. In Union Station, in the mural on the wall.

"You're Gandy Dancers!" I said, remembering what the little placard next to the mural had said. Gandy Dancers were railroad workers back in the day who laid tracks and also *fixed and repaired them.*

"THE Gandy Dancers," Turtle corrected. "And we got a job to do. Move them hammers, y'all. Don't make Mama Turtle come snappin' behind you!"

In a whirl of energy, the group of workers stormed out of the front of the train car like paratroopers diving out of a plane. I limped as fast as I could to the upper deck of the observation car and pressed my face against the window, but I couldn't see anything. I ran back downstairs, only to skid to a stop when the map display flickered and winked off. When it came back on, it showed a bird's-eye view of the front of the Shriek, as if someone were filming with a drone. My jaw dropped to the floor as I watched the Gandy Dancers in action.

Jock clung to the front of the Shriek with only his legs, both wrapped around an opening in the cowcatcher, the little plow-like attachment at the front of the locomotive. He swung the hammer in a figure-eight pattern. To his right, Turtle had both hands outstretched, orbs of light enveloping them. As she lifted her arms, massive hands formed out of the mist surrounding the Gray Line. They plucked and twisted and ripped chunks of cloud and placed them in front of Jock's hammer.

That's when I realized they were each a kind of summoner, too!

All around the train, the Gandy Dancers laughed and shouted as the wind roared in their faces. Half of them hammered, the other half channeled, and between them they managed to create a shining set of railroad tracks that glimmered like the tail of a comet in the night sky. The Shriek blasted a whistle as it began to follow the new set of tracks back down into the mist, and slowly the rough, jostling motion of the train became a gentle sway.

Turtle took a break and backflipped into the air. For a brief moment she hovered there, letting the momentum of the train carry itself beneath her. Then, just when I thought she'd be lost overboard, she reached out and snagged a handhold on the Shriek and swung herself down to the door. I turned as she entered, laughing and shaking her hair back down over her shoulders.

"Wooeee! That's better than coffee. Look here, Jax my boy, 'bout time for you to get your friend and get ready. You know how to disembark?"

I nodded. "Yeah, but...where am I going to go?"

"Oh, there's only one place and one person to go to to heal up injuries like his, 'cause she fixes the living and the dead. Get your friend and you'll see."

I limped back to the rootwork car and gently lifted Devin in a firefighter's carry over my shoulders. When I got back to the observation car, the rest of the Gandy Dancers were back inside, forming an aisle for me to walk through. A few clapped me on the shoulder gently, or wished me well, and I nodded at as many as I could.

"You ever wanna swing a hammer, you come find us," a bushy-haired man with more beard than face said.

Jock shoved him aside. "You ain't gotta tell him that—that's my line! Go comb your mustache or something, ol' broom-looking face." He turned to me and put a hand on my shoulder. "But he's right. You need help again, or want to lay down steel with the Gandy Dancers, give us a call."

I nodded, then thought about it. "Wait...How would I call you?"

Turtle pounded on the slam door. "When the tracks get to singing, we come a'swinging. Here's your stop! Ready?"

The Shriek dipped, and the mist parted to reveal a small valley surrounded by cliffs. A house nestled between the coal-black rocky walls—a tiny cottage with smoke drifting up from a chimney. An old set of railroad tracks ran just in front of the house before crossing a bridge whose supports looked shakier than me on a skateboard. The phantom tracks of the Gray Line descended to the valley floor, briefly joined the cottage's old tracks, then curved back up into the mist. I took a deep breath. That house was our destination. But who lived there?

"Ready," I said, nodding.

Turtle stepped aside, and I grabbed the train car's door handle, shifting Devin's weight on my shoulders. I visualized the cottage, then yanked the door open and stepped out as light bloomed and the ancient ticket appeared above my right arm for a second. My feet stepped from a carpeted aisle to soft grass and a gravel path. The Shriek rumbled away behind me, disappearing into the mist overhead, blowing dust and dandelion seeds into my face. I scrunched my eyes closed.

"Well, well, well," an old, familiar voice said. "Look what the cat dragged half-dead onto my porch."

I opened my eyes, then sagged with relief, only to stiffen in shock. I'd disembarked safely. And we'd made it to the porch of the cottage. Artfully arranged bones decorated the front of the house, and a skull served as a mailbox. But it wasn't the skeleton decor that grabbed my attention.

No, it was the old woman standing in the doorway and leaning on a giant wooden spoon.

CHAPTER
THIRTY-ONE

"Miss Ella?" I said, struggling to keep Devin from falling to the ground. "What are you doing here? Wherever *here* is."

The old woman sucked her teeth as she stepped to the edge of the cottage's porch and gazed down at us. Well, actually, she was so short that even though she stood on the porch we were the same height. "*Here* is my home, at one of the crossroads between the spirit realm and your realm, with no neighbors and no soliciting. And yet here you are. Watch your feet, boy. I just mopped the porch!"

The cottage was worn but well loved. Even though mist hovered above everything, the air in the valley was clear, and the house stood out like a beacon. Light blue paint covered the planks, and white trim lined the round windows, which held boxes full of drying herbs. Conjure pouches dangled in the glass. White jasmine and gardenias grew up around the porch, some flowers even poking through cracks in the floorboards, and more dotted the field around the house. The air was filled with floral scents, and a gentle breeze blew in our faces.

It was very homey and pleasant, but still . . . there was something . . . off about the place.

"What'd I tell you about eyeing folks?" Miss Ella said, dragging me back to the present. "Still as rude as before. I tell you, some people don't learn."

"Sorry," I mumbled.

"Don't be sorry, be better."

I looked up. That was the same phrase Jock had uttered on the Shriek. I'd heard it from Miss Ella originally. I guess her influence rubbed off on people.

Devin stirred on my shoulders, and the old woman's eyes softened. She sighed and shook her head as she turned around and headed back into the house. "I told you there was a choice. There's always a choice and a consequence. Y'all come on inside."

A flare of anger swept through me as I struggled up the porch stairs. "You said if I went to my destiny, the others would be safe," I called after her. "Does this look like safe to you? Devin is burning up, Miss Naomi's summoners are basically in control of everything, and they're going to make family fight family to get their revenge."

I stumbled through the door and leaned against the entryway wall to catch my breath. Miss Ella was no longer in sight, but that didn't stop me from continuing my rant. "I almost broke the Gray Line trying to get us out of Coin territory, and I left Nina behind. I don't know if that's what she wanted, or if I'm supposed to go back and save her, or if I'm swooping in like Captain Patriarchy when she can handle her own problems!"

The words were running out of my mouth now. I hefted Devin again and walked deeper into the cottage. The entryway opened into a living room with two love seats, a coffee table between them, and little else. There were labeled pictures of flowers on the wall, along with old, faded photos of a younger Miss Ella and a young man who was laughing as she braided his hair. Purple lilac wallpaper made the interior feel like a garden—or maybe it was the shelves upon shelves of potted plants. I'm talking plants of all varieties. Ferns, succulents, flowers, and herbs. Viny plants, thorny plants, even a couple that were taller than me. These stood in the corners and sent wide, leafy branches crowding up to the ceiling.

I stared at one—a small tree?—as I walked beneath it, heading toward the clanking of dishes I heard coming from what I assumed was the kitchen.

I kept up my litany of complaints. "And not to mention I haven't even started to study, not for normal classes and not for summoning. There's going to be a big test at the end of the semester. What if I fail? What if they say I'm not cut out for school and I'm forced to—"

My voice faded. The living room wasn't next to a kitchen. Instead, I stepped out of a sliding barn-style door into an open-air courtyard with a stunning view of the rest of the valley. Homemade wooden patio furniture surrounded a fire pit, amethysts sparkled on shelves and outcroppings, and more plants filled the space with a minty aroma. A workstation covered in tools, jars, roots, and herbs stood against the exterior wall of the cottage, and there was a cushioned bench next to it. Miss Ella stood on a stool near the workstation, crushing herbs and stirring a small pot on an electric burner. She raised an eyebrow at me, then nodded at the bench, and I gently laid Devin down. He was still unconscious.

"It seems," Miss Ella said, "that you need a lot of help."

"Story of my life," I muttered. Then I sighed. "But can you help him? Devin? The Gandy Dancers said you could."

Miss Ella pursed her lips as she ground bright blue flower petals with a bit of water and crushed mint. "S'pose I could. Don't turn away the ill, anyway. But what's wrong with him? Why he need my help?"

"I don't know."

"Well, that's your first lesson—figuring out what ails a person. Do you know why that's important?"

"No!" I snapped. "Why does everything have to be a lesson?"

"Because you keep making the same mistakes," she retorted. "Stop sulking—you slouch when you sulk, and you'll ruin your spine. Good. Now use that brain of yours and tell me what happened and how I can help."

I fought back a swell of frustration and blew out a puff of air. "Devin was summoning his brogres—I mean, his spirit defenders—while battling this bald guy who looks like he chews cinder blocks. But he couldn't keep up, and the bald goon hurt him. I think he's hurt bad."

"I believe this boy tried to borrow too much power from the spirits," Miss Ella said. "Got greedy. No hospital is gonna be able to do anything about that. No wonder that loud, greasy gang of fools sent you here. It's his spirit that needs fixing, and that's what I'm gonna do."

"Thank you," I said, sinking down onto one end of the bench.

"Don't thank me yet. Here, drink." She handed me a cracked mug full of tea.

Flower petals and mint leaves floated on top, and I grimaced but then took a sip. I paused, then took another. It tasted like mint with a hint of citrus, like lemon or lime. "Oh," I said, sitting up and staring into the cup. "That's actually pretty good."

"Of course it is," Miss Ella grumbled. "I made it myself. Now get up—we got work to do." She pulled a basket from under the workstation, then turned and held out a hand.

"Me?"

"I'm not talking to the flowers, Jackson Freeman. Your friend needs a medicinal salve, and you need to learn how to defend yourself the next time a shadow summoner tries to crack your ribs. We can fry two birds in one pot over yonder in the valley."

The memory of Cinder's blow made me wince again. It also reminded me that there were people back in Chicago stirring up trouble. I didn't know how to stop them, but I had to try.

"I can't take the time, Miss Ella. I gotta go back. Nina's mother and her gang—"

"I don't care," Miss Ella said, her eyes flashing. "Do I look like I care? Is this the face of an old woman who cares what foolishness fools are up to? No. I'm looking at one boy who did too much and is paying the price, and another fixing to follow in his footsteps. No, Jackson Freeman, this is the price you pay. You want my help with your friend? You gonna work, right here, and learn, until I say you can go. Is that understood?"

"Learn what?"

"How to get out of the way of things that'll run you over. How to stand up to something trying to knock you down. Maybe even how to fix up a medicinal salve when your silly tail gets hurt."

I clenched my jaw and stared up into the sky—or where the sky would be if the mist weren't drifting overhead. As much as I wanted to get back to Nina, I couldn't leave Devin alone here. Our friendship might be in the early stages, basically running on fumes, you might say, but it was still a friendship. "Fine," I said.

Miss Ella raised her eyebrows in exaggerated surprise. "Well, don't do me no favors. You'd think I was taking your money. It's not my fault you—what is it the kids say? You suck?"

My jaw dropped. "You can't say that," I said as I climbed to my feet and offered her my arm.

"It's true."

"Yeah, but . . . you're a mentor, right? Like a wise old centaur or something like that?"

"You just call me a horse?"

"No!"

"Mm-hmm."

She latched on to me with more strength than I expected, and together we headed out of the courtyard and into the valley, me still grumbling all the way.

"I bet Percy Jackson never had to deal with this."

CHAPTER THIRTY-TWO

"EVERYTHING HAS SPIRITUAL ENERGY," MISS ELLA said as I pulled a medium-sized sled carrying her up a hill. "From the rock to the bird to you and me. And when we're done on this earth, the body might fade, but that spiritual energy remains, eventually migrating to a mirror realm, a spirit realm, connected to our own. Two rooms separated by a wall. That make sense?"

"Grrmph," I said.

"Good. Pull faster. Now, in some places, that wall gets thin. We call them places 'crossroads.' Anybody can get to a cross-road, provided you can find it. Only crossroads that folks can't go to on their own is Conjure Station, on account of you need a porter to get inside. But crossroads like this valley? Anybody can visit. Not that I encourage it." She sniffed, then flapped a hand at me. "Oh, I know you're a porter, child—that's why you're here. Anyway, powerful things happen at a crossroad because that's where spirits cross over."

As I huffed and puffed, I scanned the area again. Is that why this place was so . . . still? We were between the worlds of the living and the dead? Neat. Anyway, back to my lungs being ripped out.

"In the beginning," Miss Ella continued, "when the families were first granted the power, they would find lost spirits and escort them back to a crossroad before someone got hurt. Or the spirits would help out a descendant. All this was so the two realms would be in balance. Understand?"

"Grrmph."

"Now, when we light incense— Pick up the pace, boy, we ain't sightseeing. When we light incense for our ancestors, we're communicating with their spirits. When we thank a plant for its fruit, or a river for its water, or a tree for its shelter, we are speaking to their spirits."

"Grrmph."

"Will you stop whining? It's messing up my groove. Oh, for the love of—fine, if you gonna be a big baby, go ahead and take your silly little break." Miss Ella folded her arms and leaned back on the makeshift futon she was sitting on. The sled had baskets mounted on the sides and seat cushions. ("For my bad back," Miss Ella had explained.) Ropes were fastened on the front, and I currently held the ends in my hand, looped around my arms. I dropped them, then myself, into a heap on the rocky ground.

We were partway up the hill behind Miss Ella's cottage.

Next to the hill was a collection of stones and boulders arranged in a circle that she called the Old Crossroads, but I didn't have a chance to explore it. Not while I was working like a mule. The hill we were on sloped gradually, but there were rocks sticking out everywhere, and I'd already stubbed my toes once. We were supposed to be gathering flowers for the salve Devin needed, but so far, I'd been the only one doing anything. I hauled the sled, plucked the plants Miss Ella pointed out, then returned to the sled to pull it farther up the hill.

"Remind me why can't I just pick the medicine plants without the workout or the history lesson?" I asked after I caught my breath.

"Remind me who won the last fight you were in," she answered.

Fair. Totally fair. "But how will this help me fight?"

"You'll see. And besides," Miss Ella continued, "you always need history. If you didn't learn from history, you'd touch a hot stove every time you saw it start to glow."

"That's different," I said, taking a deep breath before climbing back to my feet. "I have to learn that so I don't hurt myself."

Miss Ella raised her eyes and both hands to the mist above. "Y'all, help me with this boy." Then she turned back to me. "The only way you gonna hurt yourself is by thinking too hard."

"Hey!"

"Hey yourself," she said. "Tell me, why do we need to understand our history?"

I shrugged, exhausted. "I don't know. To get a good grade in Social Studies."

The crack of her hand against the side of the sled sounded like a gunshot. "No! Three times no! Why do we need to understand our history?"

"I don't know! Can't you just tell me?"

"I've watched whole summoner trees tear each other apart because they couldn't remember how to survive together. They couldn't remember their history! You found out your ancestor wasn't a coward but a hero. That's history!" Miss Ella sighed, and the tension left her as she reclined against the pillow and closed her eyes. After a second, she sighed again and spoke, one hand massaging her temple. "You have no control. Or very little."

The change of subject threw me for a loop. I'd summoned the Shriek. What more did I have to do? "Control?"

"No control over your summoning. You just ... hope for the best." She pointed to a place above us. "Do you see the clusters of flowers up there? The marigolds?"

Still reeling from her outburst, I squinted. High up on the hill, at the foot of the cliffs that stretched into the mist, there were groups of bright orange-and-gold flowers, like drops of sunshine in the gray. They grew out of rocky crags, in between fallen boulders, and even on the cliffs themselves, surrounding shadowy alcoves like wreaths.

"I see them," I said.

"Good. Here." She unhooked the baskets from the sled, and they fell to the grass. "I need you to fill all these to the top and bring them down to me."

"That's it?"

Miss Ella raised an eyebrow. "Oh, so you think it'll be easy? Wonderful. Sooner you bring me them flowers, the sooner I can get the salve ready for your friend. Till then, all I can do is head home and help him sleep."

I looked back at the cliffs, calculating how many baskets to take up with me. "How are you going to—" But when I turned around, I stopped in mid-sentence because Miss Ella was running down the hill like something was chasing her. Looking like FloJo in her prime. Like, she Usain Bolt–ed outta there. If I didn't know better . . .

"Watch out for the puppies!"

Her voice came floating back up the hill even though she was out of sight.

"Puppies?" I muttered under my breath as I grabbed two baskets and headed to the cliffs. What is she talking about? And if she could run like that, why did I have to pull her up here on the sled like I'm Rudolph the Red-Faced Asthmatic?

After a few more complaints, I reached the cliffs. I dropped the baskets and started yanking up the first cluster of marigolds I could find, ripping them out by the handful. I tossed them into the baskets, clumps of dirt and all. I had a pretty good rhythm going when I heard a low, rumbling growl on my left.

I froze, my mistake immediately becoming clear.

The cliff wasn't dotted with shadowy alcoves—those were caves! There was one only two feet away from me, and that's where the growl had come from. I scooted back, the marigolds immediately forgotten. The puppies! Miss Ella must have been talking about some sort of wild dog. Coyotes, or maybe even wolves. I had to get out of there. Maybe there was something in the sled I could use as a weapon....

The growls intensified, and I flinched. My mind conjured a giant wolf foaming at the jaws, starving and ready to eat me whole. Maybe drag me back into the den, where I'd never be seen or heard from again. Maybe eat half of me and save the rest for later. Maybe...

A tiny dog no bigger than my foot trotted out of the cave. All black with floppy ears that fell over its snout. It sat down, its tongue sticking out, and started scratching its head. Its eyes were huge compared to its face, making it look like it didn't have two thoughts going on inside its brain. As if to confirm my suspicion, the dog noticed its tail mid-scratch and growled at it before trying to bite it, spinning like a barking tornado in the process.

"You," I said, "are ridiculous."

The dog immediately stopped spinning and started growling again. This time at me. The problem was, it was facing in the wrong direction. As if realizing that, it hopped around, spotted me, snarled, and backed away.

"That's fine," I said, standing up and dusting off my pants. I reached for a cluster of marigolds to continue to gather them for Miss Ella. "I just need these—"

The dog disappeared in a puff of charcoal-gray smoke. Not even a second later it reappeared on the cliff wall near my hand, standing there like some friendly neighborhood spider-dog, and yoinked the flowers out of my grasp.

"Hey!" I shouted, but it had already swallowed them and

*poof*ed away again. I stood there absolutely bewildered. This Chihuahua-looking creature could flicker?

I reached for a different group of flowers, keeping an eye out for the dog. "Don't even think about it," I warned its invisible self, feeling around for the flower stems.

The dog reappeared right next to me. It cocked its head and lifted an ear.

"You heard me. I don't know what you are, but—"

Instead of the leafy stems of the marigolds, my hand grabbed a spindly, furry leg. I swiveled my head to find myself holding a second stealthy Chihuahua, its bug eyes staring at me as it chewed on the flowers I'd been reaching for.

"Aah!" I shouted, dropping the appendage. Instead of falling, the dog flickered away, landing next to the first. "How many of you are there?"

The two dogs yipped at the same time. Answering yips echoed from every cave. A head poked out of one, then another. Three, four, five. Dozens. There were dozens of them up here. Now I knew what Miss Ella had meant by *Watch out for the puppies.* They all started growling and inching closer, and I grabbed the basket I'd filled a third of the way up and held it close to my chest.

"Oh, no, you don't. Stay back."

They didn't listen. Rude! They stalked forward, tiny bodies trying to creep like I couldn't see them, walking along the walls, bug-eyed and panting.

"I said... Oh, forget it, I'm out of here." I turned but saw a flash of movement out of the corner of my eye. One of them flickered to the lip of the basket and I swiped it off.

That was the cue.

Suddenly, they all began flickering at the same time, *poof*-ing into existence around me, on my shoulders and head, try-ing to get at the flowers in the basket.

"Stop!" I shouted, shaking and wriggling to get them off me. "I need these!"

I began to run downhill. The shadow pups followed, yip-ping and trying to flicker up to the basket, forcing me to carry it overhead as I barreled toward Miss Ella's cottage.

"No! Leave me alone! Stop it, you rats! Quit it!"

I stumbled up to the courtyard behind Miss Ella's house to see her stirring a cauldron that simmered atop an outdoor stove. "Help!" I called out to her.

She lifted her oversized spoon at me. "You fill all them baskets?"

"You didn't tell me there were angry vegan dogs up there!" I shouted, panting from exhaustion. "They're eating the flowers! I grabbed what I could." I turned to point them out, but I was alone. They must've stopped chasing me after a bit.

Miss Ella cackled. "Yeah, them spirits love the marigolds."

"Spirits? I thought they were dogs? I grabbed one!"

"They're stone spirits. Solid in this realm. A bunch of 'em live here near the crossroads. Just wait till it rains and you can smell 'em, too. Saw some river spirits the other day—they looked like otters—and I had some Tinker Bell–lookin' house spirits lingering a while back. Expect they took off when the Shriek came roaring through."

"So," I said, trying to work out this new wrinkle, "you got spirits just roaming around like wild animals? Eating flowers?"

"They probably eat 'em for the same reason I need 'em for the salve. The marigolds enhance the spirit." The smile fell from her face, and she nodded toward her doorway. Inside, I could see Devin lying on the love seat in the living room, a compress over his eyes. Wait, how had he moved? Did he sleepwalk there? Was Miss Ella sneaky strong? Did she own an enchanted stretcher? "Speaking of, we still need more. That little bit you brought ain't gonna be enough."

I snapped back to the problem at hand, then sighed. I was still sweating and trying to get my breathing under control. "But how do I get them? Those dogs are like toddlers with turbo boosters."

Miss Ella wagged a finger before returning to her cauldron to stir the bubbling concoction. It smelled like ginger and honey, and the longer I stood there, the more I felt my stress leaching away. Not that I could stand there for long.

"You wanna help your friend?" Miss Ella said. "Get me them flowers! Or maybe y'all wanna hang out with Miss Ella outside of time for a while. I have plenty of chores that need doing. No, I didn't think so. And don't leave my sled out there unattended! That's how things get stolen. Now go!"

I groaned. This was unbelievable! I turned around and stomped out. On my way back to the hill and cliffs, I psyched myself up. "All right, just go, grab as many flowers as you can, dodge the ankle biters, and get back to the sled. They can't eat everything."

Boy, was I wrong.

On my first attempt I grabbed a handful of marigolds, but three stone spirits that looked like bulldogs flickered between my feet, tripped me, and ate the flowers right out of my hand while I lay groaning on the ground.

On my tenth attempt, a large spirit shaped like a rottweiler flickered out of the cliff face and scared me so bad I threw the flowers at its face. It snatched them out of the air and trotted away as smug as could be.

On my thirty-fifth attempt, twenty of the original Chihuahua spirits swarmed me, and I tumbled down the hill, landing upside down with my feet in the air, screaming like a two-year-old as Wack Russells yipped and circled me like tiny sharks smelling blood.

I was on my sixty-third attempt, cradling my basket as I hid behind a boulder to avoid a cross between a pug and a labradoodle, when three of the Chihuahua-shaped spirits raced by, dragging a clump of marigolds I'd abandoned. The labrapuggle (give me a break, I'm trying), sensing an easier meal, chased after them. Two of the spirits scattered, but the one left dragging the flower bundle didn't. The larger spirit lunged at it, but the Chihuahua flickered off, appearing a dozen feet away on the cliff face. The labrapuggle flickered to land behind it, but the first spirit was off to the races. What followed was a chase scene straight out of a spy movie. The two flickered all over the valley and up the cliffs, the labrapuggle slowly gaining.

Marigolds forgotten, I sat on top of the boulder and watched, fascinated. The Chihuahuas were fast and agile, able to flicker here, there, and everywhere at the drop of a dime. Like, they could change directions almost instantly. So how was the labrapuggle keeping up?

It happened so fast I almost missed it.

The Chihuahua disappeared . . . then reappeared in my lap! I was so stunned I didn't move. It didn't weigh anything. All I could feel was a chill, like a cool breeze in the summer. The labrapuggle *poof*ed beneath the boulder and sniffed the air. The Chihuahua held completely still, marigolds drooping from its mouth. Just when I thought the bigger dog would go away, the labrapuggle froze, then jerked around to point its nose at the boulder.

There was the faintest pressure—a tingling, really—on my left side, and the Chihuahua flickered away, right as the labra-puggle leaped, mouth outstretched and aimed at my face. I yelped and acted on instinct.

I flickered to my left.

When I reappeared, I was near the cliffs, and the Chihuahua was standing sideways on the rocky surface, ready to chomp down on the flowers right next to my head. I think we were both stunned I was so close, so when I reached out and plucked the flowers from between its paws, it cocked its head at me like *I can't even be mad right now.*

"I . . . *felt* you flicker," I said to it.

Its ears popped up.

"I could sense it." I was talking more to myself than to the stone spirit. "Right before you flickered. Is that what the labra-puggle feels? Is this what Spider-Man feels? Is this a Jax sense? I wonder if... If you have it, do all the stone spirits have it? All spirits, period?"

The Chihuahua twisted its head to the other side, eyeing the marigolds, and I sighed and held them out. "Here. I guess I owe you for revealing your secret. And you probably need a name, too, if you're gonna keep eating the marigolds before I can get them down to Miss Ella. You're a tiny stone spirit, sooo... how about Pebble?"

The spirit—Pebble—twitched its ears before gulping down the rest of the flowers. Then it plopped down on the cliff face the way a normal dog would lie on the floor, and its tongue lolled out its mouth as it waited for me.

I nodded. "Okay, Pebble it is. I'll make you a deal, Pebble. You let me collect the flowers I need for my friend, and I'll save some for you. Teamwork makes the dream work, right?"

Pebble licked its nose with its tongue.

"Um... right. Okay, here we go." I flickered back to the boulder and grabbed the basket I'd dropped at its base. As soon as I stooped to reach for the handle, I felt the tiniest sensation behind me. Instantly, I flickered to the top of the boulder, just in time to see the labrapuggle bite air. The large spirit looked around in confusion. It thought it had an easy marigold meal but got nothing.

I laughed. "Up here!" I shouted.

The labrapuggle growled and dropped into a crouch as it stared up at me. It sprang forward and disappeared, but again

I was ready for it. I flickered down to where it was before, waving as the spirit barked in frustration. I left it behind, flickering back up to the cliff face. I started picking marigolds, collecting a full basket in just a few minutes. I tossed a handful to Pebble, who yipped in what I guess was thanks and started devouring them as I flickered to the sled to drop off a full basket and return with an empty one.

I repeated the process again and again. I'd finally realized that Miss Ella had warded the sled to keep spirits away. I began carrying empty baskets up four at a time, stacking them on my arms like a waiter delivering meals, and I'd carry two full ones back down. I lost count of how many times I did this. Up and down. Sometimes I'd flicker to a target; sometimes I'd walk.

I filled up a sledload and pulled it down to Miss Ella. She was still at the cauldron and grunted in approval, then she motioned for me to dump the flowers into the concoction while she continued to stir. Steam hissed, and the liquid turned amber and thickened into a honey-like consistency almost immediately. Miss Ella began to dip bandages into the mixture and laid them aside to cool.

"More," she said, and I set off again as she carried the bandages over to Devin. Did I grumble? Maybe. Not a lot. Just a smidge. Nothing she could hear. Probably.

"I heard that!" she shouted.

Whatever.

I collected more flowers. Hauled more sledloads. Dumped more baskets. More stone spirits tried to snatch away flowers. Most were satisfied when I tossed them a few blossoms. The rest

I avoided by flickering, leaving the spirits confused and frustrated as I practiced my timing until I could go when I felt the slightest hint of power emanating from them. I easily evaded the rockweiler (Get it? Rockweiler? I'm on fire!) that had scared me before. As soon as I sensed it was about to flicker, I would disappear and then reappear right behind it. It was almost like a game of tag. A mildly terrifying game of tag, yes, but you get the picture.

I also practiced summoning my heirloom, the neon-blue ticket. Every time the glowing rectangle winked into existence, I couldn't help but marvel at it. An heirloom, from an ancestor who believed in me and what I was capable of. There was something new to notice with each summon.

Like the circle bisected by a cross in the middle of the rectangle, what Dr. Clayton had called a kosmogram.

Or how, no matter which direction I was facing, a capital *N* would appear to indicate which way was north. Handy if (when) I got lost again.

So, between flickering to avoid stone spirits, summoning my heirloom, and also gathering marigolds and trekking back and forth to the sled, time passed. Hours maybe? A day? It felt like forever.

Finally, I loaded the last basket onto the sled. Pebble sat a few yards away, shaking its head and sneezing because of the wards. I waved at it.

"Bye!" I shouted. "I'll come back and visit sometime. I'll bring some roses or something for you to eat."

Pebble's tail thumped the ground as I looped the sled's

ropes around my shoulder and started to haul it downhill, mentally preparing my gracious acceptance of Miss Ella's praise, imagining the compliments she'd shower me with, and Devin, bandaged from head to his expensive sneakers like a mummy, awake to tell me how great I was....

BOOM!

The ground shuddered beneath my feet. An explosion rocked the valley and sent me and the sled toppling over. I was at the top of the last hill before Miss Ella's cottage, maybe thirty feet away, not that far at all. Close enough that I could witness everything.

I saw when the tiny house's roof collapsed, plumes of dust shooting into the air like a volcanic eruption. I could see it—but I couldn't stop it.

I also saw two figures marching toward the cottage and disappearing into the wreckage.

I was running now, sprinting, baskets and sled and marigolds forgotten, hoping I wouldn't find what I feared. By the time I reached the courtyard, it lay in ruins. The cauldron was overturned, the stool and workstation smashed to pieces. I could smell smoke—the cottage was burning somewhere inside.

"MISS ELLA!" I shouted. Tears streamed down my face. I didn't know if they were from the smoke or not. "MISS ELLA! DEVIN! DE—"

I felt it. Someone had flickered. It was a more obvious sensation than with the stone spirits. I turned just in time to see the two figures from before appearing at the top of the closest hill, a third supported between them. Were they stealing Devin?

"Jackson," a faint voice said nearby.

I spun around. "Miss Ella?" I called out. "Where are you?"

The cauldron wobbled, and I raced to lift it. Miss Ella was crouched underneath, her tiny frame covered in dust. She coughed several times, then pointed a wrinkled finger behind me.

"Go after him," she whispered. "Don't let him go alone. Go after him!"

I looked behind me. The two figures with Devin were about to flicker again.

"Go!" Miss Ella hissed, shoving at my hand and wincing in pain as she did. "Don't let 'em take our boys again. Don't let 'em! Go after 'em! Go!"

As the people on the hilltop began to flicker, one of them looked back, and it was like a punch in the stomach as I stared up at a face I recognized.

"Two-Saint?" I whispered.

The boy who'd welcomed me my first morning in the Freeman House. Goofy Two-Saint. Weird and awkward Two-Saint, who'd never made it back from the botched summoner's link in class a couple days ago. He had done this? I was up and running toward him before I could think twice about it.

"Hey!" I shouted at the top of my lungs.

I was halfway up the hill when Devin finally glanced back at me. My friend's chest and arms were bandaged, but he could stand on his own now. He looked frightened. Terrified! The larger of the two people taking him away pulled him forward, and I tried to put on a burst of speed. Then Two-Saint glanced down at me, and I stumbled to a stop on the hillside.

He looked... sad. Almost reluctant. Then, slowly, he pulled the hood of the cloak I just realized he was wearing up over his head.

His charcoal-gray hooded cloak. A hooded cloak I'd seen before.

On a shadow summoner.

With a slow, nearly imperceptible shake of his head, Two-Saint turned as his bigger, still-hooded companion took a piece of chalk out of his pockets. Stooping, he drew something on the ground, and a bright flare of silver-blue light bathed them all, blurring their immediate surroundings, until it sharpened and resolved into a familiar circular shape: a summoner's link.

Two-Saint stepped into it first, disappearing from sight. Devin shot me one more panicked stare. Before I could respond, he also stepped into the link, pushed by the second hooded figure, and then they were gone.

"No!" I shouted. I raced up the hill, desperate to reach the link before it closed. The light was just beginning to fade when I finally made it to the top. I hesitated, only for a moment, because I had no idea where I would emerge. What if there were avarice spirits or shadow summoners there?

I shook my head. Didn't matter. Miss Ella said to help Devin, and even if she hadn't, I would've followed after him.

After *them*. Because Two-Saint's mysterious return was equally as important.

Right as the circle was about to disappear, I took a deep breath and lunged forward...

...and reappeared in the middle of an attic.

I stood confused at the center of another kosmogram drawn on the floor in chalk. Withered marigolds were scattered around the attic, while a pair of binoculars lay on the sill of a small circular window. I carefully stepped out of the kosmogram, crossed the room, and picked up the binoculars. The window overlooked a side alley with junk scattered everywhere, and there was a barbershop pole on the top of...

Wait. I knew that alley. It was Papa Coin's workshop. Was this a spy's lookout?

Tires squealed to a stop on the street below, and I raced to a larger window. I pressed my face against the glass to see a black luxury sedan pull up in front of the barbershop. One of the Coins' limos! And there were Devin and Two-Saint, climbing into it. Had Miss Naomi completed her takeover of the Coins? Now she was using the limo service? Where was she taking Devin? And Two-Saint was working with her, too?

"Hey!" I shouted, pounding on the window before turning and sprinting down the stairs. The house was abandoned, and the door opened onto a side street. I dashed outside, racing to the corner and rounding it only to see the sedan take off, tires peeling, burned rubber lining the street, and I came to a stop.

What was going on? What was I supposed to do now?

"Friends. Think you've got them figured out."

That voice. I knew that voice.

When I turned around, a man in an oversized sweater stood only a yard or so away from me, leaning against a familiar car parked in the street. Graying hair and a sour expression, narrow eyes softened by the hint of a smile I'd never seen on his face before. He raised a hand in a little wave.

"Almost as bad as family," Uncle Moe said. "Come on. Let's go for a ride."

CHAPTER
THIRTY-THREE

We rode in silence for a few blocks. Uncle Moe still drove like an out-of-work stunt-car driver, and I could barely focus on the life-threatening near-misses. The dashboard clock read nearly five o'clock. It had only been two hours since Nina, Devin, and I had gotten out of school. Only ninety minutes since we'd found Nina's mother waiting for us, someone who for all intents and purposes was the leader of the shadow summoners, and I'd fled to the Shriek with Devin.

Ninety minutes.

Time really did stand still in the spirit realm. It felt like weeks had passed. The marigolds, the stone spirits. Two-Saint. All that in ninety minutes. My body ached like I'd aged ninety years. And Miss Ella . . . still there in all that destruction and chaos . . . was she going to be okay?

At that moment Uncle Moe pulled up to the sidewalk, put the car in park, and sighed. "We need to talk, Jax."

I looked up to see that we'd made it to the Freeman House. The house itself looked like something out of a fairy tale, with smoke curling up from the chimney and frost covering the roof. The sign next to the front door read THANK GOODNESS YOU'RE SAFE, and I gave it a small wave before glancing back at Uncle Moe.

"Talk about what?" I asked.

He shifted to face me in the seat and rubbed his hand through his thinning hair. Then he reached into his pocket and pulled out an envelope with AMTRAK stenciled on the front. He held it out to me, and after a second, I took it.

"Is this—" I started to ask.

"Ticket back to Carolina," Uncle Moe said, nodding. "This Sunday. Couldn't get you first class—too expensive. But I did get a deal on business class. No coach for my nephew."

I just stared at the envelope.

Uncle Moe smiled. "I know it's a surprise. Was gonna wait until the weekend, but I figured better now, before... well, before anything else happens. Gran talked to your parents, and they agreed. Said it was probably for the best."

"I don't understand," I finally said, thinking of what Papa Coin had told me.

He rested his hand on my shoulder and shook me gently, like he was waking me up. "You get to go home. Isn't that what you wanted? To go back? Back to your friends and the school you were attending, and getting ready for football?"

"Yeah, but you said I couldn't. And I—"

Uncle Moe sighed. "Truth is, we're worried about you. Gran and I. You've had a bunch of stuff thrown at you all at once. And when you start running with the wrong crowd, it's only going to make things worse for you, especially someone who's supposed to be lying low and following rules."

"But..." I said, still staring at the ticket. "My friends..."

"You were runnin' deep in Coin territory, chasing after the grandson of the man who did this to us." Uncle Moe gestured at the Freeman House. As if it had overheard, the roof seemed to tremble, and snow slid to the ground in a mini avalanche. "Gran said you came home late last night. That you're buddy-buddy with kids whose families want to see us suffer. Don't want that for you. Want you to be safe."

My shoulders slumped. I should've been ecstatic. I should've hugged my uncle and fist-pumped until I sprained my elbow. Seventy-two hours ago, I probably would've done just that. But... something had changed.

"I don't want to go back," I whispered.

"What?"

I held out the envelope to Uncle Moe, who looked surprised, and also... not? "I don't want to go back to Raleigh. I'm a summoner. I want to learn more about how to do it, how to control it, and I can't do that back home."

"Maybe. But you can come back next year, in the fall, and start off properly. The way you were dropped in the middle of lessons with students already ahead of you—it's not optimal.

You can try again from the beginning, be in a much better position to succeed."

"But my friends—"

WHACK!

Uncle Moe slammed his palm on the dash behind the steering wheel. "That's your problem! They *ain't* your friends! Don't you get it? You're a Freeman. That's what got them interested in you—the name! You are an oddity. Something new and strange that they will use up and toss aside once you become familiar. And that's if you don't get into trouble first by trying to run 'round behind them, doing what they do."

I shook my head, refusing to believe it, and yet a sliver of doubt, the tiny voice that I thought I'd squashed, reemerged in the back of my head and whispered *You're odd, you're weird, you're odd, you're weird, no one likes you.*

Uncle Moe must've seen something in my expression because he clapped my shoulder again and sighed. "I know it's tough to hear, but trust me, it's for the best. And besides, you don't want to be around those Coin kids anyway, not with the trouble they're in."

"Trouble?" I asked, looking up.

"Yeah, the congregation's been watching Papa Coin and his little empire on the South Side for a while."

"But isn't he part of the congregation?"

"Don't matter. In fact, that makes it worse. Let's say there've been some . . . inconsistencies . . . with how he's been running his tree, and it's not only him. Word is those kids have been abusing their summoner powers, too. Yesterday a little birdie told me a report came in about their flickering without approval, and summoning spirits where non-summoners can be harmed. And that's just the start. Looks like the whole family is corrupt, and they're going to face the congregation tomorrow, after the Glimmer Fest Games." He glanced at me. "But you didn't hear that from me, understand? Look, I'm only telling you this for your own good, because you, of all people, should understand how making bad choices can send you down a dark path that's hard to recover from. Right?"

I swallowed and nodded, and he smiled. "All right. So come on, let's enjoy these next couple of days. We Freemans may not have a lot, but we have each other. How about after school tomorrow we go catch a movie or something? That sounds good, right? Popcorn and a movie. Come on, let's go in and have dinner."

Uncle Moe got out of the car, whistling as he navigated the snowy sidewalk to the Freeman House's porch. I clenched the Amtrak ticket. *Go home.* I guess Chicago really wasn't for me, not yet at least.

But if you attempt to leave the Freeman House...

If Papa Coin was going to get in trouble, he'd be too pre-occupied to care if I left. He'd probably be too busy defending himself to make good on his threat. Maybe it *would* be better for me to return to Raleigh.

Except it wasn't just Papa Coin, was it? Nina and Devin were going to get in trouble, too. For using magic.

My eyes widened.

Flickering? Summoning spirits? Were they talking about

the avarice-spirit attacks? But all that was in self-defense! Did the congregation know that? What if Devin and Nina weren't allowed to give their side of the story? Would Miss Naomi stick up for them? Or would she only care about Nina? That wasn't fair! It was one thing to face the consequences for your choices, but not if those consequences weren't your fault. I could speak from firsthand experience that being blamed for something, like the fight in Raleigh, was crushing.

The sign at the front of the Freeman House had changed again. YOUR ANCESTORS NEED YOU.

I shook my head. My friends needed me, and I knew what I had to do to help. All I had to do was go to Glimmer Fest, find the congregation, and talk to them before they could come to any sort of conclusion about Devin and Nina. Easy enough, right?

Right.

CHAPTER
THIRTY-FOUR

GLIMMER FEST WAS INCREDIBLE. IT WAS HELD IN Grant Park in downtown Chicago, and it sprawled over all 313 acres. Think of the biggest festival you've ever been to, with live bands and performing artists, food trucks with mouthwatering aromas, and all the tents and stalls filled with whatever shopping you could possibly want. Limited-edition sneakers, designer shirts, toys, and jewelry—you name it, they had it. It was one of the biggest winter festivals in the world, and they really leaned into the mood. Strings of light decorated every tree, and ice sculptures of castles and creatures stood tall on chilled pedestals. Light-up snowflakes the size of Boogs hung like lanterns from branches and poles.

And then multiply all that awesomeness by ten, because that was just the reggie part of the festival. I haven't even mentioned the magical nooks and crannies tucked beneath trees and in pockets outside of time.

Like Mr. Cranes's Ten-Minute Names. An old man in a pair of heavily patched overalls sat on a rocking chair next to a bookshelf stuffed with dusty brown bottles with names scratched on the glass. Supposedly, you could drink one and for the next ten minutes exactly, every document, piece of identification, and website with your information on it would say that you were named whatever was on the bottle. I thought it was neat, but there were some sketchy people buying from him, so I moved on.

Then there was Margarita's Pitas, where a short woman covered in flour sold pocket bread stuffed with emotions. You heard me right—emotions. Tired of feeling sad? One bite of her contentment-stuffed pita would have you whistling and thinking life was perfectly fine, yes it was. According to rumor, it could also give you gas that made you cry, so I wasn't too keen on trying it out.

And let's not forget Tina's Adapta-wigs, and JJ's Fairy Traps. I saw Kelvin's Cryptid Colognes, and Caterina's Catcall Catchall, a charm that absorbed every unwanted comment and converted it into an embarrassing secret before returning it to the sender. I got to see it in action when Caterina, the young summoner who'd designed the charm, ran into some trouble with the shop owner next to her.

"Heeey," he called over, leaning on a stack of custom T-shirts. "You can catch my attention anytime, sweetheart."

Caterina ignored him as she wrapped a wooden charm in

paper and handed it to the customer in front of me. "Have a great day," she said. "Next?"

I stepped up just as the loud shop owner cupped his hands around his mouth. "Why don't you take my number down? It's eight one eight"—Caterina's hoop earrings began to glow—"two one four...ONE TIME MY TOOTHBRUSH FELL IN THE TOILET AND I FORGOT TO WASH IT BEFORE BRUSHING MY TEETH FIVE MINUTES LATER."

The man clapped his hands over his mouth as everyone around him stared openmouthed at his confession. Fury crossed his face and he pointed at Caterina, obviously about to yell at her, but I guess the charm was still working.

"You little...I'VE ONLY WASHED MY HANDS SEVEN TIMES IN THE LAST THREE YEARS!"

Someone snickered, and it was like a fuse had been lit. The entire crowd around the two stalls started laughing. The man was so embarrassed, he packed up his stall and disappeared in no time flat.

"I guess your charms really work," I said. Maybe they'd be useful when someone tried to hit me with fat jokes disguised as helpful comments.

Caterina smiled, though I could tell she was still a little upset. "I'd rather they not be needed at all," she grumbled before turning to me and taking a deep breath. "Now then, how can I help you?"

"I'm looking for the congregation," I said, lowering my voice. "Do you know where they are?"

Her forehead wrinkled. "The congregation? I think they're judging the Summoning Games."

That was the second time today I'd heard something about games. "What kinda games? Like 2K, or *Madden*? *Apex*?"

"No," she said, laughing. "Summoning Games. Competitions between the top ranked summoners from across the Midwest! How do you not know about them?"

I shrugged. "I don't get out much."

"Well, let's change that," she said. "Come with me. I was just about to go over."

Caterina stepped out from behind her table and extended her hands. An heirloom shaped like her earrings appeared in front of her, and suddenly everything in the tent started putting itself away. The charms went into a briefcase, which, along with the tablecloth, went into a trunk. The table folded itself again and again until it was the size of a napkin, and then it, too, hopped into the trunk, which Caterina locked before motioning for me to follow her.

We traveled along the center aisle of the festival, a flag-lined path decorated with different kinds of branches arranged in various patterns. When I commented on them, Caterina explained that they represented the five summoning trees, so summoners could know which territory they were in.

"Oak for the Baskets; pine for the Coins," she said, as if reciting a nursery rhyme. "Walnut for the Skulls; willow for the Wands; and myrtle for the Knives."

"What if someone wanted to create a new tree?" I asked.

Caterina thought about that as she led me away from the

center aisle toward a blue-and-orange tent. "I don't know," she finally said. "It's always been just five families, since they're the ones who escaped together. Buuut, if I had to guess, as long as most of the congregation agrees, it could probably happen. That's how they handle most disputes—by majority rule.

"Here we are," Caterina said.

She walked into the tent, and I followed. Inside, a line of children waited to get their faces painted by a sullen teenage boy. There were posters of different animal faces hanging on the walls, and each child would point to the one they wanted. Pretty normal stuff, right?

Wrong.

Because the boy wasn't using ordinary paint. He summoned different colored light and painted in elegant, glittering swirls. The children squealed and laughed, then scampered off as rabbits, bears, and even eagles.

He brightened when he saw Caterina. "Hey, Ms. Cat," he said, clearing his throat when his voice cracked. "What's up?"

"Need a pass to the Games, Trey. Somehow— What's your name?" Caterina asked me.

"Jax," I said, looking at one kid who scurried away with a tiger's face painted over his own. Was it just me or were those actual whiskers on either side of his nose?

"Right," Caterina said. Then, to Trey: "Jax didn't get a pass."

Trey's smile faded some when he glanced at me. "Wellll, all passes are supposed to be distributed via the tree representatives. We can't really hand them out to random individuals. I could get in trouble."

"Aw, please?" Caterina said. "Just this once. Besides, you said you'd take me to watch. Why not right now?"

"Seriously?"

Caterina nodded.

"I mean…" he said, blushing. "I guess I could check to see if it's okay. Maybe they'll let you in. I'd go ask, but I have a couple more face-paint charms to do."

"I'll do them," I volunteered.

"You?"

"Sure." I mean, how hard could it be? I painted in my sketchbook sometimes. This couldn't be much different, right? Even if it was magic paint.

"And I'll go with you," Caterina said, linking the boy's arm in hers.

"Okay!" Trey said, his voice cracking again as he turned to me. "I mean, okay. Just remember it's really simple. Paint-by-numbers type of deal. Summon the animal from the wall in front of the kid's face, and paint the light onto them. If they start acting like animals, it's only the magic taking hold. Gives them a random trait from the animal they selected. But make sure you pay attention—too much paint and they can get a little wild. I'll watch you do the first one."

I stepped up to the line and grabbed a paintbrush. Concentrating on the wall, I summoned the animal face the same way I would summon my heirloom. A cheetah appeared directly in front of a small brown girl with bangs, and she giggled.

"Ready?" I asked, and when she nodded, I carefully painted the golden fur and dark brown dots over her cheeks and eyes, then brushed cream-tufted ears over her own. It took a few minutes, but when I stepped back, she giggled again and then gave a practice growl. The other kids oohed and aahed as she sprinted out of the room.

"You're pretty good at this," Trey said with a nod of approval. "Okay, I'll be right back with a pass, and then we can all go to the Games."

Someone tugged on my sleeve. "Can I go next?" a tiny Black kid with glasses asked.

"Sure," I said. "What sort of animal do you want to be?"

Several other kids his age—maybe five or six years old—crowded around and watched, their conversation as random as the animals they chose.

"Look at him," one kid said, pointing at me. "He's taller than my dad. He *has* to be a grown-up."

"I bet he's rich," said another kid. "All grown-ups are rich."

"Are you rich?" a third kid asked me.

I nodded, not really paying attention, as the first boy picked an antelope with huge horns from the wall. I summoned it, overlaid it on his face, then started to paint. A few minutes later, he bounded out of the tent, laughing. Cheetah Girl spotted him and immediately gave chase. The next kid stepped up, and I turned back to my task.

Meanwhile, Glimmer Fest continued all around me. A band from a local HBCU marched down the main aisle, stopping every fifty yards or so to let a trombonist play a solo or the drumline bang out a snappy beat. A balloon artist charmed her creations to scamper along the shoulders of the crowd, dropping candy and her card at random, and leaving squeal-ing children in her wake. There was even a guy on a unicycle slinging kebabs. I was having so much fun I almost forgot what I'd come here to do—to testify on behalf of my friends.

Too bad my plan came to a screeching halt.

"No, I'm sorry."

I looked up to see Trey and Cat walking back toward me behind an older Black woman in an elegant dress. Her arms were folded over her chest, and she was shaking her head. "No more passes. The Games have started, and it's too dangerous to cross now. You'll have to find a spirit-cast to watch."

"But—" Caterina began.

"No. And that's final," the older woman said, walking away.

Trey and Caterina looked at each other and shrugged, and I let out a small groan. There went my chance to get to the congregation. Now what was I supposed to do? I was running out of options.

Six or seven kids had already galloped, slithered, or flapped out of the tent when a flash of white flickered in the corner of my eye. I looked up from the rhino I was painting on a freckled girl and froze.

It was the Veiled Woman.

I couldn't believe it. Here, in front of everybody? I watched as she stopped in the main aisle, her dress fluttering even though the air was still. Two adults with flowering myrtle twigs pinned to their collars—Knives, then—walked straight through her, never once stopping their deep conversation.

So, nobody could see her but me.

I watched carefully as the freckled girl left and another kid took her place, then another and another. The Veiled Woman just stood there, waiting. But . . . for what?

Suddenly, she whirled around and began to glide off the path, passing by the face-paint tent and disappearing behind it.

"Hey!" the kid whose face I was currently painting shouted. "You didn't finish!"

"Sorry," I said, hastily slapping the charmed light onto his features. "There. Done." I turned to Trey, who'd returned to take over. "Thanks for trying, but I gotta run. Lunchtime."

"It's ten thirty in the morning!" he said, confused.

"I eat early!" I called back, then raced out of the tent after the Veiled Woman.

I thought I'd lost her, but a flicker of movement put me back on her trail. She was cutting through a grove. There wasn't a path for me to follow, just a break in some large flowering bushes and ornamental trees where someone could slip through. I hesitated, looked around, then took a deep breath and rushed in behind her.

The Veiled Woman was waiting several yards ahead. Without looking at me, she started moving forward again as soon as I approached. She trailed her hands behind her in midair, light rippling at her fingertips as if she were skimming her hand across a watery surface. Then she disappeared beneath the shadows of a giant weeping willow.

Follow me, I heard her say in my head.

This tree, y'all. It was practically a living curtain. Its branches dangled so low they piled on the ground like golden hair, as if Rapunzel lived up in its limbs. I brushed the wispy leaves and branches aside and walked between them.

The noise of Glimmer Fest faded behind me as I pushed, pulled, and navigated my way through the willow. Something crunched under my feet, but I kept my eyes straight ahead. I could barely make out the Veiled Woman in front of me, her gown flickering between the yellowish leaves. Silence fell over me, and the willow branches grew stiffer and stiffer, pressing me back until it felt like I would be forever trapped among its roots. To my horror, when I looked down, I saw that the skeletons of small animals and birds littered the ground. That's what I'd been stepping on! I shoved forward, desperate to leave, no longer focused on the Veiled Woman but on trying to survive. Right when the pressure grew so heavy it felt like I was sinking beneath the ocean...

I burst out of the branches, straight into the oncoming path of a huge rolling wheel!

"Get out of the way!" someone shouted.

"What?"

"MOVE!"

At the last second, I dove aside, and the rolling wheel thundered past me. *What in the world was that? Had a monster truck lost a tire?* That thing had almost flattened me into a Jax tortilla!

Three older kids raced past, wearing different-colored uniforms, like this was a soccer game or something. A roar of noise exploded around me. I was in the middle of a flat grassy field. The willow tree was nowhere to be seen; instead, rows of elevated bleachers surrounded me on five sides, their base forming the walls of a pentagon.

"MOVE!" a girl shouted again as the ground began to shake under me.

I climbed to my feet and turned to see the giant wheel rolling back in my direction. It was weirdly colored and shaped—a brown-and-green hula hoop the size of a dump truck, with markings like a face painted on one section. I started to run toward the nearest bleachers, but I couldn't see a way to climb into the stands. There were no doors or stairs in the walls of the arena. Even worse, the rumbling wheel was coming right at me!

The three older kids began waving at me. "Get away from the oooznate!"

"What?" I shouted back, retreating until I was pressed against the wall.

"Get. Away. From. The. Hoop. Snake!"

Hoop snake? HOOP SNAKE?

I grasped the truth just in time. The huge reptile had been biting its own tail and rolling around. Now the tail came out of its mouth and sliced through the air like a whip... aimed straight at my heart.

I acted without thinking. I flickered a dozen yards to my left. I stumbled to the ground right as the hoop snake's tail collided with the wall, shaking the stands with a loud *BOOM*! The crowd roared in approval, but the hoop snake wasn't done yet. It yanked its tail free, hissed, then resumed its wheel shape and began to roll after me again.

"Oh, poop," I said, then got to my feet. I looked at the stands behind me and tried to flicker up to the seats, but it was like a giant invisible rubber wall protected them. I bounced off with a grunt and fell back to the grass.

"You can't escape," one of the older kids shouted at me. "There's a force field, you know!"

I did not, in fact, know that. "Double poop," I said. "Triple poop with one-ply toilet paper."

The uniformed kids tried to summon a giant net made of light and sparks, but it appeared slowly and in unconnected sections. And anyway, the hoop snake wasn't paying attention to them. Just my luck. This thing wanted a Jax-sized snack.

I flickered around the arena, trying to find an exit that wasn't warded or protected, but of course there wasn't one. The hoop snake rolled after me, hissing as it tried to skewer me into a Jax-kebab, and rumbling when it tried to flatten me.

"This way!"

The other kids waved. Their net was finally complete, hovering in midair like a giant spiderweb. All we had to do was get the hoop snake over there. And I guess we all know what that meant, right?

I flickered to the middle of the arena, a few yards in front of the net, and took a deep breath. Then I started to jump up and down. "Hey! You oversized pair of lemon pepper steppers, here I am! You want a snack? Come on! What are you waiting for?"

The arena went silent, like everyone was holding their breath, as the hoop snake pivoted and rolled toward me, beginning to pick up speed. It rolled faster and faster, dust kicking up in the air.

Thirty yards.

Twenty yards.

Ten.

Five.

I flickered. Not to the left or to the right, but straight up.

The hoop snake's stinger tail sliced beneath me as I reappeared in midair, the snake's snout right in front of me. Oops. I'd managed to avoid the tail, but now it looked like I was in for a snaky headbutt.

The impact was like being hit by a truck.

"Oomph!" I grunted as I was driven back into the net. Clouds of dirt and grass arose, forcing me to close my eyes. A giant weight pressed on my chest, and my arms were wrapped around something smooth and scaly and mildly terrifying.

The dirt settled.

I opened my eyes.

The crowd erupted in a deafening roar. I looked up to see the eyes of the hoop snake inches from my face. I was hugging its nose with my arms and legs. The net was pressed against my back, preventing me from letting go but also preventing the snake from shaking me off. I was stuck, but also safe...I hoped. I let out a sigh of relief as the uniformed older kids came sprinting up, shock written in their expressions.

"I'm okay," I called down. "I'm just...booping the snoot. I'm a snoot-booper."

"Yo, that was amazing!" one of the boys shouted, both hands on his head.

"Who are you?" the girl asked.

"Are you a wild card?" asked the other boy. "Have you chosen a team yet?"

A previously invisible door opened in the stadium wall, and adults in gray-and-black uniforms ran onto the field. To my great relief, they took charge of the snake. They sheathed its stinger and snout in green light, and then summoned the image of a bleating lamb to lure the creature to the exit. The net disappeared, and the muzzled snake and I both dropped to the ground at the same time. I flickered out of the way, rubbed my sore chest, and waved as the hoop snake grabbed its tail once again and rolled out of the stadium and out of sight.

I let out a sigh before I said to the older kids, "Sorry I got lost and ruined your game."

"Ruined?!" The first boy finally dropped his hands. "That was the quickest we've ever captured the hoop snake! Are you a freshman? What school do you go to?"

"Uh, DuSable," I said, fiddling with my coat.

The girl wrinkled her forehead in confusion. "DuSable? That's not a high school. My brother went there for middle school before we moved."

"Yeah," I said sheepishly. "I'm in sixth grade. My name is—"

"Jackson Freeman," said a cold voice behind me. I turned to find a new group of grown-ups walking toward us—three or four elders surrounded by twice as many summoners wearing silver masks that covered the top halves of their faces and distorted the lower halves. If you stared at the masks too long, it was like squinting through a kaleidoscope. Whirling colors and shapes filled my eyes, and I had to blink and look away.

The teens next to me quickly straightened and bowed their heads in respect. I stared at them, puzzled. When the girl peeked and saw me standing there like a giant goofball, she hissed at me like the hoop snake.

"It's the congregation," she whispered. "And their stewards. Bow your head!"

I drew in a sharp breath. The congregation? The very people I'd come to see? I finally had the audience I wanted . . . and they did not look pleased at all.

CHAPTER
THIRTY-FIVE

THEY TRIED TO HUSTLE ME OUT OF THE ARENA before the crowd could realize I wasn't supposed to be there.

"Hold on," I said, struggling as one silver-masked steward grabbed me by the arm. "I just need to talk to the congregation!"

A second steward took my other arm, and then a third stepped up. By that time, the crowd realized I wasn't being congratulated, but detained, and the boos started raining down.

"Hold him still," one steward hissed.

"I'm trying!" replied another.

I leaned away. "Just hold on! I need to speak—"

A fourth silver-masked steward stepped in front of me as the other three hemmed me in. "You will speak with them, all right," she snarled. "Put a glimmer on him."

"Wait, that doesn't sound—" I started to protest, but I was cut off by a fog that descended around me. I don't know what it looked like from the outside, but I can tell you that wearing a glimmer is one of the weirdest things I've ever done, and this is from someone who once played flower tag with little Chihuahua spirits in another realm. I could see, but only blurry lights. I could hear, but it was like someone was shouting in a tunnel and I had to decipher the echo.

Someone took my hand, and I grabbed it and held on tight. We were walking. Maybe for five minutes, maybe for five hours, I didn't know. I did hear a door *whoosh* open, then shut, and I smelled flowers, lots of flowers, but it was all jumbled. All I knew was that when we finally stopped and the glimmer was removed, the invisible band of steel that had been squeezing my chest disappeared. I dropped to my hands and knees, blinking furiously while I sucked down huge lungfuls of oxygen.

"Watch him," someone said as I squeezed my eyes shut and reopened them several times.

"Why is he glimmered?" another person asked.

"I don't know; I'm just following orders," the first voice snapped. Then I heard footsteps walk away and a door open and close.

"That's the problem around here," the second voice said. After a few seconds, they chuckled. "First time being glimmered?"

I sat up, stretching my neck and rubbing my eyes, and then took in my surroundings. They'd taken me to a...forest? An indoor forest? I'd definitely heard a door. But all I could see around me were pine trees that stretched high up to...the ceiling? Yes. But when I pressed against the ground to get up, my hands crunched pine needles and dirt as real as any I'd felt before. There could only be one explanation.

"I'm in a parallel universe," I whispered to myself.

Another chuckle echoed behind me. I turned to find a brown kid a few inches shorter than me laughing as he walked through the trees to where I stood. He had a mop of silky black hair that fell into his eyes when he shook his head.

"No, you're in Shedd Aquarium," he said. He wore a name tag that said HI, MY NAME IS MAKWA! ASK ME ABOUT THE DOLPHINS! He had on a blue polo shirt with an aquarium logo on the breast and khaki cargo pants, and he smiled so wide I almost smiled in return . . . until something rustled in the trees several yards away. Something big. I saw a tail the length of my body disappear beneath a carpet of leaves, and I gulped.

"Are you sure?"

"Yep! I help run the cryptid department on the weekends. Just got done making sure Hyacinth was okay after you startled her in the arena. She's a gentle soul, you know."

"Hyacinth?"

"The hoop snake."

"Where?" I shouted, spinning on my knees, eyes searching wildly.

Makwa started laughing again. "Easy, bro, she's harmless. Mostly. Once she's fed, which I did, so it's probably fine. As long as you don't shout."

My mouth, stretched to the max as I was indeed about to holler, shut with a snap. Makwa continued to smile at me, and

I stared at him, until, after a few seconds, I pointed at the name tag. "How are the dolphins?"

"Grumpy. They're hungry, but they're always hungry, and right now I need to prep some medicine for Hyacinth. She loves chasing summoners, but rolling 'round like that is tough on her skin. Wanna help me?"

I rubbed my temples, where the pressure from the glimmer had lingered the longest. "This is too much. I need to talk with the congregation for five minutes. Five minutes! My friends are in trouble for something they didn't do! If anything, *I* should be the one in trouble."

Makwa shrugged. "I'd say you're going to get your wish."

"Are you a steward?" I asked.

"Nope! Just an intern."

"They put an intern in charge of me?"

"That's what they think, but this isn't a prison and I'm not a warden. If you're here, you're going to help. Trust me, the congregation will call for you very soon."

"Oh. Well, all right. I guess I can help until then. I'm Jax."

"Yep, I know. I'm Makwa."

He pulled me to my feet, handed me a trowel, and then showed me the contents of a basket at his feet. Inside were familiar bunches of golden-orange flowers. "I need you to gather some—"

"Marigolds," I finished, nodding. "To help the spirit recover. Got it."

Makwa stared at me, then laughed. "I don't care what they say about you, Jax—you're pretty cool."

"Nice. But, you know, for funsies, who is 'they,' and what do they say about me?"

"Trust me, you don't wanna know."

We started walking through the trees, climbing over boulders, and harvesting marigolds wherever we found them. It felt unreal, being in a forest inside an aquarium (it would be like going to SeaWorld to climb a mountain). But then I remembered Nina's father's van and how it was charmed to be bigger on the inside for his garden. I guess this was the same thing, just on a larger scale.

Afterward, Makwa showed me small purple-and-yellow wildflowers that were allegedly like catnip to hoop snakes. I started picking those, too, while he told me about his internship as a summoner. "Anyway, I'm the teen volunteer coordinator here at the Shedd, assistant assistant to the assistant cryptozoologist, and apparently the occasional babysitter. Oh, don't include those, or Bessie will be mad."

I glanced down to see that I had picked yellowish purple flowers instead of the purple-and-yellow flowers. Trust me, there was a difference. "Why? Is Bessie a hoop snake, too?"

"Nope. Sea serpent. One of three. Triplets, you know?"

"Oh . . . of course. And, again, for future reference, where do the sea serpents come from?"

"Well—"

At that moment, the walkie-talkie on his hip crackled to life. *"Hi, Makwa. Dr. Clayton here."*

I perked up as Makwa grabbed the walkie-talkie and raised

an eyebrow at me before responding. Why was my teacher here? "Makwa here. Go ahead, Dr. Clayton."

"*Hey, dear, bring young Jax with you to the East Terrace. The congregation is ready for him. Quickly now.*"

"Yes, ma'am." Makwa reclipped the walkie-talkie and shrugged. "Guess you're off the hoop-snake hook."

"Or I just got moved to a bigger one," I muttered.

I dusted off my hands, adjusted my coat, then followed Makwa as he cut through the trees and emerged next to a plain white door in a plain white wall. There was no doorknob ... at least, not until he looked around, made sure the coast was clear, then raised his hands and summoned one. A purple handle appeared, and he twisted it and shoved the door open, dispelling the handle once he was through. I followed, a thousand questions rattling around in my brain.

"So, you're ... like me," I said, as we stepped out of the indoor forest and into a bright hallway with white walls and a linoleum floor. A sign read ABBOTT OCEANARIUM, THIS WAY! The words flickered as I walked by, as if the placard had static, and when I looked again, they had changed. It now read R. A. YOUNG CRYPTOZOOLOGY RESEARCH CENTER, THIS WAY!

"I don't think anyone's like you, Jax," Makwa said. He led me to an elevator, and when the doors opened and we were inside by ourselves, he summoned again, this time bringing forth a new elevator button that he pressed before turning to me. "I've never seen one person rile up the congregation, their stewards, whole trees, and a few ancestors like you have. The aquarium's wards have been alarming nonstop for the past half hour as people head to the East Terrace. I think everyone wants to hear what you have to say."

The doors opened and he stepped out, but I held back. "Say? Everyone? I thought I was just going to talk to the congregation?"

Makwa grinned. "Not today, buddy. Everybody was already here to witness the new tree being sanctioned, or here for the Summoning Games, or both. But then you somehow got around the heavily warded entrance that requires a pass from the highest level of the congregation. And, if I might, in front of three of the top summoners in the Glimmer Fest rankings, you singlehandedly stopped a rampaging Tier-B hoop snake. Jax, my friend, *everyone* will be there."

CHAPTER
THIRTY-SIX

So, FIRST THINGS FIRST. THE EAST TERRACE WASN'T actually a part of Shedd Aquarium. Not for reggies, anyway. It wasn't on any map; it wasn't in the app you could download for more information about the facility; and it wasn't listed on any of the signs hanging in the hallway as we emerged from the elevator. Strange, right? And once Makwa led me through the weird shimmering doors that everyone else in the hallway seemed to walk right past without noticing, it got even stranger.

"Welcome to the East Terrace," he said, gesturing for me to go first. "Also known as the Court of the Ancestors."

"You're not going in?" I asked, pausing at the threshold.

"Nope. Those cryptids aren't going to feed themselves. More likely to feed on one another if I don't get back to work. Besides, you got this. Just... be you."

"That's what got me here," I muttered, but I stepped through the doors and walked up a flight of stairs...

...and almost fell back down.

The East Terrace was a floating pavilion that looked like an island temple built for gods. Clouds drifted by underneath as I walked toward the center stage, where a semicircle of five seats created from living trees—oak, pine, walnut, willow, and myrtle—awaited, their trunks curving to form a couch, a chaise longue, and even a recliner, as their branches arched high overhead in a shady canopy. Stadium-like seats created by still-growing saplings surrounded the stage and were filled with people and spirits. The noise grew to near deafening levels when they saw me approach the podium. Some cheered, some booed, and some shouted things that made no sense.

"Free Stuart!"

"Two-dollar lattes are not ancestral libations!"

"Anyone got some incense?"

The podium stood above a living map of the region, and now the clouds I'd seen floating by earlier made sense. Maybe one day when I wasn't in a heap of trouble I could check it out. But in the meantime, as I stepped up to the lectern, its glass surface shimmered. Words appeared on it, and a soft voice read them aloud in my ear as they scrolled across its surface.

"*Welcome, Jackson Freeman, to the Court of the Ancestors. I am a figment attached to this podium, here to aid you. Below is a map of all five Great Lakes and the territories of the five families. If at any time you need clarification, just speak up and I will do my best to help. For now, please wait.*"

"Can I speak before Devin and Nina get judged?" I whispered to the figment.

"*Apologies, Jackson Freeman,*" it answered. "*There are no other cases on the docket today.*"

"But..." I said, confused. "My uncle told me—"

"*One moment,*" the figment interrupted. "*The congregation is approaching.*"

On the map below me, tiny boats sailed over the lakes as miniature waves hammered the shores. Pinpricks of light representing cars hummed along interstates and freeways. I saw a storm system moving down from Toronto to Ohio. A tiny set of railroad tracks crossed the Indiana and Illinois border. And hovering above it all was a pair of glittering silver doors made of stars, one doorknob an ivory skull, the other a golden fist. Black chains crisscrossed the double doors and were secured with multiple padlocks.

"The giant doors from my vision," I said quietly, but the podium figment must've heard me.

"*The Door of Return, also known as the Door of Gold and Bone, was once the portal from which ancestors and spirits granted their power to summoners. It is now closed for... information missing.*"

I was about to ask for clarification when another door appeared near the semicircle of trees in front of me. Eight silver-masked stewards stepped out. They fanned across the stage, glanced around, then stood to the side as three elders emerged—two men and a woman.

Members of the congregation.

I could tell who they were because the crowd grew quiet as they entered, either out of respect or anticipation. Each elder wore a kosmogram medallion—the circle bisected by the cross—somewhere on their person. A tall woman with locs had looped a headscarf through hers. A short but wide man wore his on his belt like a buckle.

Other people followed the elders, but I was so busy trying to figure out which family was represented by which person that I didn't see the last member of the congregation until she waggled her fingers at me. She moved toward an empty space at the end of the semicircle, where she sat down, looking smug.

Miss Naomi.

"Wait, what are you doing here?" I said, stepping off the podium toward her. "Where are Devin and Nina? Why—"

But before I'd gone far, two stewards appeared in front of me, blocking my way.

"JACKSON FREEMAN," a voice boomed over the terrace. "WE WOULD ADVISE YOU NOT TO MAKE YOUR SITUATION WORSE."

I scowled but let the stewards usher me back to the podium. Nothing was happening the way I thought it would. The short man standing in front of his tree—"*Tree of Skulls, Elder James*," the podium told me—stepped forward and held out his hands to quiet the crowd, even though no one else was talking. Everyone's attention was riveted on what was about to happen.

"What was *supposed* to be a celebration of the Summoning Games," Elder James said, "a time of community togetherness and renewed peace amid the violence emerging between our great trees, has now been reduced to a panel of judgment." He shook his head at me. "Son, you're in big trouble. You've been accused of theft, of unsanctioned summoning, of risking the safety of the summoning community, and the destruction of property, to name a few. Do you have anything to say for yourself?"

This was it. The opportunity I'd been waiting for. I took a deep breath and cleared my throat.

Wait...*I* was being accused?

Not Devin and Nina? But Uncle Moe had said...

"Well?" Elder James demanded.

"Oh, give him a minute, Elder. He's a bit starstruck," Miss Naomi said, leaning forward in her seat. "I'm sure this will be *entertaining.*"

"MR. SKULLS," I said, and I flinched as my voice boomed across the terrace. Several people in the crowd gasped in alarm.

The man winced. "No need to shout," he said. "Your regular voice will carry fine."

"Oh. Um, Mr. Skulls—"

"And no need for Mister this or Madame that. You can address us by—"

"Right," I said. "Honored Oldheads, I came here today to warn you about something, but I think it's too late."

"Did he just say 'honored Oldheads'?" one of the others whispered.

"She," I continued, pointing at Miss Naomi, "is plotting something terrible. Horrible. I know Devin and Nina have been accused of summoning and performing other unsanctioned magic, too, but the truth is, we all did it because *she* summoned spirits to attack us! And her father!"

The crowd exploded into noise.

(Not literally, you feel me; that's a figure of speech, which—if that's another phrase that confuses you like it did me—doesn't mean there's an actual figure. I used to think saying *figure of speech* was like saying *Jax of North Carolina*, but that's neither here nor there . . . which is *another* phrase— You know what? I'm getting carried away. The English language is ridiculous.)

Everyone started talking at once. One of the stewards leaned over to whisper in Elder James's ear, but he flapped him away as he tried to restore order. It took several minutes for him to do so, and he glared at me afterward. "What nonsense are you spouting? I'm warning you—"

"She and her gang of rogue shadow summoners sent avarice spirits to attack Papa Coin." I pointed at Miss Naomi, who was curiously calm in the face of my accusation. Didn't she know I was about to expose her whole scam?

Everyone went silent. The elders, the crowd . . . no one spoke or moved for several seconds. The same steward from before bent down to whisper to Elder James, and part of his sentence was amplified before it was cut off.

". . . magical anomaly tripping the wards . . ."

I didn't hear the rest because at that moment Miss Naomi sighed and leaned forward. "Since it's clear none of this will be resolved until this lovable but foolish boy pries his way into grown folks' business, can we end this charade? My role in it is done, anyway."

I looked back and forth between her and Elder James.

The crowd buzzed as the congregation members stared at one another. The woman with the locs—*"Tree of Baskets, Elder Lenore,"* the podium said—frowned at me. "This is no time for games or dramatics, Mr. Freeman," she said.

"Honored—"

"Elder," she interrupted. "Elder Lenore."

"Elder Lenore," I said, "I promise I'm not making anything up."

The woman shook her head impatiently. "I don't know who's putting you up to this, but Naomi didn't come here to attack her father. We sent for her. To protect him."

Every argument I had lined up fizzled out on my tongue like Pop Rocks. *Sent for? To protect him?* But...the attacks in the alley. The shadow summoners. The avarice spirits. Who else would attack, and who else could get past those wards? Who would want to take out Papa Coin?

Now each pair of stewards whispered to their assigned elder, and then, as one, they all turned to look at me. No, I realized, as I felt that peculiar sensation of someone about to flicker...*behind* me.

I turned just as someone materialized on the stage behind me, and in that second, everything clicked into place. There *was* someone who would want to take out Papa Coin. Someone who had held a grudge against him for years. Someone who would benefit from stolen heirlooms because they couldn't summon their own, not since they had been stripped of their magic. He laughed, a snort of disbelief that turned into an ear-piercing cackle that brought tears to his eyes.

"I have waited," Uncle Moe said after catching his breath, "*so* long to do this."

And before anyone could react, he held up a familiar conjure pouch... Papa Coin's! Then, in front of our eyes, he dropped it on the ground and crushed it beneath the heel of his shoe. Something shattered, and a gust of wind ripped across the podium, swirling around Uncle Moe before spiraling up into the sky. I flinched away, and when I looked back, he looked... different. His spine seemed straighter, his eyes brighter, and a smile—cruel and mocking—twisted his lips. He slipped his hand into his pocket, brought his hands chest-high, and steepled his fingers in a familiar gesture.

And then he summoned. A train ticket. The Freeman heirloom.

"Shriek," he hissed while glaring at the congregation. "You're mine again!"

A horn was the only warning we received before the miniature railroad tracks on the map rose into the air next to the stage. They grew larger with each passing second until they were standard-sized. Then—with a blast of wind and thunder—the Shriek appeared and plowed through the podium. As the elders were pulled out of the way by the stewards, the train smashed into me before slamming into Uncle Moe himself and speeding up and out into the Chicago sky.

CHICAGO DEFENDER, VOLUME CVIII, ISSUE 14, NOVEMBER 2013

Record Number of Babies Born During Storm

Chicago General Hospital's head of maternal care reported that the hospital saw a record number of infants born during the year's worst storm last week. Unprecedented lightning strikes caused power glitches, while many visitors reported seeing ~~~~~~~~~~~~

SCHOOL CLOSINGS TO CONTINUE

Protesters stand outside the Chicago Public Schools boardroom to voice disagreement with the board's decision to close upward of fifty schools. Moe Freeman, a local steelworker, led a group as they listed reasons as to why the decision would disproportionately affect marginalized communities ~~~~~~~

LOCAL BUSINESSMAN BEATS OUT NATIONAL BRANDS TO WIN CONTRACT

Dennis Bell, affectionately known around his businesses as Papa Coin, celebrated at his barbershop yesterday with the neighborhood. Bell recently won the contract to offer his much sought-after car service

ATTENTION ALL SUMMONERS, ATTENTION ALL SUMMONERS, A NEGOTIATION TO CEASE ALL HOSTILITIES HAS BEEN PROPOSED. AGAIN, A NEGOTIATION TO CEASE ALL INTER-TREE HOSTILITIES, ALSO KNOWN AS THE "FEUD," HAS BEEN PROPOSED. A MESSAGE FROM THE CONGREGATION WILL FOLLOW SHORTLY. YOUR ANCESTORS THANK YOU. to the

Chicago Bulls in a

PART
FIVE

CHAPTER
THIRTY-SEVEN

FOR THE SECOND TIME IN AS MANY DAYS I WOKE up dazed and confused on the floor of the Shriek. This time Nina and Devin weren't standing over me, threatening my very existence with ice water. Instead, I lay in the rootwork car, piles of rich black soil scattered around me. I sat up, wincing as my head pounded.

Everything had gone sideways. Uncle Moe had summoned the Shriek. He'd lied about Nina and Devin, the latter of whom was still missing. Where had Two-Saint taken him? And if Miss Naomi wasn't the one in charge of the shadow summoners, who was?

A roar interrupted my thoughts. I needed to get to the next car to check on the Gringemaw, see how close it was. A pair of lumpy garment bags were leaning against the slam door behind me, so I stood and headed to the front of the car. Then I paused when I saw I wasn't alone.

Uncle Moe sat on top of a workbench on the far side of the car. And next to him? Two-Saint, handing over clumps of leafy herbs. I wanted to confront them both, but I was distracted by what they were doing. My uncle was slouched against the wall, his head tilted up as he stared at the ceiling, his hands balled into fists on his lap. He'd discarded his sweater-vest on the floor, and his button-down shirt was untucked, the sleeves rolled up on his forearms. He took the fresh herbs from Two-Saint and squeezed them in his left hand. Emerald sparks floated from his fist. Then he opened it to reveal dry, brittle brown husks, which he let drop. Bits of herbs lay scattered across his lap and on the workbench next to him. They looked familiar. . . .

"I saw him when I was about your age," Uncle Moe said suddenly. "Twelve, maybe thirteen."

I walked closer. "What is going on with you?" I demanded. "Why did you—"

My uncle continued as if I wasn't speaking, while Two-Saint shot me a panicked glance, then looked away. "Down in Wilmington, outside my parents' store. Clear as day. He stood on the tracks in the field where we let the chickens run around. A train hadn't come through there in years. Years! But he stood there, dressed in a porter's uniform, as tall and as proud as you can be. And then, out of the darkness, came a rumbling. A great rumbling. Thunder, earthquakes, all that at the same time. And this . . . *thing* emerges from the dark. Horrible look-ing. All hands and faces, screams and claws. And he, that man, stood in front of it, and he looked at me. He looked at me. And he said, 'Tell them I'm sorry.' And then that thing . . . that thing . . ."

Uncle Moe's voice trailed off, and I stepped closer. His hands were trembling, and there was something in his right fist—something other than a clump of herbs. Whatever it was, he squeezed it so tight I was surprised he hadn't hurt himself.

"That was it for you," I said. "Your Origin of Spirits. You saw—"

"The Gringemaw," he whispered. "I saw it eat my great-grandfather." He cleared his throat, and then, to my surprise, he hopped down from the workbench with the agility of some-one a few decades younger. His movements were sure, precise. He was no longer the confused old man who drove like he wanted to become a front-page headline.

"That year I turned thirteen, things became . . . different for me. I started seeing things that weren't there. Hearing people talking when no one was around. I thought I was losing my mind. I started acting out, getting in trouble, getting in fights. My mother sent me to Gran, who told me what I was. What *we* are."

"Summoners," I said softly.

"Powerful," Uncle Moe said. "And some people can't handle that. Even some summoners can't handle it. But word among the summoners was that there was a Coins man who knew all about power and was doing great things with it. The W. E. B. Du Bois of magic, they called him. So I started working for him, doing odd jobs, sweeping up his one-chair barbershop, polishing the wheels on the two cars he had before he had a whole limo service. And I watched. Watched him summon. Watched him charm. Watched him create conjure pouches and wards to make him even stronger as he gathered more and more summoners under his influence."

Who else would attack, and who could get past those wards?

"But when I finally worked up the courage to tell him who I was and what I'd seen, you know what he did? He laughed. Laughed! Said Portis Freeman had gotten exactly what he deserved." Uncle Moe whirled around and slammed his hands down on the workbench. I jumped back, but he just shook his head and opened his hands, letting the contents finally fall to the table.

It was Papa Coin's conjure pouch, torn to shreds.

Who would want to take out Papa Coin?

"And when I started researching on my own, trying to understand what had happened to my great-grandfather, he had the nerve to reprimand me. Lecture me! *Forbid* me! So what if I took a few things from the other trees? They were looking for a reason to fight one another anyway. This was important; why couldn't they see that? Why couldn't *he* see that?"

Some kind of argument turned them against each other.

Uncle Moe stared at the bits of herbs still stuck to his fist, then snarled. As if squeezing them was too slow, he started gathering the clumps around him and stuffing them into his mouth. He chewed and swallowed as if he hadn't eaten for days. His eyes shone with a light that made me uneasy, like he wasn't completely there but instead was reliving all the slights ever inflicted on him. I started to back away, but the garment bags were still blocking the door behind me. I didn't want to go forward, either, and get any closer to Uncle Moe. I tried to make eye contact with Two-Saint, but he wouldn't look up. It was like he was terrified of attracting attention. From the way Uncle Moe was acting, I couldn't really blame him. I just wanted to know why my friend was helping this guy.

"And then..." Uncle Moe whispered. The leaves in his mouth distorted the words, so I had to strain to understand. "He took my magic. He... took it! He and that stuffy, self-righteous bunch of elitists who call themselves the congregation. More like con *artists*. They locked me up and stripped me of my ability to summon. Couldn't so much as flicker without one of them breathing down my neck. Laid a trick on me with his own conjure pouch."

The image of Uncle Moe stepping on Papa Coin's conjure pouch flashed into my memory. So that's how he'd broken the curse. By destroying the tool of the summoner who laid the trick.

"Do you know what that's like? To know that you should be able to feel something, because you can still remember feeling it, but you're cut off? To remember the taste of power before everything turned bitter? They made me a prisoner in MY OWN BODY!"

A shriek of rage ripped from Uncle Moe's mouth as he slammed his fists over and over into the workbench. I stepped forward, sure he was going to hurt himself... but before I could reach him, the wooden table splintered. Cracked right down the middle and collapsed in a pile on the floor. Uncle Moe's chest heaved as he stood huddled over the debris, his fists balled.

"No more," he whispered, letting the remaining herbs fall from his hands. A sprig unfurled, and recognition sparked in my mind. I *had* seen that plant before. In Nina's purse, when we were in Conjure Station.

Carver's vine. Perfect for restoring a summoner's energy. If you'd suddenly regained your ability to summon after several decades, you'd probably chew a handful, too.

"No more," he said again. He turned toward me and straightened, sighing and stretching. "And then you got kids like your friend here." He dropped a hand casually on Two-Saint's shoulder, who flinched. "Can't summon, just because he doesn't have an heirloom. That ain't fair, is it? So I told Toussaint here, I said, 'You help me, I'll get you an heirloom. I'll get you power. No one wants to help you but me. Because they're selfish, inconsiderate, power-hungry dictators.'"

Two-Saint finally looked up, and suddenly it all made sense. I remembered the way other summoners, like Jalen, had made fun of him for not having an heirloom. Two-Saint had wanted to fit in, the same way I'd wanted to fit in with Marcus back in North Carolina. And, after years of being pushed away by everyone else, Two-Saint had taken the first friendly hand that was extended to him. Yet not everyone who acts like they want to help has your best interests at heart. From the expression on the boy's face, it seemed that Two-Saint had come to realize that about Uncle Moe. But he was in too deep now.

"It's their turn," Uncle Moe was saying. "They think they're so powerful. So wise. So . . . perfect. I'm going to show them how powerful they really are as they watch their own precious little ones get stripped of their power. Let them see how it feels to be able to do nothing. Starting with Coin himself. I want to see him in pain. I want him to *suffer*."

Uncle Moe turned to face me, and I was confused for a moment. Then I heard someone groan behind me. I spun around, my eyes widening in horror as I realized what—or who—was inside the garment bags. I yanked down the zipper of the one on the left.

Nina's head lolled forward as she groaned again.

I unzipped the other bag, and Devin's eyes, blurry and unfocused, rolled in their sockets.

"No," I whispered.

"Move aside, Jax," Uncle Moe said. His voice could chill ice.

"Uncle Moe—"

"I said, move aside. Toussaint, go get those kids."

Two-Saint's eyes widened in panic. He glanced at me, took a few steps forward, then stopped and shook his head. He mumbled something, and Uncle Moe scowled.

"Speak up, boy," he commanded.

"I . . . don't want to," Two-Saint said.

Uncle Moe folded his arms across his chest. "What happened to earning your heirloom, boy? You forget what you wanted? You signed up for this—I didn't make you."

Two-Saint shuffled backward. "I didn't . . . I didn't sign up to hurt anybody."

"Uncle Moe," I said, cutting in. "Please stop. What will Gran think?"

His eyes softened, and then he shook his head. "I'm doing this for her. For *us*! For Freemans, and everyone forgotten by the so-called congregation. Now, Toussaint, get those kids and bring them here, or else!"

Two-Saint, breathing rapidly, took a stuttering step forward, then stopped again. He shook his head and backed up. "I can't," he whispered. "I don't want to hurt them. They're my—"

"USELESS!" Uncle Moe roared. In an instant he had his chalk out and was drawing a summoner's link on the wall. With the other hand he snatched Two-Saint by the collar, and by the time I realized what he was about to do, it was too late.

"NO!" I shouted, lunging forward. I missed by inches.

Uncle Moe shoved Two-Saint into the link. The boy's scream was cut off as my uncle smudged the symbol, preventing me from following. "Coward," he snarled. "Couldn't do what needs to be done."

"You're a monster!" I cried. I held out my arms, blocking Nina and Devin from his view.

Uncle Moe snarled in frustration before he pinched the bridge of his nose and took a deep breath. "Their grandfather hates Freemans," he said, squeezing the words through gritted teeth. "He would rather see us suffer than help. And you want to protect his relatives? Why?"

"They're my friends!" I said.

"THEY'RE COINS!" he shouted.

"IT DOESN'T MATTER!" I shouted back. "If you know what it feels like, why do it to them?"

"Because I *can*," he said, stalking forward. "Because they're weak. I'm going to show them exactly how weak they are, and why their heirlooms will never see another generation of summoners. I'm going to hurt them because I WANT TO HURT THEM!"

"Then you're a bully."

"What?"

"You. Are. A. Bully."

Uncle Moe snorted. "Look who's talking. Tough football player. Bigger than everybody else, picking on everybody else, instigating fights, damaging property! Who are *you* to label *me*?"

"I didn't start it!" I yelled back automatically, as Marcus's image came to my mind. "It was all a misunder—"

"But you didn't *stop* it, did you?" Uncle Moe stood up and laughed. "You didn't! Because it felt good. Made you feel powerful. You can stand there like a gaping fish, but I know the truth about you. You're no better than me or any of us Freeman foul-ups."

Was that true? Was I destined to a life of getting into trouble over and over again? And never speaking up for what was right?

"We are what we are, boy, and it's time to recognize that fact. Bring me those kids."

"No," I said, folding my arms. "This isn't what porters do. We *help* people." The bottom of my coat flapped against my legs. "You're taking out your anger at Papa Coin on kids who didn't even do anything. You're the one who said that only the weak hurt the weaker, and now look at you! Please, Uncle Moe, you don't have to do this."

"Jackson," he warned. "Don't make me discipline you like I did Toussaint. Do as I say."

I turned around and unzipped both bags at the same time. Nina and Devin fell forward, and I managed to hoist them up, one over each shoulder. I grunted with effort as I slowly stood up.

"Good," Uncle Moe said, wiping off the workbench. "Now bring them over here—"

If I was going to be a troublemaker, so be it. I'd start by not obeying my uncle.

Instead, I reached for the handle of the slam door behind them and stepped out into the wind.

CHAPTER
THIRTY-EIGHT

I DISEMBARKED FROM THE SHRIEK ONTO CONJURE Station carrying Nina and Devin. A cement statue with a dry fountain basin floated by, and I flickered up to it and deposited them inside. Then I collapsed onto the attached bench, my head in my hands. What was I going to do now, stay here forever? Maybe. But not with Devin and Nina...I had to get them back home safely. How had everything gotten so out of hand?

I rode the fountain like a carousel as it orbited the main welcome platform. The kiosks were just as impressive as the last time, and as I rested, I took comfort in the smells of the sizzling kebabs and other foods. The giant split-flap display hovered overhead with the same times and destinations frozen upon it. But the place was devoid of other travelers.

Except one.

"You're choosing them over being a Freeman?"

I looked up.

A food stall floated overhead. Its sign had a painting of meatballs dripping in sauce, but it didn't make me hungry. I only had eyes for the man sitting on the stool in front of it, a meatball on a toothpick in each hand.

He popped the meatballs into his mouth, made a face, then spat them out into space, where they sank into the nebula below. "Ugh. Never did see the appeal of those. Wads of ground meat smothered in tomato juice? Yuck!"

Uncle Moe rolled his sleeves up farther. "Let me show you something I learned. Did you know you could use more than one heirloom? Just gotta convince an ancestor you need the power. But they won't tell you that in that school of yours. Just like they won't tell you that a summoner in the service of another can do magic on their behalf. Really handy if, say, your magic's been stolen. Right, Toussaint? But now that the trick is gone, let's see if I can get this to work for myself."

He steepled his hands in front of his chest, and, with his face scrunched with concentration, summoned the largest heirloom I'd ever seen. A scythe the length of a motorcycle, rippling in the air between us and covered with red-orange flames so bright I had to squint. It was a vicious color, bathing Conjure Station in its glow, and it crackled like lightning. Like a bonfire.

Like what had destroyed Papa Coin's alley.

Like what had destroyed Miss Ella's cottage.

The second person who'd kidnapped Devin...that had been Uncle Moe.

A summoner in the service of another can do magic on their behalf.

No.

Two-Saint *had* been the one to cause that destruction. He'd done it while working for Uncle Moe. I'd seen him, I realized, that evening in the alley. The shadowy figure hiding behind Papa Coin's chair. He'd been right there. The pieces falling into place knifed me in the guts, and in my shocked state, I nearly became a sitting duck.

The fire surrounding Uncle Moe's scythe raged for several moments. Then the weapon disappeared, and a smaller blaze flared up in his left palm. He started launching fireballs in quick succession like his hand was a cannon. They demolished several kiosks and statues before he quenched the flame, laughing in sheer delight. "Look! It's all coming back to me, like riding a bike! Wait till they see this. Wait till they realize what's about to happen. The feud will seem like a little tantrum by the time I'm finished. Their bloodlines are done. Their genealogy is done. Their heirs and heirlooms are *done*! HEY!"

I'd turned to try to pick up Nina and Devin when I felt the looming pressure of magical power behind me. "Not thinking of leaving yet, are you?" my uncle said, grabbing my shoulder. "These children still have a debt to pay. Their family owes me."

"They don't owe you anything," I spat.

He snarled and lunged forward. Ducking from his grasp, I threw myself backward and flickered away, while clutching Nina's arm in my left hand and Devin's in my right. I landed on the nearest platform in orbit. Not a second later, Uncle Moe appeared at my side like a shadow, grabbing at me. I flickered to a fountain, and he did the same.

What came next was like a terrifying game of tag.

I flickered to a kiosk, and he followed.

I fled to a different platform only to find him already waiting there.

Bench. Statues. Food stall. Wherever I ran, he showed up.

He finally caught me when I flickered back to a train platform and slipped onto the tracks. I lost my balance and dropped Nina and Devin in the railbed. When I caught myself and started to turn around, a fireball shot past my ear, sending me reeling backward. I nearly tumbled off the tracks and into orbit, but Uncle Moe flickered next to me and snagged my collar.

"You don't see it, do you, Jax?" he said, the scythe reappearing in his hand.

My coat began to smoke. *Not my coat!* But Uncle Moe was so consumed by rage that he didn't even notice. "With the power, your parents wouldn't have to scrape and skimp to get by. No more hand-me-down clothes for you. The Freeman House would be restored to its former glory, the way Portis Freeman would've wanted it, the way *I* want it. Why don't you want it? Aren't you a Freeman?"

"I thought..." I whispered.

"You thought what? That this is all about you and your little problems at school? Making new friends? You've got to think bigger, boy. This is about your family. The people who gave you life, took you in, look after you. The Coins ain't going to do anything for you. What did you think?"

"I thought..."

"What?" He started to pull me closer, then finally noticed that my coat was smoldering. He patted it to extinguish the flames he had summoned, but by then it was too late. My coat was ruined. I shrugged it off and watched it burn on the platform floor. That could've been me!

"I thought," I said, steepling my fingers, "that you wouldn't fall for it."

Uncle Moe frowned. "Boy, what are you—"

The Shriek erupted out of the nebula at full speed, barreling along a rapidly unfolding Gray Line into Conjure Station, right on the tracks where we stood. Uncle Moe whirled around to face it, his burning scythe twirling in front of him. He extended the weapon and the Shriek slammed on its brakes, wheels screaming and horn blaring as Uncle Moe poured more and more energy into holding off the phantom train. Amazingly, it screeched to a grinding halt a few feet in front of us, rumbling impatiently.

While Uncle Moe struggled with the train, I ran over to where Devin and Nina lay. Nina was starting to come to, and I helped her to her feet before lifting Devin. "I've got to get back into the weight room." I grunted as I staggered to the Shriek. "Come on, get aboard," I told Nina.

"What about you?" she asked.

"I'll be right behind you. Here, take Sleeping Beauty."

"I heard that," Devin muttered in a groggy voice. I put him on his feet, and he wobbled uncertainly.

The two of them managed to climb aboard the train, which

was starting to inch forward. Uncle Moe was losing the battle. Any second now he'd run out of the boost the Carver's vine had given him, and then he'd either have to dodge out of the way or get on the Shriek with us. Maybe, once he was weaker, I could talk some sense . . .

A shout of frustration echoed through Conjure Station as the train began to move. I placed one foot on the step and looked back at my uncle.

He was still standing in the middle of the tracks, seemingly paralyzed as he stared into the distance.

Then a deafening howl shook the platform. It hadn't come from Moe this time.

"Oh no!" I whispered, jumping off the train step. I flickered to the front of the Shriek and tackled Uncle Moe. He grunted in surprise as I grabbed him in a bear hug and flickered to the other side of the platform.

The Shriek shot forward, blaring its horn and shooting off around the nebula before it disappeared with Nina and Devin safely inside.

Uncle Moe and I landed in a heap on the ground. His flaming scythe sputtered before fading away.

"HAVE YOU LOST YOUR MIND?" he yelled.

But I didn't have a chance to respond, because another spine-tingling howl, the kind that rattles your teeth, filled the air. My heart dropped in my chest. The Shriek's departure had been delayed, allowing its pursuer to catch up.

The Gringemaw had arrived.

Its many mouths howled as it crawled into Conjure Station.

Dozens of hands pulled it forward through rubble and destruction. Multiple pairs of eyes swam around each other, landing on fountains, on statues, on platforms, until all of them found what the amalgam spirit was looking for:

Me.

The sounds that emerged from the monster rooted me to the platform. A tortured scream echoing a hundred times over battered my ears and my core, until I could feel my sanity slipping away. The creature shambled closer, ripping up chunks of the station and cramming them into the nearest mouth.

It feeds on the energy we channel, Madame Helene had said. And what was Conjure Station but a collection of channeled energy? As the Gringemaw moved toward me, the will to flee from it drained from me like someone had pulled the plug on my self-determination. I fell to the ground.

But I wasn't the only one suffering. Uncle Moe's energy—both physical and spiritual—was nearly gone as well. He was skinny, skinnier than I'd ever seen him, as he crawled around the platform. Sparks drifted up from his skin, and as they left, his movements grew slower and slower. His gas tank was on E. His abilities had faded, leaving him a frail old man. A summoner whose time was nearly at an end, with no more Carver's vine at his disposal.

Power borrowed from the ancestors.

He'd used up all the power he'd stolen, and then some. Miss Ella had warned me about this. Uncle Moe had taken too much of what wasn't his, and now the spirits wanted it back.

With the little strength I had left, I stood.

"Jax?" he said. He was beginning to glow.

I shook my head. "I'm sorry," I said. "I can't...."

If Miss Ella were here, she could've helped him, but he'd blown up her house. Now he was paying the consequences.

He lifted his hands to his face, staring at them as a strange light gathered beneath the tips of his fingers. It traveled up his arms and his neck, into his face.

Power is provided, not purchased.

"Jax, what's happening? It hurts.... It hurts!" He started screaming, and I backed away, terrified, my own condition irrelevant as I watched the ancestors reclaim their power.

"Jax? JAX? JA—"

I closed my eyes, no longer able to watch. My arms felt so heavy, my body so tired. Was this how all Freeman summoners were destined to end up? Consumed by power or by monster?

FFFFFT.

When I opened my eyes again, Uncle Moe was gone. A faint glimmer of light was all that remained, and it drifted off the platform, sinking into the nebula below.

A thousand screeches filled the station. I lifted my head and scowled at the Gringemaw. "Hurry up and get it over with," I said.

Darkness closed over me, and the screams of the Gringemaw were the only answer I received before one of its many hands dragged me to one of its many mouths, and I was swallowed by the monster.

CHAPTER
THIRTY-NINE

THE GRINGEMAW WAS AN AMALGAM, AND AMALGAM
meant many spirits combined.

I floated on the outskirts of a crowd of hundreds. Was I a spirit now, too? Could spirits cry? My uncle was gone. I didn't know whether to be sad or glad. He'd hurt people, he'd schemed, and he'd lied, but still, he was my uncle. Should I feel pain for the hurt he'd experienced, or anger for the hurt he'd caused others?

I floated.

Would anyone mourn him? Would anyone mourn me? Who would comfort Gran? To be a Freeman was to deal with suffering, it seemed. Was I an ancestor now? Could I give Gran power to strengthen her?

I floated. I floated with the young and the old, the big and the small; with the suits and ties and the holey cargo pants, I drifted. And they weren't all human, either. There were stone spirits with wagging tails and gravelly fur, and river spirits with webbed fingers and wide eyes. There were forest spirits with dappled skin like bark and hair that flowed down their shoulders and backs like the branches of a willow tree. There were giant spirits and tiny spirits, monstrous spirits and adorable cherubs. Their mouths moved, but I couldn't hear what they said unless I touched them, and after the first few instances of accidentally getting insight into some of their thoughts and feelings, I tried very hard to avoid that. One person's sadness was good enough for me, thank you very much.

So I just floated around them, always moving, silent, a leaf falling through a forest, an unmoored boat bobbing on an ocean. The Gringemaw was an amalgam, and amalgam meant many spirits combined.

You don't belong here.

I spun in a slow circle and looked around. No spirit was within five yards of me, so what was that? Seriously? I was hearing voices now? Figured. Being trapped in the abyss of an amalgam was sure to involve some sort of hallucinations. Go ahead and drop those on me, I thought. At least I wouldn't be bored.

Are you just going to float there and do nothing?

Ugh. No one had said the voices were going to harass me! Maybe they were intrusive thoughts. Who wanted to remain for all eternity with nagging hallucinations? Ew—0 out of 10, not a fan. What was next? Were they going to insult my weight and my clothes, too?

You are bigger than this, Jax.

Oh, for the love of— Wait, that wasn't an insult. More like a stern reprimand. The kind your parents or a teacher would give, or one of your elders at a family reunion who caught you drawing faces on your reunion T-shirt because all they had for kids was a size small and if people were gonna laugh at you, it might as well be for something you'd actually done. . . .

Sorry, got a little carried away there.

I drifted on. Don't know for how long. Minutes, maybe. Could've been hours. The Gringemaw was an amalgam, and amalgam meant many spirits combined.

Jax! I know you can hear me. You've got to come back.

I opened my eyes in annoyance and floated off again. Couldn't I wallow in eternal self-pity in peace? It wasn't every day your spirit got eaten, after all. And now I had to deal with other spirits? Is this what meatballs had to deal with after I ate them?

Things could've continued like that for a long time— me complaining, circling the milling spirits lost inside the Gringemaw like a new kid watching others play at recess—if a commotion hadn't broken out nearby. A cluster of spirits exploded into a storm of ghostly hands. Silent fury erupted for several seconds before the group suddenly broke apart and drifted away as if nothing had happened . . . all except for one. A small oval of blue-and-green light that pulsed slowly.

I drifted over, curious. The light sharpened, and the oval became a child with brown skin and blue-green eyes, black hair in tight coils. When she saw me getting closer, she flinched, and I stopped. When I didn't approach, she slowly relaxed, waved, and began to drift away, blue-and-green light pulsing from her like the aurora borealis. But she hadn't even gone ten feet when a cluster of spirits descended on her again.

"Hey!" I shouted as they swarmed. "Leave her alone! HEY!"

But they didn't, and I didn't think before I acted. I steepled my fingers and summoned.

I don't know what I'd expected to happen, but it wasn't that every spirit around me would freeze and leave me feeling like I was staring at a photograph. Not just the few in my immediate vicinity. All of them. Then, as one, they turned to face me.

I watched them.

They watched me.

"Did I . . . do something wrong?" I asked.

The tiny child spirit flitted over to me and floated in front of my face. She was curious, cocking her head this way and that, and then—to my surprise—she steepled her fingers and looked up at me.

"Yeah, I was trying to summon, but it didn't work," I said. "Maybe it can't be done here." She steepled her fingers again and I shook my head. "It won't work."

But she just floated there, imitating me, and I got annoyed. "I keep telling you, I can't do it! It's not working! Look!" And I steepled my fingers again and tried to summon, ready for nothing to happen, and I was right. Nothing did happen . . . while I tried on my own. But then the child spirit placed her hands over mine.

A small, faint circle of light appeared, and beneath it, a tiny rectangle.

"What . . . What's happening?" I asked. "How did you . . . ? I don't even know what this is. And why is it so small? We can't even—"

Another spirit floated up, interrupting my babbling. A river spirit. The otter-like creature placed a webbed hand on me and smiled. I felt a surge of power shoot through me, into my fingertips, and into the glowing circle, which grew slightly larger. Then another spirit came, and another. They placed their hands—or paws, or snouts, or giant claws—on me, and soon more spirits were floating over to connect with those spirits. It went on and on, each spirit lending power to me as the circle and rectangle grew larger and larger, from a pea to a disk to a hula hoop to a giant . . .

"Summoner's link," I breathed. "This is a summoner's link! We can get out of here!"

The oval-shaped link flashed yellow, then green, before settling on the familiar silver-blue I recognized. A connecting link had been found.

"Go!" I shouted to the spirits that still drifted around me. "What are you waiting for?"

A stone spirit—looked like another rockweiler—bounded away, then ran back to me, like a dog asking to go out on a walk. A monstrous spirit lumbered forward on knuckled claws and swiped at the link several times. When nothing happened, it retreated, returning to wait behind the stone spirit. Several spirits tried, but they couldn't open the link, and soon every spirit was queued up by the summoner's link. They needed my help.

You're a porter, I remembered Madame Helene saying, *and you help spirits make their way home.*

Even if I wasn't on the Shriek, I could still help these spirits.

"All right," I said loudly, clapping my hands and marching to the summoner's link and facing the front of the line. I tried to imagine how Dr. Clayton would handle this, or my gran, or even Uncle Moe. Well, okay, maybe not Uncle Moe, but you get the picture. I had to act like an adult. "Single-file line, y'all. Don't make me . . . uh, give you homework. Don't make me lecture you! Raaah, I'm an adult! Listen to me or . . . or I'll take away your video games. Blaaaah!"

All right, so I didn't know how to be an adult. Whatever. I'm twelve.

I reached out and pushed the door, and the link flared. It opened to reveal a spiraling whirlpool of purple and violet, like I was staring through one of the amethysts Miss Ella had kept in her courtyard. In fact . . .

"All right! Here we go!" I shouted. I took a deep breath, then waved the first spirit, the rockweiler, through.

"I am the pebble in rivers, from the basalt in the mountain, the shelter from storms."

Next came the monstrous spirit.

"I am the storm, the harbinger, the thunderhead, and the maelstrom."

On and on, each spirit passed through, handing me their story like a passenger would pass a ticket to a conductor.

"I am the forest guardian, the cool shadow, the willow tree."

"*I am Douglass, the first to take that name, discarding the other, the first to see freedom and the last to see the yoke.*"

"*I am Abdullah, the hidden, who brought the secrets of the harvest.*"

"*I am Strife, the unwelcome, the scorned, the hated.*"

Until there were only two spirits left—a large man in glasses with a haunted expression, and the child with blue-and-green eyes.

"Let's go, you two," I said, looking back and forth between them. "Nothing to be afraid of."

The child glanced at the man before floating forward. She waved, flitting about like a fairy, then crossed through the summoning link.

"*I am the cymbee, the water spirit, from the lakes of the old country to the rivers of the new, with a sea in between, who welcomed you when you fled the ships, who disguised your footprints when the hounds chased you, who turned your mills and watered your crops, and I thank you.*"

She was through, and that left the giant man who wouldn't stop staring at me. He seemed familiar, but it was probably fatigue on my part. Every spirit was starting to look like someone I knew.

"You all right, mister?" I asked.

The man opened his mouth, then closed it.

"*I . . . am afraid.*"

"Well, you're the last one, so we can go through together. Is that cool?" I held out my hand, and he took it, and I heard a faint thought as I was just about to step through the link.

"I . . . would like that, but it isn't traveling I'm afraid of. . . . I am afraid of what awaits me, great-great-grandson."

I stared at him just as we were entering the link. At the wide shoulders, the round face, the features that, now that I examined them, looked so much like my own.

"I am Freeman, the name that is a celebration, the summoner, the porter, the first in the family, and I am so proud of you, Jackson. I am . . . mighty proud."

CHAPTER
FORTY

I STUMBLED OUT OF THE SUMMONER'S LINK ONTO a familiar hilltop. The high, chiseled stone of the Old Crossroads surrounded me and the spirits who'd escaped the Gringemaw.

Spirits like my great-great-grandfather.

Portis Freeman.

The spirit who was my ancestor floated in front of me. He put one hand on my shoulder, which felt like a gust of wind, and then pulled me into an embrace.

Have you ever hugged a spirit? Imagine the wind holding you aloft. Imagine the ocean supporting you as you lie on your back, floating on the waves. Imagine the warmth of the sun when you first step outside, or the rustle of leaves as you walk under the trees. Imagine being accepted as who you are, in that moment, unequivocally, without judgment, or fear, or reluctance. Imagine being loved.

The embrace ended all too soon. Portis Freeman backed up, waved good-bye, and headed down the hill. I wiped a tear from my eye as I watched him mingle with the others. Some spirits were clearly waiting on something, but the nature spirits were beginning to disperse, drifting down into the valley, sinking into the ground, or heading up into the mist. Part of me wondered what it would be like to visit the spirit realm. Maybe I could stop in one day and just take a look-see.

Below us, at the end of a winding path lined with boulders and dozing stone spirits, lay Miss Ella's cottage, fully rebuilt. I looked down and brushed aside a few weeds. I smiled. Here too, carved into the earth, was the circle and cross, the same symbol from the summoner's link and the Praise House.

"Though we may have forgotten the power of the ancestors," I said, remembering the words etched over the Praise House door, "the ancestors haven't forgotten us."

I knelt and pressed two fingers against the circle. Maybe it was my imagination, but I swear I felt a brief thrum of energy from it, like a car engine revving. But instead of a car, it was the collective attention of people who'd gone before me, of the wind and the water, of the trees and the mountains, all urging me on. Well, then, who was I to disappoint?

As I got closer to the cottage, the smell of cinnamon bubbled up, and the sound of muttered complaints echoed from inside. I went to pull up the collar of my coat, then remembered it had been destroyed. Another loss. Another thing to mourn.

The wind brushed against my face and through my fingertips, as if asking what I needed a coat for. Who was I trying to hide from? I shrugged and dropped my hands. Maybe hiding was overrated. Let the world hide from *me* if I wasn't what they were expecting.

I made my way down to the back of the cottage—restored to its previous glory, no sign of damage aside from a few scorch marks—where the sliding barn door was wide open. Something heavy clattered to the floor, and a furious stream of words I will not repeat echoed in the cool morning air.

"Hello?" I called through the door, then flinched at the response.

"Don't hello me, Jackson. Get your butt over here and help me lift this cauldron. You see an old woman struggling and you just gonna hello her to death? Children! Do better, son, because I swear upon the grave of . . ."

More complaints followed as I smothered a grin (never show amusement around a complaining adult—they'll think you're laughing at them and somehow blame all life's troubles on you) and entered. Inside the cottage, Miss Ella stood with her hands on her hips and stared shrewdly at me. Then, after a moment, she sniffed, wiped her hands on her apron, and turned to grab her giant oar-spoon. She hefted it over one shoulder, then beckoned me to follow.

Follow me, the Veiled Woman had said, beckoning me.

A hammer blow of realization stopped me in my tracks. *That's* what felt so familiar. The way Miss Ella moved, and the way she spoke sometimes.

What was your OOS? Two-Saint had asked.

"About time you showed up," Miss Ella was saying. "And

brought your little friends with you, too. Hmph. More spirits
to harass my gardens, I bet. Well, don't just stand there—put
the cauldron on the sled! I need some more marigolds, and you
apparently need to train some more, 'cause I'm not running a
motel! What do I look like? You need to get them spirits up
there from where you left them and take them to the Door of
Return, not the door of Miss Ella. And what are you staring
at? Jackson?"

I *was* staring. I couldn't help it—it was like something had
snapped into place in my mind. A puzzle piece in my heart.

"You . . . aren't alive," I said softly.

Miss Ella froze.

"You aren't, are you? You're one of my ancestors. That's
why you live here, at a crossroad. You couldn't cross over, not
without a porter, not until I came along."

"Jackson—"

"You sent the Veiled Woman, didn't you?"

"Child, that's not—"

"Why didn't you tell me? I thought she was trying to hurt
me! What was she, a friend? A named spirit who owed you a
favor?"

The old woman sighed, deflating like a balloon, and it was
as if I was seeing the real her for the first time. She turned and
leaned on her oar-spoon.

"Her name was . . . *is* . . . Eleanor Rogers."

That name . . . I'd heard it before. "The head of the Tree of
Knives?"

Miss Ella nodded. "She created a figment of herself in her

wedding gown to remind her husband not to be late to their wedding, what with him working on the spell he was preoccupied with." She smiled, her eyes lost in memory. "He'd get so lost in his work that the day would get away from him.... She was feeling a bit faint, so she asked him to bring her house slippers to the ceremony. But what she thought was nerves turned out to be their unborn son, the only child they would have together because Portis Freeman never got to finish the spell. And I stood at the altar for hours, even after they told me what happened, even after the sun set, even when the preacher came down the aisle of that tiny church, the aisle I was supposed to walk with my husband."

She turned and finally met my eyes. "Your great-great-grandfather."

"PF and ER," I whispered, remembering the locket I'd found at the Freeman House. "Portis Freeman and Eleanor Rogers."

"He called me Ella, and I hated it." The old woman laughed, tears streaming down her face. "I hated it so much. But when he died, I couldn't bear the thought of losing another part of him, so I kept the name. Same with the figment. I always meant to free that part of myself, but I kept saying one more year, let that bit of spirit roam free, waiting for her husband for one more year, and then... well, it was too late."

I sat down with a heavy *thud* on the bench in the courtyard. A stone spirit, a Chihuahua I recognized, trotted up and nosed my palm. "Hey, Pebble," I said, scratching it behind the ears. I glanced up at Miss Ella (more like looked straight into her eyes, because even sitting down I was taller than her). "So . . . you're my great-great-grandmother."

She nodded.

"Why didn't you tell me?"

Miss Ella sighed. "I panicked, child. I panicked. When your Origin of Spirits called to me, I'd given up on ever making contact with another descendant. I'd tried once before and failed."

"Uncle Moe," I guessed.

She nodded. "At first, I thought you were another one of those snake-oil types trying to steal power, so I put some goofer dust on your pecans. By the time I realized who you were, you'd been spooked and were ready to run off. All I could do was douse you with repel powder to keep you safe from malevolents and beg my figment to watch over you."

"And figments can only do their specific task," I said, thinking back to the cemetery chase, and my vision of the train. "You tried to show me the avarice spirits. And the willow path. But why didn't you tell me who you were when I brought Devin here?"

"I wanted to. I really did. But when you hopped off that train, I thought maybe it would be better not to. You already were dealing with so much. . . . I didn't want to overwhelm you."

I reclined on the bench, scratching Pebble's ears, and stared off into the valley. The cymbee spirit was flitting around with a rockweiler, while the storm spirit pretended it didn't see the horde of Chihuahua stone spirits stalking it. Then, at the last minute, it turned and roared, and they all flickered away, yapping reprimands from a distance. A few of the human spirits, including Portis, lay among the marigolds, while others drifted in a daze, barely maintaining their identities after being a part of the Gringemaw for so long.

"I need to take them to the door," I said.

"This old place handled your phantom train one time," Miss Ella said wryly. "I guess it could do so again."

I nodded, then began to steeple my fingers. As the ticket appeared and the railroad tracks running through the valley began to glow, the blast of a train's horn echoed through the hills. I stood, then paused.

"What about the Gringemaw?" I asked.

"A Gringemaw is—" Miss Ella began to say.

"An amalgam of spirits," I finished. "Yeah, I know."

She rapped me gently on the head. "If you know, then you should understand that you freed all the spirits trapped inside of it. No spirits—"

"No Gringemaw. That's a relief." I paused, then cleared my throat. "He's there. Right now. Portis Freeman."

Miss Ella let out a deep, shuddering sigh. "I expect so."

"Can I . . . take you to him?"

She pursed her lips, then shook her head. "I'll see him in time. Now that he finally made it, we'll have all the time in the world. But you still need my help. A bunch of help. I might as well stick around here for a little while longer and try to do the best I can. Lord knows if I'll succeed."

I snorted and she smiled as the Shriek swept out of the mist above the Old Crossroads, steam billowing from its cowcatcher grille. The spirits began to queue up along the tracks, all waiting to climb aboard and cross over to their realm. I got ready to embark as it rumbled closer but turned back to Miss Ella first.

"I've got to make a couple stops," I said, thinking of Nina and Devin, and wherever Two-Saint was now. "But I'll be back. I have so many questions."

Miss Ella—my great-great-grandmother—smiled and waved at Pebble, who was chewing more marigolds. "You better. I got chores and answers waiting for you. Now go."

I grinned, then flickered away. I had a job to do.

I was a porter.

CHAPTER
FORTY-ONE

A FEW WEEKS LATER, I FOUND AN OMINOUS BLACK business card taped to my locker as school let out for the day. While the rest of the sixth-graders in our wing were running around us, hooting and/or hollering, I stood quietly, Devin and Nina behind me.

"Is that—" Devin started to ask.

"A summons," Nina said, cutting him off.

I looked between the two of them, confused. "What's a summons?"

"To see the congregation? It's like going to the principal's office except for..." Devin peered around, then leaned in. "Summoners."

"Right," I said, sighing. "I guess they couldn't wait for the end of the year to kick me out."

I was barely squeaking by in my classes. My progress report

looked like alphabet soup, my last science test had been forty-five minutes of concentrated stress, and now I had to stand in front of the congregation? After the Glimmer Fest incident, I was sure they already hated me—and all Freemans, thanks to my uncle. Any moment now I could be shipped back to North Carolina, which, surprisingly, made me feel sad.

I mean, I could go back to Raleigh if I wanted to. Mom had called to excitedly tell me and Gran that the judge had ruled in my favor. I was found not guilty of participating in the Great Mall Brawl. Security camera footage showed that I'd been at Bubba Grub's Subs, a footlong meatball sandwich in my hands, at the time of the fight. I was free! *Exonerated* is the word Mom used. And Marcus had gotten in so much trouble for making me his scapegoat that he got kicked off the football team. He was also sentenced to community service at a local preschool every weekend for a year. May his clothes always smell poopy.

Truth was, I'd gotten used to life in Chicago. I didn't mind the Freeman House or DuSable. Maybe even liked them a little. Maybe. And I also felt sorry for Gran. She was . . . well, to say she was heartbroken over Uncle Moe was an understatement. He was still her son, no matter what he'd done. But I think she also knew something like this would happen. No, I didn't want to leave her just yet. Besides, who would help her take care of Boogs?

I also had unfinished business. Two-Saint still hadn't been found. No one knew where Uncle Moe had sent my friend. The elders of the congregation kept reassuring us that they had their best summoners on the case, and that Two-Saint would be located and brought home safely. But I felt we could be doing more, even if it meant I'd have to do it on my own.

And I fully expected that I'd be working by myself. After everything that had happened with Uncle Moe and the Gringemaw, I was sure I'd get ten kazillion lectures—from humans and spirits—about all the things I'd done wrong as a summoner. But nobody had come for me. There'd been no threats from the Coins, no magical detention at school, no one trying to steal my skin.

But that was before I found the card on my locker.

"Welp, I guess that's it for me at DuSable," I said, turning and heading for the exit. "And as a summoner."

"Jax, you don't know that," Nina called after me.

I spun around. "Y'all's grandfather has been trying to get me stripped of magic ever since he first heard about me. And, Nina, your mother tried to get rid of me faster than the school got rid of Bantonio Banderas!"

Professor Benjamin, the administration had learned, had started putting more and more books on the Not Approved list, including our math textbook. "They're improper fractions!" everyone had heard him yelling as they dragged him out. "*Improper!* Children shouldn't be reading them!"

"Wish me luck," I said, before rushing out the door in a crowd of students so I couldn't hear Devin's or Nina's half-hearted reassurances. Better to bite the bull by the horns. Wait, was that saying right?

* * *

I disembarked from the Shriek across the street from a small diner on the corner of 103rd and Torrence. Coin territory. The diner, Julian's, was a one-story brick building with tinted windows and a sidewalk chalkboard in front advertising today's special: BLACKENED CATFISH AND GRITS. Outstanding. As the Shriek disappeared behind me in a spiraling blur of fog and light, I looked at the business card in my hand. One side had JULIAN's printed on it in bright red letters, with the symbol of a plate underneath. But the other side... I flipped it over again even though I knew what it said by heart.

JULIAN'S, 4:00 PM.
SPIRITS WATCH OVER YOU,
THE CONGREGATION

Maybe it was the sun warming the back of my neck, or the thought of blackened catfish, but I felt more optimistic. Whatever the congregation had in store for me, I could get through it. I'd gotten through plenty worse.

As I heaved a deep breath and prepared to cross the street, a large black SUV pulled up to the curb. Out hopped Devin and Nina, who didn't say a word, just bracketed me and waited. The front passenger window rolled down, and I was surprised to see Dre there. He nodded at me, and I nodded back, and then the SUV pulled off.

"That man still owes me some gift cards," I muttered. The light turned green, but I didn't cross. Instead, I looked at my friends. "What are y'all doing here?"

"Character witnesses," Devin said. "Somebody's gotta stick up for your goofy behind."

"I'm . . . so moved by your words."

Nina elbowed me. "Seriously. You came to defend us, even if you were completely wrong about what was happening. It's the thought that counts. Besides, it can't hurt to have a Coin and a Basket back you up."

I swallowed. Both of them were taking a big risk. I couldn't ask them to do that for me. I didn't want them to get into trouble. But deep down, I *did* want them nearby. The idea of not having the ability to summon and my great-great-grandparents' heirloom made me want to vomit. I couldn't lose this part of my life, and yet, what choice did I have? None. Zip. Zilch. Well then, fine. Let them. If all I could have was the past few months, they were a few months I'd never forget.

"Thanks, y'all," I finally said, and squared my shoulders. Before I could think about it for too long, I marched across the street with my friends beside me and plunged into the diner, ready for whatever happened next.

Or at least I thought so.

The diner wasn't open, or at least it didn't have any customers at the moment. A short man wearing an apron and old-school over-the-ear headphones mopped the floor. When he saw us come in, he jerked his head at the rear of the building. Behind a roped-off corner, a set of stairs led up to a hallway, which in turn connected to a small, well-lit room filled with plants and carved wooden statues. Five people sat on one side of a long table: Elder James, another member of the congregation

I hadn't met yet, Elder Hiram, plus Elder Lenore, Miss Naomi, and Papa Coin—with an oxygen tank next to him. The leaders of the midwestern summoning community, the heads (and co-heads) of the four remaining trees. Even though it was late afternoon, the table was heaped high with the remnants of their lunches. Shrimp and grits, waffles drizzled with spicy syrup and topped with golden fried chicken tenders, and huge fluffy biscuits smeared with butter and jam. My stomach grumbled, but I ignored it, trying to listen to what the adults were arguing about.

"And I'm telling you," Elder Lenore was saying, "we have to act now. My office has been fielding messages for days from other families around the world. Questions about stability. About our ability to maintain control."

"It's too soon," Elder Hiram said, stroking his beard. "We have to assess the threat and plot a course of action."

Miss Naomi scoffed. "Really? Plot a course? Don't waste this opportunity—we can grow stronger and remove competition at the same time. The math is simple."

"Perhaps," Papa Coin said, his voice raspy but his gaze sharp as he glared at his daughter, "your eagerness to go on the offensive is the exact wrong thing to do right now."

"And being scared serves us how, Dennis?" Elder James snapped back. A massive leather book was propped open in front of him, and there was a newspaper clipping in his hand. As I watched, the printed letters thickened, shifted, and swirled on the page, and then the clipping drifted down into the book.

Could that book have something to do with the articles

on Portis's walls at the Freeman House? I wondered. Maybe the clippings were messages from the congregation? It would explain why some were old and some were newer....

Elder James was still talking. "A rogue summoner—a shadow summoner with an accomplice, the report says—terrorized our neighborhoods and caused serious damage! We have to be proactive."

The "rogue summoner" was my Uncle Moe. And the accomplice? Two-Saint. It hurt to hear them talk about him when he wasn't here to defend himself.

"No one is scared," Elder Hiram said, sighing. "But the threat of more shadow summoners, plus the return of Conjure Station, are variables we must tread carefully around."

At that point he looked up and saw us hovering in the doorway. He broke off the conversation to beckon us, so we stepped into the room.

Papa Coin glared at me. He, Miss Naomi, and Elder James looked like they wished I'd never made it back from the Gringemaw. Only Elder Hiram and Elder Lenore seemed like they welcomed my presence. The former stood and spread his arms wide.

"Jackson, son, we're so happy you're back and safe," Elder Hiram said, beaming. His grin was so genuine that it almost made up for the fact that no one else was smiling. "And you brought your friends, too—wonderful!"

"Devin...Nina...what are you two doing here?" Papa Coin asked.

"Supporting our friend," Nina answered.

"No one told you kids to come," he said. "Don't you got responsibilities, boy?"

Devin nodded. "I do, Granddad. This is one of them."

"Well, I didn't raise you to lollygag with troublemakers."

I folded my arms, exhausted by the lecture. "They came with me, and I'm here, so can we get the punishment over with? Just take away my summoning so I can go be a kid or something."

Elder Lenore looked surprised. "What do you mean, take away your summoning? Why would we do that?"

"And another thing. You— Wait, what?" I'd been revving up to really lay into them, to get everything off my chest, but the elder's question stopped me in my tracks. "Because... I didn't obey your instructions, right?"

"Well," she said, "at the time, you knew more than we did, and you acted on it. I'd say that showed intelligence, motivation, and concern for your fellow summoners. And even if you did disobey an order from the congregation, we'd never strip you of your ability to summon just for that. Why rob the bird of its wings because it flew in a different direction? Who would tell you such a thing?"

I glanced at Devin, then at Nina, and finally all three of us turned to face Papa Coin, who was conveniently adjusting his oxygen tank and pretending not to pay attention. But after the silence grew tense, he raised his head and cleared his throat, somehow having the decency to look embarrassed.

"I may have... exaggerated those threats of discipline," he

said. "But the kids were running wild! Needed to learn some respect."

"But what about my uncle?" I asked. "Didn't you take his abilities away?"

This time Elder James cleared his throat. "Moses Freeman was punished because he discovered a way to *steal* heirlooms. Powerful ones that never should've been in anyone's hands, let alone his."

"At the time," Papa Coin said gruffly, "what with the feud and all, everyone was on edge. And it wasn't just that he was stealing. He was *good* at convincing people he was being oppressed. That they had a right. The same way he convinced your friend to help him."

It took me a second to connect the dots, and then my heart skipped. "Two-Saint."

Miss Naomi leaned forward. "He saw a kid on the outskirts and convinced him that he deserved an heirloom. That stealing one would be okay, as long as it gave him power."

"Have you found out where he is now?" I asked. "Two-Saint?"

They looked at each other, then shook their heads. "We don't know. But we have some leads, and we're going to follow them," Elder Lenore said. "But that's for us to worry about. Right now, you're not getting your summoning power removed, Jax. We need it."

"You do?"

Elder Hiram nodded. "The revealing of Conjure Station is a critical development for the summoning community. Not just in Chicago, or even the Midwest. Throughout the *world*.

New modes of communication and travel are suddenly available. Ghana, Brazil, France, Columbia, Egypt, Malaysia... Summoners from around the globe are reaching out, and there are even talks of a global Summoning Games taking place for seventh- and eighth-graders next year. It'll run for a whole semester, starting with a Tournament of Spirits to open the Games. Your ancestor did a powerful thing, uniting us like this, and you should be proud of the role you played in it. In more ways than one," he added with a sly grin.

I looked around the room and Elder James reluctantly nodded. "People are still talking about your... *antics* with the hoop snake. As much as I disapprove of rewarding self-indulgence, everyone agrees... you would make an obvious choice."

"No way," I said. "You're putting me in the Games?"

"Indeed," Papa Coin said. Then he leaned forward, and his eyes became shrewd. "And you're to report back anything you discover about the other schools. Strengths. Weaknesses. Everything."

And there it was. The other shoe. "You want me... to spy."

"We want you to protect what we've struggled to build," Papa Coin snapped. "And you owe me for damage to—"

"That wasn't his fault," Devin interrupted. "He was saving our lives, too."

"Which is why you'll be accompanying him. Since you all have such a buddy-buddy relationship."

This time Devin gawked. "Wait..."

But Papa Coin cut him off. "The Games is a competition of five, boy, and a chance to impress on everybody how the

Coins do things. So you're going, and that's final." He nodded at Nina. "You, too. Since you've obviously chosen to be a part of this . . . *friendship.*"

He held eye contact, but Nina didn't look away. She stared right back, a challenge in her expression, as if she dared him to say she didn't belong. A few seconds passed and Papa Coin must've found something he recognized, because he nodded and looked away first. Miss Naomi laughed. "I told you, my Nina Bean is more than ready."

"Excellent!" Elder Hiram stood. "It's settled. We just need two more summoners, but I'm sure we can—"

"Bull and Vanessa," I said automatically. "If they want to, I mean."

The elder clapped. "We will ask. But it will not be all fun and games, children. We will send adult summoners as chaperones, and you'll spend this summer practicing."

"Can't believe you're using us to spy!" I shook my head. The audacity of adults. Adultcity.

Elder Hiram shrugged. "We prefer to call it 'minor intelligence.' And, since you made such an impression on the cryptozoologists at Shedd Aquarium, we've arranged for Summoning Summer School to take place there."

"Not Triple-S!" Devin groaned.

"And I will be running it," Elder James announced, a hard expression on his face. "So don't expect slack or gentleness."

"From you?" I muttered. "Oh no, how will we cope?"

Elder Hiram laughed, then walked around the table to usher us to the door. "Relax, children, you'll make it through your first year at DuSable yet! Look at what you've done so far! That in itself is an accomplishment, and you're already contributing to your community. Speaking of which, there's one last thing to do. Summon your heirlooms, please."

We looked at each other, then all three of us assumed basic summoning stances and began to channel power. Devin's deck of cards emerged first with a burst of golden light, followed by Nina's purple purse, and then my ticket. Elder Hiram nodded at the others in the congregation, and they all stood and summoned the heirlooms of their trees: the harvest basket, the coin, the wand, and the skull. Elder Hiram also produced the heirloom of the Tree of Knives. One by one, their heirlooms merged, shifting, morphing, and transforming into one glittering silver kosmogram. Bright light flashed, and I closed my eyes. When I opened them, my heirloom had a silver ring of light around it. So did Devin's and Nina's.

"Normally we'd wait until the end of the year for this, but I say why delay it? You have successfully demonstrated your ability to summon," Elder Hiram announced, "and thus are deemed proficient to advance to intermediate rankings within the community. You have passed your evaluations. Now, go and celebrate. Your training summons will arrive soon enough. Oh, and when you can, Jax, I think you'll want to examine your heirloom more closely. You might enjoy a small tweak I've made."

We walked out of the diner in a daze. "Did that just happen?" I asked. "I thought I was going to get expelled, or worse!"

Devin stared glumly back at the door. "Bro. Summoning Summer School? That's so traaash."

"It could be worse," Nina said. "You could have to go to reggie summer school, too."

Devin shuddered, and we all laughed. The sun was shining, there was a set of railroad tracks that would take me wherever I wanted to go, and I had my friends by my side. Friends who stuck by me. What more could I want?

"Well, what should we do now, Jax?" Nina asked. "You're not in trouble! No walk of shame as everyone blows spitballs at you, so you get to decide what to do."

"Wait," I said. "That's a thing?"

"Totally. So, you wanna go find a meatball sub?"

"Or go to the sneaker store?" Devin said.

I started walking, crossing the street and stopping at the line of weeds just off the sidewalk. I stared at the overgrown lot across the street that was partially hidden by trees and a brick wall. The railroad tracks in the middle of it seemed to gleam at me.

I shook my head at both suggestions. "No," I said. "Two-Saint is out there. Somewhere. And if I'm—we're—going to find him, we have to get stronger. We got invited to the Summoning Games. We should go train."

"Now?" Nina asked. "Before it's even summer?"

"Why not?"

She glanced at Devin, who looked thoughtfully at me, then at her, and shrugged. "I'm trying to put the Coins on the globe, so I'm down."

"I guess I am, too," Nina said.

I grinned and steepled my fingers. Neon-blue light flashed, and the Freeman ticket appeared, but that wasn't all. As the light washed over me, something began to materialize. It started at my wrists and grew up my arms to my shoulders, then around my chest and down my back, stopping at midthigh. The others gasped as I turned around, the buttons sparkling like precious gems, the seams threaded with silver. It was a navy peacoat, just like my great-great-grandfather's. I made sure the collar was popped. As the Shriek emerged out of mist and light, rumbling to a stop behind me and sending my coattails flapping like the cape of a superhero, I lifted my hands and let the wind wash over me, not caring for once about how I looked or who could see me. Their opinions were their own. I knew who I was.

"All aboard!" I said.

CHICAGO DEFENDER, VOLUME CXVIIII, ISSUE 4, JUNE 2024

Bulls Win! Bulls Win!

. . . is the headline we would have run had the Chicago Bulls won the NBA Finals this year. But since this is the second annual Troll Issue, we'd like to remind our subscribers that the best team in the NBA, and in our division, is in fact the Milwaukee Bucks

TOP SUMMER STAYCATIONS

We asked several travel agents who also happen to be Chicagoans to recommend the best locations within the city for a staycation. Our first interviewee, Naomi Greene, gushed over the fine dining and entertainment in the revitalized Calumet Park district

FORMER SCHOOL VOLUNTEER SENTENCED TO COMMUNITY SERVICE

Stuart Benjamin was sentenced to 400 hours of community service for his role in an illegitimate book-banning program spread across the Chicago public school system. Mr. Benjamin

ATTENTION ALL SUMMONERS: REGISTRATION IS NOW OPEN REGARDING NEXT YEAR'S GLOBAL SUMMONING GAMES. PLEASE SPEAK WITH YOUR LOCAL TREE'S HOSPITALITY COORDINATORS TO REGISTER. YOUR ANCESTORS THANK YOU.

maintains he is innocent, despite m

ACKNOWLEDGMENTS

First, to the ancestors. Thank you for going before me, paving the way, lighting the path, and walking beside me. Thank you to the Gandy Dancers and the Porters, the men and women of the rails who worked to build this country when this country wanted to exclude them. Your spirit still rides, and your power is still being shared.

Now this is the part that the thugs skip.

I am nothing without my family, so to my wife, Mallory—my pillar, my foundation, my inspiration—I love you, thank you, smooches. To Shani, Kendi, Nia, and Dakari, I love you and I'm writing for you always. To Doreatha Mbalia and Ahmed Mbalia, thank you for the values you instilled in me. To the Georgia Mbalias, the Milwaukee Mbalias, the *wherever it is Jelani is located* Mbalias, I love you. To the Breland family, I love you. (Deep inhale.) Jalil, Layla, Ameenah, Yasiel, Zuri,

Baby Mbalia, Kylie, Maddie, Spencer, I love you all. (Exhale, Kwame, exhale.)

Thank you to everyone at Disney Hyperion and Freedom Fire (!) for believing in this book, in me, and in Jax. Steph, Rebecca, Ashley—we're doing great things together. But there are more.... If it looks like I copied and pasted your names in, I did, but only because I want everyone to know who you are, what you do, and that it takes a village to create a book.

Tonya Agurto, SVP, Publisher

Kieran Viola, Editorial Director

Guy Cunningham, Copy Chief

Sara Liebling, Managing Editor

Tyler Nevins, Senior Designer

Jerry Gonzales, Production Manager

Matt Schweitzer, Holly Nagel, Dina Sherman, Danielle DiMartino, Maureen Graham, and Jordan Lurie in Marketing

Ann Day and Crystal McCoy in Publicity

Andrea Rosen, Monique Diman, Vicki Korlishin, and Michael Freeman in Sales

Patrice, we did it again. Super-agent extraordinaire, thank you for never ignoring my frantic texts with my story ideas. To the team at New Leaf, thanks for having my back and stepping into the ring to fight with me.

Joanna Volpe, President

Joseph Volpe, Director of Business Affairs

Pouya Shahbazian, Director of Film & Television

Katherine Curtis, Film & Television Assistant

Trinica Sampson, Literary Associate

To my #LiteralBlackFriends (and Mark), thank you for providing an outlet and a harbor. To my BFS gang, my Iron-Pen gang, thank you for the memes and the safe space to rant without being canceled. To the twelve X followers who always like my posts, thanks for supporting me. Thank you to the schools and libraries. I know your road has been tough, and I see you and appreciate you. Thank you to the book clubs, the bookstores, the TBR piles, and the book reviewers—you all keep me motivated.

Now for the youth dem.

Thank you for trusting me to write with you. Thank you for giving me stories, names, and truth. Thank you for your support, your encouragement, your energy, and your belief. Thank you for letting me into your schools, your Zooms, and your Google Meets. Thank you for reading, thank you for sharing, thank you for your curiosity. Alone I'm just a grown-up nerd; together we are a movement.

So let's move.

COMING NEXT

Jax Freeman and the Tournament of Spirits